THIS
*F*INE
LIFE

Books by
Eva Marie Everson

Things Left Unspoken

THE POTLUCK CLUB
The Potluck Club
The Potluck Club: Trouble's Brewing
The Potluck Club: Takes the Cake

THE POTLUCK CATERING CLUB
The Secret's in the Sauce
A Taste of Fame

THIS
FINE
LIFE

A Novel

Eva Marie Everson

Revell
a division of Baker Publishing Group
Grand Rapids, Michigan

Published by Revell
a division of Baker Publishing Group
P.O. Box 6287, Grand Rapids, MI 49516-6287
www.revellbooks.com

Printed in the United States of America

Library of Congress Cataloging-in-Publication Data
Everson, Eva Marie.
    This fine life : a novel / Eva Marie Everson.
        p.   cm.
    ISBN 978-0-8007-3274-5 (pbk.)
    1. Young women—Fiction. 2. Marriage—Fiction. 3. Spouses of clergy—Fiction. I. Title.
PS3605.V47T48 2010
813′.6—dc22   2010000508

10   11   12   13   14   15   16   7   6   5   4   3   2   1

To the man who has made this life just fine for me!
My husband, Dennis.
I love you.
—Snookums

And in memory of
Mr. David Lipscomb and
Mr. Tom Grantz,
for lives well-lived.

Acknowledgments

If you've heard the song "Washed by the Water," sung by NeedToBreathe, you might think this story was inspired by the song. It wasn't.

This story was inspired by a song, however, though probably not one you'd guess.

Several years ago, while I was out working in the "real world," my employer popped a Frank Sinatra CD in to the office CD player. (He knew how much I love "Old Blue Eyes.") And, as creative people do, while Francis crooned his tune "When I Was Seventeen," I immediately began to build the story of a young man who grows up in the forties and fifties with two brothers on a farm, then moves to a city, where he meets a young girl, falls in love, marries, and then . . .

And then, nothing. I had no more story.

Years later, while at a writers' conference, several other writers and I sat in front porch rockers and, in the cool afternoon air, "shot the breeze." One of those "rockers" was my good friend, Alton Gansky. Al is not only an excellent writer, he is also a retired pastor. As Al entertained us with his true-life stories, my mind began to file some of them away (another method of fiction writers, so be careful what you say around us).

Later, I heard "When I Was Seventeen" again. The story I'd created while at work (when I should have been working!) blended with some of Al's stories. After that, I went in search of stories from preachers about their first year in ministry. All I spoke to or received emails from were quite generous with their time and history. I wish I could thank them all personally, but many of their stories came in second- or even third-hand. I would, however, like to thank Reverend C. Mike Benson of First United Methodist Church in Sylvania, Georgia (my hometown), who entertained me one summer afternoon with a number of stories rich with humor and poignancy. Between Frank and Al and Mike and all those who offered stories in between, I eventually developed the character and the life of Thayne Scott.

I also learned that not everything about the first year of being a pastor can be regarded as funny, even though many years may have passed. Some things haunt God's called for as long as they live.

Still, when we do what God calls us to do and go where God calls us to go, we are blessed with a fine life. A very fine life indeed. That's what this story is designed to do, to share with you, the reader, that our steps are ordered by God, but, in the end, we have to take those steps. And if we just trust him during the journey, we are blessed.

There are a few others to thank. My mother, who was a young bride in the mid to late fifties and a young mother in the late fifties and early sixties. She regaled me with stories and methods and reminded me of the way things were "back in the day." Another thank you to Cynthia Schnereger, my "reader," but more importantly, my friend. Thank you, Cyn, for reading every word, sometimes twice, and making sure I stayed true to my craft and my characters. Thank you to Vicki Crumpton (I love working with you!)

and Kristin Kornoelje (I love working with you too!!), two incredible editors. Thank you to all the members of my Baker family who have believed in my ability to share a little Southern truth with a little Southern fiction. You're all right for Northerners.

Prologue

June 1964

The sporadic pain came initially from the center of my lower back. It wrapped itself around my middle until it peaked at my navel. I flinched, then shifted my weight so I was lying completely flat. I stretched, pointed my toes, then flexed my feet until I felt the expected—and needed—pull along the muscles of my calves. I took a deep breath, blew it out, pulled my arm out from under the bedcovers, and glanced at my watch.

It was 2:35.

Outside the window of the bedroom, the afternoon sun flickered through the branches and leaves of the old magnolia that stood like a soldier, welcoming me back from a brief nap. "I'm just tired," I'd told my mother shortly after lunch. I handed her a cloth I'd used to dry the few dishes we'd dirtied, and attempted a smile. The expression on her face—of late nothing but an etching of concern and worry—didn't change with my words. I kissed her cheek as I'd always done to pacify her. "Really, Mama. I'm just tired." I forced my voice to a level of reassurance that was both hopeful and imaginary.

But that had been two hours ago, and the nap had left me feeling even more tired than before. I took another deep breath, arched my shoulders against the soft mattress, and exhaled, all the while keeping my gaze on the slats along the bed's canopy, as though I were searching for something to concentrate on. Without them, I thought, the gentle sloping of the princess pink material would sink in the middle.

There would be nothing attractive about that. A décor nightmare.

I pushed myself up on my elbows and surveyed the room of my childhood. It had been Mama's to decorate as she pleased until I turned sweet sixteen. Then, with Mama's persistent guidance, I was given the honor of making it my own. Of giving it my signature. The wallpaper was of bouquets of baby pink roses, their stems tied off with dark pink ribbons that seemed to sway along on a white satin background. They were pretty to look at, weren't they? So then why could I feel myself frowning?

Because *everything* in the room was pink and white and in perfect order. There were no accent colors, no pieces out of place, no dirty underwear on the floor. Just pink and white and perfect. No wonder Thayne had nearly balked at being in here. Living in here.

Had it been that long ago that we'd fought over it?

I leaned to the right as I extended my left hand and studied it. The line of veins, the long fingers, the short, self-manicured nails. The ruby that winked at me, the band of gold that mocked me. "Thayne," I whispered. "What have I done?"

I got out of bed, pulled the thick eyelet cover back into place, fluffed the pillow imprinted by the weight of my head, and then walked to my old desk, where I'd once pored over high school studies and—later—Thayne had read his Bible, taking meticulous notes in a steno pad while cross-referencing his seemingly limitless number of Bible dictionaries, commentaries, and encyclopedias. The desk I'd kept tidy in my youth had, in the days Thayne lived here, become cluttered and chaotic. When I'd tried to right the mess, Thayne had stopped me. "No, Mariette, don't touch it," he'd said, both pleading and firm at the same time. "Don't try to straighten it for me." He gave me his best dimpled smile that came and went too quickly. "And for Pete's sake, tell Daisy not to dust the books."

"She's just trying to help," I argued.

"I know she is, sweetheart, and I appreciate her for it, but sometimes her dusting causes the little slivers of paper between the pages to come out, and then I lose my place."

"Then why don't you use bookmarks? Real bookmarks and not 'little slivers of paper'?" I used my index fingers to form quotation marks in the air.

It was a good question, a fair question, but he'd only shrugged, looking more boy than man, more college student than husband. "I dunno, Mariette. I just don't."

Now I sat at the desk, which was neat once more, and opened the center drawer. I pulled out my diary, the one I'd left behind so long ago, the one with notations about hanging out with friends and meeting with Sister Teresa Anthony after classes to talk and laugh and . . . listen while the sister prayed. . . . I searched for a fountain pen, found one, and then jotted a note.

2:35.

I waited, resting against the ladder-back chair for a moment, then reached for the knob on the transistor radio—white, of course—that sat perfectly straight on the right back corner of the desk. I flipped it on. Brief static was replaced by the clear voice of Connie Francis cooing "Who's Sorry Now?"

The irony wasn't lost on me.

I switched the radio off. "Oh, Lord, help me." I whispered a prayer. "If I've ever meant anything to you at all, help me."

I stood without waiting for a divine answer, walked over to the window, and peered down to the thick carpet of grass stretching from the white frame of the house to the sidewalk out front and driveway to the right, where my brother Tommy was washing an old jalopy he'd purchased with the money he'd earned as an usher down at the Liberty movie theater. I looked past my own reflection—the dark blonde hair pulled taut, the ghost of a face in spite of the extra pounds I carried, the full lips that, without lipstick, disappeared into peachy skin—and smiled at him. Sensing my stare, I suppose, he looked up and waved, soapy suds running down the length of his tanned and muscled arms.

When did he get to be so handsome? So grown up?

He motioned for me to come down and join him, but I shook my head then shuffled away from the window and toward the closet where my purse, draped with a pair of gloves I'd worn to town that morning, hung on the glass knob. I pulled them off the purse and slipped them onto my hands, adjusting one finger at a time while humming a familiar tune. Without thinking about it, the humming gave way to its lyrics.

The tears began. I choked as I continued, this time speaking rather than singing. "Come with me . . . for thee . . . I love."

Oh, Thayne! How do I get to where you are?

I closed my eyes against the pain returning yet again from deep within, took a deep breath, and exhaled as I'd done earlier. I opened my eyes, looked down at my watch, then slipped the strap of my purse over my wrist. I stepped over to the desk and reached for the pen still lying across the open diary.

I leaned over the desk and penned "2:57." Twenty-two minutes.

"Time to go," I whispered. I closed the diary and slipped it into the purse. I wet my dry lips with the tip of my tongue, took one more deep breath, and then ambled toward the door as a lingering question pounded from deep within.

Go where?

Part 1

Friendly Persuasion

1

This is not the story of my life. This is the story of my husband's life, or at the very least how the story of his life affected mine and all those he touched just by his being near them or with them. Thayne was like that, you see. Just by being, he touched lives. He was infectious, upbeat, passionate, determined. Next to the flame of his existence I was a spark looking to ignite, a matchstick never quite making it to the striker. But, in time, the same fever that burned within him burned within me.

For too long I had existed, not really going anywhere and not standing still. I just lived, always in search of something that seemed just out of my range of vision. Or, if I thought I could see it—this elusive thing I needed to be complete—it was slightly out of reach.

But the change didn't occur instantaneously after meeting Thayne. I had to come to grips with who he was, who I was when I was with him, and who I was without him. I had to open myself up to the truth he'd discovered, step into the pages of its book, pressing myself like a flower between them. I had to stop looking for the fairy tale and find the story.

Up until my eighteenth birthday the days of my life came too easily. Pampered childhood, oldest of three children, good daughter, good student, good friend. While my father planned my next academic move, my mother plotted the rise of my social status, and all the while I lived day to day, trying to figure out just where my life would go from wherever it was at that moment.

And then everything changed, all within the narrow stairwell of my father's apparel factory, exactly between the third and fourth floors.

I returned home on a warm summer's day in early June 1959. The previous afternoon I'd celebrated my graduation from Saint Margaret Mary High, a private boarding school I'd attended over the past four years. Mama and Daddy were there, of course. Daddy's mother. My brothers, Tommy and Mitch (whom I had always called Toodles, much to his dismay). After the solemn services—where I received the St. Francis de Sales award for having read the greatest number of books in the four years I'd attended—Daddy had taken us out for a pricey dinner at a swank restaurant Mama had chosen for the occasion. While Tommy and Mitch devoured hamburgers with thick, juicy fries, the rest of us dined on steak and baked potatoes loaded with gobs of sour cream and sweet butter and garnished with chives. It was the Great Feast, the Last Supper, if you will. The meal where I'd officially left the innocence of childhood and entered the sacrificial experience of adulthood with all its questions, most of which Grandmother Puttnam was asking.

"So, Mariette, what's next for you, dear?" she asked, dabbing at the corners of her mouth with the white linen napkin she'd drawn from her lap.

"Well," I began. I dropped my hands to my own napkin. I grabbed it by its seam and pulled, curling my fingers until my hands had formed tiny fists. "I'm not really sure. I'm all packed and ready to go home tomorrow, of course, and I thought maybe this summer I'd just, you know, spend some time with old friends, hang out at the beach, take in some movies. Come fall I can concentrate on what's really next."

I cut my eyes over to Mama, who added, "She's a young lady of breeding, Miss Emily. She'll do what all young ladies of breeding do."

Daddy cleared his throat. "She'll go to school starting the first of next year. We let her slide on fall enrollment, but come January . . ." His voice trailed off.

I smiled at Grandmother Puttnam. "Maybe I can combine my father's wish with my mother's wish, go to college, and come back with an M.R.S."

Grandmother Puttnam reached for her glass of water and spoke, directing her comments to my mother. "Mary Sue, what I would have given for the opportunity to have earned a college degree. Women didn't do things like that in my day, of course. Or it was few and far between. Most of us were expected to marry and participate in all that goes with wedded bliss, and so we did." Then she looked at me. "My dear, what do *you* want to do with the rest of your life?"

I didn't answer right away. I couldn't. I had absolutely no idea what I wanted to do or be, what I wanted to accomplish or earn. The thought of being some man's wife for the rest of my life—especially some man Mama might find suitable—left rocks in the pit of my stomach. But I couldn't imagine four years at a college—an all-girls college if I knew my father—either.

All eyes turned to me. I finally smiled, tilted my head, and said, "Oh, I don't know, Grandmother. Let's just see what the summer brings."

The following evening, Daddy stood at my bedroom door and said his final good night. "Tomorrow?" he asked. "Lunch at noon with the old man?"

"Like old times?"

Daddy winked at me. He instinctively knew what I was asking. "Old times" was our code for a greasy cheeseburger with fries and a fountain drink at Drucker's Rexall Drug Store. "Like old times." He disappeared from the doorway and stepped down the hall to say good night to Tommy and Mitch.

I chuckled lightly. It was good to be home, even though Mama would have a conniption fit if she knew Daddy would be spoiling me with such tempting delicacies. "She's a young woman now," she'd say. "She needs to watch her figure if she's going to land a husband of any worth."

I am a young woman now. That much was certain. I'd left for Saint Margaret Mary's a gangly fourteen-year-old and had returned after my senior year as grown and ripe for the picking as they come.

I heard the faint "good nights" whispered by my father and brothers, then listened as Daddy entered the master bedroom, where my mother was waiting. Their room was separated from mine by the wall behind my headboard.

At first no words were spoken between them. I waited expectantly for the sound of drawers sliding open then shut. The door to the bathroom closing, then opening. My father muttering something followed by my mother's comeback. These were the words I never understood, muffled by Sheetrock and wallpaper. But I'd certainly wondered about them. These were the words of a couple who still loved each other after twenty years of marriage. What were they, exactly? What did a woman say to a man she'd slept with for two decades?

Typically, after the ebb and flow of their final conversation of the day, they and the house would grow silent, then dark. I would turn off my bedside lamp and, like all the others in our home, fall asleep. But this night was different. This night I heard their words. Not the first words, but the final ones.

"This is a new era, Mary Sue," Daddy said. "A young woman can choose more than being a wife and mother. A young woman can choose education *and* following in her father's footsteps rather than her mother's."

I gripped the year-old copy of *First Love and Other Sorrows* I'd been reading. I sucked in my breath, held it, and listened. They were fighting . . . they were fighting over me. "Don't be asinine, Carroll. Mariette will now join all the social clubs for women of her age and stature. She'll do some volunteer work, I imagine, but she'll also attend parties and teas. This is her time to prepare herself for—"

"Who are you calling 'asinine,' woman?" To my relief, Daddy's voice was not demanding; it was tender and sensual. I released my breath with a sigh.

Mama's voice dropped low. "You, you old bear," she said. Then the rumble of laughter from deep within my father's ample girth. I slid low between the crisp and familiar white sheets. My father had never been (nor would he ever be) a match for my mother when it came to sparring over their children. When not another sound came through the wall, I closed my book, turned out the white milk glass lamp next to my bed, drew a pillow over my head, and went to sleep.

I slept in until ten o'clock the next morning, forced myself out of bed, then traipsed down the stairs and into the kitchen, looking for Mama and a cup of coffee. Instead I found Daisy, Mama's once-a-week help, ironing laundry and humming an old spiritual tune I didn't know the name of; but I certainly knew the melody. I'd been hearing Daisy vacillate between humming and singing it since I was five. "Wheel in a wheel, way in de middle of de air," I sang as a way of greeting her.

"Well, look what the cat done drug out of the bed," she said, shaking her head.

Daisy was a tall, slender woman with mahogany skin and round gray-blue eyes that belied her heritage. Or, at the very least, kept mine in a state of reproach. Her hair was nearly sheared, and no matter what day of the week, she wore large pearl-like earrings that seemed to elongate her earlobes. She was stunning enough to be a movie star but poor enough to be a white woman's housemistress.

I stood before her in my baby pink cotton pajamas that were too short since I had grown another two inches. Mama said I should be done by now, but I'd hit 5'9" not two months ago. I placed my hands on my hips in mock reprimand and said, "I deserve a little rest and relaxation, Daisy. I've been hard at work earning my high school diploma."

"The good Lord never meant us to sleep till the day was nearly half over," she said, pressing the iron hard against one of my father's handkerchiefs, one of those I'd embroidered his monogram along one corner of and slipped into his Christmas stocking six months before.

"Is there any coffee?" I asked, ignoring her reprimand as I often did.

"Will be when you make yourself a pot," she said.

I giggled. "Oh, Daisy. You know I don't know how to make coffee."

"Time you learned," she said. "Grab that pot over there in the drain. I've already washed it once this morning. I reckon I can wash it again."

I reached for the pot and shook out the excess water. "You really want me to make the coffee?" I asked. I looked down at the Timex gracing my wrist. "I'm supposed to meet Daddy at 11:45, and I haven't had a bath yet."

"Then I reckon you'd best hurry and do what I tell you. Now, fill the pot with water up to that there line you see marking for four cups. No, make that six. May as well have myself a cup or two seeing as you're making it."

Later, I dressed in a cotton swing skirt—white, with large luscious slices of watermelon splashed across it—a wide black patent leather belt and a red summer sweater with a satin bow at the shoulder, a pair of nylons and black high-heeled pumps. I pinched my cheeks hard for color as I looked at my reflection in the vanity mirror then raced down the stairs, ready to hop into the new cherry red Chrysler De Soto Daddy and Mama had gifted me with for graduation.

Mama met me with a smile at the bottom of the curving

staircase. "What?" I asked, stopping before her, two stairs up from the landing where she stood. "What has you so pleased?"

"I'm just happy to see you dressed like the young lady you are, and not in that tomboyish way you've insisted upon for so long, looking more like an older brother than older sister to the boys."

I stepped to the hardwood floor and turned slowly. "You like? Pretty peachy, huh?"

"Honestly, all these new sayings you children have these days." She briefly touched my ribbon. "I do like this red ribbon."

I gave my hair a light touch. Naturally dark blonde, it reached past my shoulders when straight, but in a flip, as I wore it now, it grazed the top with a light bounce. My hair was an asset, and I knew it. I took great care to brush it repeatedly before bed, to use the best products, and to drench it in egg yolks at least once a month, allowing the yolks to dry to a crisp, stiff mask before rinsing. "Thanks, Mama." I gave her a light kiss on the cheek, wiped off the lipstick imprint of my affection with my thumb, then left my childhood home to begin my life as an adult.

I just didn't know it yet.

2

The Fox & Hound Manufacturing Company—which took up the entire block between Azalea Avenue and Dogwood Drive—was my father's creation, an innovative business that gave hundreds of our town's residents secure jobs and brought additional prosperity to our corner of the world, Meadow Grove, Georgia. Hundreds of sewing machines whirred on the second floor, producing a durable line of sports and casual wear that was shipped out to stores across the nation from the first floor loading docks. The third floor was divided, with the mailroom and the operations manager's office on one side and the employee break area on the other. The fourth floor was used exclusively for my father's suite of offices, a boardroom for executive meetings, and storage rooms for mannequins, overstock, and office supplies. The entire building smelled of dye and fabric.

I entered by way of the front double-glass doors, humming a tune by the recently deceased Buddy Holly I'd heard on the car radio, then paused to greet Donna Springfield, a contemporary of Mama's who'd worked for Daddy as far back as I could recall. Donna was tall and wore her red hair in the traditional Lucille Ball poodle cut so she'd look even more like the entertainment icon despite the fact that she carried about twenty more pounds than Lucy did. Unlike most of the women in town, she accented her facial features with gobs of makeup. Mama said she looked like a clown. But, I said she'd always been nice in spite of her obsessions.

"Welcome back home, Mariette," she said, rising and then coming from around the simple desk where she greeted visitors to the factory, answered phone calls, painted her long red nails, and read Hollywood magazines and cheap romance novels, the kind sold at the five-and-dime downtown. She wrapped me in a hug. "Good to see you, good to see you." She stepped back, took my face in her hands, and said, "My goodness but aren't you the prettiest thing I ever did see?"

I batted my lashes and hoped I blushed appropriately. "Thank you, Miss Donna."

She stepped back, drawing my arms straight out with her hands, then pulled them wide as though I were a dress on display. "Simply stunning. Cute as that new actress Sandra Dee ever dreamed of being. Have you seen anything of hers yet? She's adorable, that's what."

"My girlfriends and I went to see *Gidget* a couple of months ago."

She dropped my hands. "You haven't seen *Imitation of Life* yet?"

I shook my head. "No. Not yet. The last few months at school were really busy with other things. You know, finals and dances and stuff like that."

She laughed. "Of course. How quickly we forget. But do try to see it if you can find it still playing somewhere. Maybe the drive-in will have it. That old place is always showing yesterday's hits."

I smiled dutifully, ready to get upstairs to my father. "I will."

"I suppose you're here to have lunch with your daddy."

I nodded and felt the curls bounce off my shoulders. "I am."

"Well, you know where the stairs are," she said, returning to her seat. "I've told that father of yours a hundred times or more, we should be thinking about getting an elevator, but he won't hear of it."

I moved toward the door leading to the stairwell. "A little exercise never hurt anyone."

She took a sip of something from a Dixie cup and said, "Easy for you to say. You're young and with your whole life in front of you."

I smiled. "Now, Miss Donna, you know you're still young," I said, then slipped through the partially open door of the stairwell before she could answer. When it closed behind me, the sound echoing all the way to the fourth floor landing, I breathed in the familiar odors. No matter the time of year it was always cold and smelled of paint and half-smoked cigarettes and Daddy's cigars, the ones Mama didn't let him smoke at home. An odd combination that blended well with the lime green paint that coated every inch of it, including the railings but not the stairs themselves. More peculiar than its look and scent was the way it always made me feel safe and at home. These were the stairs that led to my father's offices.

I clutched to my chest the small white purse I'd been carrying, and began my ascent, careful not to bound up the stairs as I would have done four years or even six months ago, but to take each step slowly, one at a time, like a lady.

I rounded the first short flight of steps, then headed up the second. I paused at the door to the second floor and peered through the small window near the top, observing the workers in their tasks. I took a deep breath and sighed. I couldn't imagine being a factory worker. Day in. Day out. The same thing. I couldn't imagine answering phones like Miss Donna, either. "Good morning"—or afternoon, whatever the case might be—"Fox & Hound Manufacturing. How may I direct your call?"

I wondered then what it was like to be Miss Donna or any

of the number of women who worked the lines for my father. Then I thought about other women I knew who'd made being a wife and mother the center of their world. Cooking, cleaning, raising children. Like Miss Donna's work, day in, day out, the same thing.

If Daddy had his way I'd go to college, get a business degree, and then come back to Meadow Grove, work alongside him, and eventually take over the business. But if Mama had her way, I'd be *her* replica, marrying a man of means, spending my days ordering the lives of my children, going to luncheons at the club on Wednesdays and dinners at the homes of all the right people on Saturday nights. My "spare time," like her "spare time," would be spent tending to civic and volunteer duties.

I frowned. Mama had made a fine life for herself, but it was *her* life. She'd accomplished exactly what she'd always wanted and more. But it wasn't *my* life's ambition. Still, I wasn't sure I wanted to go to college as Daddy wanted me to, either. I blinked a few times. He was sure to discuss it with me today. "You've successfully managed to avoid this conversation for a year now, young lady," he'd say. "But now it's time to get serious about it. I am perfectly amenable to you having your summer of fun, but by January we can have you registered, in a dorm, meeting new friends . . ."

"For Pete's sake," I said to no one, then turned and headed up the next two short flights. As I'd done at the second floor, I peered into the window of the third floor door, cutting my eyes one way, then another, looking for Mr. Schneiders, the operations manager. When I saw his short, slightly bent frame passing by, I opened the stairwell door and followed after him. "Mr. Schneiders!" I hollered like a twelve-year-old.

He immediately appeared at the doorway down the hall. "Land of the living, land of the living!" he said, then jaunted toward me.

I smiled at the aging, white-haired man who wore black-rimmed glasses and whose height barely reached my shoulders. I bent over and gave him a hug. "Could you get a bit taller?" he asked. "How many inches do you have in those heels there?"

I stuck my foot toward him and twisted my ankle to the right. "Four," I said.

"Look at you," he said. "All grown up. Wearing your mama's heels, this time for show and not for play."

I laughed. "They're my heels, Mr. Schneiders." He made a "pshaw" sound. "How is Mrs. Schneiders?" I asked. Before I had left for Saint Margaret Mary's, Mrs. Schneiders had been my piano teacher for eight painstaking years.

"Fat and sassy."

I laughed again. "Does she still play as beautifully as she did last time I heard her at CKLC?" Christ the King Lutheran Church was our church home and where Mrs. Schneiders had played the piano since coming there as Mr. Schneiders's bride.

"Like heaven's pianist."

I pointed down the hall, toward his office. "How's work going for you, Mr. Schneiders?"

"Same." He gave a nod then pointed a finger upward. "Oh! We've got a new boy working the mailroom though. Right fine boy. He's living over at Harriett Gleason's boardinghouse."

I nodded. "Oh, really?"

"According to the missus, Harriett is his aunt. Mama's sister, I believe she told me."

"Fresh out of college?"

"No. He's taking classes part time, though. I think he's got about two more years to go. Pretty sharp young man," Mr. Schneiders added with a nod of his head.

I gave him a half smile. "Better be careful there, Mr. Schneiders. Next thing you know, he'll have your job."

Mr. Schneiders snorted. "Ah, go on now. And don't say things like that around the missus. She'd give her right arm if I'd retire. Says it's time for the two of us to hit the open road or some such nonsense."

I placed a hand on my hip. "Well, maybe it is."

"Go on now," he repeated, this time placing his hands on my shoulders, turning me away from him, and giving me a light push toward the door. "Last thing I need in this world is me and that woman of mine alone in a car or one of those homes on wheels for any length of time."

I laughed as I gave a half turn and waved good-bye. "Nice seeing you, Mr. Schneiders."

He waved back then headed to where I'd called him from.

Once again in the stairwell, I made my way from the third floor to the fourth. Nearly halfway to the landing I heard a door from the floor above open, then close, followed by quick, heavy footsteps. I stopped and glanced upward just in time to see and hear a young man bounding down the stairs, arms laden with manila envelopes and whistling Pat Boone's "Friendly Persuasion." It slipped from between his lips like honey dripping over hot baked bread. Realizing there was another body below, he stopped short and then, taking in the full length of me, smiled. "Oh, hey there," he said, dimples deepening. "Sorry, I didn't know anyone was in here."

I bit my bottom lip as I pushed myself against the wall of the stairwell. My breath caught in my chest. "That's okay," I said, nearly swallowing the words. Then I opened my mouth to say something else but nothing came. It was like one of those dreams I had as a child with me yelling at my friends or my brothers but nothing coming out of my mouth. But this boy wasn't one of my childhood friends or one of my brothers. He was like no boy I'd ever seen before.

For that matter, he wasn't like *anyone* I'd ever seen before.

3

"Name's Thayne," he said, taking one step at a time, coming down toward me. "Thayne Scott. Yours?"

I had to think. "Mariette," I said finally, pressing my back more firmly against the wall.

His feet came to rest on the same step as mine. I looked down; his scuffed penny loafers pointed toward shiny peep-toe heels. My eyes traveled north. He wore cuffed light blue pants and a plaid cotton shirt, the long sleeves rolled up just below the elbows, unbuttoned at the neck and collar. I noted the tan skin of his arms and around his throat, where his Adam's apple bobbed a bit as he swallowed. "Nice to meet you, Mariette," he said.

I took in his eyes then, nearly drowning in them. Dark blue. So dark they could pass as black in the right light, or lack thereof. His hair was a mass of soft blond curls he tried to tame, combed back in the style of Robert Wagner. But it was his smile that made my heart flip. Broad, white teeth showing, dimple digging into his right cheek.

I saw then that he'd jutted his hand forward as best he could, what with his arms overloaded as they were, with some manner of etiquette. I slipped my hand into his, a jolt of electricity slipping up my arm, and quickly retrieved it.

"You work here?" he asked, taking a step, then another, toward the third floor.

"Um . . . no. I'm just on my way up . . ." I pointed a nail toward the fourth floor.

He continued down, nodding. "Oh yeah. Yeah. Mr. Puttnam's office? Mr. Schneiders told me there might be a new position opening up here." He glanced up then. "Good luck getting in. This is a real cool place to work."

Cool. That part of slang we weren't allowed to say at Saint Margaret Mary's. I took a few steps up, keeping my back to the wall, my eyes on him. "Oh. Cool," I said. "Thanks."

"Bye now," he said, then darted through the third floor door, resuming his whistled tune.

I took a deep breath, blew it out, then continued on to Daddy's office.

Lunch with Daddy went exactly as expected, with him telling me the value of a being a woman today with a college diploma.

"And I don't mean this 'M.R.S.' business either."

I snickered. We sat across from each other at one of the eight white wrought iron soda shop tables clustered in front of the fountain counter at Drucker's. We'd nearly devoured our cheeseburgers and fries, Daddy keeping his eyes toward the front door of the drugstore, ever aware that Mama could waltz through it at any minute.

"Daddy," I said. "If I go to college—*if* I go to college—it surely wouldn't be to get an M.R.S. Besides, that would be just what Mama wants, and then where would we be?" I smiled at him, hoping he got my joke.

"Your mama just wants the best for you."

"I know she does, Daddy. And I know you want the best for me too. For that matter, so do I. I just don't know what is best for me. These last four years away were such a long time for me. I missed being here. Being with you and Mama and the boys. Missed my old school chums. I feel like I hardly know any of them anymore."

"Anything else, folks?" the soda jerk called over the counter, where a sprinkling of customers sat eating their lunches. Daddy and I—along with all the others sitting at the tables—looked over to him. Then Daddy turned to me. "Princess?"

"Maybe a malted?"

"One malted," Daddy called over his shoulder. "Two straws."

I crossed my arms in mock horror. "Who said I'm sharing?"

Daddy patted his stomach. "Your mama is after me to lose a few. So, I'll just have a sip."

"Mmmhmm. I guess that cheeseburger and those fries don't count."

"Proteins and vegetables are good for you," he said with a chuckle. "Now, don't try to change the subject."

I narrowed my eyes playfully. "What were we talking about, anyway?"

"Let's start with what you want." Daddy pulled a cigar out of his pocket, chomped it between his teeth, then lit it, puffing a few billows of smoke into the air.

"What I want . . . That's just it, Daddy. I don't know what I want. But if you and Mama will give me the summer to think about it, I promise I'll have an answer for you by the end of August."

The soda jerk, whom I recognized as Missy Deerfield's sixteen-year-old brother, brought the malted over with two straws and said, "How ya doing, Mariette?"

"I'm doing good, Pete. And you?"

"Working this summer for my uncle here at the drugstore."

I smiled up at him. He was a handsome boy, if one could get past the ruddy face and thick black-rimmed glasses. "So I see. How's Missy?"

"She's good. She's getting married, you know."

"No, I didn't know." The last I'd heard, Missy Deerfield and Chadwick Marshall, the cutest boy in our town, were an item. "To Chad?"

"Awww, no. Chad's heading to the University of Georgia. She's marrying Ward Hill."

"Ward Hill?" The name didn't strike any chords of remembrance. "Did he graduate before us?"

My father cleared his throat and shifted in his seat, capturing my attention. He shook his head. I furrowed my brow at him, then gave the same look to Pete, who blushed, his pimples turning crimson. "No. Ward Hill, the insurance guy. You know, Hill & Hill Insurance Company?"

I knew of the Hill Insurance Company, but Hill & Hill . . .

My father was now pressing the toe of his shoe against mine. I decided it was best not to ask any more questions. Instead I smiled up at Pete and said, "Tell Missy I hope she is very happy. When is the big day?"

"In two weeks. June bride and all that."

"And all that," I repeated. "I'll have to scold Mama for not telling me." I placed my elbows onto the glass tabletop as I laced my fingers together and rested my chin on their bony peaks. "Tell Missy we'll get together after she's back from her honeymoon and gets settled into her new home and life."

"Tell her yourself when you and your family come to the wedding."

"Oh," I said, not realizing we'd even received an invitation.

I watched as he turned and lumbered back behind the counter. I swung my face toward my father and said, "What was that about?"

Daddy shook his head. "Ask your mother. She's got more of a scoop on it than I do."

"I will," I said with a nod of my head, then leaned over to take a sip of "our" drink. I rolled my eyes then winked at

Daddy. "Heaven," I said. "You don't get malteds like this at Saint Margaret Mary's."

Daddy chuckled. "I imagine not."

As soon as I returned home I went in search of Mama. I found her upstairs, sitting cross-legged in the middle of her bed, talking on the telephone to goodness-knows-who. As soon as I flew into the room, she looked up, startled, as if I'd caught her doing something she wasn't supposed to do. Her fingertips flew to the hollow of her throat and she said, "Goodness, Mariette. You scared me half to death." She turned her attention back to the person on the other end of the call. "Doris, let me call you back."

She hung up the phone, which was on the bed in front of her crossed legs, then returned it to the bedside table. We were one of the few families I knew of in Meadow Grove with a phone in a bedroom. Daddy had one in his home office, of course, and there was one in the kitchen. But Mama had insisted there be one in their bedroom after I went away to school. "If something happened in the middle of the night," she told Daddy, "and we didn't hear the phones ringing downstairs, I'd never forgive myself."

"Young lady," she said, now giving me her attention. "What in the world is so important I had to end a call with Doris?"

I plopped on the bed; my legs dangled off the side. I kicked off my shoes then massaged the bottom of one foot with the toes of the opposite. "Don't 'what in the world' me. I should be saying that to you."

Mama leaned back, resting her weight on the palms of her hands as she uncrossed her legs to stretch them. I took in the length and the look of her. She was an adorable excuse for a fashion ad, keeping her dress as contemporary as any teenage girl I knew. She wore a play set. The pants were orange and cropped. The white top had a large orange nautical sash held in place by a white loop. Mama tied the whole outfit together with two jangle-bangles—one white, one orange—worn on her right wrist. Her short blonde hair—touched up once a month by her hairdresser—framed her face in soft curls, the bangs brushed to the left, away from her low forehead. "Explain yourself to me, Mariette," she said.

"Missy Deerfield?"

Mama's face paled. "Oh. How did you hear about that?" Her eyes quickly narrowed. "Don't tell me your father took you to Drucker's for lunch." I watched as her shoulders dropped with a dramatic flare only Mama could produce. She swung off the bed, dipped her feet into a pair of orange flats, and then stepped over to the dresser. She peered at herself in the mirror, pretending to primp by raising a hand to her hair, and said, "Honestly, Mariette. Did we not discuss the importance of where you go, what you do? Daddy should have taken you to the club. Introduced you to—"

"Mama!" I exclaimed, turning my body to have a better view of her. She swung around to look at me, feigning shock at my sudden outburst. "Don't change the subject."

Mama sighed. "Oh, all right. Missy Deerfield has nearly driven her poor mother to the loony bin."

I patted the mattress in front of me. "Sit. Sit. I want to know."

Mama returned to the bed. "Well, you know she dated that wonderful Chadwick Marshall for the last year or so. Everyone—including her mama and daddy, I might add—thought they'd get married, you know, after Chadwick had a couple of years of college under his belt. I saw Sally Deerfield in the grocery store one day, and she was nearly beaming in anticipation of the nuptials."

"Who is Ward Hill?"

"I'm getting to that. Don't be impatient." Mama took a breath. "Ronny Hill—"

"Hill Insurance."

"Don't interrupt. Yes. Hill Insurance. Of course, Ronny has lived here for—what—ten years now. He and Virginia Hill have been an important and contributing part of our community and of the church."

"Mama."

"I'm getting there, Mariette. Do you want to hear this or not?"

I nodded. "Go ahead."

"Last year, right after you returned to Saint Margaret Mary's, Ronny's younger brother moved here to go into business with Ronny. From what I understand, he'd just gone through a divorce and wanted to start over."

I began to sense where the rest of this story was going. "A divorce? How much younger is he than Mr. Hill?"

"Five years. Or so I've heard. I haven't actually seen his birth certificate."

I began to calculate, or at least I tried to. "Wait a minute; how old is Mr. Ronny Hill?"

"Ronny Hill is my age." My mother had not quite hit forty, though she was closing in. Not that we ever discussed it. "Ward Hill is just shy of thirty-five."

"Missy Deerfield is marrying a thirty-five-year-old man?" The very idea was caught somewhere between nauseating and intoxicating. An older man. I wondered if he were handsome like Cary Grant, who, at any age, was completely dreamy.

"You can imagine how horrified everyone is."

"How did they meet?"

"It's the school's fault. This is one reason I have no regrets sending you away to school. The school system is to blame for this travesty." Mama pointed at me, I suppose to make sure I knew how sure she was.

"How so?" My curiosity was now at an all-time high.

"This past year the school offered seniors a new program where they could take a job as an apprentice in a number of the businesses here. Just for the experience. Not for money.

Missy took a job filing and doing light secretarial work at Hill & Hill."

"She met Ward . . . their eyes met over a stack of claim files." I sighed for effect. "And the rest is romantic history."

"Don't dramatize it any more than it needs to be. It's a travesty. Sally is nearly beside herself, doing everything she can to make this look acceptable, but you know she's just dying inside. Just dying."

"So why didn't you tell me?" I pretended to have a child's hissy fit—temporary of course—by bouncing a bit on the bed.

Mama slipped off the bed again, this time heading for the door. "You and Missy haven't been close for years—not with you attending school out of town. There was no need to take your mind away from your schoolwork."

Suddenly my good grades were her lofty goal. I followed my mother into the hallway, stopping just outside the bedroom door. She was near the top of the staircase. She paused, one hand on the railing, the other on a hip. "We'll attend the wedding, of course. Sally is, after all, my friend. And I've already gone to a tea and a luncheon in Missy's honor. I gifted her with two pieces of her china pattern. Your father had a fit over the price, but I told him I'd rather spend the money on something she can use more than a set of bedsheets *after* the marriage fails."

I nearly swallowed my tongue at the reference.

"Let's not romanticize this, Mariette. Ward Hill is not only too old for Missy, he's divorced and has an eight-year-old son. The marriage stands little chance for survival, and this is just a fine example of young people thinking Hollywood love stories are real. Believe me when I tell you how important social propriety is."

I stepped over to the railing, rested my hands and weight against it. "But, Mama, what if Missy and Ward are in love? What if this is the real deal?"

"Don't be silly, Mariette. Missy just wants to hurt her mama and daddy, though only the good Lord knows why. They've given her everything she could ever want or ask for. She knew good and well they were counting on her marrying Chadwick Marshall." Mama paused. She seemed to collect her thoughts then reached over and cupped my chin. "Just promise me you'll never do anything like this." Her hand dropped. "Oh, Mariette. For my sake as well as your own, find a nice young man who can provide well for you and marry him. None of this college nonsense your father would have you consider. What does a pretty young woman like you need with more education?"

I pursed my lips and shook my head. *This again.* "I don't know what I'm going to do, Mama. Maybe I don't need more education, but I don't see myself falling in love anytime soon. Old man, young man, rich man, poor man. I have to figure out who *I* am as a woman before I can be any man's wife."

Then—and it was the strangest thing—the face of Thayne Scott appeared just over my mother's right shoulder. As quickly as it appeared, it faded from view.

"What?" Mama asked. She glanced over her shoulder as if she felt the presence of the mailroom clerk behind her, then looked back at me.

I felt my face grow hot. "Nothing," I said. "Nothing at all."

"Mmmhmm. Just remember what I've always told you: men don't like to marry women who might appear to be smarter than they. A college degree, my dear, is a great threat to your future."

I narrowed my eyes teasingly. "I have absolutely no recollection of you ever saying those words."

Mama was nonplussed. "Haven't I?" She shrugged. "Oh, well. I'm sure I meant to."

4

After dinner that evening, and with the dishes all washed, dried, and put away, I ran upstairs, pulled my hair into a ponytail, changed into a pair of blue, white, and yellow striped Capri slacks with a matching white top, the striped pattern repeated at the V-shaped neckline. I dug around in my closet until I came upon a pair of yellow canvas Keds. I slipped my feet into the sneakers, tied the laces, grabbed a book off my nightstand, then darted down the stairs. "Mama," I shouted. "I'm going out."

Mitch appeared then, stepping out of the living room. "Hey," he said. He wore a light cotton button-down shirt and a pair of dungarees cuffed at the hemline.

"Hi." I walked over to him. At just ten years of age, Mitch was everyone's baby boy. He had dark red hair, a sprinkling of freckles across an upturned nose, and demanding green eyes. I placed my hand on a shoulder and said, "Tell Mama and Daddy I'm going out, will you?"

"Where ya goin'?"

"I thought I'd go to the Bean." The Bean was short for our local hangout, the Village Bean. "You know, see if any of my old friends are there." I waved my book at him. "And if not, I'll sip coffee and read like a beatnik."

"Aw, whatcha wanna go do that for?" He twisted his shoulder from under the weight of my hand. "I thought maybe you'd hang out here and play a game of checkers with me." Disappointment registered on his face in the form of a flush.

"Sorry, Toodles."

"Aw, geez. Do you have to call me that? I'm ten-almost-eleven years old now."

I smiled. "You'll always be my Toodles."

"Knock it off, will ya?" He sauntered back into the living room where, to my dismay, a checkerboard was set up and ready to be played on Mama's highly polished coffee table.

I frowned. "Okay." I walked in behind him. "I'll make a deal with you." He turned and looked at me, hopeful. "I'll play one game of checkers"—I held up a finger—"and in return I get to call you Toodles."

He mulled it over. "I'll make you a deal," he said. "You win and you can call me Toodles. But if you lose, all name-calling is out."

I extended my hand. He did likewise and we shook on it, then sat on the floor and faced each other like worthy opponents. Half an hour later, I was losing badly. I dropped an elbow to the coffee table and my chin to my palm. "When did you get so good at this?"

"This year . . . while you were gone."

I frowned. "I see. So this is what happens while I'm away."

"Well, at least I'm not going all gaga over girls." He sneered and blew air out of his nose like a bull.

"And just who is going all gaga over girls?"

He rolled his eyes. "You know."

I leaned in. "Tommy?"

"It's sick," he said. "I'm talking Pukesville."

I pressed my lips together to keep from laughing. "Well, he is twelve-almost-thirteen," I said, playing on his age calculations from earlier. "I guess that's about the right age to start noticing the opposite sex."

"Gross," he said, then grabbed a checker and hopped over one of my kings. "Gotcha. You're down to two kings." He rubbed his hands together in victory.

I decided to turn my attention back to the game. I stared at the board a good long time, mentally calculating my strategies. Or, at least, what was left of them.

"Hey, Mariette?" Mitch's soft voice broke my concentration.

I looked up at him. The green of his eyes had turned misty. "You going away again?"

"I don't know. Why do you ask?"

"I dunno. I mean, I don't like it when you're gone." He gave another shrug of his shoulder, an indication I was not to make a big deal out of what he'd said.

"Really?"

"Really. I mean, Tommy used to play with me a lot, but now he only wants to hang out with his friends. They go skating all the time and, you know, talk about girls, and dances, and junk like that."

"Junk like that, huh?"

"Yeah."

"So, why don't you go skating with them? Don't you like to skate?"

Mitch shook his head, glanced down at the checkerboard, shifted a checker from one square to the next and then back again. "Tommy says little brothers shouldn't be tagging along all the time and that I need to play with my own kind." He looked up at me again. "What do you think that means? My own kind?"

"Well, I think it means he wants you to play with friends your age. What do you like to do, Mitch? When you're playing?"

"I like playing board games, mostly. Checkers. Life. Monopoly . . . when I can find someone who wants to take that long to play a game. Jeffie and I ride bikes a lot and play with our BB guns sometimes . . ." Another shrug. "When Mama lets me. Boy, she watches that thing like the old hawk up in the McGordys' backyard tree."

The McGordys, who were Catholic, had been our neighbors forever, it seemed, having moved in shortly after Mama and Daddy moved to the neighborhood. Their home—one level rather than two, like most of the houses around here—had been filled to overflowing with children from Day One, including Jeffie, who was Mitch's age but by no means their youngest. "They're like rabbits over there," I'd overheard Mama saying to Daddy one afternoon in the kitchen. "Not that I don't like them, of course. But still . . ." A few days later I learned that Mrs. McGordy was pregnant again; I put two and two together and figured out who Mama'd been talking about.

"Well, I'll make another deal with you," I now said to Mitch. "Every day this summer you and I will play at least one board game. Deal?"

"Deal." Mitch grinned and then added, "Cool."

"Now, are you going to finish me off here or make me suffer a long checkerboard death?" I smiled at my baby brother, and he grinned back.

Two moves later, the name "Toodles" was laid to rest.

I arrived at the Bean just as the light of day turned gray and settled around the town. The Village Bean was a small building with cement picnic tables and benches clustered along the outside. On this night a few of the boys from school stood around them, some with a foot propped on a bench, smoking cigarettes and sipping Cokes.

Inside, to the right of the front door, were several chrome table sets, their colors red and silver. The chairs were thickly padded, making them more comfortable than they looked.

Along the walls were booths whose seats matched the table sets. From outside I could see that the number of patrons was down. Then again, as late as it had gotten, they'd probably all eaten and gone home or to the drive-in.

Just inside the front door was a serving counter that formed an elongated U. The barstools matched the chairs and booths. They stood high and swiveled, which was a good thing because people rarely faced forward. At least no one in my crowd, or what was left of it.

Neil Price was the owner of the Bean. "Chief cook and bottle washer," he'd add. His wife, Cathy, was the head waitress. Most summers and weekends found some of the local high school girls working there as well. Tonight it was just Cathy and some young girl I didn't recognize.

Cathy waved to me and I waved back. "Home for good?" she asked.

I nodded. "At least for the summer," I said a little too loud, attempting to speak over the music from the jukebox; Bobby Darin was crooning his latest hit, "Dream Lover."

My voice attracted the attention of a few old friends sitting in the back corner booth. I pointed in their direction and then said to Cathy, "A cup of coffee?" She nodded to me.

I went toward my old chums, Sandy, Anne, Toni, and Bobbie Sue, who were now sliding out of the booth and heading toward me. I was aware of groupings of older folks sitting at the tables, a few who called out, "Welcome home, Mariette." I smiled toward them, not really taking the time to say much more than "thank you" back.

The girls grabbed me by my hands, jumping up and down, ponytails bouncing, and dragged me back to their booth, all the while asking about a hundred and one questions.

We squeezed back into the booth, settled down, and my coffee was served. "Okay," I said. "One at a time, please. I can hardly think." I reached for the sugar dispenser, poured two teaspoons of the white granules in, then reached for the small pitcher of milk, which was shaped like a black and white cow.

"Are you home for good?" Sandy asked.

I took a tentative sip of coffee from the thick cream-colored ceramic mug. "*That* is the question," I said. "Never mind 'to be or not to be.'" Everyone giggled at the schoolgirl humor. "My parents are making me crazy, asking me all the time."

"So, what are they pushing?" Toni asked.

I explained my situation and they gave me their plans for the future. Sandy was going to work as a secretary in a law firm. Anne was dating Anthony Pierson and was expecting a ring for Christmas, so her parents insisted she just take it easy between now and then and enjoy the last days of singledom. Toni had decided to go to college to study early childhood education, and Bobbie Sue, in spite of her parents' warning, was soon to enter classes in Atlanta to be an airline stewardess.

"I'm going to fly the friendly skies," she said, eyes cast upward.

"She's going to be the friendly skies," Sandy teased. "She's already daydreaming about meeting some handsome pilot—"

"Or rich businessman," Bobbie Sue interjected, then looked at me. "I'm not choosy."

I nearly spewed my coffee across the table. Swallowing hard I said, "Just keep your virtues. I've heard a lot of stories about the life of a stewardess." Just what the stories were I didn't know, but the line sounded good.

"What virtues?" Sandy asked, cutting an eye at Bobbie Sue.

Bobbie Sue, in turn, slapped her friend's arm. "I'll have you know . . ."

Sandy leaned over the table at her. "You and Joshua Black dated nearly all of last year."

"King and queen at the prom," Bobbie Sue said to me.

46

"Never in the history of Meadow Grove High have two people ever traded so much spit on campus and off." Anne rolled her eyes. "Bobbie Sue isn't saying what or who caused them to break up, but right after prom . . ."

I pointed toward the window. "Isn't that Joshua outside with some of the guys?"

As if on cue, we all turned to look out the window as the cluster of boys—the ones who'd wolf-whistled at me but who I'd greeted with no more than a wave and a toss of my ponytail—jumped into their cars and revved up the engines. I noted then that Chad Marshall was among their number. He was even more handsome than I'd remembered, and I thought Ward Hill must really be something for Missy to have broken up with her longtime beau. "There's Chad," I said absentmindedly.

"I suppose you heard about him and Missy," Anne said.

I nodded. "Have any of you met Ward Hill?"

"Have we ever," Sandy said. "He's positively adorable."

"Ew," Anne retorted. "He's practically old enough to be her father."

"I wouldn't mind if he were *my* father," Sandy shot back, placing imaginary quotes around "father."

Toni giggled. "He's older, I guess you heard."

"I heard."

"But he's a really nice guy. Kinda religious, you know. Like the real deal. But nice."

A divorced father of an eight-year-old marrying a girl seventeen years his junior. Sounded odd to me.

Toni ended the topic of conversation by glancing at her watch and saying, "It's almost 8:30 now. Hey, we should scoot."

Bobbie Sue looked toward me. "We're all meeting at the drive-in." She glanced out the window, then back. "Wanna come?"

"What's playing?"

"Cat on a Hot Tin Roof."

"With Elizabeth Taylor?"

"Who cares about Elizabeth Taylor? Paul Newman's who I'm going to see."

The girls on the outside of the booth started to slip out as Sandy, who was near the wall and across from me, said, "I could absolutely drown in his blue eyes."

"Coming?" Toni said to me.

I shook my head. "No. Maybe another time." I pointed to my nearly forgotten book on the booth's seat. "I'm going to do some reading."

"Oh, come with us," Anne said. "School's over, friend. No more reading. No more books. No more teacher's dirty looks." She wrinkled her nose at the old verse. "Anyway, everyone who's anyone is going to be there, and it's been ages since you hung out with the old gang." Then she leaned down and whispered, "One of the guys is bringing the beer."

I shook my head. "I'm really kinda tired and I'm dying to finish this book. But, next time. I promise."

"Come on, Anne," Toni said, dismissing me.

I looked up at Bobbie Sue, who was gazing wistfully out the window. "Hey, Bobbie Sue. What did happen between you and Joshie?"

She cast a sideward glance at me, then looked back out the window. "Nothing, really. We love each other but we both want different things. We're headed in totally different directions." She turned her attention back to me. "It happens, I suppose, and if it's meant to be, it will be. Maybe after he's done with college and I'm done flying the friendly skies . . ." Again she cast her eyes upward, then smiled wryly.

With all her dreams, I thought, there was sadness in her eyes. There she was, with her future all mapped out, and still she wasn't sure.

"Good luck with that," I said to her as she walked away.

I watched my friends leave the joint, then motioned for

Cathy to bring another cup of coffee my way. I went about preparing it to my liking, swirling the spoon around and around until I was nearly dizzy watching the mocha-colored brew spin. I pulled my book onto the table, laid it flat open, and read the first three words of the next-to-the-last chapter. Just then the bells over the door chimed, and I looked up. I felt my eyes go wide and my face grow hot.

It was Thayne Scott, in all his glory.

5

"Well, hey there," Thayne called to me, sauntering toward the booth, then stopping long enough to give Cathy an award-winning smile along with an order. "Cup of coffee, Cathy, and a piece of your delicious apple pie."

"You've got it, Thayne."

I noticed the young waitress—the one whose name I didn't know—blushing furiously as she watched the boy-turning-man sliding into the seat opposite mine, all the while saying, "Mind if I join you?"

I squared my shoulders. "Would it matter if I did?"

He looked at me and grinned. "Oh yeah. I guess I could have waited for an answer, huh?"

"I suppose."

He jutted his thumb toward the front of the restaurant. "Do you want me to leave? I can, you know."

Cathy arrived then with Thayne's cup of coffee and the thickest, widest slice of apple pie I'd ever seen cut and served at the Bean. "Here you go, Mr. Scott."

Thayne gave Cathy a wink, then said, "This is some slice of pie, boy."

Cathy patted his shoulder, said, "You're still growing. You

50

need your fruit in any form you can get it," then moved back to the counter.

Thayne held the fork Cathy had placed alongside the pie between his thumb and index finger and extended it to me. "Want a bite before I dig in?"

I shook my head. "No. Thank you, but no." I closed my book but left it on the table.

"Your loss," he said, grinned, then did exactly as he'd said: he dug in. I wondered if he'd eaten within the past twenty-four hours and said so. He laughed. "No. See, I live with my Aunt Harriett—she owns a boardinghouse—serves dinner early every night. Six o'clock even if the creek *does* rise. She serves a pretty good meal, but by eight o'clock I'm starving." He winked at me. "Like Cathy says, I'm a growing boy."

"So I see."

"On the nights I go to school, I near starve to death." He took a sip of his coffee and rolled his broad shoulders at the same time. "This is the best coffee in town." He paused, then looked at me directly. "Good book there?"

"Very good."

"What's it about?" He took another bite of pie.

"It's a collection of short stories by Harold Brodkey. His first, I think." I shrugged. "Anyway, it has a variety of themes: the fears of childhood, adult social issues. Things like that."

Thayne nodded as though he cared, which was endearing if nothing else. "So . . ." He smiled. "Did you get the job?"

"The job?"

"Yeah. Isn't that why you went up to Mr. Puttnam's office?"

"Oh. The job."

He took another bite of pie then, shoved it to the side of his mouth, and said, "I forgot. They don't usually let you know right away. May be a day or two. Hang in there, kid. You'll get it." Then he swallowed.

I thought it wise to move away from any conversation about my possible employment at the factory. "What about you? How'd you get your job?"

He blushed.

"What?" I couldn't help but smile. His boyish charm only intensified with the added pink in his cheeks.

"It's not a very pretty story."

I leaned back. "I've got nothing but time." I wasn't usually so forward, and especially not with boys. I'd hardly had contact with them in four years. But, I couldn't help myself. I was more than a little intrigued by Thayne Scott, and for some inexplicable reason, I was nearly bursting inside with joy that I'd chosen to come to the Bean on this glorious Monday evening.

"I grew up near Vidalia. You know where that is, right?"

"Sure I do. It's where they grow the sweet onion."

Thayne nodded. "That's right. My father is a farmer there."

"Is there a high demand? For the onion, I mean."

"He does all right. Makes a living at it. Of course he grows more than onions, but he's pretty proud of his place amongst the sweet onion farmers of the world." He nodded a couple of times. "Pops says that one day the sweet onion will be what the area around there is known for."

I thought about that for a second. "Maybe they'll have sweet onion parades and festivals and things like that."

He pointed his fork at me. "You joke, but one day . . ."

I smiled. "So you grew up on a farm?"

"I did. Me and my two brothers."

I brightened. We had something in common. "I have two brothers."

"Hey, whaddya know? Younger or older?"

"Younger."

Cathy returned to the booth and refilled our coffee cups. "You're going to float home, little missy," she said to me.

I laughed lightly as she stood there but frowned as she walked away. I prepared my coffee, then noted that Thayne took his black. "So you take it straight, huh?"

He nodded. "What's a sweet girl like you adding more sugar to your coffee for?"

I tilted my head and gave him my best "oh, come on, now" look. Inside, though, I was pretty much a goner. "What about you?"

"Me? Yeah, I'm sweet enough to not need sugar in my coffee."

I laughed, then tossed my ponytail on purpose. "No, I mean, brothers. Younger or older?"

"Younger. Dana is two years younger than me. Carter is two years younger than him."

"Your parents must have had it all planned out."

"Mama did. Everything in that woman's life is orderly. Planned out to a T. She and Aunt Harriett are sisters shelled out of the same pea pod."

I laughed again. I was already in love with his pattern of speech and growing to like him more and more by the moment.

"What about your brothers?" he asked.

"Tommy is twelve-almost-thirteen," I said, smiling again in remembrance of my earlier conversation with Mitch. "And Mitch is ten-almost-eleven."

Thayne frowned. "So what does that make you, fourteen-almost-fifteen?"

"Goodness, no. I'm eighteen-almost-nineteen," I said, which made him laugh. "My parents aren't the planning kind. Well, not in that department anyway." I felt my face grow hot, and I placed the palm of my hand against my cheek. "Let's not talk about that, okay? Teenagers talking about their parents' love life over coffee and pie just doesn't seem right somehow."

"Sure. Whatever you say. Personally, it's not something

I ever think about." Then he shook as though he had the willies.

I smiled at him, folded my arms along the edge of the table, and leaned in. "What do you think of Meadow Grove?"

Thayne winked. I'm not sure if it was voluntary or involuntary, but it was cute just the same. "I like it. It sure is a lot bigger than where I come from. But, you know, not quite a city and not quite a town."

"That's one of the things I love about it. Hometown qualities but still enough places to go and things to do."

He nodded. "It's got that. And a small college, of which I'm appreciative."

About that time the song on the jukebox changed to the Frankie Lyman and the Teenagers hit "Why Do Fools Fall in Love." Thayne slapped his hands together and said, "I dig this song. Wanna dance?" He was up and out of the booth before I had time to say yes or no.

The crowd had thinned out so there was really no need for me to be embarrassed by the whole thing, but I was nonetheless. I enjoyed dancing. I'd been to a few of the dances held at Saint Margaret Mary's over the past four years, the ones where the boys from Saint Luke's were invited to join us for punch and cake and dancing as long as no bodies touched and no one snuck away to neck and smooch. Mostly my dorm mates and I danced together, learning all the new dance moves of the day—whatever they happened to be. My friends at school said I was pretty good at doing the West Coast Swing.

We made quite a show of ourselves. The few patrons left—along with Cathy, Neil, the nameless waitress, a couple of cook's helpers—were standing in a circle, cheering us on with the rhythmic clapping of their hands. I was laughing freely and Thayne was keeping up with me, grinning all the while.

When the song changed to "Who's Sorry Now," Thayne

54

pulled me to himself as though we'd been dancing together our whole lives and, in perfect time, shuffled into the box step. At school I'd always played the male role with my dorm mates, but I found it easy to allow him to lead. I caught a glimpse of Cathy then, hands clasped together and held near her heart, head against Neil's shoulder. Neil's arm was around his wife, and then he turned her toward him and they, too, began to dance. When I was facing the counter again, I noticed the waitress vigorously wiping a circle on the linoleum. Another couple—older than we but not as old as our parents—had joined in the dance, and the cook's helpers had disappeared. I dropped my forehead to Thayne's shoulder and squeezed my eyes shut. In turn, Thayne's breath blew across my ear, and for a split second I caught a delicious whiff of coffee and apple pie. It was a marvelous combination of senses—swaying back and forth, the warmth of his body as close to mine as propriety would allow, and the smell of his dessert blowing warm across the side of my face. I felt an involuntary shiver run down my spine, and I wondered if Thayne felt it too.

"Who's sad and blue . . ." Thayne sang lightly in my ear, keeping harmony with the crooning of Connie Francis.

Not me, I thought. Not me at all.

I went to bed that night feeling lightheaded. Giddy. I'd pulled my diary out of the center desk drawer and written:

> I've never felt like this. His name is Thayne and he's dreamy. A doll. He works for Daddy. I wonder if Daddy likes him. Mama would die. She'd say I was like Missy Deerfield. Shameful.
>
> So, this is what this feels like! Is it love? Goodness, no. Not so soon. Then what is it? Maybe I'll find out tomorrow. I gave him my phone number. He said he'd call. He will, won't he?

Maybe.
Oh, I hoped so.

He didn't call.

Wednesday evening after church and while Daddy was going over some paperwork in his home office, I stepped up to the door and knocked lightly, then waited for him to say, "Come in." When he did, I opened the door just enough to slip through, peeking my head in first.

"Got a minute?" I asked.

"For you, princess? All the time in the world."

I stepped inside, walked over to the chair near the desk, and sat down. It was an old chair Mama refused to have in any other room. Sort of low and worn. Downright lumpy in some spots. But it wrapped around a body like a pair of big bear arms. When I sat in it, I drew my knees up to my chest and balanced my feet along the edge of the seat. "Daddy?"

"Uh-oh. The sound of my name sounds like we're about to get into some dangerous territory."

I shook my head. "Oh no. Nothing dangerous, I promise."

"What then?"

I pressed my lips together, then licked away the dryness with the tip of my tongue. "I was just wondering if maybe we could go to lunch again tomorrow. I mean, if you have some room in your schedule."

"Didn't we just have lunch on Monday?" His eyes twinkled.

"Is there a law somewhere that says we can't have lunch twice in one week?"

"None that I know of."

I shrugged. "Okay then." For the briefest of seconds I had a glint of guilt that my invitation came not at wanting to be with him but on the hope of seeing Thayne again.

He chuckled. "Okay then."

I stood, gave him a quick hug, then left the room and headed up to bed. Mama stopped me halfway up the staircase. "Oh, good. There you are."

"You were looking for me?"

"Tomorrow let's go shopping, shall we? The Kellys—Tish and Jack—are having a barbecue on Saturday night, and your father and I have been invited. I told Tish you were home and she said by all means we should bring you." She smiled as she patted my cheek. "You are, after all, a young lady now. An adult."

The Kellys were wonderfully known for their get-togethers. The very thought of being invited was divine, and I said so. "But, I'm having lunch with Daddy tomorrow," I said. "Can we meet afterward and then go shopping?" No one would ever accuse me of passing up a shopping trip, but I was itching for the possibility of seeing Thayne again.

"Lunch? Again?" Her shoulders dropped. "Please don't tell me you're going to Drucker's."

Where we'd eat hadn't even crossed my mind. I'd only thought of my ulterior motive. "Not if it makes you unhappy," I said.

Mama thought for a moment before patting my shoulder and saying, "I know. I'll tell Daddy that you and I will meet him for lunch at Marjorie's Café." I felt my mind spinning as she leaned in. "A lot of young businessmen go there for lunch. You know, to seal the deal, that kind of thing." Then she squared her shoulders. "Oh, this is perfect."

I opened my mouth to protest but couldn't think of a thing to say. My chances of seeing Thayne again were thinning out to nil.

"Then," Mama said, "we'll go to a few of the Main Street boutiques." She nearly skipped down the stairs, leaving me behind to stare after her, dumb with how quickly my plot had dissipated.

The next morning I woke early, even before my parents. I went downstairs, made a pot of coffee, dropped two pieces of bread into the toaster, then got the butter from the refrigerator. I prepared my toast and ate it without waiting for the coffee. By the time the perking had stopped, my stomach was full and I had devised another plan. I poured a cup, preparing it to my liking, took a sip, and then headed upstairs, cup in hand and a wry smile on my face.

Mama and I were to meet Daddy at noon at Marjorie's. Mama said we'd leave the house no later than 11:45. "So be ready, dear."

"I will," I'd said.

At 10:30 I found Mama at her vanity getting ready for a bath. She took one look at me and said, "My goodness, but aren't you ready early. And don't you look all grown up."

I was wearing a form-fitting dress—white with bursts of black across the fabric—which was less loose than the new straight shifts and didn't have the full skirt of many of my dressier outfits. This was the most adult femme fatale dress I owned. I wore it well and I knew it.

I placed my hands on my hips. "I thought it would be appropriate for lunch."

"And I have to agree." By now Mama had stood from the vanity's stool and made her way to me. She touched the pearls dropping from my earlobes. "Nice touch."

"Thank you." I took a deep breath and then exhaled slowly. "Mama, do you mind horribly if I meet you at Marjorie's?"

"Meet me? I thought we'd go together?"

I acted as nonchalant as I knew how. "Oh, I know. But I was really wanting to stop by the library. I've been dying to read *Doctor Zhivago*, and you know me when I get in a library." I swallowed past the knot forming in my throat. "Is Mrs. Bartlett still there? The librarian?"

Mama gave me "the eye." "I know who Mrs. Bartlett is,

Mariette. She's been the librarian for nearly twenty-five years. What I don't know is why this can't wait."

"Really, Mama. *Doctor Zhivago* was released a year ago, it was a bestselling book for crying out loud, and I haven't even read it yet. Me! The winner of the St. Francis de Sales award."

Mama sighed. "Well, all right."

I brightened. "Why don't I pick up Daddy and then he can drive my car back to the factory after lunch."

"Then how, pray tell, will he get the car back home? One man can't drive two cars, Mariette."

I was already ahead of the question. "Of course not. After you and I shop you can take me back to the factory and I'll drive the car home." Thereby allotting two opportunities for seeing Thayne . . . in case the first one failed.

Mama shook her head. "You are a silly child. Go." I was halfway to the door when she added: "And don't be late."

6

Until that day, I had never knowingly lied to either of my parents. Like any teenager I had avoided questions. I had skirted the truth. But I had never out-and-out lied.

On my way to the Fox & Hound I stopped by our local library, which had been some rich person's home way back at the turn of the century. The story, as I remember it from our fifth grade field trip, was that a woman named Lillian Allen had bequeathed the family home—a mansion, really—to the county as long as it became and remained a library. "Miss Lillian," as she was called, had never married. Her father, Dr. Allen—or "Doc Allen" as he was called—had pressed into his only child a love for reading and an even greater passion for passing that zeal to others, especially children. "Miss Lillian" had worked with her father from her early teen years and had become as competent in the area of medicine as any college graduate, though she'd never attended school past the eleventh grade. She simply read and absorbed. In her spare time, when she wasn't working for Doc Allen, she visited her father's patients as they recovered in their homes and brought books to their young children.

The old home—now the library—sported a grand staircase that curved gently from the marble of the first floor foyer to the landing of the second floor. The walls were paneled in pink and white; within each panel was a portrait of a member of the Allen family—Doc Allen, Mrs. Allen, Lillian, her sister Beth (who married a Yankee and moved up North), and their brother Jonathan, who died tragically at the age of ten in a riding accident. Most of the rooms—large and filled with shelves of books that smelled of paper and leather, dust and musk—were divided by genre. The more mature the subject, the more likely the library patron was to climb the stairs.

While most of my time at the library had been spent downstairs, today I knew I would be ascending the great staircase. Had I the time, I could wander aimlessly for hours. But my visit today would be cut short by a more pressing matter—that of seeing Thayne Scott. Still, when I slid my car into an empty parking space at the factory, my backseat floorboard was graced by a short stack of books, including *Doctor Zhivago*, which I'd already read three times.

I nearly skipped inside the front door, said a quick hello to Donna, who was, blessedly, busy answering the phones. She did, however, point to me, eyes wide at my appearance, and make an "OK" sign by placing her index finger against the tip of her thumb.

I dashed into the stairwell then smoothed my dress over my hips, pulled a small compact out of my purse, and gave myself a quick once-over. I took in a deep breath, exhaled slowly, and began the climb toward my father's office. I offered a meager prayer to God, begging, really. "I'll do anything," I whispered, as though the Almighty were right next to me. "I'll even listen to the preacher on Sundays instead of thinking about—"

I heard a door open then slam shut. I stopped and gasped, casting my eyes upward, hoping against hope until I heard a sweet voice singing the lyrics from "Friendly Persuasion," the tune Thayne had been whistling the first time I'd seen him.

I waited until he would have a clear view of me before I said, "Hi."

I expected his usual smile, the deepening of dimples, the twinkle in his eyes. Instead, he slowed his pace, scowled, and said, "Oh. Hey." I noticed he wasn't carrying any parcels or interoffice memo envelopes.

I felt my heartbeat quicken. Something was amuck. "That's not a very friendly hello. Is something wrong?"

He seemed to gather his wits. He straightened his shoulders, cleared his throat, and began the descent toward me. "I'll tell you what's wrong," he said, keeping his eyes on me.

I slid toward the wall—just as I'd done on Monday—and pressed my back against it. I felt the cold penetrate the fabric of my dress as I raised my chest in a boldness I wasn't sure of. Then I swallowed. Hard.

When he reached the step where my feet rested, he continued. "Why didn't you tell me who you are?"

"I don't know—"

He raised a hand. "Don't."

I struggled to keep my voice low. Anything said within these cavernous walls might be heard on the floors in the echo. "Don't what? I don't understand . . ."

He jutted his face toward mine. "You're the boss's daughter. You're Mariette Puttnam."

The well of tears that had begun to sting the back of my eyes suddenly dried up. "Well, you don't have to say it like it's a curse word."

He took a step back, blinked at me a few times before saying, "You led me to believe you were here looking for a job."

"That's not true. I never said—"

"You never said anything. Nothing to change what I thought. You deceived me."

In one day I'd become both a liar and a deceiver. The tears returned. I felt my bottom lip quiver. I looked down at my gloved hands—the fingers of one clasping the fingers of the other—and said, "How'd you . . . how'd . . ."

"How'd I find out? I'll tell you how."

I looked up at him, and as I did a tear slipped down my cheek. I tried to imagine when I'd felt this kind of turmoil. I'd allowed myself to feel something for a young man I hardly knew. Hadn't it been just days ago I'd said I wasn't ready for a relationship—rich man, poor man, no man?—and yet here I was, weeping over a broken relationship that hadn't really gotten started.

"As soon as you left the Bean the other night in that sporty car of yours, which should have told me something right there, Cathy says to me, 'So, you and the boss's daughter are a hot item.' And then Neil says, 'Not a shabby way to climb the old ladder to success.' Like I *knew*." He spewed the last word.

"Thayne, listen . . . please . . ."

"You can't say anything to me right now. Nothing I want to hear, anyway." He took a few steps toward the landing, then looked back at me. "I thought you were special, you know that? I told my aunt about you. Told her I thought I'd met someone different than anyone I'd ever met before."

A flicker of hope leapt in my chest.

He snickered then. "I guess I wasn't far off, boy. I guess you are different. A rich girl playing on the wrong side of the tracks." He shook his head. "I'm just glad I never kissed you. Man, that would have been even worse than this." He poked himself in the chest a couple of times for effect. "This I'm feeling." He shook his head again. "Man," he said again, then turned and continued down the stairs until he entered the second floor. I wondered if he had any business there. If that was where he'd been heading.

Then I slid down the wall, buried my face in my hands, and cried like a five-year-old.

Before walking into Daddy's office, I slipped into a restroom, washed my face, pinched color back into my cheeks, and steadied myself. If Daddy knew what had happened he'd

fire Thayne for sure. Of course if Daddy knew I'd been dancing with and daydreaming about a mail clerk, he might just
blow a gasket and skin me alive.

Not that he ever had.

The rest of the day was painfully long. Mama and Daddy
had a bit of a tiff over lunch about my future. Although I
said little, the thought of leaving town again suddenly ap-
pealed to me.

Mama asked if I was okay more than once during the meal
and about a half dozen times during our shopping spree. I'd
already lied to her once that day, so I added another. "It's nearing my time of the month," I said. "You know how I get."

It was enough to satisfy her.

Saturday evening finally arrived. Mama and I dressed in
our new outfits—complementary clam diggers and madras
blouses—and Daddy looked sporty in a pair of casual black
slacks and a pale blue and white panel front sports shirt.
Tommy was left to "sit with the kid," as he put it. When I
saw Mitch setting the Monopoly game out, I winked at him
and he winked back.

We arrived fashionably late to the Kellys'; a train of cars
streamed down both sides of the street before their luxury
home nestled behind clusters of magnolia and dogwood trees.
Mama scanned them and announced who had arrived to
Daddy and me, as if we actually cared.

"The festivities will be held outside," she told me as we
walked up the wide drive, me keeping step between my parents. "You haven't seen their backyard since Jack had all
the work done. It's simply marvelous." She beamed toward
Daddy. "Isn't it, Carroll?"

With the extra weight he carried—albeit well—Daddy
already looked miserable. "It's going to be hot," he said with
a huff. "It already is. I hope Jack remembered to have some
fans set out."

64

I looped my arm in Daddy's and said, "Daddy, you should have brought your bathing suit. Don't the Kellys have a pool?"

Daddy smiled down at me. "That'll be the day," he said. The lilt in his voice had returned.

The party being held in the backyard or not, we entered by way of the double front doors, escorted in by the Kellys' maid, Delores, who also happened to be Daisy's baby sister. Although they worked doing the same kind of job, the difference in the two was that Delores was a full-time maid and Daisy only came to our house once a week.

"Good evening, Delores," Daddy said.

"Mr. Puttnam. Daisy told me you had come home, Miss Mariette," she said. "I know your mama and daddy is proud to have you home again."

Mama smiled at Delores but said nothing. Daddy had already made his way toward the back of the house, where a large living room opened out to the patio area via four sets of French doors framed with ceiling to floor tie-back muslin drapes. The entire house was decorated in a Caribbean motif, and I sighed at the breathtaking beauty of it.

From the direction of the patio came the sound of someone tickling the ivories, drawing me toward the rest of the partygoers. I noted that Mama had found our hostess and was already making small talk with her. Daddy had all but disappeared.

The pianist, it turned out, was Mrs. Schneiders. She was finishing up "Daddy's Little Girl," which brought a smile to my lips. "Perfect timing," she said when she saw me.

At first I thought she was being her usual kind self, but then she raised her brow, and I wondered exactly what she meant by the words. "How are you, Mrs. Schneiders?" I asked, ignoring my instinct. "I didn't know you'd be playing here this evening."

"I always play for the Kelly parties," she replied. "But

I'd say you wouldn't know that, this being your first adult party."

I leaned against the grand piano, resting my elbow on its ebony finish. "That's true."

"And what do you think so far?" Her aging hands returned to the keys, and she began playing "No Other Love" as though she didn't expect an answer.

I looked around the room, trying to take it all in—this adult party—as Mrs. Schneiders added her lovely voice to the music of the piano, sounding more like Jo Stafford than Jo Stafford as she sang about love and warm hearts and the comfort of a man's arms.

I felt a twinge within my chest cavity. I looked at Mrs. Schneiders, who, as she sang, kept her eyes on me.

She knows, I thought. *She knows about Thayne and me.*

She changed from singing the lyrics to humming the tune, raised her chin just a bit, and looked over my shoulder. I turned to see a group of men standing around the indoor bar, glasses clutched in their hands, one and all in a casual stance as they laughed and chatted about whatever men talk about. But it was the bartender who caught and held my attention. He stood behind the bar, dropping ice from silver tongs into two Tom Collins–sized glasses, looking too young to drink, much less serve.

Thayne.

I looked back at Mrs. Schneiders, who smiled up at me, her fingers keeping perfect time on the piano keys. "Go," she said. "Get yourself a Coke. Perfect on a hot evening like this."

"It's not ladylike," I whispered back. "To approach a bar." I looked at Thayne once more, then again at Mrs. Schneiders. "Is it?"

"All is fair in love and war, my dear. Just ask Mr. Schneiders." She looked down at the keyboard.

I walked over to the end of the bar, glancing around briefly for signs of Mama or Daddy—of which there were, thankfully, none.

Thayne smiled when he saw me, but the smile quickly faded. Mrs. Schneiders's voice rose as she sang as though she were trying to get his attention, which worked. He cast his eyes toward her, flinched, then looked back at me, this time making his way to where I stood.

"What can I get you?" he asked, then added, "Ma'am."

"Thayne, don't . . ."

"Cocktail? Dry martini? Manhattan?"

"No." I kept my voice low, my eyes on my hands, which clasped the bar's padded edge. "No, thank you. I'll just have a Coke please."

"Ice?"

"Yes. Please."

"Be right back with the lady's pleasure."

I watched him prepare my drink, the way his hands deftly dropped ice from the tongs with one hand and poured soda with the other. His final touch was a cherry, dropped into the dark liquid. It rested between pieces of ice, bobbing over like a buoy on water. He placed the glass on a white cocktail napkin and brought it to me, extending it in midair. I took it from him. Our fingers touched. Electricity shot through me, the same as I'd felt when he shook my hand on Monday and held me in his arms as we danced on Wednesday.

"You okay?" he asked.

"What?"

He took the glass from my quivering hand, its liquid sloshing from side to side.

"Are you okay?" he asked again.

I took a jagged breath. "Thayne, I'm sorry. I'm so sorry. I didn't mean to deceive you. I didn't. And if you'll just give me a chance to see you . . . to talk to you . . . to explain."

Thayne looked around nervously; his eyes told me he didn't want to chance anyone hearing what I had to say.

Once again I glanced down at my hands then back up to him. Another jagged breath inhaled and exhaled before I said, "Three hundred."

He furrowed his brow. "What?"

"That's my number, in case you've forgotten. Call me tomorrow at two o'clock on the dot and I promise I'll answer." I swallowed. "Please, Thayne. Don't make me beg you to forgive me."

From behind me I heard a man's voice. "Vodka highball, young man."

Thayne snapped to attention and I did too, but we somehow managed to keep our eyes on each other. Then—though barely perceivable—he nodded. "Two o'clock," he said. "Three hundred."

As I stepped away from the bar, clutching my drink, I heard a new tune from the piano: "My Foolish Heart."

7

I avoided Thayne the rest of the evening by nursing the one soft drink he'd prepared for me. The one with the cherry on top.

As it turned out, Missy and Ward were also guests at the party. Mama later expressed dismay, to which I remarked that of course they would be; after all, the Deerfields and the Kellys were longtime friends. Mama told me then that Tish Kelly had hosted a tea for Missy two weeks ago.

Missy glowed in Ward's attentiveness. In fact, she looked more beautiful than I remembered. Not that she wasn't always gorgeous; she was petite with golden skin, short blonde hair (that Sandra Dee had nothing on her), and startling blue eyes, but love had brought out in her something almost exotic.

She showed me her diamond—a one-karat, round cut solitaire set in white gold—while describing its accompanying simple, thin wedding band. I oohed over the engagement ring as much as I thought appropriate. It truly was lovely. A little ostentatious for a girl Missy's size, but she seemed quite pleased with it. "I lie in bed at night, I tell you I do, and I hold my arm out and let the moonlight through the window catch like fire in it. It just sends shivers up and down my spine. I cannot believe it's mine." Then she leaned into Ward. "Or that he's mine."

Ward Hill—six foot if he was an inch and every bit as gorgeous as I'd heard—leaned down and kissed the top of Missy's head.

I smiled at him and then back at Missy. "Something tells me that if Mr. Hill here had come on bended knee with a Cracker Jack ring, you would have still said yes."

Missy nodded like a little girl as Ward said, "I know I'm a little older, but I'd prefer to be called Ward."

I nodded. "Ward," I said.

"What about you?" Missy asked. "Found anyone special since we last spoke?"

Ward chuckled. "Okay. This is my cue to leave in all fairness to my own sex."

Missy pouted playfully, obviously fine with Ward's departure. When he'd sauntered away, she practically pounced. "Okay. Tell me everything you've heard."

I was taken aback. "Me?"

"Yes, you. We're not best friends so you have nothing to worry about—you know, like I'm not going to ask you to be my maid of honor or anything. We've not seen each other in—what?—nine, ten months. Just tell me what you've heard."

"Okay," I said, then told her what I'd heard from both Mama and the girls at the Bean, ending with, "And he is. He's totally dreamy."

She smiled, showing off a slight overbite. "He is, isn't he?"

"Explain to me," I said, "about this 'religious' statement Toni made."

Missy shifted her weight and took a sip of her drink, also a Coke, and shrugged. "It's no big deal." Then she rolled her eyes. "Well, unless you talk with my parents about it. He was raised in an independent church; he actually likes to read the

Bible—he talks about it a lot—and has a very . . . well . . . personal relationship with God."

I'd been in a private Catholic school for the last four years, and still I wasn't sure what that last comment meant. "Personal."

Missy nodded. "Mmmhmm. I guess you could say I have a personal relationship too. That's why, when Ward and I realized how we felt about each other—no matter the age difference—he said we should get married." She cleared her throat. "'I say therefore to the unmarried and widows, it is good for them if they abide even as I. But if they cannot contain, let them marry: for it is better to marry than to burn.'" She paused. "Paul's first letter to the Corinthians, chapter 7, verses 8 and 9."

I blinked. "Doesn't the Bible say something somewhere about divorce?"

She looked down, then back up. "So you know that Ward's wife left him."

"Actually, no. No, I didn't know. I just heard he was divorced."

She turned a pleasant shade of pink. "Well, it wasn't his idea; it was hers." She shrugged. "She found someone else and . . . well, don't advertise that, will you? He's pretty devastated about it. Never talks about it with anyone. Hardly even me. They have a son together, after all."

"How do you get along with him? The little boy?"

She beamed. "Oh, marvelously. He's adorable, just like his daddy. Ward goes to get him about once a month, and after the wedding and the honeymoon, we'll have him the remainder of the summer."

"Speaking of which . . . Pete tells me the wedding is in two weeks?"

She held up two fingers. "Two weeks from today." Then she blushed. "Two weeks and I'll be Mrs. Ward Gregory Hill." She sighed. "I don't mind telling you I'm about to burst for the honeymoon."

I looked down at my sandaled feet, wiggled my toes, and said, "Well . . ." Then back up to her. "So, where is he taking you?"

"On a Caribbean cruise."

"Wow."

"I know. I'll come back all tanned and happy." She bit her lip.

Without thinking, I looked over my shoulder at where Thayne continued in his work as bartender. He looked at me at the same time, smiled faintly, then went back to his task. I looked back at Missy, who'd obviously not missed a thing. "He's cute," she said.

I nodded. "He is."

"Do you know his name?"

"Thayne," I said. "Thayne Scott. He works for Daddy."

Missy raised her chin. "Uh-oh. Scandal, here comes Mariette."

I tried to dismiss her words with a wrinkle of my nose and a shake of my head, but the flush I felt across my cheeks gave me away. Missy—God love her—winked. "Tell you what; you keep Ward's secret and I'll keep yours."

"But there really isn't—"

Missy placed her left hand on my arm and said, "Mariette. I'm practically a married woman. If I don't know the look of love about to bloom, then who does?"

The following afternoon at about 1:30, after church had been attended, lunch had been eaten, the dining room had been cleared, and the kitchen had been cleaned, Daddy declared it was a perfect afternoon for a family drive.

"How long has it been, Mary Sue, since we had the three kids in the backseat, windows down, enjoying the countryside around here?" Daddy wiped the back of his neck with one of his starched handkerchiefs. "A hot day like today? It'll feel good to get out of the house."

Mama thought it was a marvelous idea and said so. "I can put some iced tea in a thermos, bring along some of those Tupperware tumblers."

While Tommy complained about wanting to play softball with his friends over at Anderson Park and Mitch nearly flew upstairs to get the latest Superman comic to read in the backseat, I bit my lip in angst, trying to think of a reasonable excuse that wouldn't land me in a liar's pool again.

Mama caught the look and asked, "What is it, Mariette?"

I glanced down at my watch then back to my parents. With the exception now of Mitch, we were sitting in the den where the newspaper had been strewn across the floor and oscillating fans drove warm air from the outside to the inside at the opened windows, causing the papers to flap lazily in the breeze. "Well, I . . . actually I was waiting for a phone call."

"The gang doing something this afternoon?" Daddy asked. He chuckled. "Look at her, Mary Sue. The child has only been home a week, and she's already out having the time of her life with her old friends."

The "gang" most assuredly was. They'd talked about it after church as we'd clustered together on the sidewalk in front. Boddiford's Bridge was *the* swimming hole, complete with a rope swing dangling from an old cypress tree, its roots deeply imbedded in the soil beneath the glassy surface of the water, and a low bridge, perfect for diving into the deepest part of the creek. A hot day like today drove young people there en masse.

"We were talking about going down to Boddiford's Bridge for the afternoon," I said.

"It's a good day for it," Daddy said. Then he slapped his knees and hoisted himself up from his chair. "Well, that leaves us and the boys, my dear," he said to Mama. "Go get that tea ready and I'll get the car to humming."

Tommy was fast on Daddy's heels. "Oh, come on, Pop," I heard him say before his voice faded to a boy's whine. "If Mariette doesn't have to . . ."

I looked at Mama and she at me, and we smiled. "Boys," I said.

Mama stood from her place on the sofa and headed for the door. "Does your old bathing suit from last year still fit?" she asked. She turned to face me.

I nodded. "It should."

"All right then," she said, then left me sitting alone with my anxious thoughts, wondering if the family would be out of the house by two.

It was 2:02 when the phone rang, and within the past two minutes I'd nearly chewed my fingernails down to shredded nubs.

I'd practiced saying hello, had said it a dozen times or more. Maybe two dozen times or more, always attempting to sound older and wiser. Maybe a little sexier. After all, Thayne was a college student. Part time only, but a college student nonetheless. The girls he'd dated in the past two years were probably attempting higher education as well. (Score one for Daddy.) Or, if not, they were primed and ready for marriage. (Score one for Mama.)

When the phone finally rang, I grabbed it and practically barked, "Hello!"

"Whoa!" the infectious voice on the other end said with a chuckle. "I thought you *wanted* me to call."

I was sitting at Daddy's desk, having moved from the den, thinking that being around all the business papers would help with the whole mature-sounding voice issue. I now attempted to relax a bit in his high-backed chair as I said, "Oh. Sorry. The phone in here is so loud . . . it startled me, is all."

He was silent for a moment. Then he said, "So, then. Did you enjoy yourself last night?"

"I did. It was my first adult party." I squeezed my eyes together and pretended to pound my fist against the desk. *What a stupid thing to say!* "What about you?" I asked, hoping to retrieve the moment.

"Well, I was working, so . . ."

"Oh yeah. That's right. Sorry." I took a deep breath. "The Coke was good."

He chuckled again. "Just doing my job, ma'am," he said.

I relaxed, this time resting my back against the tufted leather of the chair. "Very funny."

"So, what are you doing today? I hear a bunch of the kids are heading out to Buddiford's Bridge."

"Kids? I'll have you know—"

"I know. Your first adult party. You and your friends aren't children anymore."

"Very funny." I should have been incensed, but I smiled anyway.

"So," he said again. "What *are* you doing today?"

I shrugged as though he could see me. "I dunno. I was hoping maybe you'd have a suggestion." I felt my face grow hot. When had I ever been this brazen?

"Well, I'll tell you. I'd really like to get to know you better." He paused. I felt my heart skip a beat, waiting and wondering what he'd say next. "But it's like this; you're Mr. Puttnam's daughter and I'm Mr. Puttnam's employee and—"

"But we can . . . I can . . ."

"What, Mariette? Get another job for me when the axe comes down on my head? I gotta have this job. I have to get myself through school and pay rent. I'm not like you; I worry about next week and next month and even next year. What have you got to worry about?"

I had no answer.

"That's what I thought."

But I felt a glimmer of hope. "You said you want to get to know me better."

Again, he paused. Again, my heart skipped.

"I said I wasn't going to do this," he said, more to himself than to me.

"Do what?"

Another pause. This one longer than the others. "Never mind. You want to meet at the Bean? Say, like old friends who just happened to bump into each other? All right. Let's do it."

I became a mixed bag of emotions. I was both tentative and exuberant, all at once. I'd never done anything behind my parents' backs—well, until the day I'd made up the whole *Dr. Zhivago* story—and now here I was planning to meet a boy I knew they'd disapprove of. Still, he was Thayne Scott and he was adorable, and I'd never—not once, ever—felt like this about any boy. He'd taken my breath away from the moment I met him. I'd explain all that to my parents if I thought I could first explain it to myself.

But I couldn't. So, I said, "Okay. I'll meet you at the Bean."

And later? If my parents found out?

Come what may.

8

It was a day to be remembered forever. The most exciting Sunday of my life thus far. I'd never felt so completely put together and yet so undone. I was coming into my life's purpose while at the same time losing sight of any future I'd contemplated, even if only for my parents.

Thayne and I met at the Bean, where we had cups of coffee and shared a piece of lemon meringue pie. We looked at each other as though we were each trying to memorize the other's face. I noted a small crescent-shaped scar near his right eye, and when I asked him about it he chuckled a bit, then touched it with his index finger and said, "I think this is the evidence of a fight over a stick Carter and I had when we were kids."

"Over a stick?"

He nodded then shook his head. "Kids can fight over the stupidest things. It was one of those days when whatever I had, he wanted, and whatever he had, I wanted. I think I was about ten at the time. Carter was about six. Mama had had enough of our fussing and she sent us outside to the yard, where we fought over the tire swing until Dana came along, shoved past both of us, and got in it. Then we fought with Dana, screaming like banshees for him to get out of *our* swing." Thayne laughed again, took a sip of his coffee, and continued, "Until Pop came around the side of the house and told Carter and me to 'get a move on, now.'" His voice deepened as he quoted his father. "Eventually, the fight progressed to a stick, which landed right here." Thayne pointed to the scar.

"Tell me more about your father."

He shrugged. "What's there to tell? He's a good man. A hard man, but a good one. Farmer, but you know that."

"I know that."

"Loves his wife and kids, but he didn't mind slinging a strap across our backsides when we acted up."

I jerked a bit. "He beat you?"

Thayne cut his eyes up to me, hunched over the table with his forearms against the side of it, and said, "I wouldn't say 'beat' exactly." He paused. He looked straight at me. Straight through me, really, as if he were living out a moment somewhere else. "You know that old saying about this hurting me more than you? You know, that thing parents say when they're disciplining their kids?"

This time, I shrugged. "Not really, no. I've never had a spanking or even much of a verbal thrashing."

His eyes widened. "You're kidding."

I shook my head and said, "No, I'm not." I pursed my lips. "I think maybe Tommy got a spanking from Daddy once but . . ." I didn't want to talk about my family. I only wanted to hear about his. "What's your father's name?"

"Emmett. Emmett Johnson Scott. Mama is Lena Marie Scott."

I blinked. "What about you? What's your full name, Thayne Scott?"

"Thayne Johnson Scott. Johnson was Pop's mother's name. You know, before she married my grandfather. It's a traditional thing now, I guess. She named Pops after her maiden name; they named me after it too." He pinked. "I suppose my first son will have Johnson for a middle name as well."

"I think that's a fine name," I said. I felt heat flush my face when the implication of what I'd said hit me. Thayne only laughed at me, then pointed toward the jukebox—which had just begun to play Sam Cooke's "You Send Me." "Dance?" he asked.

And I said I would.

Was there anyone else in the café? I have no idea. To this day I don't remember another living being, not even Cathy or Neil Price, though I'm sure they were there. All I remember is getting to know a little bit more about this wonderful young man and swaying in his arms, feeling the muscles under his shirt against the softness of my breasts, of breathing in the scent of him and him breathing in the scent of me. "What is that perfume?" he whispered in my ear, which caused me to shiver and him, in turn, to laugh lightly as it seemed he was always doing at me.

"Evening in Paris," I said when I'd found my voice. I swallowed. "I hope you like it."

He drew back to look at me. His eyes danced as he asked, "Did you wear it just for me?"

I nodded. "Daddy gave it to me for Christmas last year."

He pulled me to him again and said, "Your daddy should be ashamed. Doesn't he know what perfume like this does to a man?"

I dipped my forehead until it rested on his shoulder. "I don't think he thought about that at the time. It's a pretty safe bet I wouldn't be wearing it for the nuns at Saint Margaret Mary."

He stopped dancing with me, ran his hands down my arms, and then gripped my hands. "Are you Catholic?"

I shook my head. "No."

He looked at me for so long I thought there must be something wrong. A song by Roy Orbison replaced Cooke's.

Thayne's eyes searched mine, shifting back and forth like a pendulum in rapid motion. I started to ask what the matter was when suddenly he said, "Did you know I saw him once?"

"Who?"

"Roy Orbison." He dropped my hands.

"Seriously?"

"Yeah." We continued to stand where we'd been dancing, near our booth. "Him and his band. The Teen Kings."

"Wow."

"Johnny Cash and Carl Perkins were there too."

I didn't say anything. I honestly didn't know what to say.

"He sang 'Ooby Dooby.'"

I started laughing at the silliness of his words. Years later he told tell me he was just trying to get his emotions under control; that what he wanted to do right there on the floor of the Bean was to ravish me in front of Neil and Cathy and all the patrons who were enjoying a Sunday afternoon slice of pie and cup of coffee. I said to him, "There were others there?"

To which he said, "Oh yeah. And they could all call your daddy and tell him Thayne Scott was making love to his daughter in public and I wouldn't have cared."

"But you did care." I smiled at him. "You didn't ravish me."

Then Thayne winked. "Not right then, no."

But that conversation was years later when I understood the makings of a man better. Or, a man's undoing, if nothing else. Thayne insisted, after my giggles over "Ooby Dooby," that we go for a drive. Get out of there.

I asked him if he wanted to take my car or his, to which he replied, "We'd better take yours, seeing as I don't have one."

Thayne paid our tab, and we walked out into the heat of June. "How can you not have a car?" I asked, digging into my purse for the keys to my De Soto. I handed them to him, thinking it would only be proper for him to drive. He hesitated, then took the keys.

"Sure about this?" he asked.

For a second I wasn't sure what he meant. Leaving to go anywhere with him or allowing him to drive my car. Either way, I was fine with it, and so I nodded and smiled.

Thayne and I slid into the car's hot interior, him behind the steering wheel and me somewhere between the middle and the passenger window. He keyed the ignition and then, after acclimating himself, put the car in reverse and eased out of the parking lot. "I had a car," he said. "Well, a truck. Pop's old truck."

"What happened to it?" The searing breeze tussled my hair. I reached into my purse again and pulled out a white poodle scarf, draped it over my head, then secured it under my chin. I finished the look with pink cat-eye sunglasses that I had to fish from the bottom of my purse.

"I do believe," Thayne said, his voice upbeat, "my little brother Dana is now the proud owner." He cut his eyes over at me. "I told you there was an ugly side to my past. That's just a part of it."

"Losing the truck to Dana?"

"Mmmhmm."

He slowed the car to a stop at a traffic light, then reached over to turn on the radio. My hand shot up and grabbed his. The electricity I'd learned to expect whenever our skin touched shot through me again. "Don't," I said.

"Something wrong?" His fingers slipped between mine and then rested on the vinyl of the seat between us.

"I just don't want to listen to music right now. I want to talk. To get to know more about you."

He smiled then. I turned to look out my window. This being a Sunday, few people were out in their cars; no one walked the sidewalks. A few folks sat on the benches around the town's fountain located in the center square in front of the towering courthouse. The light changed from red to green, and he eased the car through the intersection.

"And just where are you taking me, Thayne Johnson Scott?"

"A secret place."

"What kind of secret place?"

"You'll see." He focused on the road ahead, and so did I. We were leaving the city limits; that much I knew. The rows of dogwoods and azaleas that lined the street gave way to a few buildings followed by rambling houses and then open spaces of land.

"I was the star of our baseball team," he said, breaking the silence.

"You were?"

"Yeah. Had a scholarship to ABAC."

"ABAC?"

"Abraham Baldwin Agricultural College. Over in Tifton."

"Oh. Did you go?"

"For a while. Like I told you before, Pop was a hard man. Strict. And Mama was all about God and the Bible and stuff. Every morning, that woman got up before the chickens and sat at the kitchen table, reading her Bible, then she'd pray for her boys. All four of us." He cut his eyes over to me again. "Pop too."

"Nothing wrong with that, I guess," I said, though I couldn't imagine my mother getting up before the sun to read anything, much less the Bible.

"Not a thing in this world. Every Wednesday night she had us all dressed up and ready for prayer meeting down at the little country church where both sides of my family have gone as far back as anyone can remember. Then, on Sunday morning, like it or not, we went to Sunday school and church. Came home. Had a big dinner. Pretty traditional."

"We're Lutherans," I said, as though it mattered.

He looked at me for a moment. "That's nice. You religious?"

I shook my head. "Not really. I mean, I went to Saint Margaret Mary for four years. That's a private school about three hours from here. We had mass and I participated as I could, not being Catholic and all."

"If you aren't Catholic, why'd you go to a Catholic school?"

"Daddy wanted me in an all-girls school, and the best in the state, to his determination, was Saint Margaret Mary's." I pressed my lips together. "Daddy made quite a donation to the school, which is how I got in, if you're wondering."

"What about your brothers? They go?"

I laughed lightly. "Oh no. Daddy doesn't worry as much about their virtue."

Thayne gave me a peculiar look then slowed the car and turned down a long and narrow paved road.

"Where *are* you taking me?"

"It's a surprise. So, is what I hear about Catholic girls in private schools true?"

I bristled. Crossing my arms, I said, "I don't know. What have you heard?"

He just shook his head. "Never mind. Anyway, not being Catholic and all, how did you get along with the other girls?"

I looked down at our hands, still intertwined. "Okay, I guess. Sometimes—most times—I felt like the girl left out in the cold."

"How so?"

I felt a familiar ache from deep inside. "They have their ways, you know. Their traditions. Lutherans have some of the same but not the same, if that makes sense. Sometimes I felt like—because I'm not Catholic—I was always three paces behind. I hung out with them and all, but . . ." My voice trailed off as Thayne turned the car from the paved road to a dirt lane, thick with foliage and vines of ripe blackberries on both sides. A tuft of grass grew between the ruts in the narrow road. I felt my brows knit together.

"Don't be nervous," Thayne said, as though reading my mind. "You want to talk about church? This is my church."

"I don't understand."

"You will in a minute," he answered.

I remained quiet as the car bounded down the road. When we reached a clearing on the left, he turned into it, then parked the car. "Thayne," I whispered. I'd hardly been on a date before, much less parking.

I braced myself, expecting him to reach for me, to kiss me or paw me or whatever it is men do to women who find themselves parked in the woods, alone together. Instead, he let go of my hand, opened the driver's door, and said, "Come on."

I pulled the scarf off as I scooted out of the driver's side. His hand found mine again. For several minutes he guided me from the clearing, to the outskirts of the woods, and then into its deepest parts. I kept a watch on the earth beneath my feet, my eyes darting in search of snakes or other creatures that might have made their home there. I avoided briars and brambles as best I could, but occasionally one sliced across my bare legs. My one-piece halter top shorts set with a button-down, full open skirt wasn't really the best attire for this particular outing. Thankfully I'd worn a pair of flat shoes.

"What do you think?" Thayne finally said. His voice was breathless.

"About what?" I pulled my sunglasses from my face and looked around, then up. The vine-wrapped pines seemed to stretch on forever; they completely blocked out the sky and clouds. Dusty sunrays fell like shafts between their branches, giving the world above me an ethereal feel. "Wow," I whispered.

84

"Listen." Thayne's voice was so low I barely caught the word. He stepped from in front of me to behind me, wrapped his arms around my waist, crossing them and squeezing ever so lightly.

"Thayne . . ."

"Shhh." He tilted his head up, causing mine to do the same. "Listen, Mariette."

I stayed completely still and quiet, waiting to hear whatever it was he wanted me to listen to. But I heard nothing. Not a bird, not a twig cracking or breaking, not a trickle of water, or—blessedly—not a single forest creature. The world around us was totally silent, as though time had been suspended and somehow we'd gotten caught in the balance.

"I don't hear anything," I finally said.

"I know. You talk about church? This is God's sanctuary, Mariette. This is where I come to pray. To think. To get away from everyone and everything."

I turned then, slipping casually into his embrace. "You pray?"

"Sure. Don't you?"

"At church. Sure. I guess." I licked my lips with my tongue, thinking that if he didn't kiss me soon, I'd die. I'd simply die right here in this church of his. And now, because Thayne trusted me, I supposed, mine.

"Mariette," he said, then drew me to him, tenderly at first, his lips barely touching mine. My knees buckled and his arms flexed to catch me. "Mariette," he said, this time against my face, then deepened the kiss, pressing the fullness of his lips against mine until I thought my brain would explode.

I pushed away from him. "Oh," I said, stumbling a bit.

He reached for me, helped me steady myself. "I'm sorry," he said.

"No." I brought my hand to my mouth and held it there for a moment. "It's okay, it's just . . ."

Thayne looked down. "How many men have you kissed, Mariette?" he asked, bringing his eyes up to mine.

One, I thought. But I said, "I've kissed plenty of boys." I stretched my back and squared my shoulders. Another lie from my lips. I'd kissed exactly three, and none of them memorable enough to write about in my diary.

"Boys," he said, taking a step toward me. I took one step back. "Boys," he said again, this time walking past me. "I didn't say boys."

I watched him as he stepped deeper into the woods. "Don't you dare leave me, Thayne Scott," I said, running to catch up to him. When I did, he reached for my hand and squeezed it tightly in his.

"I would never leave you, Mariette Puttnam."

I smiled, but not at him. I just smiled as he hummed the tune to "Friendly Persuasion."

"So," I finally said. "What happened at ABAC? And what brought you here to Meadow Grove and into my life?"

9

As we walked a ways farther, Thayne told me what he'd been skirting for the hours we'd been together. He'd been the high school baseball star, but it was his good marks that had earned him a number of scholarships. Although a semi-pro team's scout had looked at him, at his father's insistence he'd chosen to go to ABAC. "Not that it's a bad place. It's actually a wonderful school," he said. "If you want to be a farmer. Which I do not."

"What do you want to do?" I asked him. By now Thayne had directed us back toward the car. The air had turned cool around us, the sky a grayer shade of blue.

"I don't know, to be honest with you. I just know what I don't want to do."

He'd gotten into a few skirmishes while at ABAC the half year he'd attended. "Drinking too much, mostly," he said. "Pop got a call." He grew quiet, then said, "That was a day to remember, when he headed down to the school. I thought he'd take a strap to me right there in front of my school chums. Instead he took me out for dinner and said, in no uncertain terms, that I would either straighten up and fly right or I'd pay dearly for it. He never said what that payment would be, but I got the picture."

I wasn't so sure I would like Mr. Scott, and I said so.

"Nah. Pop is okay. He just had his dreams pinned on me, and I blew them."

"So then what happened?"

Thayne's carousing stopped, but only for a short period of time. One night, while out with some of the boys, he'd met a girl. "Prettiest thing I'd ever seen in my life," he said, then looked at me. "Until I met you."

I wasn't sure whether I should be pleased or put out.

"And?" I asked.

"My grades really plummeted then. I couldn't get this girl out from under my skin."

I felt heat rush to my cheeks. I wanted to know just how well he'd known her, how deeply involved they'd become, but I didn't dare ask.

"She was a pretty girl but she was a girl with one thing on her mind."

"And that was?"

"Getting married. Any way she could. In my head I knew she was destroying me in more ways than one, but my heart wouldn't let me let her go."

I frowned. "Did you marry her, Thayne?"

He stopped and gave me a peculiar look. "Goodness, no."

I forced myself not to grin. If Mama thought the Deerfields had a scandal, wait till she heard *this*.

"But," he said, "while I couldn't let her go, ABAC could surely let me go." He chuckled. "Pop was so mad. And Mama; God love her, she was hurt. Scared too, I think. She called her sister—my aunt Harriett—and asked if I could come stay here. Aunt Harriett said she had a boarder who worked for your father and he thought he could get me a job down at the factory. So, in January, I came here."

I thought about what he said for a few moments. By the time I'd sorted it all out in my mind, we were back at the car. Thayne opened the passenger door for me. I sat on the seat and swung my legs in. Just then he looked down at the open skirt, seeing the cuts on my legs. He squatted, ran his hands down one, then the other. "Oh, Mariette. Honey, I'm so sorry."

I shivered at his touch and at his words; it was his first endearment toward me.

"It's nothing," I said. "I don't even feel it."

He stood. "You'd best get home," he said. "And get something on these scratches so they don't fester up."

He closed the door. I'd best get home, all right. But not because of the cuts on my legs. My parents were going to have hissy fits when I told them who I'd been with all day.

If I told them at all.

"I thought you were a second year student at the college," I said as we headed back toward the city limits.

"Nah. I don't even have a major yet. I'm just taking some classes, mostly because of Aunt Harriett's influence." He chuckled. "Aunt Harriett; she's a character."

"I'm afraid I don't know her well."

"Loves classical music—which she's drilled into me these past six months. And, like Mama, she loves God. She's had me going to church with her every Sunday but, more than that, really thinking about the Lord and my life and the role he plays in it."

"That seems to be important to you."

"It's getting to be."

"Do you know Ward Hill?" I asked him. I don't know where the words came from; I just blurted them out.

He looked at me kind of funny and said, "Yeah, I know him. He's marrying Missy Deerfield in about two weeks."

I nodded. "Yeah. I've heard he's kinda religious."

Thayne laughed a bit. "Even more than my Aunt Harriett. I see him down at the Bean some nights. He's down there reading his Bible and sipping on coffee, and we talk some. Nice guy."

"Is he?"

Thayne didn't answer the question. Instead he said, "Do you know Missy well?"

"As well as I know any of the gang from around here, I suppose."

"What does that mean?"

We were now blocks from where we'd started. I looked down at my Timex. It was a little before six o'clock. Mama would be frantic if I wasn't home by suppertime. "I grew up with them, most of them. But then I went away, remember? Every Christmas I'd come home for two weeks and try to catch up and summer breaks too, but—just like at school—I was always a few steps behind. By the time I got caught up on all the news it was time to go back to school. During Christmas, I mean. And then during the summer, everyone seemed to be flitting here and there. I ran into some of the old gang the other night at the Bean—the night I saw you there. They were all going to the movies but I . . . I don't know . . . I couldn't seem to muster up the enthusiasm."

"You don't like movies?"

"I like them fine. I just . . . Well, for sure, I'm glad I didn't go."

He reached for my hand then and squeezed. "I'm mighty glad too."

"Thayne," I said as he parked the car in front of the Bean. "What are we going to do from here? I mean, you don't want my father to know about us because of your job, and I can accept that, but eventually someone is going to say something to him or Mama. You have to know that much is true."

He nodded and turned the ignition switch to "off." Then he shifted, bringing his right knee up to rest on the seat and his right arm along the back. "Yeah, I was thinking about that.

I'm not going to stop seeing you, Mariette. Not after today. You're making me crazy, I can tell you that much."

I smiled. "I am?"

"Oh, boy. Yeah." He curled his fingers along the back of my head and drew my face to his for a kiss, simple and sweet. "But I can't lose my job. I've come too far in the past six months. Getting my life back on track. So, I'm going to have to think about all this."

"I see."

"Trust me until I do?"

I nodded. "I do."

If we had known that some well-meaning patron of the Bean had called Mama and Daddy—called them and called them and called them until they answered, according to Mama—we wouldn't have sat there wondering what our next step was going to be. We might have even lingered longer, seated a breath away from each other, and kissed until we were dizzy with passion and let everyone else be hanged. But we didn't know.

Two seconds after I walked into the house, though, there was little doubt. Thayne wouldn't be any wiser until I called him later, until I told him of Mama and Daddy standing there in the foyer, grim looks on their faces, and of how Tommy and Mitch were ordered to their rooms. *Now.*

"But what about supper?" Mitch asked, marching his way up the staircase, while Tommy leaned toward my ear and said, "You'd have done better to have gone with us, lovebug."

I gave him my harshest look while Mama barked, "Thomas Darrin Puttnam!"

Daddy said, "Young lady, shall we go into my office where your mother and I can talk to you?"

I took a deep breath and then exhaled in some lame attempt to calm my nerves. I nodded, then stepped down the hall between my parents. When we'd reached the door, Daddy stepped to one side to allow Mama and me entrance. I stood with my hands clasped in front, trying to find my courage, but flinching when Daddy shut the door behind us.

"Sit, Mariette," he ordered. I automatically went for the low and lumpy chair. But this time, I didn't draw my feet up. I sat as prim and proper as I could.

Daddy sat in his chair while Mama rested on the arm of it, farthest from me.

"Do you care to tell us where you have been?" he asked.

I pressed my lips together, then said, "Out. Driving."

I watched Mama's eyes flutter, then close, then open again. For a moment I thought she was going to faint.

"Let's not play games. With whom, Mariette?" she asked.

It was no use. They knew the truth. No amount of white lies would suffice. "Thayne Scott." I forced myself to brighten. "You know him, Daddy. He works for you. Mr. Schneiders says he a fine young man. Anyway, we met when I had lunch with you—the first time—and then we ran into each other at the Bean and—"

"I know who Thayne Scott is, Mariette. And I know he's a fine worker. Schneiders has never sung anything but his praises. I also know that young ladies of your breeding don't need to be gallivanting off all Sunday afternoon with a boy like him."

I was incensed for Thayne's sake. "What does that mean?"

Mama sighed. "Oh, Mariette. Don't you think we've heard from our good friends this afternoon that the two of you were practically all over each other today?"

That couldn't be true, I told myself. No one could have seen us. We'd been so deep within the woods, who of my parents' friends would have ever seen us out there? I felt myself blush. "I don't . . . I don't know what you mean."

"At that café you like so much," Mama said. She stood, crossed her arms, and then stepped behind Daddy's chair. "Apparently Janice Ruffin called Sally Deerfield, who took great delight in calling me. You made quite a spectacle of yourselves."

"We had pie and coffee!" I scooted forward in the chair.

"And you danced, according to Janice, so close a feather couldn't have passed between the two of you. She also said that the heat *outside* the Bean was nothing compared to what you two were stirring up."

I never cared for Janice Ruffin. She was a back-stabbing busybody who'd never cared for me either, especially since my days at Meadow Grove Elementary, where she served as my eighth grade teacher. She was just snobby Janice Boldman then, not quite the social snit she became the following year.

My eighth year of school I'd grown uncharacteristically sullen and withdrawn—hormones, no doubt. Between Miss Boldman and hormones, this also became the year Daddy declared me heading to Saint Margaret Mary for my high school years.

"That's not true," I lied. "You know Mrs. Ruffin never liked me."

Daddy cleared his throat then leaned his beefy arms on his desk. "Mariette, I want you to listen to me. While I do not approve of your mother's plan for you to find some—as she says it—nice young man and settle down at this stage of your life, and while I would like nothing better than to see you in college in January where you can advance your education, I will not have you seeing Thayne Scott. No, ma'am."

I scooted up a little more. "Daddy," I pleaded. "Can't you tell me why?" I felt tears stinging the back of my eyes.

"There are things you don't know," he said.

"Like what?"

"Things I make it my business to know when I hire someone for my factory, no matter if he is just a mail clerk."

"If you are talking about his being asked to leave ABAC, I know about that."

Daddy turned scarlet. For a moment I thought he was going to have a heart attack. Then he said, "Young lady, I have never punished you in any way I can remember, but if you see this young man—even one more time—I will fire him and send him packing out of this town so fast his head will spin. And you won't be able to sit down for a week."

I looked up at Mama, who jutted her chin in victory.

Then I stood, hands clenched at my side. "That is unfair, Daddy, and you know it." I kept my voice low and as respectful as I could.

"Unfair or not, you are my daughter and this is my house. You will live by my rules."

I stared at him, then dropped to my knees. "Daddy." I began to cry. "Daddy, please don't do this. I . . . I . . ."

Daddy must have been moved by my display of angst. He reached for me and pulled me into his lap, resting my head on his shoulder. "There now, Mariette. It was just one date. This is not Shakespeare and you're not Juliet to his Romeo."

I leaned back, wiping my tears from my cheeks with my fingertips. "But I am, Daddy. I love him."

"Love?" Mama all but spat. "What in the world do you know about love after one afternoon of eating pie, dancing, and driving around?" I watched her face grow white. "Unless . . . Mariette." Mama came around to the front of the chair and rested against the desk as she grabbed my shoulders and shook me. "Tell me! Tell me now. Have you . . . have you?"

"Have I? Have I what?" I realized then what she meant. "Mama!" I stood from Daddy's lap and then stepped away from the two of them. "Is that what you think of me? Don't you know me better than that?"

Mama buried her face in her hands. "I thought I did, Mariette. But then . . . today . . . my mind has just run wild with imaginings."

Daddy spoke then. "Get a hold of yourself, woman," he said to her. Then to me, "You can call Thayne and tell him what I've said. I will give you five minutes and not one second more." He reached for the phone and extended the handset toward me.

I took it but not without saying, "Daddy, won't you just try to get to know him. To know who he is?"

Daddy didn't answer. Instead he escorted Mama toward the door as he said, "Five minutes, Mariette." He opened the door and turned back to me. "Don't make me come in here after you. Do I make myself clear?"

I nodded. "Yes, sir."

He gave me a weary smile. "Good. Mama," he said, turning his attention to her as he closed the door behind them. "Let's start dinner."

10

I wouldn't see Thayne again until the Deerfield-Hill wedding, and even then it was only across the crowded church. The last two weeks had been miserable for me and, though dressed fine for a wedding, I'm sure I looked just horrid. I'd hardly come out of my room, barely eaten, and said no more than necessary to my family. Except Mitch. Mitch and I played a game every afternoon on the plush rug in my upstairs bedroom. I was happy for the time-consuming Monopoly and the childishness of checkers.

The wedding was as beautiful as the bride. At the reception Mama did everything she could to make sure I danced with first one boy and then another. She oh-so-casually mentioned that David Snow was now the chief mortgage officer at the bank and doing quite well. Then she waved David over and asked if he remembered her daughter, Mariette, and "Wouldn't the two of you like to dance?"

David wasn't fooled, but he did ask me if I'd like to have dinner sometime, to which I replied, "Why don't you call me?" all the while hoping he wouldn't.

Thayne wasn't at the reception. I didn't know why at the time. Later he told me he was invited but just didn't think he could handle seeing me there, being so close and not being able to speak to me. "Or touch you," he added.

The days dragged by. David Snow called on Wednesday and asked me if I had plans for Saturday, and I told him I did. I'd gotten so good at lying I amazed myself. He said, "Maybe next Saturday then?" He sounded so hopeful and I felt like a heel.

"Call me next week," I told him. "I should know something by then."

On Friday Mama cornered me in my room and told me she'd run into David at the bank and he told her he'd asked, and I'd declined because of a previous engagement, but he was hoping to see me the following week. Mama had assured him my previous Saturday night plans had been cancelled and I would be ready for his arrival at seven o'clock. "This is silly, Mariette."

I narrowed my eyes at her, something I'd never done in my whole life. "What is?"

"This insistence you have for a young boy you went out with exactly one time."

I turned from her, walked to the window, and looked out across the front lawn and then down the street. "Mama," I said. "How did you know you loved Daddy?"

Mama went to the bed and sat under the canopy. She patted the cover and said, "Come here, Mariette."

I did. I was honestly too weak to argue.

"Your father courted me properly, just as I know David Snow will do to you." She reached for my hand and held it long enough for a quick squeeze. "You know this story, but I'll tell it to you again if it will make you feel better. My parents sent me to camp every summer, and every summer the girls from the girls camp would have dances with the boys from the boys camp. Your father was a camp counselor, four years my senior." I watched as Mama smiled faintly then pinked. "Oh, he was a magnificent specimen of a man." Then she giggled and, heaven help me, so did I. "We danced." She pointed to me. "Properly. But I was totally infatuated from the first moment he held me in his arms."

"Properly."

Mama arched a brow.

"Don't you see?" I asked her. "That's exactly how I feel about Thayne. I don't know why, Mama, but the minute he shook my hand in the stairwell at the factory, I felt like I knew why God had placed me on this earth."

Mama raised her chin. "The difference, Mariette, is that your father and I were on equal footing socially." She sighed. "There are things I know about Thayne Scott that you don't know and you don't need to know." She patted my hand. "Now, I'm sure he'll grow to be a fine man and he'll marry someone of his"—she paused—"own social standing. He'll be a fine addition to our community or wherever he happens to settle. He'll be a good father and then a grandfather and on and on it goes." Then she squeezed my face between her hands. "And you, my darling, will do the same. Only you'll be a mother and a grandmother, and you'll forget all this ever happened."

She stood then, as if that were that, and left the room.

David Snow took me to dinner at an Italian restaurant where candles dripped in the center of small tables and a large, dark-haired woman served red wine and oval plates of pasta I only picked at. David droned on and on about himself while I nodded and pretended to listen. I stayed awake by making internal comments on his looks. He was handsome, that much was for sure. Tall, lanky, with dark blond hair and piercing green eyes. His facial features were angular. Sharp. He was a catch. He was even swell. But he wasn't Thayne.

After our dinner was whisked away and coffee served, I began to perk up a bit. Soon the date would be over and I could go home, crawl under the covers, and—hopefully—

sleep the memory of the night away. David asked if I'd like to go somewhere for a nightcap—no doubt thrilled that I'd actually said more than two words during dessert—but I said no. "I'm tired," I said. "But this has been fun."

He looked disappointed as he said, "I'll take you home then."

But instead of driving me home, David drove to some out-of-the-way place, reminding me vaguely of Thayne's "church" in the woods. I realized too late where we'd been heading since leaving the restaurant. Before I could demand to be taken home, David reached across the front seat for me, pulling me to him in one swift and almost violent move. His lips found mine, which were open in protest. He kissed me as if he were starving and I were a full-course meal. His lips groped mine, bruising them, just as his hands were working their way under my summer sweater.

"Stop!" I screamed, pushing at him with the pads of my hands.

"You stop," he said back. "You've been giving me this look all night. You know you want what I've got to give."

I was against the passenger door; the handle dug into the flesh of my hip. "What are you talking about? I've done no such thing."

He slid closer, reached for me again, pulled my neck to his mouth, and began nibbling, biting, and sucking in a way I'd never experienced. This was unlike when Thayne touched me, when Thayne's lips had brushed against the tender flesh there. This wasn't electric butterflies fluttering through me. This was disgusting, like a wet vacuum.

Then David wrapped my face in his hands, the fingertips digging into my skull. "The way you looked at me. Like you could eat me for dinner."

I tried to shake my head. "No," I whispered.

His breath was a mixture of garlic and red wine. Sickening. "So what's it going to be, Mariette? You a woman or a little girl?"

The question was rhetorical and didn't deserve an answer. "Take me home," I said. "I mean it, David. Take me home and I'll forget any of this happened."

He slid back to the driver's seat. "A little girl. I should have known." He jerked the gear shift then looked back at me. "Your mother thinks she is so smart. 'Mariette is a fine young woman, Mr. Snow,'" he mocked. "'You could look the whole world over and not find a girl like her.' Like I don't know what that meant. She wants a husband for her little girl. Well, not me, little missy. Women are good for one thing only, and marriage isn't it."

"You repulse me," I said. I jerked the door open and rushed out of the car.

"What are you doing?" he yelled as I marched toward the road.

"I'm walking home!" I heard the engine rev.

The car slid up next to me, but I didn't look toward it. "You're an idiot."

I stopped then. I placed my hands on my hips and said, "Maybe. But I'm not a cad. You, David Snow, are a cad." I started walking again.

"A cad? Who uses words like that anymore?"

"If the shoe fits."

"You are such a baby."

"Well, maybe so. But this baby has kept her virtues."

"That's not what I hear."

I stopped again. "What does that mean?"

"You and Thayne Scott? Oh yeah. Wiped that self-righteous look right off your face, didn't I?"

"You don't know what you are talking about." I continued walking.

"Get in the car, Mariette."

"No."

"Get in the car. Don't be silly."

He drove alongside me for what seemed like hours. My feet hurt and I was growing weak, having only picked at my food in the past weeks. I knew I had no choice. "Do you promise not to lay a hand on me?"

He held a hand up. "My word as a gentleman."

I gave him my best "oh, really?" look.

"I swear."

I reluctantly got in the car, but I sat as far from him as possible. The ride to my house was silent with only the rise and fall of cicadas singing outside the windows until we got into the city limits, where they hushed their song. But it resumed again as we drove between the houses of my neighborhood, a friendly reminder that I was safe at home. When the car glided to a stop in front of the house, my hand jerked the door handle and I exited as quickly as I could. "Thank you for the ride," I said.

I heard him opening his door. "At least let me walk you to the door."

"Have you lost your mind?" I spoke as loud as I dared, staring at him with my arms folded.

He nodded his head toward the house. "What about them? What are you going to do, let Mama and Daddy know you were compromised tonight?"

I marched up to him then and said, "I most assuredly was not compromised."

His eyes bore into mine. "Take a good look at your neck, Mariette, when you get inside." He grabbed for my purse, jerked it away from my arm, and then opened it. Before I could protest, he pulled the poodle scarf out, shook it, then wrapped it around my neck, tying it gently at the right side. "There you go."

He returned my purse to me while I wondered how he'd even known the scarf was there.

"Now," he said calmly. "Walk with me to the front door. I'll kiss your cheek good night in case Mama Bear is looking from the living room window, you'll smile appreciatively, and then you and I will part, never again to meet, God willing."

I nodded, but I didn't say anything. True to his word, David did exactly as he said he would. Inside, I found my parents were already in bed, hopefully asleep. At my bedroom's vanity mirror, I surveyed the damage to my neck. It looked as if I'd be wearing a scarf for a month.

I didn't bother to wash my face or brush my teeth. I just went to bed and cried myself to sleep.

The following morning I told Mama I wasn't feeling well, that my monthly had started, and that I'd prefer to stay home buried beneath the covers. She thought nothing of it. But as soon as I heard the family car drive down the street, I jumped out of bed, bathed and dressed, then slipped down the stairs and out to the driveway. I checked the security of the scarf around my neck in the rearview mirror of my De Soto, then backed out of the driveway. Minutes later, I was bouncing down a narrow dirt road, heading to Thayne's "church."

My heart leapt when I saw a car parked where mine had been just weeks earlier. It had to be Aunt Harriett's car. It just had to be.

I turned off the car, then scurried out, running in the direction of where I hoped I'd find the love of my life. "Thayne!" I cried. "Thayne!"

I leapt over the vines and brambles, the broken and rotting branches, and the clusters of pine cones. "Thayne!" I screamed again.

I ignored the dark and silence of the world around me. I just kept running, hoping I could remember where he'd taken me before. "Thayne!"

"Mariette?" I heard my name echo between the trees.

I stopped running, breathing in and out as though living out the last of my days.

"Mariette!"

Then I saw him. He was running toward me, one arm waving, eyes looking wild and afraid. I ran toward him, crying like a lost child who'd found her father. When we reached each other, arms flailing, we kissed. We cried. We fell to the spongy earth and held on to each other as though dying.

But then he jerked up, looked at me, brow furrowed. "What?"

He tugged at the scarf. "What is this?"

I shook my head. "Thayne, don't. It was—"

"Who did this to you?" He was on his knees now, pulling me to him. He unknotted the scarf, then slipped it away and dropped it to the ground.

I wrapped my arms around his neck. "Thayne, don't! Don't ask me about it. It was horrible."

He pushed me back. "Did someone . . ."

"No! No, Thayne. No."

"Who did this?" he asked again.

"Some man my mother thought perfect for me. That's all. I'm okay and I'm here in your arms now and that's all that matters." I threw myself against him again.

But Thayne was having nothing to do with my passion. He sat me down, then followed, cross-legged, hands on my knees. "I've been thinking," he said. "God knows that's all I've done since you called me. I certainly can't sleep. Can't eat. Can't study. I barely get by at work, and your old man is just itching for a reason to fire me."

"I know."

"Listen, Mariette. I don't care anymore. I've been a bit of a rebel my whole life." He shook his head a bit. "I've not had a chance to tell you everything . . ."

"Then there *is* more?"

"More? Of course there's more. I could spend a lifetime telling you what a mess my life has been up till now."

"And I could spend a lifetime listening to you tell me."

103

He stared at me then, long and hard. "Mariette, I'm only going to ask this once."

I furrowed my brow. "Ask what?"

"Do you love me?"

I threw myself against him again. "Yes! Oh, Thayne! Yes! I do. I know I do. I don't know much about love, but if this isn't it, I can't imagine anything more. I'd die if it were any better than this." I kissed his neck then, butterfly kisses up and down and then front to back.

He pushed me away gently. "Mariette, listen to me. If you don't, you'll kill me."

"I'm listening."

"I love you."

I burst into tears then.

"I love you, which makes no sense, and I know it. But it's what I feel and . . . and I want to marry you. Right now. Leave with me right now. I know a place we can go. No parental consent necessary. All they want is two people sane enough to sign the papers and two witnesses, which we can find off the streets if we have to."

I stalled. I didn't mean to but I did. Thayne gave me a hard look. "You *don't* love me."

"It's not that. It's just . . ."

"You don't love me enough."

"Oh no, Thayne. I love you more than I have words to say. I just wasn't prepared for this."

He shifted his body until one knee was raised and an elbow rested against it. "Well, I tell you what, Mariette. You've got about one second to decide because, quite honestly, I can't live like this anymore. I'd rather quit my job and leave this town than continue on, knowing you are no more than a few miles from me and yet I can't see you, talk to you, or touch you. That wedding? That wedding nearly killed me." His eyes grew wide. "Ohhhhh, I get it. You want a wedding. Like Missy Deerfield."

"No." I shook my head. "Really, I don't."

"Then, what's it going to be? Stay here and be Daddy's little girl and Mama's pawn or, this time tomorrow, my wife?"

His wife. The words were heady. But I didn't like the references to Daddy and Mama, no matter how put out with them I'd been.

Thayne leapt to his feet. "Good-bye, Mariette," he said.

I scrambled up. Before I could steady myself he was paces ahead of me, a light disappearing in the dark of the forest. "Thayne, no!" I ran after him, grabbed his right arm, and swung him around, pushing myself into him. "I want to be your wife," I said. I wrapped my arms around his shoulders and buried my face into his neck. "I want to be your wife." And then I cried again.

"And I want to be your husband."

"Daddy will kill both of us, you know," I said, drawing back to look at him.

"As long as he buries us side by side, I don't care." And then he kissed me, kissed me with more passion and abandon than three weeks earlier. As if that were even possible.

The following morning, I awoke on a lumpy mattress with musky sheets in a ramshackle motel room located at the edge of a strange town. When my eyes fluttered open, crusty with deep sleep, the most adorable face I'd ever seen so early in the day was peering down at me. And then, from between sweet lips, came the words to a song by Miss Dinah Shore. "On a dilly-dilly day you'll be wed in a dilly-dilly dress of lavender blue."

"Good morning, Mr. Scott," I said, stretching.

"Good morning, Mrs. Scott," he answered, then gathered me to his arms one more time.

Part 2

Wings of a Dove

11

June 1960

Our first wedding anniversary arrived quicker than I could have imagined, brought to us on wings of love and the thrill of being Mr. and Mrs. Thayne Scott. Because Ward and Missy Hill had become our best "couple friends," we'd decided to celebrate together, as theirs was one week before.

A lot had happened in the year since we'd married, and facing the music of my parents' wrath was but a small part of it. I called them collect from a phone booth that Sunday afternoon on the way toward the sleepy little town where a justice of the peace pronounced us man and wife. Mama cried on the other end of the line while Daddy made demands from the office extension. But I remained firm inside that hot and cramped booth while Thayne held my hand and nuzzled my neck. I also gave my parents the impression we'd gone north when, in fact, we'd gone south. Then I silently promised God I'd stop lying as soon as a band of gold was on my left ring finger.

That band of gold wasn't a long time coming, but it would be a long time before I lied to my parents again.

A year earlier, when we arrived back in Meadow Grove, our first stop was Thayne's Aunt Harriett's. While I waited in the parlor—as she called the cavernous room at the front of the rambling Victorian near the end of South Main Street—she and Thayne went to the kitchen "to talk some things over." Occasionally I heard their voices rise and fall, mainly when I went to the double doors and leaned my head into the foyer. For the most part, I spent the time fingering the figurines and tiny tea sets that gleamed from crocheted doilies, all the while thinking about Mama's living room, which was ultra modern and sparsely furnished. I imagined how we—Thayne, Daddy, Mama, and I—would no doubt be sitting in that foyer within the hour and how that encounter might play out. Not a single scenario turned out well.

Finally Thayne sauntered into the parlor looking a little worse for the wear. He wrapped me in his arms, kissed my nose, and said, "Well, good news. It's all settled."

"What's all settled?"

"Aunt Harriett says we can live here until we find a place of our own, however long that takes."

I stepped out of his arms. "Live *here*?"

He looked like I'd slapped him. "Sure. I thought you knew that's what I was doing when we came here."

I opened my mouth to speak, but nothing came out.

"Mariette?"

Finally I collected my thoughts and choked out a humorless laugh. "I thought you were coming here to pack."

He shoved his hands into his front pants pockets. "And live where?"

"I guess I hadn't gotten that far." I walked over to the velvet camelback sofa. "How much money do you have?" I asked, sitting.

He joined me, hunched over. He rested his elbows on his knees and intertwined his fingers. "Not much." He winced as he gave me a sideward glance. "What we did yesterday, it wasn't exactly planned."

"I'll say."

He straightened, reached for my hand, then drew me close, his right arm wrapped around me. "We'll figure out something, sweetheart. For now we can stay here. I told Aunt Harriett you'd be a great help to her in the house. Cooking, cleaning. That sort of thing."

I drew back. "Thayne, I just learned how to make coffee not three weeks ago."

He patted my hip. "Good for you, sweetheart."

I laughed then. "I don't think you get it. I mean, that's all I know how to do. I've never really *had* to cook. Ask me how to boil an egg. Go ahead. Ask me."

"How do you boil an egg?"

I shook my head. "I have no idea. But I think water is involved."

Thayne smirked. "But you know how to clean, don't you?"

"Well, sure. The nuns made us keep our dorms spotless. I can even miter the corners of my sheets."

Thayne looked puzzled. "Well, all right then." He took a deep breath and exhaled. "Ready to go get your things?"

My heart sank. "Not really. I've been thinking about it and I just can't imagine how this can possibly turn out well for those of us involved. And, by 'those of us,' I predominately mean you and me." I sighed. "But I guess we have to sooner or later. I can't very well not go. Unless I can start wearing your clothes."

He kissed me again, then spoke into my ear, "But what I like best is when you wear no clothes."

I blushed in spite of being alone with my husband. "Thaaaaayne!"

He chuckled and we stood, then walked toward the door, hand in hand. Thayne's squeezed mine. "Actually, that's a good lead into the other thing I need to tell you."

We stopped under the arch of the door frame. "What other thing?"

"We're the only married couple here."

"I kinda figured that."

Then he reached over and whispered in my ear. "Aunt Harriett says we have to keep our lovemaking to a minimum."

I gasped. "What does she mean by that?"

He kissed me then, full and hard. "No more of this in the middle of the parlor, Mrs. Scott."

We lived with Aunt Harriett for three months. For Thayne the days were no different from what they'd been before. He got up every morning, had breakfast (a full course, which Aunt Harriett cooked), went to the Fox & Hound, and then—at a little after five o'clock—returned home. Three nights a week he went to the college for his classes. I accompanied him, taking the opportunity to go to the library.

My days, on the other hand, were spent learning how to cook, clean, sew, and crochet, all at the "knee" of Aunt Harriett. The first I was horrible at, the second I was mediocre, but the sewing and needlework I took a liking to. I'd always been good at embroidery, and this was an extension of that talent.

Some days I drove to the house, mainly to see Mitch and Tommy. Mama was speaking to me, but only barely. I'd never known the woman could hold a grudge for quite so long. And, Daddy! Daddy was downright brutal toward Thayne at work, insisting he think in terms of advancing far beyond the mail room.

Then, in late September, as the weather turned cool and the leaves on the trees threatened to change to fiery colors, Mr. Schneiders announced his retirement. With little to no fanfare, Daddy advanced Thayne to operations manager. He didn't ask Thayne if he wanted the promotion; he just gave it to him with a "this is now yours" attitude that was not open to debate.

I couldn't tell if Thayne was pleased or not, especially seeing as how it was Neil Price's comment about climbing the corporate ladder by dating the boss's daughter that had sent Thayne over the edge where I was concerned. But if this new position at the Fox & Hound bothered Thayne, he didn't let on.

"It means we can afford a place of our own," I reminded him in an attempt to get him to talk about it.

He only nodded.

By the middle of October we'd put a deposit on a small four-room apartment we planned to rent. The following day I surprised Mama by dropping in and telling her she simply *had* to come with me somewhere. I took her to lunch at Marjorie's Café, then drove her to the line of quadruplexes at the center of 7th Avenue.

"Why in the world are we here?" she asked from the passenger seat.

I pointed to the middle of the rectangular brick building. "See that window there? The one with the curtains drawn?"

Mama nodded. "Yes, I see it."

"Thayne and I rented it. It's not much—a living room, dining room, and kitchen in one area, and, of course, a bedroom and the tiniest bathroom you've ever seen. But it's all we need. Except, well, I'll need to do laundry now over at your house."

Before she had a chance to remark, I coaxed her inside, where she turned in a slow circle in the center of the "living room."

"It's actually no more than a closet," she said.

"Help me decorate it?" I hoped the prospect of such a project would help bridge the months-long chasm.

She beamed in spite of herself. "Oh, that might be nice." Then she frowned. "Mariette, I know what your husband makes, and so I daresay you don't have any money for furniture. What are we supposed to decorate with? Orange crates and refrigerator boxes?"

I shrugged. "I'll sell the car if I have to. Thayne says we don't need such an expensive car anyway."

"Oh he does, does he?"

I hated her tone when she spoke of my husband, but I wasn't ready for another war so I pulled her into the bedroom, a spacious area with wide windows sheathed in gauzy curtains, gray painted walls, and scarred hardwood floors. "I asked Mrs. Brown, our landlady, if I could put up some wallpaper and she said I could, as long as it is tasteful."

"You will not sell your car, Mariette."

I placed my hands on my hips. "Mama, I don't need such a fancy car, but I surely need a bed!"

Mama flushed, then began pulling off her gloves. She kept her eyes on her rigid fingers as she said, "I'm glad you brought that up, Mariette." Then she shoved the gloves in her purse and snapped it shut. "Please tell me you are being . . . how can I say this delicately . . . careful."

It took me a moment to understand. "Of course I am. I mean, we are. The last thing we need right now is a baby."

Mama held up her hand to stop me. "I don't want to hear another word about it," to which I chuckled. "I also don't want to hear another word about selling your car. Your father and I have been wondering what to do for you two—should this marriage actually survive longer than six months—and now I know the answer. We'll furnish your home."

And thus it was so.

In all honesty, there was a scare after the first of the year. I didn't say anything. Not to Thayne and certainly not to Mama. Not even to Missy, and lately we were talking about nearly everything. When my monthly finally showed up—two months later than it should have and with a vengeance—I was grateful I'd not shared my fears. It would have led only to worry, which none of us needed another dose of.

On a happier note, at Christmas Missy had placed a small box containing two pale yellow duck-head diaper pins under the holiday tree for her husband, and then when he looked up from the opened box, she squealed "Surprise, Daddy Bear."

At least, that's the way he told Thayne it all took place. We were not there, of course.

By the time June rolled around and we were ready to celebrate our anniversaries together, Missy was in her seventh month and absolutely glowing. And why wouldn't she be? Ward's business was thriving, they lived in a sprawling house he'd bought from the Blackaby estate, and they were about to add another child to their family. After their announcement of impending parenthood, Thayne asked me repeatedly if I regretted marrying a poor blue-collar worker, and time after time, I told him no.

"But if we had the money," he said, "you'd be trying to make a baby right now."

I slapped his arm. "Thayne Scott. Do not talk like that." To which he laughed.

For the first anniversary celebration, Missy and I decided a cookout for the four of us was in order, and their country house on the lake was the perfect place for it. On Wednesday I called Missy and asked her if she would like to come over for lunch the following day so we could plan out our menus. She thought it was a fine idea and offered to bring soda crackers, which I noted would go nicely with the tuna salad I intended to serve on leaves of iceberg lettuce.

Thursday morning I busied myself as I usually did. While I sipped my second cup of coffee, elbow on the table and chin resting on my cupped palm, Thayne munched on toast slathered with butter and some of Daisy's homemade strawberry jam. He kept the newspaper folded next to his plate, reading one small section at a time, looking very much like a businessman on his way to the office. Occasionally I said something mundane, to which he groaned a response.

One thing I'd learned about Thayne that I'd not known before our nuptials (and that list could go on for miles) is that he is a man of few words first thing in the morning. I'd also learned that while I was pretty adept at keeping him satisfied with love, after a short period, my lack of attention to kitchen duties wore thin.

One afternoon back in February we'd had quite an argument about it. I'd called Thayne to the kitchen table for dinner, which was grilled cheese sandwiches and tomato soup. As soon as he saw it, he groaned.

"Ah, come on, Mariette. I've eaten enough grilled cheese to make a cow weep."

I had been cranky that whole day—though I couldn't explain why. I opened my mouth and barked, "You know, Thayne, if you wanted a good cook for a wife, you should have married Aunt Harriett."

He looked at me like I had three heads. Without another word, he turned and left by the same door through which he'd entered an hour earlier. Of course I ran after him; out the front door, across the porch, and down the steps. I hurried down the walkway then came to a stop on the sidewalk that stretched between Main Street and its houses. I looked first to the right, then to the left. There he was, ambling toward town, hands shoved in his pockets and head ducked between his shoulders. Just as I started after him, to my horror, Janice Ruffin's sleek Continental rolled to a stop in front of me.

"Why, hello, Mariette! My, aren't you something; all grown up and married, gazing after your husband as he strolls toward town." She smiled at me, a half smile from painted red lips, a sharp contrast to her bleached blonde hair. She wore an embroidered linen sheath dress and matching hat. I noted a complementary colored jacket was thrown over the back of the passenger seat. "It's like a scene from a movie."

The last thing in this world I needed was Mrs. Ruffin reporting a feud between Thayne and me to my mother. Not to mention the entire community. I smiled sweetly, then took a step toward the car, hands crossed in front of me. "Oh, hello, Mrs. Ruffin," I said. "You look nice."

"Tea at Marjorie's," she reported. "I saw your mother there, as a matter of fact. We were having a board meeting for the Garden Club." Another smile came and fell within a breath. "Really, Mariette, you should consider joining."

"Whatever for?" I was barely holding on to my sanity in the kitchen. I couldn't imagine attempting any sort of success in a garden.

She shrugged. "Might do you good. Give you something to do." She pursed her lips. "Better than running down the sidewalk after your wayward husband for the whole neighborhood to see." She looked over her shoulder toward the place where Thayne had become nothing more than a speck on the horizon.

I forced myself to laugh lightly. "Oh! No . . . well, Thayne was just heading out to pick up a few things for me and he . . . um . . . he forgot his wallet."

She looked at my hands. "Apparently you did too, dear."

I felt my face grow hot, and pointed back toward the apartment. "I . . . um . . . left it inside." Then I shrugged. "Oh, well. He'll realize it soon enough." I laughed nervously.

"Mmm," she said. "I wonder."

My embarrassment collided with my anger. I glared at Mrs. Ruffin, trying my best to quell the fiery darts in my eyes as I fiddled with the thin gold wedding band on my left hand. "What do you wonder, Mrs. Ruffin?"

She cut her steely blue eyes toward mine. "I wonder, Mariette Scott, just how much of a paradise this little love nest is."

I hated her. God help me, I hated her. I pictured myself dashing over to her car, digging my fingernails into her eyes, and ripping them right out of their sockets. Then, as suddenly as my flash of outrage came, it subsided. A new thought came to mind, causing me to smile. "You know, Mrs. Ruffin, I forgot to thank you." I cocked my hip to the right.

"Thank me?"

"Yes!" I positioned my right index finger against my chin. "If you hadn't called Mama and Daddy . . . you know, told them I was out with Thayne that Sunday, why, they'd have never separated us. I suppose, after all, it was the separation that caused us to run off like we did." I widened my eyes. "My, but aren't you the Shakespeare to our Romeo and Juliet?"

The inflection of my voice, mimicked so close to hers, hit its mark. She gasped, then turned forward. "That's very funny, Mariette. I can see married life has done nothing to tame your saucy tongue." She jerked her car into gear then eased away.

Thayne returned two hours later after a full meal at Aunt Harriett's, who he proclaimed—with a bit of mischief in his eyes—to be his "other wife." I was too angry to speak and too embarrassed by my encounter with Mrs. Ruffin. That night, while he slept in our bed, I slept on the sofa, rewarded the next morning with a backache and a crick in my neck. . . .

And Thayne, who blew kisses along my cheek, all the while whispering his apologies, which I readily accepted.

That evening he brought home a gift for me: a Betty Crocker cookbook for the new bride.

12

"I'm glad you like tuna salad," I said to Missy at lunch that day as she waddled toward the kitchen table. "It's about all I know how to prepare for lunch."

Missy eased herself down into a chair at the kitchen table. She laughed lightly and said, "You still haven't mastered the art of cooking." Then she tapped the top of the new Formica table Mama and I had picked out and said, "I'm thinking of having our kitchen remodeled with Formica. Did I tell you that? One thing about buying an old house; there's plenty to do to keep you busy."

I brought plates of tuna mounded over lettuce to the table and placed one on the placemat before her, another on the opposite. "Want some coffee? I can perk it while we eat."

Missy shook her head. Her hair, which she'd recently cut to look—as she said—"more like Marilyn's," shimmered in the natural light of the kitchen. In her own way, Missy did look a lot like the famous actress, only younger. She had the same dreamy eyes and pouting lips. Seeing how darling the cut was, I'd toyed with the idea of cutting mine, but hadn't quite gotten up the nerve.

"No, thanks," she now said to my offering. "Lately coffee makes my chest hurt."

"Sounds like fun," I said, now bringing over tumblers of iced tea. I placed them near our plates, then sat. "By the way, thanks again for having the cookout over at your place."

After Missy said a quick blessing over the food, we speared the tuna with our forks.

"I really like what you've done here," Missy said. "It's tiny, no doubt, but you've made it look like a million."

I smiled. If there was one thing I apparently *was* good at, it was taking the unadorned and giving it charm. "I didn't want to overdo," I said, looking around. "Mama said to keep the furniture simple, so I did."

Mama said the place had a real Doris Day feel to it. Simple lines. Simple colors, she had said. I opted for a few throw pillows of various shapes and sizes on the sofa and bed, a couple of knickknacks on the low coffee and end tables, a mirror on one wall of the living room and a large landscape on the other. To round things out, she and Daddy had thrown in a console TV, which Thayne had to admit he liked. "Even if I didn't pay for it."

Other than that, there wasn't much else in the apartment. Tish Kelly had insisted on throwing a shower for me after our return, which garnered us the necessary items such as dinnerware, towels, sheets, and—of course—small appliances like a toaster, a coffeepot, and an iron. Thayne's mother—whom I met in July, shortly after our wedding—had given us a quilt made from scraps of Thayne's baby and childhood clothes, which I kept folded at the end of our bed.

"I wish I had your touch," Missy said as she reached for a cracker from the plate between us. "Honestly, I wish I could even *care*."

I smiled at her. "But you have the cooking thing down."

She laughed lightly, rubbed her swollen belly, and said, "And apparently the baby-making thing down."

This time I laughed. "Oh, Missy. What would I do without you? I'm glad we're friends."

"Me too." She took another bite of tuna, chewed, then swallowed. "Hey, have you gotten an invitation to Anne's shower? The one Janice Ruffin is throwing?"

I told Missy about my last encounter with the woman. "But, no," I concluded. "I haven't gotten it."

"Mine just came in the mail yesterday, so yours may arrive today."

"Or, it could have been addressed to both Mama and me and just gone to her house."

"Probably."

After lunch we moved to the sofa with pads of paper and pencils to plan out our Saturday evening. We decided to keep it very simple. Hot dogs and burgers from the grill served with all the fixings, potato salad, and a cold green pea salad for the main course. Homemade ice cream for dessert. "I'll bring the ingredients for that," I said. "Including the rock salt."

"We have a churn," Missy said. "And two strong men to turn the handle."

When we had it all mapped out—including games and snacks—Missy said, "Why don't y'all stay out there for the night? Go to church with us the next morning? I know Thayne loves going to church with Ward."

"He loves talking theology with Ward," I said. "That much is for sure."

Missy opened her mouth as though she wanted to say something, then closed it as if she'd thought better of it.

"What?" I asked.

She shook her head, looked down at the pad of paper in her lap, and said, "Oh, it's nothing."

"No. Tell me. What?"

She looked at me directly then. "What about you, Mariette? Where do you stand with God?"

I didn't answer her. I couldn't answer her. Her query was the $64,000 question, not to mention the key to much of my anguish. Since we'd married, Thayne seemed to have become even more addicted to the time he spent in Bible study and often spoke to me of God as though the Almighty were his constant companion. It never occurred to Thayne, I don't think, that I didn't feel exactly the same. After all, every Sunday morning I sat in a pew at Christ the King between my father and my husband like the dutiful daughter and wife I tried to be. On some Sundays I was between Aunt Harriett and Thayne at the small country church where she was a member. My dress was always appropriate and my attitude above reproach. After all, I wasn't like many of the young people in our age group; I didn't drink or smoke (not even socially), I didn't swear even when I was mad. In fact, I was rarely mad.

The real question for me wasn't where I stood with God. It was why I couldn't seem to grasp what my husband and best friends—Missy and Ward—had. Some nights, after Thayne and I made love and he'd fallen into a deep sleep, I lay awake, staring at the tiles in the ceiling, tracing lines between their swirling pattern with my eyes, feeling pretty much the way I had at Saint Margaret Mary's. The outsider looking in. The one who, though she went through all the motions—saying and doing the right things at all the suitable times—was in fact six steps behind, always trying to catch up but never quite making it.

A few months before our anniversary, in March and much to the delight of every young girl in America, Elvis Presley returned home from his time stationed in Germany. And, much to my delight, the month after our anniversary, Mama bought me a copy of Harper Lee's *To Kill a Mockingbird*, which I devoured no less than six times before the year's end while Thayne found pleasure in watching Wilt Chamberlain on the basketball court and some guy named Cassius Clay in the boxing ring.

Thayne and I had settled into a nice routine for a married

couple of one year. We'd grown accustomed to the other's idiosyncrasies, arguing about them less and less. Between school and a job I knew he only tolerated for the sake of income, Thayne was typically tired when at home. In spite of his full schedule, he still had plenty of energy when it came to the end of the day, to lovemaking. As for me, I seemed to come more to life during these moments than any other time. I tried to keep my days as full as possible. Once a week, after dropping Thayne off for work, I went to a nearby laundromat, having chosen that over washing at Mama's house. While our clothes washed, I spent time talking to some of the other young wives who, like us, couldn't afford a washing machine. Sometimes I played with the children who ran wild under and around the stainless steel tables where their mothers sorted or folded their laundry. Other times, when engrossed in a good book, I kept my nose buried between the pages.

Laundry day was an all-day event. With Daisy as my instructor I'd learned to wash, sprinkle, and roll the clothes, then bring them home and place them in the refrigerator. The following day, Tuesday, I took them out, unrolled them, ironed them, and put them away. Between regular house chores and that, those days were completely filled. Wednesdays I scrubbed the bathroom and kitchen and on Thursdays I bought groceries because that was the day the local A & P had their "specials." Fridays I dusted, vacuumed, and mopped, and once a month I buffed the hardwood floors until they shone like new. But, try as hard as I might, I was still a terrible cook.

And so 1960 came and went, one day, week, and month at a time. As normal as life was for me, it seemed our nation— indeed our world—was on the cusp of something I couldn't identify much less wrap my mind around. By December everyone—even many of the staunch, protestant Republicans of the South—spoke about how well John F. Kennedy, a great debater if I'd ever seen one, would lead our country, especially with Texan Lyndon B. Johnson as his vice president. President Eisenhower had signed the Civil Rights Act, so it was not just white voters who elected the new president. But the South was experiencing something else that was altogether new, and not just the recently elected Leader of the Free World.

Actually, equal rights for all men was becoming a popular mantra since four Negro students in North Carolina had gone up to a Woolworth's lunch counter, sat, and waited for service. It would take six months—from February to July—before the service came, making it apparent *something* was stirring in the air.

In December, Thayne and I took a trip to see his family. Thayne had taken Friday the 16th and Monday the 19th off so we could spend a long weekend on the family's sprawling farm in the middle of nowhere. I'd never warmed to Thayne's father, who—to me—was a dark and surly man, but I adored the rest of his family, including the extended members. And I most especially loved his mother. We enjoyed sitting for hours at the kitchen table with cups of steaming coffee and our handwork, knitting one and purling two and talking about Thayne as an infant all the way through his boyhood. Mrs. Scott—who I called Mama Lena, for that was her name—grew distant as we climbed the years toward adulthood but beamed and laughed whenever we talked about his younger years. I filled her in on her son as a husband, leaving out the best parts, of course.

At some point during the weekend Thayne and his mother went for a long walk. "Why can't I go?" I asked him in the privacy of his old bedroom, now ours when visiting. Mama Lena had changed it completely from the first time I'd come, no longer displaying high school pennants or shelves of trophies. The walls had been painted a cheery blue, the boyish artwork removed and replaced by portraits of family members who had long been laid to rest. The windows displayed white Priscilla curtains, and the bed—no longer covered in dark blue—boasted a quilt Mama Lena called "The Wedding Bouquet" in our honor.

"Not this time, sweetheart," he said. He wrapped his fingers around my shoulders and kissed my nose. "I want to talk to Mama about a few things."

"Like what?" I wiggled out of his hold and plopped down on the bed.

He looked down at me and smiled, his dimple growing ever deep in his cheek. "It's a surprise. Can you just give me this time with my mother? You've hogged her all weekend."

"I have not." I pretended to pout, but deep down inside I wondered if this had something to do with Christmas and, perhaps, a gift for me under the tree we'd yet to put up.

Thayne and Mama Lena were gone for the better part of two hours. When they returned I noted she'd been crying, which alarmed me. But she seemed perfectly happy, leaving me more confused than concerned. She dabbed at her eyes occasionally during dinner, and when I pressed her for information while we cleared away the table and washed the dishes, she said only that I would "find out soon enough."

On Saturday, Thayne, Dana, and Carter had gone in search of a tree with Mr. Scott. That night we'd decorated it, sung Christmas carols around the piano—which I played—and sipped hot apple cider. The next morning we all oohed and ahhed over the gaily wrapped packages that had somehow found their way into a merry jumble around its base. "Little elves," Mr. Scott said, and then everyone laughed. Including me.

On Sunday after evening church we exchanged gifts in the expansive living room and in the glow of the fire and the twinkling light of the tree. Thayne sat in a chair and I sat beside him, an arm wrapped around one of his legs. I'd changed into a long red velvet skirt and sweater set, Mama Lena was still in her church dress adorned with a pretty strand of pearls, while the boys and men still wore black pants, white shirts, and ties. The only difference from an hour earlier was that they had taken off their coats. I thought the whole scene was like something out of a Norman Rockwell painting and whispered so to Thayne, who kissed me gently on the lips in return. "It is nice, isn't it?" he asked, though not as if he expected an answer.

By the end of the evening Thayne and I were the proud owners of a knitted afghan (from his parents), dress socks (from Dana and Carter to Thayne), and a book, *Better Homes and Gardens Decorating Ideas* (for me from the same). "Because Thayne says you're good at making a house pretty," Dana said by way of explanation.

All the way home on Monday I vacillated between reading the book and staring at Thayne, who, reading my thoughts, would only say, "On Christmas. I promise I'll tell you Christmas morning."

I had great plans for our second Christmas as a married couple, and was most pleased when they came together so nicely. On Friday evening, the 23rd, Thayne and I decorated our tree—tiny though it was—and then kissed under the mistletoe until I was drunk with love. On Saturday afternoon we visited Ward, Missy, and little Kay. We exchanged small tokens of our friendship and sipped on coffee while listening to Bing Crosby croon about a white Christmas. At one point Ward and Thayne stepped away and spoke in whispers from the adjoining room. "Do you know what that's about?" I asked Missy.

"I do, but I'm not saying," she said. Kay, as beautiful a baby as I'd ever seen, started to get fussy, effectively thwarting any further questions I might have asked.

That evening we went to Mama and Daddy's for homemade eggnog, singing around the piano, and another gift exchange. Mama insisted Thayne and I bring our gifts for each other so we could open them with the family, but I resisted. "No," I said. "We'll open gifts in the morning like the lazy married couple we are, then meet you for church at eleven," I told her. She argued, but in the end I won.

When morning arrived, I woke Thayne with a cup of coffee and plates of buttery cinnamon toast served in bed. We ate, drank, and smooched a whole lot, then wrapped ourselves in warm robes and went into the living room, where I'd already lit the furnace and turned on the Christmas tree lights. We sat on the cold hardwood floor and exchanged our gifts.

Thayne insisted I go first but I insisted the same and he finally gave in. He ripped the silver foiled paper away from a long, slender box. As it fell to the floor near his crossed legs he said, "Wonder what this could be."

"Just open it," I said with a shiver.

He did. "Oh, Mariette," he said. "It's the most handsome pen and pencil set I've ever seen."

I pointed toward it. "I had your name engraved on the pen and your initials on the pencil."

He leaned over and kissed me. "You have no idea how handy this is going to be."

"Operations managers of successful factories need their pens and pencils, I always say."

He kissed me again but not before his face stained as though he were uncomfortable with my one-liner. "Open yours," he said, shoving a small square box toward me.

I could tell it was a ring box, or at least about the size of one. "Thayne," I said. "Is this what I think it is?"

His dark blue eyes twinkled. "I don't know, Mariette. What do you think it is?"

An engagement ring, I thought. I'd never said anything to him about it, of course. Never dared chance hurting his feelings about not being able to afford it. After all, we'd married so quickly. No formal proposal. No months of preparations, teas, and dinners and showers and such. No rock the size of a patio table, like Missy's, to show off to everyone who came to the festivities. But I'd always wanted a ring to wear with my slender gold band.

I opened the box and gasped. "Thayne . . . my gosh," I whispered, blowing the words out as though I'd faint.

Thayne took the box from me and then the ring from the box. "It was my mother's," he said. "And my father's mother's before her." He took my hand in his, then slipped the antique filigree ruby ring onto my finger. "My grandmother was born in July, so that's why the ring isn't a diamond." He smiled a crooked smile. "That and, most likely, my grandfather couldn't afford a diamond."

"It's beautiful," I said. I shivered again, but not because I was cold.

"You're beautiful," he said.

I held my left hand up and allowed the morning's muted sunlight from the frosty windows to dance and play on the white gold band with interwoven floral engraving down its sides. "This is the best gift you could have given me. Honest to Pete."

Thayne sighed then. I looked up at him. His eyes were hooded, his lips thin. "I hope so," he said. "Because there's something pretty important that I need to talk to you about."

13

He said he was ready to talk about it.

"Not fully, maybe," he said. "But mostly."

My heart's joy at the morning's offerings plummeted. "Thayne," I said. "You look positively ill."

Thayne shrugged. "I just don't like talking about it."

I shimmied closer to him. The ruby ring slipped to the left on my finger, and I mentally noted I'd need to get it sized. "About what?" I placed my hand on his knee, ran it up his thigh, though there was nothing sexual in the motion. "Thayne, what's going on?"

His head was low between his shoulders. I looked at his hair, the blond curls that refused to be tamed first thing in the morning, the thick feathering of lashes, the straight line of his nose. He'd changed a bit from the very young man I'd met in the stairwell, now a year and a half ago. He'd aged, but nicely. Before, he'd been adorable and cute, and now he was striking and handsome, reminding me a little of Troy Donahue. And he still stirred my senses in ways I'd never imagined possible. Being with him—whether talking over coffee and toast first thing in the morning or wrapped in the throes of passion last thing at night—gave me a sense of belonging I'd not felt since eighth grade.

He looked up at me then. "Sweetheart." He bit his lip. "Remember I told you I'd done some pretty stupid things before I came here?"

I nodded. "But you've never really talked about them. My mother—when I got the 'you're forbidden to see him' speech . . . before we married—said there were things I didn't know about. She indicated she knew about them, but she's not elaborated. Not ever."

Thayne chuckled. "There are things neither she nor your father could possibly know."

"Like?"

His face flinched. "Like when I was in high school, when I was the golden boy of my class, I let everyone down by dropping my all-American image." He shook his head. "I don't know what I was thinking or who I was mad at, Mariette. But I stopped hanging out with all the right people and started hanging out with the hoods." His eyes locked with mine. "You know the type. Hot rods and hot girls. Cigarettes and beer. I was drunk more than I wasn't during my senior year. Stumbling home on Friday nights after the game." He smiled a bit. "Oh, I led the team to victory because I was fast on the field. So, no harm done there. But I was also fast off the field. A new girl every weekend as though I was somehow due."

I felt myself growing colder. My hand left his leg and reached for the fingers of my other. Clasped together, I laid them in my lap.

Thayne caught the motion. "I know," he said. "You don't like to think of me with any other girl any more than I like to think of you with any other boy."

"But there were no other boys. You know that, Thayne. You were my first. You have to know that."

He jerked. "Oh, baby, I know *that*. I mean—"

"What are you saying? You think I was a—"

"No!" He now inched his way closer to me. "Just listen, okay? No more talk about what a mess I made of things. I'll just wrap it up by saying that between my daddy's strap and my mama's tears—not to mention her prayers—I ended up at ABAC."

"I know that part."

"And you know how much of a mess I made that too."

And I knew about the girl. The one who wanted to marry him. At any cost.

"Thayne, where is this going?"

He chuckled then. "Mariette, when it comes to God, where do you put me?"

I felt my brow knit together. "I don't understand the question. I don't think you're God."

"No, no. What I'm asking is, where do you think I stand with God?"

I swallowed. Hard. It was Christmas; why were we talking about God, for Pete's sweet sake? "I don't know. I guess you stand just fine with him. You certainly read that Bible of yours enough. You don't miss church unless you're sick, and that's only happened once that I can remember."

Thayne tapped his chest a couple of times. "See, Mariette, I came here to Meadow Grove to start over and ran smack into Aunt Harriett and her faith. Just like Mama's but without an agenda. Sure, Aunt Harriett loves me, but she doesn't have—or didn't have—the same desperation to see me on my knees before God. She just loved me. Listened to me. Showed me some verses in the Bible to get me to looking for myself. And when I did, do you know what I found?"

I ran my tongue over dry lips. "No, I don't suppose I do."

"I found that God loves me very much. That I matter to him. And never mind the mess I'd made of my life. I knew he'd forgive me for *that*. What struck me was that he has a plan for my life that leads to good things. Not anger over my father's strap across my backside because I didn't harrow a field right or guilt over my mother's tears because I came home late and drunk."

I nodded, not because I agreed or even because I under-stood, but more because I felt uncomfortable. Where *was* this conversation going?

"So you understand?" he asked.

"Sure, Thayne. God loves you. I understand." I tried to speak as gently as possible.

He took a deep breath then exhaled. "Good, because, well, I've already talked to Mama about this. And Aunt Harriett and Ward too. I wanted his advice."

Again, my brow furrowed. "About what? Thayne, if you don't just say whatever is on your mind, I swear I'm going to get a headache."

Another deep breath. Another sigh. He straightened his back and leveled both his chin and his shoulders. "Okay, here goes: Mariette, God has called me into the ministry."

Thayne's eyes were locked with mine. "Okay," I said.

He smiled at me, that crooked smile I love so much. "I don't think you understand. I'm going into the ministry. I've prayed about this until my knees were calloused, and I know I'm doing the right thing. I'm quitting my job at the factory and I'm going to seminary." He reached under the Christmas tree skirt and pulled out a thick envelope I'd certainly never noticed before.

The envelope was extended toward me, and I took it numbly. "My acceptance letter from the seminary. It's an hour from here, Mariette. I can drive it—back and forth—every day." Thayne's words came at me like bullets from a machine gun. Rat-tat-tat-tat-tat . . . "Because of the courses I've already taken, and if I double up on some new classes, I can be out and preaching in two years." He grabbed my knees and shook them. "Think about it, Mariette. Two years and I can be behind a pulpit! And you'll be the pastor's wife."

My hand shot to the nape of my neck as though a bolt of lightning had just penetrated the skin. I felt the stiff remain-ders of last night's bouffant and wondered—ridiculously—

how awful I must look at that moment. Last night, exhausted from the day's activities, I'd not washed my face. *I must look a mess*, I thought. Mascara smeared. Lipstick faded. Teased hair pushed to one side.

And then I choked out a laugh. My husband had just told me he was quitting his job and that I was going to be a preacher's wife, and I was worried about how I looked.

And not just quitting any job. Quitting his job at my father's factory, a job I knew Daddy had given him only so as to be able to support his only daughter.

"Say something, Mariette."

I looked down at the envelope, pulled the flap away from where Thayne had tucked it, and then slid out the tri-folded papers. My fingers trembled as I spread them open, my vision blurred as I read the words: *congratulations . . . accepted . . . winter quarter . . . campus housing vs. off-campus living.*

I swallowed again. "When do you start?" I asked, my voice barely above a whisper. A lone tear plopped on, of all things, the word *congratulations.*

"January ninth." I felt his eyes on me. "You're not happy," he said.

I looked up at him then, my own eyes burning with fire and tears I tried desperately not to shed. "Not happy. Not happy?" I snapped my fingers. "Just like that, you want happy? Mariette, I'm going away to college. I'm going to be a preacher. Be happy for me, Mariette." I swiped at the disloyal tears that slipped down my cheek as Thayne slid away from me, eyes hooded, his face reading both angry and heartbroken. I'd not caught his vision, and in one second he went from handsome man to little boy, a hurt tiger slouching to a corner to lick his wounds while the hunter readied herself to fire off another round. "Well, did it ever occur to you to discuss this with me? Not your mother. Not your aunt and surely not Ward Hill. Me? Your wife? After all, it will affect me greatly, won't it?"

"Mariette—"

I raised a hand. "No, Thayne. No. I won't hear of this. No quitting, no seminary, no pastor's wife."

"You won't hear of it? You—" He jumped up, stared down, and then pointed toward me. "Now you listen here, Mariette. I've played this your way. I've dragged myself to that factory every day doing a job I absolutely hate just to keep your father satisfied and a roof over your pretty head and food in our stomachs."

I stood, still clutching the papers. "Oh, really? Well, pardon me for living, Thayne Scott. I didn't know I was such a burden to you. Poor thing. You have to go to work every day while I just sit at home and eat bonbons and watch TV. Well, how awful that you come home every day to a clean house and clean clothes and hot food." Thayne started to say something, but I stopped him. "Oh no you don't. Don't think it, much less say it. I know I'm not a good cook, Thayne, but the meal is—if nothing else—filling, and so far you haven't died from food poisoning." Then I pointed toward our bedroom. "And how terrible, having a woman in your bed who wants you and loves you before you go to sleep every night." I paused. "Or nearly every night."

Thayne's eyes narrowed. "Like you don't enjoy that too."

I dropped the acceptance letter and its envelope to the floor. "That was unnecessary and you know it."

Thayne raised his hands then dropped them to his side like a balloon that had been deflated. "Here we are," he said quietly. "Fighting in our pajamas and robes."

Matching, no less. Last night's gifts from Mama and Daddy along with a set of breakfast glasses etched in gold maple leafs. The ones I'd planned to serve fresh-squeezed orange juice in after we'd opened our gifts and after we'd made love. At least that's the way I'd dreamed it would be. Just like last year, only with more to celebrate.

"So we are," I said, but not in concession.

134

Thayne took steps toward me, stopping just shy of where I stood. "Look, I know I should have talked to you, but I thought you'd be happy for me. I wanted it to be a Christmas surprise . . . thought it would be. I finally feel like I know what I want to be when I grow up, so to speak." He cupped my shoulders with his hands, then ran the pads of his thumbs in small circles. "I want to be a preacher, Mariette. I want to tell others about God. About Jesus and the difference he can make in their lives. Like he's made in mine."

I stared at him for a moment before speaking. "This is just so out of the blue, Thayne. I mean, I know you like God and all, but . . ."

"I more than 'like him,' Mariette. Don't you know me well enough to know that?"

Apparently not. Apparently I'd been so caught up in who I was with Thayne that I'd missed who Thayne had become with God.

But I was hardly ready to admit that to myself, much less to him. "I don't understand why you have to quit your job."

"If I go to school full time, which I intend to do, I can't very well keep my current schedule too." His hands fell away.

"And how will we make a living?"

Thayne blew air from his lungs. "I've thought about that too. We've got a choice. You can work, just for the two years, while I'm in school. Or—and this is the really big 'or'—we can live with your parents and I'll take a weekend job."

I blinked. "Live with my parents," I said, though I can't say whether it was a statement or a question. I just repeated his words. *Live with my parents.* What would that mean? My first thought was of the wall between my parents' bedroom and mine, and I embarrassed myself at the notion. Then of the pink and white bedroom Mama and I had decorated during my sixteenth year and of Thayne living in it.

"Or, you can get a job," my husband said, shredding my imaginings to dust.

"Me? Doing what?"

"I heard a few days ago that Ramona down at the A & P is quitting and they're hoping to replace her right after the holidays. The timing is perfect."

I placed my hand over my mouth for a moment. "You want me to work as a cashier at the A & P?"

He crossed his arms. "You're not incapable, Mariette."

I laughed. "Thayne, it wouldn't do for the daughter of Carroll Puttnam to work at the A & P." Heaven help me, I sounded like my mother.

Thayne's jaw flinched. "You're my wife now, Mariette. Not his daughter. But if you don't like that idea, maybe your father can put you to work. I know of an operations management position that's gonna open soon."

I opted to ignore the last line. "Okay, let's say I go to work. Who would take care of the apartment?"

He waved a hand back and forth between the two of us. "We will. I'll chip in."

"When, Thayne? When will you have time? An hour to school. Then school. Then an hour home. You'll have home-work to be sure. When will you help?"

He took another step then, wrapped his arms around me while I stayed stiff. "Mariette," he breathed into my hair. "Please. Oh baby, please. I want this so bad I can taste it. Please work with me. I know it won't be easy, but I promise you a good life after I become a preacher. A fine life." He jerked as though he was crying, which was confirmed when I felt the moisture of his tears slipping down my neck. They wrapped around my throat and then trailed down my chest and between my breasts.

My hands slipped up his sides and gripped his shoulders. My husband needed me, I thought. He needed me. If he was going to accomplish this, my assistance was necessary. More than cooking or cleaning or washing or ironing. My role was vital to his success. It was . . . wifely.

I nodded, almost unperceivable at first. "Okay," I whispered. I hushed him as though he were a child.

He squeezed, and the tears came harder. I'd never seen a grown man cry before, and I grew uncomfortable with the emotions of a husband so moved by my acceptance of these new terms of our life together.

But then Thayne said, "Thank you, God."

And in that moment, a wall of bricks began to form around my heart. That night, before bed, I slipped the too-big ruby ring from my finger and placed it back in the box from which it had been presented to me, telling Thayne I needed to have it sized.

It would stay there for a good long time.

14

At my insistence, we waited until after Christmas but before New Year's Day to discuss Thayne's entering seminary with my parents. As I expected, they both balked at the notion of me working at the A & P, which only managed to increase my desire to find employment there. Not that this surprised me; their initial disapproval of Thayne a year and a half ago had made me defensive of my husband. Sometimes it seemed at every turn. As charismatic as he was with everyone else, Thayne couldn't quite convince my parents of his devotion to and love for me.

For the big announcement, we asked Daddy and Mama to come to the apartment (Thayne said it put them on our turf) at midweek for coffee and cake, which I'd baked—and pretty well at that. When they arrived, Mama balanced an apple pie in her hands "just in case." I served small slices of both desserts for her and me and large pieces for Thayne and Daddy.

We sat at the table. When there wasn't another crumb to eat and enough small talk had been spoken, Thayne cleared his throat, took a last sip of coffee, and then broke the news.

I've never seen two people look so completely shocked.

Mama cried as she muttered something to Daddy about

knowing "something was wrong . . . didn't I tell you?" Daddy insisted if Thayne were going to go through with this "hare-brained idea," we should move in with them, to which Thayne said, "We've discussed that option, sir."

I looked across the table at my father, and for the first time I could remember, the wind was completely out of his sails. As much as I felt loyalty to Thayne, I felt sorry for my father.

When Daddy regained his composure he said, "And what conclusion did you come up with, son?" The endearment was spoken with sarcasm.

Thayne flinched before he said, "I'm leaving that matter up to my wife."

Pride swelled within me. If I lived to be a hundred I'd never tire of hearing him call me his wife. It didn't sound possessive or dictatorial but rather protective and loving. I smiled at him and reached my hand across the table. He took it, winked, and then said, "Mariette? What do you want to do, sweetheart?"

I looked at my parents, who glared at me. "I haven't decided quite yet," I said. I squeezed Thayne's hand and he squeezed back. "But I wouldn't mind working to help support Thayne in his calling." The look on my parents' faces was like that of the four presidents on Mt. Rushmore.

"So what do you propose to do?" Mama asked. "Take in laundry?"

"Don't be silly, woman," Daddy said. "She'll come work for me."

"There's also a job opening at the A & P." I blurted the words without thinking.

Daddy blanched, then flushed.

"Mariette, get your father a glass of water," Thayne spoke gently.

When I placed the glass of cold tap water before my father, I ran my hand over the width of his shoulders, then laid my cheek on top of his balding head. "Daddy," I said. "I'm not your little girl anymore. I'm Thayne's wife. Helping him is what I want to do." I wasn't being 100 percent truthful, but I figured if I said it enough, my heart and my words might somehow connect.

Mama kept her eyes on Daddy. "What would you have her do, Carroll? Because no daughter of mine is going to work at the A & P." She looked up at me. "Not that there's anything wrong with a good day's labor, but we have a reputation to uphold here in Meadow Grove."

I looked at Thayne, who was staring down at his half-empty cup. I knew my husband; he was trying not to laugh at the similarity of Mama's words to my own on Christmas Day.

Daddy looked up at me and sighed, then wrapped his arm around my hips. "Jack Kelly came by to see me the other day," he then said to Mama. "His first cousin was an operations manager of a small company over in LaGrange that shut down about a month ago. Said the man has enough savings to live on for six months but can't find a job in their area along the lines of what he's used to. Asked about Schneiders's old job." Daddy's attention went to Thayne, who nodded; man-to-man language taking place at my kitchen table. Language without words. "I'll see if he's still looking. Mariette, you'll take Thayne's old job of mail clerk."

I walked back to my seat at the table. "But who will lose their job as mail clerk if I take it?"

"Me," Thayne said. His face was still pointed toward his coffee cup, but his eyes cut toward me with a slight lift of his head. "I've been doing both jobs."

I placed my hand on his arm. "Are you kidding me?" I looked at Daddy. "Why didn't you hire someone to take Thayne's old job?"

"It's okay, Mariette," Thayne said. He looked now from me to my father and back to me again. "Your father and I had an agreement. It was extra work, but it was also extra pay."

But it wasn't okay, and I said so to Thayne later that night

140

as we wrapped ourselves in each other's arms. The winter moonlight slipped through an opening in the draperies, casting pale blue shadows across the blankets and quilts. "What's bothered you most about it, Mariette? That I was doing more than my fair share of work down at the plant, or that you didn't know about it?"

I turned my face and kissed his neck. "Both."

His arms tightened around me. "I didn't mind, really. I hoped it would give me a chance to prove myself to your father."

"Do you think it worked?"

Thayne didn't answer right away. "No," he finally said. "I'm not sure what I have to do to prove myself to him."

I kissed his neck again. "You only have to prove yourself to me," I said.

He shifted so as to look at me, face all scrunched in the moonlight, neck like a turtle's. "How am I doing so far?"

I rose up and kissed him on the lips, a sweet kiss, meant only to tell him how much I loved him and would always love him. When our lips parted I touched my nose to his and gazed into his eyes. Then I smiled. "You're doing all right."

By the first of March, when cold mornings had given way to warm afternoons and the dogwood and azaleas began their burst of bloom and color, I was aware of three things.

The first, Thayne thrived in seminary. Every weeknight, on our drive to and from Mama and Daddy's (where we'd have supper, in order to keep costs down), he'd regale me with stories from class, of professors and of other students. I felt as if I were a part of everything he was experiencing. He also shared with me what he was learning about God. About the Bible. About the history of God's people and of the church. Some of it was entertaining. But some of it added to the conflict in my heart.

The second thing I knew was that without a student loan,

Thayne wouldn't be able to afford a second semester. I'd spoken to him about it one evening on the way to dinner; one of those rare times I could get a word in edgewise. He didn't say anything at first. "Thank you for looking after the finances on top of everything else," was his eventual comment.

On top of everything else. I had resigned myself to not cleaning the house during the week, but on Saturdays the dust flew. I got up early, and while Thayne studied at the library, busied myself scrubbing and polishing. On Friday mornings I ran a week's worth of laundry to the laundromat. Sarah Beth, the young colored woman who worked there, greeted me with a wide smile, saying, "Just leave it be. Leave it right here with me and I'll take care of it. You come back; it'll be all ready for you." She was right. When I returned a little after five, there it was, sprinkled and rolled and ready to be taken home for ironing on Saturday. I entertained myself by doing so at ten o'clock, which was when the old Tarzan movies ran on Channel 6.

Tarzan and Jane were Thayne and me. Passionate and carefree. At least, that's the way we used to be. Now we were both too tired, it seemed, to do much more than get through the day and then fall into a deep sleep that never seemed to be long enough.

On the night I discussed our financial situation with Thayne, he surprised me by asking Daddy if he could discuss something with him after dinner, in Daddy's study. After the two men had left the room and Tommy and Mitch had gone upstairs to get ready for bed, Mama and I cleared away the dinner dishes from the dining room table and then cleaned the kitchen until it was spotless, all the while making small talk. When we were finished she told me Tommy was itching for a summer job so he could start saving for a car.

"But he's fourteen this summer," I said, draping the drying towel over the oven door handle. "What is a fourteen-year-old going to do with a car?"

142

"Not to buy one this summer. Just to start saving for one. Your father told him to start a lawn service."

"Sounds reasonable."

"He's already made the flyers." Mama opened a cabinet drawer and pulled out a piece of typing paper with a pretty nice-looking advertisement on it. I took it from her. "Who did this?" I asked.

"He did."

My head jerked up. "Really? Who knew he had this kind of talent?"

"He's always enjoyed art."

I returned the flyer to her. "He should go into advertising when he's older. I'd hire him if I had a lawn."

Mama placed the flyer back in the drawer, then closed it. "Mariette," she said, continuing to look at her slender hand on the drawer. "You seem to have something on your mind."

"Well, I . . ."

She whirled to face me. "You're pregnant, aren't you?"

I opened my mouth to protest, but nothing came out but the sound of air being let out of a balloon. That was the third thing I knew. I was pregnant.

"How did you know?" I squeaked.

She pointed to the table. "Sit down," she said. "I'll make some hot tea."

We said nothing while she prepared our mugs of hot ginger tea, its aroma filling the room. The nausea I'd been experiencing over the past two weeks seemed to dissipate as its scent reached my nostrils.

When Mama placed the mugs on the table along with a bear-shaped jar of honey, she said, "Ginger kept me from being so sick to my stomach when I was pregnant with the three of you."

I stirred honey into my tea, took a sip, and said, "How'd you guess?"

"You're hardly eating." She bobbed her head from side to side. "And you have that look about you that all women get when they are expecting."

I felt heat rise from my stomach to my face.

"Does Thayne know?"

"No."

"Why not?"

I wrapped my hands around the mug and allowed the heat to penetrate the bones of my fingers. It felt good, as though it were warming the very core of my being. "Because I'm not sure how he's going to react. This wasn't in his plans."

"I don't imagine it was."

"What about you and Daddy? Did you plan the three of us?"

"No. Not a single one of you." She laughed lightly, which surprised me. Mama was typically uncomfortable talking about anything remotely close to the birds and the bees. "But you were welcomed, all three of you." Her shoulders sank. "Oh, Mariette. How could this have happened?"

I leaned toward her. "That's just it. I have no idea."

"You have no idea?" She took a sip of her tea and, in the process, swallowed a bit of embarrassment, I'm sure.

"Thayne and I have hardly . . . well, you know. He's tired. I'm tired. Unless we were asleep at that time . . ." I let my words drift off. There was no need in embarrassing Mama or in pushing her to a place her mind just couldn't reach.

She placed her hands flat on the table, then brushed the linen tablecloth as if it were laden with crumbs. "We need to see about getting you to a doctor," she said. "And you need to tell your husband."

I sighed. She was right, of course. Near poverty was no excuse for not taking care of my baby.

Our baby.

Minutes later we heard Daddy and Thayne shuffling down the hallway. When they met us in the kitchen Thayne looked worse for the wear and Daddy looked beat. "Ladies," Daddy said. "It's settled." I looked from Daddy to Thayne, whose eyes were downcast, like a little boy who'd gotten caught with his hand in the cookie jar. "Thayne and Mariette are moving in with us, Mama."

I felt my spine turn to rubber. "Thayne?"

He looked up then. "I'll talk to you on the way home. Your father has made a very generous offer. We can stay here and I'll work at the factory on the weekends."

"But—"

His eyes shot a warning. "Not now." He looked at Mama. "Thank you again, Mrs. Puttnam, for a delicious meal." He took the necessary steps to where I sat, cupped his hand on my elbow, and said, "Come on. I'm tired and I still have to study."

We didn't speak on the way home, but as soon as we walked through the door I turned on him. "Why do you do this?" I asked. "You make all kinds of decisions without asking me for my opinion."

Thayne reached for my sweater, a pink cardigan with pearl buttons his mother had made and sent to me as a special surprise for my birthday the month before. I shrugged out of it and then waited until he'd hung it on the peg to the right of the door. I waited until he'd taken off his jacket and hung it next to my sweater. When he turned to look at me I saw not a man who hadn't even reached twenty-five but a man who looked more like he'd lived out forty-five years of hard labor. In spite of my anger I reached for his hands, which he placed in mine, and then I guided him to the sofa, where we sat and talked for nearly an hour.

As much as he loved school and studying about God, this was more difficult than he had originally expected it to be. He was tired. He knew I was tired. "It's all over your face," he said. "I can't ask you to keep trying to balance a checking account I'm not putting any money into."

We sat, knees drawn up, elbows resting on the back of the sofa, faces leaning onto fists, both of us staring into each other's eyes, devoted to the conversation. With my free hand, I stroked his face. "I don't mind," I said.

"I know you don't," he said.

I pressed my lips together. "But I guess this all happened for a good reason."

Thayne brightened. "And we know that all things work together for good to them that love God, to them who are called according to his purpose," he quoted, then added, "Romans 8:28."

I sighed. "Yes," I said, as though I recognized Romans 8:28, which I didn't.

Thayne reached over and tapped the end of my nose with his fingertip. "So why is this such a good time?"

I pressed my lips together, then spoke softly. "Because, Thayne, I'm pregnant."

15

It took Thayne minutes of changing color to come to the same conclusion as the one I had between my mother's kitchen table and our living room sofa. There was that one night . . . when we'd reached for each other in the midst of sleep's deep slumber . . . without precaution. It would have been forgotten forever had it not been for the evidence growing within me.

From that moment, we were both united and separate, torn between what we wanted for ourselves and our child and what my parents wanted for their child and grandchild. All the while, Thayne and I managed our marriage, however well or poorly, in a pink and white bedroom meant for a teenage girl.

To my husband's credit, he was willing—especially after we'd moved in with Mama and Daddy—to allow for my parents' opinions on our current "situation." After much debate, the four of us agreed that I would continue to work with Daddy until my pregnancy began to show.

"It wouldn't be right," Mama said in a whispered tone, "for you to go to work every day displaying your pregnancy."

"Why?" I asked. "I'm not a teacher." We were sitting at the dining room table, the four of us, where we had our nightly "talks" after dinner and before Thayne "hit the books." I looked from Mama to Daddy, then to Thayne and back to Mama again. "I'd understand if I were, being around the children and all. But, I'm practically hidden from view in the mailroom or the stairwell all day."

Thayne had swallowed more than enough pride in the month since we'd moved in with my parents, and I knew he'd swallow much more before we moved out. Still, I hoped he would defend my side of the argument on this one subject. But he didn't. "Mariette, you probably don't need to be on your feet so much," he said. "Once . . . you know . . ." Thayne's discomfort at discussing my pregnancy in front of my family hadn't changed since the day I had told him. To him, it was—I think—a not-so-subtle reminder that he and I had been intimate. It's like Missy said to me when she told me she was expecting: "When you come back from your honeymoon, everyone *assumes* you have. But when you get pregnant, everyone *knows* you have."

"Thayne," I said. "We have to have money for the baby."

Daddy cleared his throat. "We'll take care of that."

"Our gift to the baby," Mama said, I'm sure to save face, though I'm not sure whose, theirs or ours.

Thayne sighed, shoulders hunched, then nodded and said, "I'll keep working on the weekends, of course."

Daddy nodded along with Thayne as Mama said, "You're doing just fine, Thayne." I'm not sure who was more shocked by her accolade, her or Thayne, but it was nice to hear.

Thayne worked from 7:30 Saturday morning until 8:30 in the evening with a half hour for lunch, which I always brought to him. We'd sit in the car, under the shade of one of the large oaks lining the back of the employee parking lot, eat sandwiches and pickles, and drink iced tea from Mason jars. Somewhere in the middle of his second semester of school and my second trimester of pregnancy, he added a paper route, Friday through Sunday mornings, which I initially accompanied him on. As I grew more and more pregnant, it became harder to get out of bed and stay awake. By the time I was in my seventh month, I'd stopped going altogether.

None of it seemed to matter much anyway. Thayne and I rarely spoke, and on those occasions when we did, our voices were pulled taut and tinged with sarcasm. I knew Thayne was exhausted—what with traveling back and forth to school, keeping up his grade point average, working two jobs—and though I wanted to feel empathetic to his plight, I was too busy being miserable at my own pity party.

Even at six months, I was fat. Unsightly. Mama had said it would be best that I not work out in public, and I conceded she was right. It was no wonder teachers weren't allowed to stand in front of impressionable youngsters while in a family way! If they saw the condition of impending motherhood they might grow up resolved never to procreate and then there'd be no more people in the world.

I was not only fat, I was despondent. I missed my husband. I missed the apartment and my old schedule of wifely duties and expectations. I missed watching at the living room window for Thayne to pull into the little one-car driveway in front of our apartment, anxious to see him, to hug him, and to be kissed and hugged in return. I missed the fun-loving, carefree man I'd married. Over the past seven months we'd been the proverbial ships passing in the night. Even then we hadn't come close enough to each other to exchange glances.

It was a hot, sticky Wednesday in July when Missy came to see me. I was lying on my bed, wearing a smock dress, feet shoeless, legs spread against the heat while an oscillating fan near the open window worked tirelessly to keep me cool. A light tap at my door woke me from a nap that hadn't quite settled in. "Come in," I said, rising up on my elbows. The door cracked open, and Missy's face appeared around its edge. "Missy," I said, breathing out her name like a pent-up sigh.

She crossed over to the bed, sashaying in a shirtwaist dress of navy blue and large white daisies with orange middles. "Hey, ladybug." She smiled. "Don't get up." I heard the clomp of her shoes hit the floor as she climbed onto Thayne's side of the bed, the one nearest the door, where I'd slept until the day I married him.

"You are a sight for sore eyes." I touched the skirt of her dress—silk—and said, "You look like the cool part of summer. Wherever that is."

"Thank you." She rubbed her hand in wide circular motions over my protruding belly then leaned close and whispered, "Hello, Baby Scott."

I giggled, lying back. "Stop."

"What? Rubbing or talking to the baby?"

I shook my head. "Making me laugh. Keep rubbing. It feels good." I closed my eyes. "Speaking of babies. Where's yours?"

"With Mama. It's my afternoon off."

I looked at her. "How's Ward?"

"Handsome. Incredibly sexy." She beamed. "We're having another one of these." She pointed to my stomach. "In six months."

I rose up again. "Oh, Missy! How wonderful."

She straightened, crossed her legs, fluffing the bouffant skirt over her knees, and said, "So, how are you feeling?"

I pushed up. "Horrible. Is this normal?"

"I don't know. Define horrible."

"I ache."

Her blue eyes danced. "Oh yeah. That's normal. Even my toenails hurt, I think."

I took a deep breath. "And . . . down there?" I cast my eyes southward.

150

Missy's dark brows drew together. "You mean . . . down there, down there?"

I nodded. "It's like a heaviness. A throbbing."

"Have you called and talked to your doctor?"

"No. I have an appointment coming up and . . . it really just started."

"When?"

"A few days ago."

Missy laid her hand over the lower part of my abdomen. "Have you said anything to Thayne?"

I snorted. "I've hardly said 'boo' to Thayne."

Missy sighed. "Ward and I have been worried about you two, especially living here and all. How much time do you spend alone together?"

"Awake or asleep?" I asked in half-jest.

She didn't take the bait and laugh. "Right here." She patted the mattress at her knee. "Between these sheets."

I sank down again. "I can't remember the last time."

"Oh, dear." She tucked her blonde hair—cut shorter now like everyone else's, copying our new First Lady—behind her ears. "I'll have Ward talk to Thayne."

I shot a warning glance her way. "You'll do no such thing. Thayne would die."

She looked up for a moment, then unfolded herself and laid back, her head at my feet. "You still have a canopy, huh?"

"Don't start. You sound like Thayne, poor guy."

She took my hand in hers and squeezed. "How much longer before you can get out of here?"

I giggled again. "You make it sound like a prison."

"Isn't it? That's probably why . . . if I remember correctly, your parents' bedroom is just beyond that wall behind your head."

"It is and it'll be a while. I don't see us leaving here until after Thayne graduates."

"When will that be?"

"June of '63. He's expecting to get his first assignment shortly after that."

"And then you, Mrs. Scott, will be a preacher's wife." We rose up on our elbows then, as though choreographed and synchronized, and looked at each other.

"Heaven help us," I said.

"Mariette." Missy's voice sounded like a warning. "Have you talked to Thayne—truly talked to him—about how you feel? About God, I mean?"

I shook my head. "No."

"Why not?" She sat up fully, crossed her legs again.

"Because, Missy. I don't even know how I feel about God. I go to church and I listen to the preacher and I think, *Okay. Sounds good.* But it means little to me. I know God is up there and he's watching us and all, but it's not like I talk to him or him to me or anything like that." I sighed. "I listen to Thayne ramble on and on about God and the Bible and how exciting it all is. I smile and I nod and deep down inside I think, *Why can't I get this?*" I looked toward the window and then back to her. "You get it. You got it, I guess, when Ward explained it all to you. Why can't I get it?" I started to cry then. "And why am I crying about it?"

"Hormones." She leaned over, pressed her cheek to mine, then drew back. "You'll get it. You will. God will reveal himself to you in a real way and then you'll know for sure like I know for sure."

"How do you know? I mean, how do you know he will reveal himself to me?" I wiped the tears away from my jaw and the hollow of my throat, thinking, *And what if I don't want him to?*

"Because I pray you will, and God's Word says the fervent prayers of a righteous man availeth much."

"Where does it say that?"

"James 5:16." She swung her legs off the bed, then slipped to the floor. I watched as she reached for her shoes, put them on, and then said, "I've got to fly. So much to do. So little time." She winked. "Promise me you'll talk to your doctor about the pressure you're feeling."

I nodded.

"And that you and Thayne will do something . . . fun . . . together."

I rolled my eyes, and this time she laughed. Then she looked at me and said, "Want me to pray before I go?"

I shook my head. "But you can keep praying for me privately," I said.

"That goes without saying, my friend."

My next appointment with Dr. Franklin, the obstetrician who'd delivered me and nearly every child in Meadow Grove and would now deliver my child, was on Friday. After Missy's suggestion that I alert him to the pains I was experiencing, and with the twinges and heaviness becoming more frequent and severe, I decided to do just that. Thayne, of course, would be at school at the time of the appointment. I was determined not to alert him to any concerns I might have. His answer would be to miss school and accompany me to Dr. Franklin's office, which is the husbandly thing to do. And I would have to tell him I'd rather have Mama, who always went with me and brought great comfort in her experiences with pregnancy.

Sometime between midnight Friday morning and around three o'clock when I awoke, I dreamed I was at Saint Margaret Mary's, standing in the back of the old chapel. As always, candles flickered at the stained glass windows—the ones depicting scenes from the life of Jesus—and the light from the bulky wrought iron chandeliers had been dimmed. The walls and pews, the altar railing and pulpit, shone dark and rich from years of age and polish.

Compelled by the sound of moaning—animal or human I could not determine—I moved up the aisle, one tentative step at a time, looking between the pews for its source and seeing nothing but the upturned kneeling benches and neatly placed prayer books.

Then I stood beyond the altar, the moaning growing more intense. It came from a small Crusader-arched window where a statue of Mother Mary stood, dressed in a white gown and blue headdress. Her eyes—mournful more than reverent—were turned heavenward.

I neared her. Her eyes shifted, peered down at me. I heard the moaning again. It was coming from her, louder now, unmistakable. Her eyes moved again—deep blue against porcelain skin, to the front of her dress, which grew red with blood, spilling between the folds.

I gasped awake, blinked at the canopy overhead, then shifted my head to the left to read the clock rhythmically ticking on the bedside table. It was minutes before three. I looked at Thayne, lying flat on his back as he always did, arm crooked over his head, face washed by moonlight.

I had to go to the bathroom, or perhaps I already had. Something wet—something gooey—was sticking to my inner thighs, making them warm and uncomfortable. I jerked back the sheet and stared in horror at the dark red stain spreading across the front of my crisp white nightgown.

"Thayne . . ."

My voice was not my own. It was agony and fear. It was nightmare becoming a reality. It was a voice belonging to a mother losing her unborn child.

16

Mama cried, probably harder than I'd ever seen her cry about anything, and that includes the death of her father. Daddy brought a box of chocolates and a bouquet of flowers to the hospital where I spent the next week lying flat on my back, staring up at the ceiling and asking God in every way conceivable, *Why?*

Thayne cried too. After Dr. Franklin had left and then Daddy and Mama, Thayne walked over to the window, peered out as though he were watching for someone, then laid his arm against the wall, buried his head, and cried like a child who'd been sent to the corner for misbehaving.

I pressed my lips together to keep the great gulfs of sobs at bay. Somehow, after waking from delivering a stillborn child and hearing Dr. Franklin's verdict of death spoken with all the professional courtesy one would expect, I refused myself the right to cry.

For days I lay in the hospital bed, being waited on by nurses who took vital signs, helped me to and from the bathroom, gave sponge baths, and brought magazines for me to read. Mama came and sat with me daily until Thayne returned from school, and then he sat with me until bedtime, at which point he was shooed out by Miss Brown, Charge Nurse.

A few friends came by. Most of them didn't stay long, only to say they were wishing me well. Anne—the recently wed Mrs. Anthony Pierson—stayed long enough for Mama to take Mitch for his annual physical. She caught me up on the latest news: Sandy, who was still working for an attorney, had seen Missy's old beau Chad, who was working in the DA's office as an investigator at the courthouse, and now the two of them were an item. Bobbie Sue was continuing to fly the friendly skies but, so far, was sans pilot. Anne said she received postcards from all sorts of exotic locations. "She's living the life," Anne said.

Toni was still in school, but Anne had heard from Sandy that she'd fallen madly in love with one of the professors and was going to drop out so she could date him publicly. I found that bit of news totally distressing, but Anne thought it was funny, and in spite of my situation, I laughed along with her.

Ward came by but without Missy. He said she wasn't feeling well, but I knew that wasn't true. Or, at least, not true entirely. It would be difficult, I knew, for a woman carrying a child to face another who has just lost hers.

When the week was over and I was pronounced well enough to return home, I did. After that, time seemed to slip by without my noticing or being a part of it. Oh, I looked and acted all right on the outside, but on the inside, some small part of me had died with our daughter, whom we named Rachel, and was buried alongside her in the family plot at Meadow Grove Memorial Gardens, where an angel stood guard over what remained.

Life returned to normal. I went back to work—despite everyone's protests, including Missy's—at the Fox & Hound. I had nothing better to do, I argued, except sit at home and think of what might have been or what might be if some night Thayne and I reached for each other once again.

All too soon, hot weather gave way to cool, and cool to

cold, and it was Christmas. Thayne and I made our annual holiday visit to his family farm, where Mama Lena doted on me. Mr. Scott was remarkably kind, never mentioning the loss of the baby directly.

One afternoon I took a long stroll down the dirt lane running alongside the farm's acreage while Thayne and his brothers were off doing something brotherly and Mama Lena was lying down "for just a spell." When I returned to the house, Thayne's father was standing next to the bed of his old truck, arms leaning against the sides, puffing on a pipe filled with sweet tobacco. I could smell it before I could see him.

He nodded at me as I neared and said, "Mariette." The words were spoken like a command to come, and I surprised myself by doing just that. I walked over to the truck, stopping on the opposite side from where my father-in-law stood.

For a while, he said nothing. He puffed on his pipe while staring out across the fields that brought both his livelihood and, sometimes, his distress. I took the time to study his face. It was weathered, older than I'd realized before. His thick brow was as gray and coarse as the hair on his head. It sprouted wild in places, poked over the rim of his thick black glasses. His eyes, a watered down blue I imagined had at one time been as vibrant as Thayne's, shifted slightly—left to right, right to left—as though he were taking in more than the scene around us. I wondered how his facial features would rest or grow on Thayne as he aged, and the thought made me shudder. Finally he cleared his throat and said, "Missy, now you know I don't talk much. Never have." He paused.

"No, sir," I said. I rested my arms on my side of the truck. Instinct told me to draw as close to him as I dared, and the truck's bed was the perfect distance between us.

"But I've got something I want to share with you." Again, he paused.

"Yes, sir?"

"When I was a young man—younger than your husband,

my son—I went off and joined the Air Force. Thayne ever tell you that?"

"No, sir, I don't believe so." I tried to imagine Mr. Scott in uniform, saluting those in command over him, learning the mechanics of war, carousing on leave with his buddies, thinking about fighting.

"Well, I did." Still he looked straight ahead. "I was stationed in Denver, Colorado, for a while. You know where that is?"

"Yes, sir."

"Ever been there?"

"No, sir. I've pretty much never been anywhere."

"It's called the Mile High City. Did you know that?"

"Yes, sir."

"Pretty place. The mountains, now, they're something else, let me tell you. Those Rockies. A far cry from this flat dirt 'round here."

"Yes, sir." I shifted my weight. Although tired, I was mesmerized by where this conversation was going.

"I met a gal there. Prettiest thing I'd ever seen up till that point. Name was Nina. Had red hair. Green eyes." He coughed a laugh, then puffed on his pipe some more. "Had a temper to go with it too." His eyes shot toward mine then, holding my attention. "She was all fire and life, that Nina was. Spirited, you know what I'm saying?"

I pictured Nina in my mind, then said, "Yes, sir."

"We did everything together. Went dancing—hard to imagine me being light on my feet, I know, but we did. Laughed and palled around with our good friends. I fell in love so quick I hardly knew what hit me. We'd known each other exactly two weeks when I married her."

I felt, more than heard, my intake of breath.

"I never said a word to my family. Not one word. Wasn't quite sure how I would." He looked past me again. "We were married no more than a couple months when she told me

158

she was going to have a young'un." He chuckled. "Not to be disrespectful, but we musta hit pay dirt right off the bat, if you get my drift."

I felt my face grow hot in spite of the chill outside. "I do."

"Happiest I've ever been in all my born days, but still I didn't tell my family. My daddy was a hard man and my mama wasn't much softer. I knew they'd be upset, what with me marrying a Northern girl. A girl with family they didn't know. I figured I'd just come home on leave one day, bringing a wife and a baby with me, and they'd get over it." He shook his head. "God must have had other plans, though." His eyes found mine again. They were even more washed out than before. "Nina died in childbirth. I buried my wife and my son in Denver, Colorado, and in time returned to Georgia a broken man, but a live one, nonetheless."

I opened my mouth to say something, though God only knew what. In five short minutes I'd gone from seeing Mr. Scott only as my husband's father, to a man who'd enjoyed a youth and who'd had a life—like mine—filled with the inexpressible pain of losing a child. But, my father-in-law had lost more than just a child. He'd lost a wife too. A lover. A friend.

"Mr. Scott, why are you telling me this?" I asked. It seemed to me the metal of the truck had become a block of ice, and I began to shiver.

He looked past me once more. "I want you to know something, little girl. Life is good when it's good, but it's pretty awful when it's not. God gives and God takes away, is what the Bible says."

"Yes, sir." I wrapped my arms around my middle.

"I came home when my time with the Air Force was over." He sighed deeply. "Came home. Ran across Lena up at the five-and-dime. My, my. She'd been just a child when I'd left four years earlier. She didn't have Nina's fire, but she was pretty and she was good and she loved me right off."

I felt myself growing defensive for my beloved mother-in-law. He must have sensed it because he added, "Don't think I don't love that woman, because I do. Love her more than I ever thought I could. She's been a good wife. Good mother. Good helpmeet."

Relief poured warmth through me. I thought I couldn't bear it if I knew Mr. Scott didn't love my mother-in-law. "Does Mama Lena know? About Nina?"

Again his eyes found mine. "No, ma'am, she doesn't. I actually called her Nina once, what with the names being so close. She didn't catch it. Leastways I don't think she did." He cleared his throat, puffed on his pipe once or twice more, then added, "I'd be obliging if Lena went to her grave not knowing, if you don't mind. She'd never really understand, I don't think." He cleared his throat again, and I wondered if he were becoming ill, standing out in the cold for so long. "I'm telling you this because it's all I know to do. I see in your eyes the same sadness was once in mine, and it breaks my heart. I know I'm not much of a touch-and-feel kind of man. But I have emotions like everyone else. That was my grandchild you was carrying, but more than that, she was your child." He turned and looked back toward the house. "See all this? It's what I've got now. A good wife. A nice home. Three boys I'm proud of, though I don't tell them near enough." Again he looked at me. "And the prettiest little daughter-in-law a daddy could want for his boy."

"Thank you." I swallowed. "But why are you telling me this?"

"Consider it my Christmas gift to you. Just between us, you hear me?"

"Yes, sir. But—"

"Life will come back around, little one. You'll see. You'll have a pack of babies you won't know what to do with. Mark my words."

I giggled sadly then. "I hope so."

"You'll see," he said again. "You'll have a fine life because that's the way of it."

I remembered Thayne's words then, the ones he'd spoken when he told me he wanted to go to seminary. He'd promised me a good life. A fine life. All we had to do was get him through seminary. Then, if Thayne lived up to his word, life could begin . . . would begin again for me.

17

For Christmas that year I gave Thayne an LP, Elvis Presley's *His Hand in Mine*. His face registered surprise as he ran his hand over the photographed face of the young crooner dressed in a dark suit and looking over his left shoulder while sitting at an organ, hands placed strategically on what I thought looked like an E chord. "Elvis singing gospel," Thayne said, his voice almost inaudible. He looked at me, eyes filled with tenderness. "I heard 'His Hand in Mine' on the radio a couple of weeks ago . . . on my way back from school. That Elvis sure can sing."

We sat on the floor of my parents' living room in our pajamas and robes, legs crossed, knees touching. The boys were nearby, tearing into their gifts. Foiled paper was ripped and scattered around them. Mama, dressed in a festive holiday lounging set, was on the sofa, still holding the box displaying a diamond bracelet Daddy had given her. She fingered it as she watched us. Daddy, I knew, had left the room as I'd arranged for him to do earlier that week.

"It's not much," I said to my husband.

Thayne leaned over and lightly pressed his lips to mine. "It's perfect," he spoke against them.

From over Thayne's shoulder I saw Daddy's head appear

in the doorway. He winked at me and I nodded. Thayne, catching the movement, turned his head—looking first at Daddy, then back at me. "What's going on here?" he asked with a smile.

Daddy stepped into the room. He wore dark green pajamas with a thick matching robe and slippers. He looked round and happy as he leaned against the doorframe, crossed his arms, and said, "So, now. What do you have there, son?"

Thayne showed him the album.

"An album? You got an album from your wife for Christmas? I believe I'd leave a woman who gave me a dollar-ninety-nine album for Christmas."

Thayne pinked and I swallowed to keep from laughing. "It's Elvis," Thayne said, trying—I'm sure—to be supportive of my inexpensive gift. "Singing gospel."

Daddy shook his head. "Good of that boy to sing for the Lord while he's gyrating all over the world."

"He's got a nice voice, Mr. Puttnam. And I've heard he has a background in the church."

Daddy shook his head again. "Well, I'm glad you like the album. But you mark my words, he'll never be a Frank Sinatra or a Dean Martin."

I grinned as I stretched my spine. "Or a Perry Como."

Daddy pointed to me and winked. "Now you're talking." He looked at Thayne again. "So, do you have a phonograph to play that thing on?"

I giggled. "Daddy! A phonograph?"

Thayne looked up at Daddy, seeming—always and forever—like a little boy. "Well, sir," he said, "we used to have the hi-fi, but we sold it when we moved here." Thayne winked at me. "That and everything else." He looked back to Daddy. "Maybe we can get a little record player for our room." He looked back at me just as Daddy pushed himself from the door frame and stepped back into the foyer. "What do you think, Mariette? We'll go shopping at Western Auto

163

after New Year's Day. There's sure to be some good sales then."

Daddy returned to the room then, arms laden with a large box wrapped in Christmas paper and tied off with an over-sized red bow. Thayne jumped up to help. "Boy, sir! What do you have here?"

Daddy allowed Thayne to take the package as he huffed and puffed. "The other gift from your wife."

Thayne enjoyed ripping into the present, Mitch and Tommy now at his side. It was, of course, a stereophonic record player. I beamed as Thayne said, "Look at this. Look at this."

Mitch and Tommy were equally ecstatic. "Boy, Mariette," Tommy said. "A Jonell Mk III. This is a beaut!"

Inside, I was more than happy. I couldn't help but watch my family—my husband, my parents, and my brothers—as they oohed and ahhed over the gift. Mostly, though, I marveled at what Thayne had managed to do: change my parents' perception of him with his charm and charisma, eliminating the tension from our earliest days together.

But more than a sense of excitement and relief, I felt for the first time in months that I was again connected to someone. To *something*. Feeling as though, perhaps, the words of Mr. Scott were coming true for me. Life was returning to good and happy. For a fleeting moment all thoughts of Rachel were lifted off my shoulders, though they remained deep inside.

After the initial thrill died down, Thayne reached under the tree for my gift. "It's not a record player but . . . well, it's from my heart." He kissed me and then whispered, "I hope you like it."

I opened the small present, the box the size and shape of a book. "I'll bet it's a book," I said, to which Thayne frowned.

"Just open it," he said with a pout.

Under the shimmery silver paper was a narrow black box, and inside it a white leather-covered Bible, my name embossed in gold lettering across the lower right corner of the cover. *Mariette Elizabeth Scott*, it read.

I pulled it out slowly, my eyes filling with tears. Thayne mistook my emotions. Or, at least, I thought he did. He reached over and squeezed my hand, then pointed to my name. "I wanted you to have something with my name—our name—on it. If we'd married in a church, you'd have carried a white Bible, like this one." He took the book from me, opened it to the page displaying a family tree. There among the branches he'd written the names of our grandparents, our parents, and ourselves. A narrow gold line from our names dropped to several boxes, the first one neatly printed: *Rachel Elizabeth Scott*.

I took in a deep breath, exhaled slowly through my nose. "Rachel," I said, then looked up at Thayne, who reached over to wipe away the tears that pushed their way past my stubbornness to puddle in the corners of my eyes.

"Look," he said, tilting my head down toward the book. "There are other boxes, Mariette."

Daddy knelt down as Mama slipped to the floor behind me. I felt her arms wrap around my shoulders, her lips press against my temple. "For all the other babies you will have, my darling," she said.

My family, all staring at me, loving me with their eyes. It was as if a dam had burst. I attempted to keep the floodwaters below the knot that had formed in my throat, but they refused. I gasped. Once. Twice. Then began to sob, to weep over the death of a child I'd not once cried over since her birth.

Thayne took me from my mother's arms, cradled me, rocked me, cooed *shushes* over and over until my head lay in his lap and I had no energy left to spend. When I looked up, it was to find only my husband's face. Everyone else had left the Christmas-cluttered room, leaving the two of us with my sorrow and anguish. To my freedom from grief.

"You needed that," Thayne said. Then he smiled. "Though this wasn't the reaction I thought I'd get."

I hung my head. "All this and on Christmas too."

Thayne pulled me back into his arms. "Christmas is about the birth of a baby boy who came to draw all men back to God." He kissed the top of my head. "My fear is that the death of our baby girl has pushed you even further away from God's love than you think you already are."

I drew back. "That's not true."

"It is too true, Mariette."

I set my jaw. "What has Missy told you?"

I saw the look of surprise as it flashed across his face, then settled to husbandly wisdom. "Missy hasn't told me anything, honey. You have."

I pressed my hand against my chest. "I haven't said anything, Thayne. Nothing to make you think I'm not a Christian. I am a Christian. I'm a graduate of Saint Margaret Mary's Academy, after all."

He laughed lightly, then brought me back to his arms. "I'm not saying you aren't a Christian. I'm saying that God hasn't grabbed hold of your heart so hard you feel like it's going to burst wide open if you don't shout it from the mountaintops. And there's a difference, Mariette."

With my ear pressed against his chest, I heard the steady beat of his heart. I closed my eyes against the sweet sound of it. "Thayne . . ."

"Shhh," he said. "It has been the things you haven't said, Mariette. Not what you have said. But that's okay. You'll know one day. You'll know and you'll understand me and how I feel, better than I'll understand it myself, I'd venture to say."

I smiled against the wrinkled cotton of his plaid robe. "I already know you better than you know yourself."

He tilted my face up to his, kissed me lightly, and said, "Your mother is making pecan pancakes. Let's go eat. I'm starved."

I smiled at him. "Me too."

And I was.

It wasn't until later that I read the inscription in the front of the Bible. *"To Mariette,"* it read, *"my wife, on this Christmas Day, 1961. I know the words herein don't speak to you quite yet, but I pray every day that they will. That's my forever gift to you."*

Thayne's everyday prayers, I thought, might just be what it would take. In spite of everything my husband believed, my best friend professed, and the years of church and mass I'd sat through, my heart just didn't get it. But more than my concern that I never would was the reality of what else was to come. Soon, too soon, I'd be a pastor's wife. Then, whether I felt it or not, I'd at least have to pretend I did.

As June 1963 zoomed toward us, I thought quite often of a movie I'd seen when I was fourteen. Mama, Daddy, and I had made a special date that evening to see the local opening of *A Man Called Peter*, the story of Dr. Peter Marshall, a man who grew up in Scotland. As a young man he came to America and received the call of God on his life—the same call my husband had heard—and then went on to be the beloved and charismatic chaplain of the U.S. Senate.

But Dr. Marshall had married a young woman far removed from me. Although we both came from good families, Catherine Wood Marshall was a wife any preacher-husband would be blessed to have. Her faith never wavered—or so Jean Peters had portrayed her—while my faith had yet to take root.

I wanted desperately to be the wife for Thayne that Mrs. Marshall had been for her husband. I went to the library to get the book the movie had been based on, written by Catherine Marshall herself. I read it many times, continuing to search for some sort of recipe or blueprint that would make me better, more qualified, for the role I found myself in.

But, other than for church, I didn't pick up the Bible Thayne had given me.

Daddy assumed that after Thayne's graduation, life would return to his version of normal. Or so he said after dinner one Sunday night in mid-May as we settled in the family room. That evening, bathed and in their pajamas, my brothers geared up to watch *Bonanza* while Mama readied herself to watch the finale of *The Dinah Shore Show*.

"I can't believe we won't have it to watch anymore," she said as she sat in her favorite chair. Thayne and I sat hip to hip on the sofa, Daddy in his chair, and the boys sprawled on the floor. Tommy, I noted, looked leggier and more muscular at the shoulders than I'd noticed before, turning into a young man right before my eyes.

Daddy stretched, crossed his ankles, and said, "What I can't believe is that our boy Thayne here will be graduating in a month."

I looked at Thayne, who smiled. "If I can pass these last few tests," he said.

I patted his leg. "You'll do fine."

"Then," Daddy continued, "I suppose you'll want to come back to work at the factory. You and Mariette will get your own place, move out, start a whole new chapter of your lives together." He shook his head. "I have to admit, it won't be the same around here without you."

Thayne leaned forward, rested his elbows on his knees, and said, "I'm sorry, Mr. Puttnam, I don't understand."

I looked at Mama then back to Daddy. "I don't understand, either," I said as my mind raced forward to decipher Daddy's message. He expected Thayne to come back to work for him, to advance within the company as he'd been slated to do before he enrolled in college. Daddy pictured us moving out, moving on, and moving up. Now, I could envision it too. A house, maybe like Missy's and Ward's. In the country with wide, sweeping views. And filled with children, like the boxes in the gifted Bible would be.

I turned to look at Thayne, and I was smiling.

168

"What?" he asked me. Then he pointed, first to Daddy and then to me. "Wait a minute. You all think . . . what? You all think this was just something I did for nearly three years to say I'd done it?" He stood, flexed his fists and his jaw muscles. His face ran scarlet to white, and his piercing eyes bored a hole in the opposite wall, then went downcast. "I'm sorry," he said. He cleared his throat, turned to my mother. "I'm sorry, Mrs. Puttnam, for such an outburst."

He turned on his heel and left the room.

For a moment, all I could do was blink. Then, taking a deep breath, I stood.

"Wow," Mitch said. "That was some anger, boy."

"Mitchell," Daddy warned.

I swallowed. "I'd better get upstairs," I said with a nod.

I found Thayne standing at the bedroom window, left hand resting against the ledge, head down as though he were watching life on the lawn below. He didn't move when I entered the room or when I closed the door behind me. I waited to see if he would, or if he would say anything. He didn't. He just kept on staring down at the lawn.

"Thayne?" Part of me trembled; I'd never seen my husband that angry, though the fury only seemed to last for a second.

There was a flinching of his shoulders before he turned. "I'm sorry," he said. He rested against the window frame. "I didn't mean to get so angry."

"It only lasted a second." I kept my hands on the doorknob as I supported myself by leaning against the door. What a picture we made, I thought. One at the window, one at the door.

He crossed his arms. "I thought you knew. I thought your parents knew."

"Knew what, Thayne?"

"That after graduation, I'd become a pastor."

"Maybe Daddy thought you'd become a part-time pastor."

"What does that mean?"

I stepped over to the bed that separated us and placed my hands on the quilted spread. "You know, like you would preach on Sundays and work a real job during the week."

Thayne moved to the other side of the bed, pressed his fists against the spread, and leaned under the canopy. "Is that what you think? That being a preacher is not a real job?"

I crossed my arms. "No. I mean . . . I . . . I don't know what I thought, to be honest with you. I knew I'd be a pastor's wife, but I guess I hadn't stopped to think about what that would mean . . . for you."

Thayne coughed out a laugh. "So you had it all figured out for you but not how it would affect me?"

My entire mouth had gone dry. I ran a thick tongue over my lips. "That's not what I meant, Thayne."

Thayne took a deep breath, straightened, then sat on top of the bed with one leg under and one leg forward. I watched the cover bunch up under him, and I fought the urge to remind him his shoes were on the bed. "Well, I tell you what, Mariette. Why don't you tell me just what you did mean?" He patted the bed beside him. "Just climb right up here and let me hear what you have to say."

I did exactly that, but not without saying, "You don't have to be sarcastic about it. After all, this is *our* life we're talking about."

Thayne leaned against the wooden post of the bed. "Absolutely," he said, though his voice remained tinged with derision.

I clutched my hands together. "Why don't you tell me?" I kept my voice low and sweet. "Tell me what you have in mind for us."

"Are you sure?" he asked, though not pleased. "You're sure you want me to go first?"

"Yes."

"Mariette, I expect that after graduation, I'll be called to some town somewhere—probably remote because it's my first assignment—and I'll be a pastor over a small church. That's the way it works. Seminary students graduate, get an assignment, and go. Then, if they do well, they advance. Better locations. Larger churches. As I grow in my ability to spread God's Word, my position will . . . I guess you could say, increase." The excitement was returning to his eyes, replacing the anger.

"You, you, you. What about me? Have you stopped to think where that leaves me?"

"You're my wife. You'll do the things a preacher's wife does."

"I don't know what that means, Thayne. I don't know what a preacher's wife does, and you've never really asked me if I wanted to do whatever it is I don't know to do."

He shrugged. "But you agreed to my going to school. Surely you knew."

I shook my head. "I didn't think it through, I guess."

"And in the years since I've been in school you haven't once asked yourself, what next?"

A chuckle escaped my throat as tears stung my eyes. "I guess I've been a little preoccupied. You know . . . working, moving, being pregnant, losing a baby, working again. Forgive me." Cynicism dripped from my tongue.

Thayne bit his lip, took a breath, and then blew it out. "Look," he said finally. "I know you've been through a lot since I enrolled, and I know this isn't exactly the life you signed up for. But when you married me I was just a mail clerk in a factory, with little ambition, a shaky past, and no real plans for the future. I hardly had two dimes to rub together. All that, and that didn't stop you from marrying me."

He had me there. I pondered it for a minute before saying, "We sure were crazy in love."

"Lust," he said, then blushed. "I'd say we were in lust before we were in love." He looked at his hands then back at me. "But I do love you, Mariette. I love you so much it hurts, and I want you to love me that much too."

I leaned forward. "I do! Thayne, do you think I would have forsaken my parents if I wasn't all gone over you?"

He leaned forward too and—as it had always been between us—our hands sought each other, followed by our lips. "Here's our problem," he said with a smile.

"Just tell me what I'm supposed to do," I said against his face. "Don't assume I know what we're doing or what I'm doing or even what you're doing. You've kept me in the dark, Thayne."

He blinked, and his lashes fluttered against my cheek. "Not on purpose."

"But still, you did."

"Okay. I will. I promise."

"And you'll make me a part of what you're doing. Promise me that too. We'll go in as a team and not you the preacher and me the preacher's wife."

He kissed me again. "I promise," he said. He pulled me into his arms as he leaned back, drawing me on top of him, oblivious to the edge of the bed. We both tumbled to the floor, landing with a thud.

Our eyes wide, we asked each other, "Are you all right?" then burst out laughing. Within seconds there was a knock on the door, followed by Daddy's voice.

"Is everything okay in there?"

We smothered our giggles against each other. I raised my head. "Everything's just fine, Daddy."

Even still, somewhere deep inside, I wondered if my words were true.

Part 3

"Sugar Shack"

18

In June of '63, Thayne graduated with honors from seminary. My family and his—meeting for the first time—sat proudly in the college chapel, clapped wildly as he accepted his diploma, and then rallied around him once all the black caps had been tossed—tassels flying and swirling, then falling back to the graduates.

A few days later, Thayne went before a review board to begin the process of ordination within his denomination. He came home (we were still living with my parents and probably would be for some time), looking exhausted but pleased. During dinner he shared with everyone how the meeting had gone.

"Three pastors and three of my professors were there, lined up on the other side of a table. I sat in a chair, feeling like the Lone Ranger, let me tell you."

"What did they ask you, honey?"

"Well, first . . ." Thayne pinked. "They asked me to give my testimony." He kept his eyes focused on the fork he held.

I looked from him to my parents and back to him again. Knowing them, the idea of a "testimony" was foreign, but it would also raise questions about Thayne's past, a past I still didn't know completely.

"What's a testimony?" Mitch asked.

Thayne looked at my brother. "It's the story of how you came to know and love God."

Mitch shrugged one shoulder. "Gee, boy. I've always known about God."

The adults and Tommy laughed before Thayne continued. "Then I was asked a series of questions. You know, theological questions. What I believe and why. What the Bible says about this and that, and where. I'm not sure how I did when we got into some of the more controversial doctrines, but I answered honestly and within my own conscience." He cleared his throat. "They asked about my concept of what a pastor does." He looked at me. "They asked about you, Mariette. About how we met, how we married." He eyed my father. "I'll admit they looked down a little at the fact that I married you without your father's approval."

"Hear, hear," Daddy said.

We all smiled, even Mitch.

"Go on, Thayne," Mama encouraged.

"Thank you, ma'am. Um, well . . . they liked that I'm a simple man from a simple family with a godly heritage and good work ethics. I could tell they liked the fact I was willing to move here. One professor said, 'That could easily be a pride issue, Mr. Scott. Seems to me you put your wife ahead of yourself on that one.' Which I thought was pretty positive."

I patted his hand. "Me too, Thayne."

The tops of Thayne's ears turned red as he added, "They wanted to know about your background in the church too, Mariette."

"Mine? Whatever for?"

"Well, I hope you told them she was raised properly," Daddy all but boomed.

Thayne nodded. "I did, sir. I told them about being raised Lutheran and about how you and I, Mariette, started going to church with Aunt Harriett."

176

I noted he hadn't mentioned my having been sent to Saint Margaret Mary's. I'm sure my parents noticed it too, so I quickly said, "Oh, well, that's nice."

"So when will you know something?" my mother asked. "What comes next?"

Thayne bobbed his head a bit. "They'll call tomorrow. If I'm recommended for ordination, my next step will be waiting for the district supervisor to determine where I'll have my first assignment."

"And until then?" Daddy asked.

Thayne cleared his throat again. "Until then, Mr. Puttnam, if you have any extra work I can do at the factory, I'd be obliged and grateful."

Thayne was ordained. And we waited three months before an assignment came through. In the meantime, he preached occasionally at the church Aunt Harriett and Ward and Missy attended. One such Sunday, I sat, back straight, in the front row, with my Bible in my lap, and listened intently, nodding my head at the appropriate times. When the sermon was over and Thayne had shaken the last of the church members' hands, I told him how wonderfully he'd done and that I thought his message was meaningful and impactful. Thayne didn't seem to buy it.

"I stammered too much," he said. "I was boring even myself."

"You'll get better," I said. I looped my arm through his. "I'll bet that Mr. Billy Graham didn't start out as good as he is right now."

Thayne teared up. "You think so, Mariette? You think I could be as good as Billy Graham?" He shook his head. "I'd settle for half as good."

I squeezed his arm with mine. "You're already halfway there."

I realized then how important my praise and approval was

and would be for Thayne. It was the first of the pastor's wife's duties I'd come to recognize and embrace, but it would hardly be the last.

Thayne received a phone call in September, three months after his graduation and one month after Dr. Martin Luther King cried out, "I have a dream!" My husband was to meet the state supervisor for the denomination the following day in Atlanta. Thayne took our car—still the De Soto—and drove up, alone. I asked if he'd like me to come with him, but he said no. This was something he felt he had to do alone. "Time to pray on the way up," he'd said.

So that day I waited. I paced, I prayed in my way, and I waited. Mostly, I worked. In spite of Thayne's increased work at the Fox & Hound, I continued on in my position, unwilling to give up what I'd grown accustomed to. Once we had our own place, I told both Thayne and Daddy, I'd quit. Until then, it kept me busy and added cash to our bank account.

It was nearly eight o'clock in the evening when Thayne arrived home. I was standing at our bedroom window when the car pulled into the driveway. I dashed out of the room, down the stairs, and into the warm late-summer air without a word to anyone. Thayne was unfolding himself from behind the steering wheel, planting his feet on the concrete, when I made it to the driver's side of the car. "Well?" I asked. My cotton seersucker shirtwaist dress swished around my knees.

He smiled at me, but wearily. His hair was windblown, his tie pulled to half mast. His suit coat was lying across the backseat. His white short-sleeved shirt was wrinkled and damp.

"Well?" I asked again.

He leaned against the door after closing it and said, "We leave for Logan's Creek, Georgia, in two weeks."

"Logan's Creek?"

He took my hands in his. "Dr. Carnes—he's the state supervisor—said we won't need a thing. There's a house we'll be using, and it's fully furnished."

"A house? We'll have an entire house?"

He nodded. "We will. It's owned by a woman named Alma. Alma Stoddard. I don't know a whole lot about her or it, only that it's next door to her house and that it's fully furnished."

"You said that." I squeezed his hands. "What kind of furniture?"

"Goodness, Mariette. I don't know." He sighed. "Dr. Carnes said that whatever it's like, it will be a good sight better than his first assignment." He chuckled. "Dr. Carnes said the first house he and his wife lived in after he became a preacher had rugs covering the holes in the floor. He said you could see clear through to the dirt underneath."

I pulled back slightly. "But you don't know about this house? Where we'll be living? Hasn't Dr. Carnes ever been there?"

I heard the front door open and turned toward it. Daddy and Mama stood framed by it, looking anxious. "Mariette? Thayne? Why don't y'all come on in now?" Daddy hollered.

"They're anxious," I said to Thayne.

"Come on, then," he said. "Let's get this over with."

"What about pots and pans?" Mama asked. "Will it have pots and pans in the kitchen?"

"I'm assuming so, Mrs. Puttnam."

"Every woman needs her own pots and pans," Mama said. "No matter what, Mariette, I'm sending you there with new pots and pans. We'll go shopping tomorrow."

Daddy had brought an atlas from his desk drawer. "I can't find a Logan's Creek," he was saying.

"It's near Savannah," Thayne said.

"That's across the state," Mama said as though we needed a lesson in geography.

179

"Four hours by car," Thayne said.

I pressed my lips together. "That's not too far."

Mama began to cry. "It might as well be the moon."

Two weeks later, Thayne and I packed all our earthly possessions—clothes and personal items—along with several boxes of Thayne's books, two boxes of kitchen items, another box of new linens freshly washed and pressed by Daisy, two new pillows, and a quilt my grandmother had made for my mother when she'd married and Mama had put away after a few years of use. "The wedding ring quilt," she called it. "Circles and circles of eternal love."

We left Mama and Daddy, Tommy and Mitch, in a flurry of good-bye hugs and soggy kisses. Two hours later, hungry, we stopped in a small town, pulling right up to a curbside café with red checkered curtains and matching tablecloths. Near the kitchen was a long bar graced by a row of red vinyl covered barstools where three waitresses bustled about, taking orders, pouring coffee, and whisking two plates full of steaming food toward a table near the back. Thayne and I ordered cheeseburgers with fries, cola, and for dessert, apple pie with coffee. We laughed easily about our first "date," back so long ago at the Bean, where Thayne had ordered apple pie and Cathy had said he was getting his fruit "any way he could get it."

"A whole lot has happened since then," Thayne said. "Married four years. The apartment, moving back in with your parents, college for me, work for you."

"Rachel," I said.

"Rachel." He looked out a nearby window. "It's getting awfully gray out there."

"We'd best get going then," I said. "Before it pours."

We shut the doors of the De Soto seconds before the first drops fell. Two hours later, it was still raining, harder than I'd ever imagined it could. At one point I begged Thayne to pull over, just pull over, but he wouldn't. "I'm fine," he said. "I can see."

But when the front tire blew out, we were forced to wobble to the shoulder of the road. For a moment, I thought Thayne was going to swear, but instead he swallowed hard, clutched the steering wheel, and said, "Father, you know all things. And all things work to the good of those who love you. We thank you for this minor setback."

Ten minutes later, Thayne—soaked to the bone—slid back behind the wheel, turned to me, and said, "I'd appreciate it very much, Mariette, if you'd get out one of those new towels your mama gave us so I don't catch my death."

I jumped, ashamed I'd not thought to do that. I leaned over to the back seat of the car, found the appropriate box, and pulled out a fluffy pink towel. *Pink*, I thought. I fished around the box again until I found one in sea foam green. "Here," I said as I handed it to him.

Thayne dried off, wrapped the towel around his neck, started the car, shifted to first, and then pulled back onto the road.

"How much farther do you think it is?" I asked. I stared out the window. The trees grew thicker and closer to the road. They swayed in the wind, sending even greater torrents of rain toward us.

"Can't be much further. We've been on the road two hours since we left that café."

"But the rain has slowed us down some."

"Some."

I noticed the road narrowing. Occasionally the line of trees and shrubs—so thick they blocked out the light, darkening the road as though we were driving at dusk—broke away, revealing stretches of farmland. A speed limit sign, cocked to the left and rocking in the wind, appeared around a bend. Power poles sprang up from the earth, offering hope of finding Logan's Creek sooner rather than later. "Thayne," I ventured. "Just how big *is* Logan's Creek?"

"I went to the library and looked it up. It's not a big place. The last census reported less than two hundred people."

"Less than two hundred?"

He nodded.

"Two hundred?"

"Yes, Mariette." His Adam's apple bobbed. "Look, it's my first assignment. What'd you expect? A metropolis?"

"But less than two hundred, Thayne. Is that enough people to even have a church?"

Thayne laughed. "Most of the folks there are related in some way or another. Dr. Carnes said many of them don't even attend services anymore. There was some feud or some misunderstanding between the members. The pastor who used to be there, Reverend Dorn, left the town a month or so ago. Gave up, if the truth be told. He'd been there only two or three years. Dr. Carnes said Reverend Dorn just couldn't get the people to catch on to God's love over their own set ways."

"So what were they doing for a preacher between then and now?"

"Lay pastors, mostly. Or just not having services."

"Oh."

"Dr. Carnes said he believes my youth and passion will influence this town." Again his Adam's apple took a dive down his throat, then popped back up again. "Help bring the people back to Jesus."

I looked out the windshield. Rambling white frame houses dotted the side of the road. Most of them seemed to strain under the weight of their roofs. All were shrouded by green and brown shrubbery and wiregrass gone wild.

Thayne slowed the car to about thirty miles an hour. "We're obviously coming up on a town. Start looking for a sign."

"What kind of sign?"

Thayne laughed then. "The sign that says 'Logan's Creek. You are here.'"

The houses gave way to a small row of brick buildings, a set of three on one side, another set of four across the street. As soon as we'd passed them, the car rambled over a double railroad track, for which there'd been no sign, jarring us both.

"I didn't see that coming," Thayne said.

"Shouldn't there be some kind of warning posted somewhere?"

Thayne didn't answer. "Keep looking, Mariette," he said finally. "It's got to be around here somewhere."

Fifteen minutes passed. With the exception of heavy rain, farmland, and foliage, there was little evidence of life. On a whim, I reached into the glove compartment and pulled out a map Daddy had placed there when he'd given me the car but that I'd never needed to use.

"It's not there," Thayne said as I unfolded the paper. "I looked, after I met with Dr. Carnes."

"Then how do you know you're going in the right direction?" I refolded the map and laid it between us.

Thayne pulled a piece of soggy paper from his shirt pocket. "Before the flat, this was legible."

I held it up to the window, hoping for enough light to make out the blurred lettering. "What is this?"

"It was the directions Dr. Carnes gave me." Thayne squinted. "We've gone too far."

I whipped my head forward. "How do you know?"

An index finger rose from the steering wheel and pointed. "That's Highway 301. Dr. Carnes said if we hit 301 we'd gone too far." Thayne slowed the car and turned it around on the shoulder, then picked up speed as we headed back where we'd just come from.

"We couldn't have gone too far. There wasn't a sign anywhere. Are you sure Logan's Creek is on this road?"

"This is 17, right?"

I shook my head. "I haven't seen a sign in I don't know when, Thayne. But the last one I saw said it was."

"Dr. Carnes said it was on 17."

I sighed. "Maybe he meant you had to turn off 17."

"No. He said it was on 17." Thayne slowed the car.

"It's not raining so hard now," I said, rolling the passenger window down. The air felt thick but cool as it blew into the car. "Open your window too, and let's get a draft through here. I think I might actually be sweating."

Thayne did, but didn't respond to my attempt at humor. "Here're those buildings again," he noted. "What do you think this is?"

"I have no idea. It's not big enough to be a town. Maybe just some out-of-the-way businesses?"

"Look and see if anyone is standing around now that the rain has slacked off. Maybe they'll know where Logan's Creek is and can guide us in the right direction."

I pointed. "Over there, Thayne. The building with the Sunbeam sign on it. There's someone standing at the window."

Thayne stopped the car between the buildings and rolled his window down the remainder of the way. He waved to the person, a man wearing a soiled butcher's apron, who waved back and then ambled over to the double screen door. The wooden front doors—made of more glass than wood, and painted dark green—were wide open. "Can I help ya?" the man called as he pushed open one of the screen doors, then kept it open with the toe of his boot. He was an older man—in his late forties or early fifties—thin with hunched shoulders and slicked-back hair.

"Yes, sir!" Thayne hollered back. "I'm trying to find Logan's Creek."

"Logan's Creek?" the man shouted back.

"Yes, sir! Logan's Creek, Georgia. My wife and I are trying to find it!" Thayne lowered his voice so only I could hear. "Dear Lord, please tell me he's heard of it."

The man's shoulders shook as he chuckled. "Well, son, I'd say your worries are over! You're parked slap dab in the middle of it!"

19

As it turned out, the grocer was the son of Alma Stoddard, so he knew "'xactly where she lives!"

"You must be the new preacher Mama was telling us about," he said as he ambled over to the car.

Thayne sat up straight and proud. "Yes, sir. Yes, sir, I am!" He jutted his arm out the window. "Thayne Scott."

"Reverend," the man said as he pumped Thayne's hand. Then he dipped his face toward the opened window. "Missus."

"My wife," Thayne said. "Mariette."

The man nodded. "Mrs. Scott, nice to meet ya."

I smiled as broadly as I dared. "Nice to meet you too."

"Clarence. Clarence Stoddard. You'll be staying in the little house next to my mama's."

"Well," Thayne said, "I'll tell you, Mr. Stoddard, if you can point me in the right direction, we'd be more than relieved to get there."

"You do look a little damp there," Mr. Stoddard said.

Thayne pinked. "We had a flat."

Clarence Stoddard nodded as he stuck his bony finger in the same direction our car was headed and said, "You see that street right there going over to the right? Turn there. Head straight down the road. It's only a block, and it dead-ends into Mama's driveway. You can't miss it." Then he grinned. "And I hope you brought your appetites, 'cause Mama's been cooking all day long."

I hadn't thought of dinner or what we'd do about it, but the notion of eating at a stranger's table didn't seem right.

"And one other thing," Mr. Stoddard said as Thayne shoved the car into gear. "You'll see the church to your left just before you turn. One end of the street is where you'll work and the other end is where you'll live."

Thayne smiled. "Isn't that fine?"

Clarence Stoddard grinned back. I noticed he had an upper tooth missing, one next to his front teeth. I turned my gaze toward the windshield.

Two silent minutes later, we were pulling into the packed dirt-and-grass driveway of Alma Stoddard. Hers was a simple box-style house with a tin roof, a screen-and-lattice-wrapped front porch accessed by three gray concrete steps flanked by two overgrown bushes. With the exception of clusters of leafy tree branches sprouting overhead behind the house, the yard was devoid of shrubbery.

"Well, Mrs. Scott," Thayne said. "Here we are."

"I wonder where the house is. The one we'll be living in. I don't see anything next to the house that looks like a guest-house."

"Maybe it's behind the house," Thayne said.

About that time the screen door swung open and a bespec-tacled woman, short, with cottony, white, well-coiffed hair, stepped forward, waving a hand as though it were broken.

Thayne grinned like a boy. "That must be Mrs. Stod-dard."

"Well, I can only hope!"

Thayne got out of the car, then ran around to the passen-ger side to open the door for me. Hand in hand we walked toward the house and Mrs. Stoddard.

"Oh, I'm so glad you made it!" she said. "I was worried you'd get lost. Lord knows we're out here in the middle of nowhere."

When we reached her, she grabbed Thayne in a tight hug and slapped his shoulders as she said, "God bless you. God bless you." Then she leaned back and looked at Thayne. "Son, you're soaked through and through."

Thayne laughed lightly. "We had a flat," he said for the second time in ten minutes.

"Well, come on. Let's get you settled in your place and then you can change."

She led us around the side of the house and toward the back where, just as Thayne suspected, a tiny unpainted cottage nestled behind a white picket fence draped in ivy. A flower garden grew untamed and unkempt between the fence and the door. The short pathway between the gate and the front of the house, which had only two windows—one to the right and one above the door—was made of bricks and nearly drenched with the scent of late-blooming tea olive.

I felt my heart sink. Thayne must have sensed it because he squeezed my hand in a way that told me to stay quiet and appreciative. "Now, it's not much," Alma Stoddard said. "But it's clean and it's got indoor plumbing." She laughed.

She was correct about the inside. It was clean. And, it had plumbing. "Now these walls haven't been painted in a while," she noted as she opened the front door to reveal a large room which was a combination living room, dining room, and kitchen. "But if you want, Reverend, you can buy some paint over at Boykin's Five and Dime. They have paint there and goodness knows just about anything else you could think of. Feel free to buy yourself a brush and a gallon of paint and go to town." She laughed again as she moved toward the sofa. "Now, this was mine when I married. It's what they call a camel-back sofa. I think the roses on the covering is right pretty." She touched a nearby white wicker rocker. "This used to be on my front porch, but I thought you might like a place to sit and rock, so I had my boy bring it in here."

"We met your son," Thayne said. "Clarence."

"That's my boy," she said. "I had two, you know, but one died in the war."

"I'm sorry to hear that," Thayne said.

"Me too," I said.

Mrs. Stoddard seemed to pass over the moment. "Now over here is the kitchen. I don't have many pots and pans but, again, whatever you need you can buy at Boykin's."

Thayne chuckled. "Oh, no worries there. My mother-in-law packed several boxes of kitchen items for us."

It seemed to me Mrs. Stoddard blushed. "Oh, I see," she said. "Well, that's fine then." She pointed across the room. "Over there is the bedroom and the bath." She looked at Thayne fully then. "Do you mind, young man, telling me just how old you are?"

It was Thayne's turn to blush. "I'm twenty-three," he said. "But I'll be twenty-four soon."

Mrs. Stoddard laughed. "I'll be sure to bake you a cake." She patted my husband's arm, then added, "Why don't y'all go get your things out the car, settle in, and be at my back door in, let's say, two hours. Clarence and his family will be joining us for dinner."

"That'll be nice," Thayne said. "We look forward to it and we appreciate it."

"One other thing. The windows in the bedroom needed new screens, but they haven't been put up yet. I wouldn't open the windows in there without them."

And with that, Mrs. Stoddard left. When the door had closed behind her, I took a deep breath and sighed. "I guess we'd better get the things out of the car."

Thayne wrapped me with his arms. "You okay?"

I pushed against his chest with the palm of my hand. "You're wet," I said. "Let's get our things and then you get into a tub of hot water." I turned from him and walked toward the door.

"Mariette," he said from behind me. "Honey . . ."

I stopped. "Don't, Thayne. Not right now. Let's just do what we have to do."

It took four trips to the car to get everything into the cottage. We took one of the trunks full of clothes into the bedroom, which was sparsely decorated. An unpainted wrought iron bed frame and mattresses took up the majority of the small room. The walls were unadorned. There was a ladder-back chair in front of the only window, which overlooked the trees and bushes of the side yard. Against the wall with the bathroom door was a chest of drawers, and at the foot of the bed was an old hope chest. Once the first of the trunks had been deposited onto the red brick floor, I stepped over to open it.

"I need to go to the bathroom," Thayne said. "Be right back."

When he returned it was to find me standing before the opened chest, my arms dangling lifelessly at my sides. "What is it?" he asked.

"Look around you," I said.

He turned in a small circle. "What?"

"Do you see a closet?"

His footsteps faltered. "No, I'd have to say I don't."

"There's a chest of drawers, but where are we supposed to hang our clothes?" I asked.

"Well, now . . . that's a good question. I suppose we'll have to ask Mrs. Stoddard when we go to dinner."

"Mrs. Stoddard." I kept my eyes on the opened and empty hope chest.

"What's wrong with Mrs. Stoddard?" He walked over to the stripped mattresses of the bed and sat down, peering at me.

I looked him in the eye. "Did you not notice she never said one word to me?"

"Sure she did."

"What, Thayne? Repeat one word she said to *me*."

He studied the question for a moment before answering, "I . . . um . . ."

"Exactly," I said, then turned on my heel and headed back for the car.

An hour later everything was unpacked and Thayne had taken his bath in the narrow claw-foot tub. While he did so, I made the bed with the fresh linens Mama and I had packed, then draped it with a chenille bedspread. I placed the quilt Mama had given me, folded, at the foot of the bed and the quilt from Thayne's mother—the one made from his baby clothes—folded on top of the empty hope chest. I went outside, broke a few flowers off, low on the stems, then came back inside and placed them in a glass I found in the one and only kitchen cabinet, over the sink. When I returned to the bedroom to place them on the chest of drawers, Thayne was exiting the bathroom, wrapped in a towel and smelling of soap. "Nice touch," he said, pointing to the flowers.

"I'm going to have Mama send my sewing machine," I said. "It's portable. I can make some things to help with this place."

"It's not bad, Mariette."

I cut my eyes to him before heading toward the bathroom. "Get dressed, Thayne. We have a dinner to attend."

Considering I was in a strange bed and, to my way of seeing things so far, an even stranger town, I slept like a rock that first night. I dreamed Thayne and I had gone to Missy and Ward's, ate barbecue chicken and potato salad and sweet peas, and then got into their small rowboat to be alone on the water. We glided across as Missy and Ward waved goodbye. Even in the dream, I felt a deep sadness, an ache for the companionship of our friends. As we drifted to the middle of the lake, the sky grew dark. Thayne said something about needing to make some changes to the boat, and suddenly he was on his hands and knees, a small tool chest in front of him, digging around for a screwdriver. "Thayne, stop!" I said. "You'll sink the boat." And then it began to rain, an absolute downpour, just as it had been during our drive to Logan's Creek. But Thayne just kept on working, unscrewing the rusty screws that bolted the seats to the boat's frame. The turning of the screws, the squeaking, became louder . . . and louder . . . and louder . . . until . . .

I bolted up in bed. "Thayne!" I gasped as I reached for him. But he wasn't lying next to me. He was standing at the window, dressed only in his underwear, parting the blinds of the venetians.

"It's okay," he said.

I pulled the sheet close to me. A glance at the alarm clock next to our bed revealed it was only 6:30.

"Um . . . good morning!" Thayne said toward the window.

I blinked several times. *Who is he talking to?*

"Well, good morning," a man's voice from the other side of the window called back.

"Thaaaaaaayne."

He ignored me. "Do you mind my asking who you are and what you are doing here?"

A chuckle came from the other side of the window. "Not at all. I'm Oscar White, the head of the finance committee over at the church. I'm the man who'll sign your paychecks, Reverend!"

Thayne made an attempt at laughter. "Well, then, Mr. White, I'm pleased to meet you. But . . . what are you doing?"

"I'm putting your screens up."

"Are you aware, Mr. White, of the time?"

"Yes, sir. But I have to get to the bank—that's where I work—and this is the only time I have today to do this."

I sighed as I threw myself, face first, into Thayne's pillow.

"Mariette." Thayne poked my hip. "Go wash your face and then make a pot of coffee."

"Do we have coffee?" I said, my face still in the pillow.

"I saw some in the cabinet last night when I was plundering."

I raised my head to look at him. "When was that?"

"After you went to sleep. I was too wired, so I kinda walked around the house and plundered." He gave a sheepish smile.

I swung my legs over the side of the bed. "I'd hardly call this a house," I sneered.

"Ugly is not very pretty on you this early in the morning," he said with a wink. Then he turned back to the window. "Mr. White, when you're done, please come inside for a cup of coffee with my wife and me."

I groaned as Oscar White said, "I'd be obliged."

Oscar White was a man who, like Clarence Stoddard, appeared to be in his late forties. Although he was balding, his eyes still held a twinkle and his smile was intoxicating. There was a space between his front teeth, a distinction that added to his charm. He sat at the dinette table—just big enough for four mismatched chairs—and regaled us with stories of the people in town, as relaxed as if he were king of the castle.

"How'd you find Alma?" he asked.

"Good cook," Thayne said. "I won't mind being asked for dinner any time she takes a notion to it."

"That woman can sure fry a chicken." Then he looked at me. "How about you, Mrs. Scott? Can you fry a chicken?"

I smiled at him. "Please call me Mariette."

"Only if you call me Oscar."

"Oscar."

He winked at Thayne. "Sounds kinda pretty coming from your wife, Reverend." Then back to me. "So, can you?"

192

"Can I what?"

"Fry a chicken."

Thayne choked on his coffee. "My wife has many talents, but cooking isn't one of them, I'm afraid."

I pressed my lips together to keep from word-thrashing him. How dare he embarrass me in front of our new friend?

"Well, she'll have to learn," he said to Thayne. Then to me, "Yes, ma'am. Preacher's wife needs to know how to fry a chicken and make potato salad and sweet iced tea." He raised his coffee cup. "Your coffee's good, so you're obviously teachable."

I blinked. Mr. White's charm was beginning to fade.

Thayne cleared his throat, I'm sure in warning, but to me or to Oscar White, I'm not sure. "Oscar, I take it you are married?"

He nodded. "I am. Married to a lovely young lady named Rose."

"Rose White?" I asked. "That reminds me of the Brothers Grimm story, Rose Red and Snow White. Not to be confused with the story about the princess and the seven little men."

Thayne and Oscar looked at me as if I had three heads. Then Thayne said, "My wife enjoys reading."

"I don't suppose you have a library here," I added.

"Ah . . . no," he said. "We hardly have any commerce at all. The grocery store. I take it you met Alma's son, Clarence?"

"And his wife Minerva and their son Kevin," Thayne provided.

"Kevin's a good boy. He and my youngest are in the same first grade class. Clarence married late in life, a woman twenty years his junior, but I guess you gathered that when you met Minerva. How'd y'all get along, Mariette? Y'all ought to be about the same age."

I'd learned the night before that Minerva Stoddard was indeed the ripe old age of twenty-eight, so she had about six years on me. When I'd seen her busy-beeing in Mrs. Stod-

193

dard's kitchen, I'd hoped for a new friendship, but she'd snubbed me as easily as her mother-in-law had.

"She seemed nice enough," I lied. Then, to change the subject, "So, there's a school here?"

"Not exactly," Oscar said. He took a swallow of his coffee. "It's in the county seat. About fifteen miles or so from here. Called Hudsonville. County busses come and get the young'uns every morning, bring them home every afternoon."

"What else is here?" I asked. I poured more coffee into Oscar's cup, hoping that if he stayed long enough I could get plenty of information about Logan's Creek.

"Well, like I said, there's the grocery store and the five-and-dime." He pointed around the room. "Be sure to go get some paint there, Reverend. This place could sure use a fresh coat."

Thayne's dimples deepened as he smiled. "I plan on it, Oscar."

"Let's see now, we have a post office, a barber, a feed and seed. Got to have a feed and seed, what with all the farmers around here." Then he smiled at Thayne. "And in all that, one church." He reached over and patted my hand. "Now, you, Miss Mariette, will most definitely want to meet the Bishop Sisters."

"Who are the Bishop Sisters?"

"Four little ladies who run this town and, subsequently, the church. Miss Viola is the oldest. She married Edward Oglesby. Now Miss Viola and Mister Edward never had any children, but that didn't stop them from adopting nearly everybody else's in town." He winked at Thayne. "Miss Viola is a prayer warrior. I wouldn't want her against me come prayer time. She'd call down the fire from heaven as good as Elijah ever thought of doing." He laughed. "She's in charge of all youth-related classes, and don't even *think* about trying to change her methods."

"I'll keep that in mind," Thayne said.

"And," Oscar continued, "if you like to read, Mariette, you'll love Miss Viola. She's got a library of books that won't wait. Just knock on her door, ask to borrow a book, and you'll be her friend for life."

I smiled. "What about the rest of the Bishop Sisters?"

"Well, there's Edith. She's married to William Willoughby. That man could plant a rock and get a crop. God has blessed him and I do mean God has blessed him. They have one son, Will Junior, and he's the postmaster. You'll come to know him real well. Then there's Leila Freeman. Married to Mister Osborne Freeman, who passed away about a year ago. Never was there a man meaner who walked the face of this earth. Miss Leila and Mister Oz had two children, Charles and Treena. Treena moved away as soon as she was old enough to hitch a ride out of town, but Charles is still here. Husband to Jane—they're both teachers over at the high school—and father to Charlie, Judy, and Andrew, all teenagers. That brings us to Miss Carolyn. She's married to Wilbur Boykin. They own the five-and-dime and have twin girls—Sylvia and Helen."

I'm sure my face registered panic. How would I remember all these names? All these people? I felt as if I were at Saint Margaret Mary's all over again. That first day, knowing no one and being fully aware of being an outsider.

Oscar winked at me this time. "Don't worry yourself, young lady. There won't be a test on all this." Then he winked again. "Leastways, not for another week or so."

20

Logan's Creek had a total area of just two-tenths over one square mile, most of which was land. The part that was water was, of course, Logan's Creek, so named for a Mr. Jeremiah Logan, who was the first to settle in the early 1800s, though no one knows the exact date. He and his wife, Mozelle, had three daughters and one son, who died at the age of six months. While the Logan name died with Jeremiah, the residents of Logan's Creek who are of his lineage by the daughters are quite proud of their heritage.

The Bishop Sisters were a part of that pedigree.

This was not information that came all at once; it came over a period of time, after several run-ins with the townspeople who knew far more than we could hope to know in such a short period about the history of Logan's Creek and its townsfolk. Although learn we did. We surely did.

Thayne thought it important that his first morning be spent at the church, looking over where he'd preach, the room he'd call his office, and then maybe walking around the town—if it could so be called—getting to know the residents. I noticed, as he dressed that morning, an unusual kick in his step. Before the mirror, as he shaved, he smiled a lot. When

I came up behind him and asked what all the grinning was about, he said, "Have you noticed, Mariette? They all call me 'Reverend.'"

"Well, you are, aren't you? You are the reverend."

To which he straightened and said, "I am the reverend."

I laughed lightly, swatted him on the behind, and said, "And yet, still, I can do that."

He turned to face me, grabbed my waist, and pulled me into his arms. We were nose to nose. I studied his eyes, their deep blue color, the way the light danced within them. It was as if he studied mine too, the way his looked at mine so intently. "Hey," he finally said.

I drew back enough to see his whole face, to watch the dimple deepen. "Hey back 'atcha."

"Wanna mess around with a reverend?" He pretended to look at his watch—the one I knew was still on the bedside table.

I slipped my arms around his shoulders, laced my fingers when they met in the middle, and pressed myself against him. "Well, I don't know. Do you know of a reverend I might mess around with?"

"It's been a while, you know," he said. "I mean, just you and me. Alone. In a house."

I felt the warmth of love weaken my knees. "Oh, Thayne," I said and kissed him. "It has been a long time. A very long time."

With that he scooped me into his arms and led me into our bedroom, where he gently laid me on the bed I'd yet to make. He lay next to me, kissed my face with fluttering kisses as I clung to him, part of me madly in love and another part of me more scared than I'd been in my life.

Our lips came together with a spark of the old flame, the nearly forgotten chemistry igniting and—as it had been with us years ago—I felt myself slipping away. I closed my eyes and imagined we were not in Logan's Creek at all. Thayne was not the reverend and I was not the "preacher's wife." We were newlyweds, lying in a musky room, wrapped in passion, just hours after we'd spoken our vows. We were a bride and groom, with none of the last four years between us. We were starting over. Beginning fresh.

Everything was going to be okay . . .

A knock at the front door brought us bounding to our feet. I pressed my hands to my cheeks, then my chest. My heart beat wildly—from our lovemaking or the unexpected rap at the door, I wasn't sure. My blouse was unbuttoned and untucked. "Thayne," I said.

Thayne was already at the bathroom sink, running his fingers through his hair, glaring at himself in the mirror with panic-filled eyes. "Mariette," he said, looking at me in the reflection. "Go see who that is."

I scoffed. "I'm hardly in any condition—"

"Mariette."

The knocking continued.

I tucked my blouse into the dark pink pleated skirt and then shifted it so the seams lined up over my hips. "I'm going," I said, then slipped my feet into the pair of flats I'd kicked off my feet and over the bed at some point. At the bedroom door I paused and said, "You know, it's not like we're teenagers making out in the backseat of a car."

Thayne made a sound—a laugh or a whimper, I'm not sure—as I left, crossed the living room, and jerked open the front door, where Alma Stoddard was still knocking. "Oh, there you are," she said. Although she'd spoken to me as needed at dinner the evening before, these were her first direct words.

I took a deep breath, pressed my fingertips against my stomach, and said, "Good morning, Mrs. Stoddard. Can I help you?"

I noticed then the casserole dish cradled in her hands. "I made a breakfast pie for you." She stepped past me and into the house. "A quick, I think they call it."

"Quiche?" I closed the door and followed her into the kitchen area.

She placed the dish on the table as she surveyed the coffee cups and saucers still in the sink. "I see you had your coffee."

"Yes, ma'am. Mr. Oscar White was here and—"

"Mrs. Stoddard," Thayne said as he burst from the bedroom on the opposite side of the room. "Good morning."

Mrs. Stoddard beamed. "Well, good morning, Reverend. Isn't this a fine morning? A fine and beautiful day the Lord has given us."

Thayne nodded. "It is, Mrs. Stoddard. And I thank him for it."

"I brought you a quiche," she said. "I know your wife hasn't had time to shop yet, and there was little in the cupboard."

"But there was coffee, so we thank you." Thayne now had the old lady by the hands, pumping them, smiling down at her as though she were the most precious thing he'd ever seen. I sighed.

"And Oscar made it by, I understand."

"Mariette told you?" He led her over to the sofa and they sat while I just stood and stared like a stranger in my own home. "Yes. What a nice man."

Alma patted Thayne's knee. "He's the salt of the earth, that man is. Now you listen to me. He's the head of the finance committee, so you be sure to keep him happy."

"And why is that?" I ventured to ask. I walked over to the white wicker chair and perched on the edge of the seat.

Alma looked at me as though I had not a scintilla of sense. "Because, my dear, he will hold your husband's paycheck."

"He can do that?" I asked, horrified.

"If he wants to, he surely will."

"I'm sure he won't do that," Thayne interjected. "Now, Mrs. Stoddard, would you like to have some quiche with us?"

Alma giggled like a schoolgirl. "No, no. I've already had my breakfast. My Clarence came over early and we ate together. He likes to do that sometimes because Minerva's eggs are runny." She stood and we stood with her.

"Thank you for the breakfast pie," I said, using her words. I clasped my hands low in front of me and rocked slightly forward on my feet.

"Yes, thank you," Thayne said. "I can't wait to dig into it."

To which Alma patted him on the cheek and said, "You're a fine young man, Reverend. I can see that already."

And with that, she was gone.

Thayne and I ate our "breakfast pie" in silence. I was too incensed to speak. And Thayne, I believe, knew better than to push it. After we ate, I dumped the dishes into the sink, ran water over them, and then went into the bathroom to brush my teeth. Thayne was slipping his arms into the sleeves of his suit coat. "How do I look?" he asked.

I nodded. "You look fine, Thayne."

He smiled, but it looked forced to me. "What are you going to do while I'm gone?"

"I'm going to the grocery store. I'm also going to go to the five-and-dime. See about getting that paint."

"Sounds good."

I blinked. "I'm going to brush my teeth now. Do you think you'll be back in time for lunch or . . ."

"Yeah, yeah. I'll be back." He walked over to me then, kissed me on the cheek, and muttered, "Sorry about this morning." His nose nuzzled my cheek. "If you'll let me, I'll make it up to you tonight. I promise."

I melted with a sigh. "Okay," I said, then kissed him swiftly and walked into the bathroom.

Thayne was gone when I returned to the front of the cottage. I picked up my purse from the floor where I'd dumped it the afternoon before, grabbed the keys to the De Soto, and then walked out the front door. Alma Stoddard was hanging out laundry on her backyard clothesline. I took a deep breath, said, "The quiche was delicious, Mrs. Stoddard," to which she nodded.

Then I got in the car and drove the one block necessary to reach the five-and-dime. I entered by the only door—like the grocery store's, made of mostly glass—and the overhead bell tinkled. There were a few small appliances near the front, many of them displayed in the window. A row of school supplies was tucked into neat bins. The blended, familiar aroma of number 2 pencils and erasers permeated the air, and as I walked toward the back, it merged with the scent of bicycle tires and paint. Across the back of the store was a high counter. Behind it, I could see the head of a woman who was sitting at a desk, and behind her in a glassed-in office was another desk—littered by papers and dirty coffee cups and a tumbler full of pens and pencils.

"Good morning," the voice from behind the counter said.

I reached it and spied on the other side a middle-aged woman, stout with dark hair and eyes that slanted when thin red lips smiled. "Can I help you, young lady?"

"Good morning," I said, then paused to smile. Whatever it was Alma Stoddard had against me, I would make sure this woman didn't. "My name is Mariette Scott and I—"

The woman jumped up, clapped her hands, and came from around the desk. "Oh, my goodness, look at you! You're here!" She reached for my hand from the other side of the counter, squeezed it, and said, "Aren't you pretty, aren't you pretty?" Her cheeks jiggled as she spoke.

"Thank you," I said.

"We're all so excited about you and your husband coming. And, my goodness! I'd heard you were young, but you're just a child. Oh, you are most definitely going to bring some fresh air into this dried-up town."

The pressure my husband thrived in—to be that breath of fresh air—wasn't something I was comfortable with. "Right now I'd just like to put some fresh paint on Mrs. Stoddard's cottage walls."

The woman laughed out loud as she propped her elbows on the countertop. "How is old Alma treating you?"

I must have blushed because she said, "Never mind. I declare that woman does beat all. As soon as I saw how pretty you are, I thought, Oh Alma's going to eat her up and spit her out. But, honey, don't you let her."

I stuttered for a moment before saying, "Do you mind if I ask who you are?"

She straightened as she laughed again. I might not know who she was, but she had to be the happiest person I'd ever met. "I'm Carolyn Boykin. My husband and I own this store." She leaned forward. "And I'm one of the Bishop Sisters."

I felt a funny tickle of excitement rush up my spine. "Well, then, I've heard about you too."

"I daresay you have. Who told?"

"Oscar White."

"That adorable scoundrel." She walked from around the back of the counter. "Okay, dear one, tell me what kind and color of paint you want, and I'll get you all fixed up."

I followed her to the paint aisle, which didn't offer a lot by way of color or texture. "Thank you, but what can you tell me about Mrs. Stoddard? I mean, why would she—how did you say it?—eat me up and spit me out?"

"Alma doesn't like pretty girls so much," Carolyn said, then shook her head. "Oh, it's a long story and one you don't need to worry about. Just be who you are and she'll come around. You'll see." She looked back at the gallons of paint. "Now . . . what shade of white would you like?"

21

I made it home from Boykin's and Stoddard's Grocery & Meats in time to meet Thayne as he ambled near the corner of Church and Bishop, where Mrs. Stoddard's house—and subsequently, ours—stood. Upon seeing me, he jogged to the car, then reached for the driver's-side door handle as I parked. He opened it, gave me a perfunctory kiss, spied the groceries in the backseat, and said, "Looks like I'm just in time."

"I'd say you are."

We unloaded the groceries and paint. While I prepared sandwiches and Saltine crackers, he talked incessantly about the church. "It's not big," he said as though I expected a cathedral. "I'd say if it were packed to the gills it might hold two hundred." Then he laughed. "That would be sitting hip to hip, mind you, but I can picture it."

"Uh-huh," I said. "What about your office?"

"Well, let me tell you about the inside of the sanctuary. It's old, okay? The walls are wide pine boards, painted white, and the altar is not really an altar at all. There's a rise near the front of the church and a podium that looks like it has been polished about a million times and—oh! Stained glass windows, Mariette. The prettiest colors you've ever seen just dance all around first thing in the morning when the sun comes through, and I bet in the afternoons when the sun goes down it's just as pretty. Different, but still impressive. There are some cobwebs that could stand being swept out. I looked for a broom but couldn't find one, so I thought I'd ask Mrs. Stoddard for one before I go back."

I raised a finger. "That reminds me," I said. I darted out the front door and down the path to the car, opened the trunk, and brought out a broom, mop, and tin pail, then headed back in. By now Thayne was at the window. Seeing me approach, he opened the door. "Now you don't need to bother Mrs. Stoddard," I said. "Your wife has supplied your every need."

He kissed me again as he smiled broadly at the broom, looking like a boy who'd scored a BB gun at Christmas. "I'm going to take the car back to the church, unless you need it," he said as he propped the broom next to the front door.

"No, I don't need it."

"I want to take my books to the office. My office has a bookcase, you know."

"I would imagine so."

"So what are you going to do the rest of the day?"

"Me? Well, I thought I'd read a book, listen to some music, eat bonbons. You know, that kind of thing." I screwed up my face as playfully as I could. "There isn't a TV in this cottage, so I suppose watching *General Hospital* is out."

Thayne looked at me as though I were an alien from outer space, one of those *War of the Worlds* creatures straight from the mind of Orson Wells. "Seriously."

"Seriously?" I slipped a paint brush from out of the paper bag from the five-and-dime. "I'm going to teach myself how to paint."

Thayne blanched. "Oh, now wait a minute . . ."

"I can do it, Thayne. I know I can. I may not be a good housekeeper or cook, but I'm gifted in artsy kinds of ways. Give me a chance."

He splayed his fingers around his waist and sighed as he looked around the room. "Start with the bathroom," he said. "If it doesn't go well, at least only you and I will see it."

A television and a fresh coat of paint weren't the only things missing from the cottage. There was also no phone. After lunch, when Thayne had left with the car and a few boxes of books, I strolled back up to the center of town—if it could so be called—to the lone phone booth I'd seen on the corner of Main and Railroad Street. All in all, it was a three block walk, and it brought me to the very end of Logan's Creek's city limit.

I called Mama collect.

"Oh, Mariette! I've been so worried. Your father said not to, but I just couldn't help it. Tell me. Tell me everything."

"Well, first I'm sorry to have to call you collect. We don't have a phone in the cottage."

"Cottage?"

I sighed in sweet relief at hearing her voice. For once, her bit of social snobbery comforted me. "That's what I'm calling it. It's practically no bigger than my old bedroom and yours and Daddy's combined."

"Oh, Mariette!"

I giggled. "It's not so bad. I bought paint and I'm thinking . . . well, if you could, would you send my sewing machine? I can get material here at the five-and-dime—goodness, they have everything in that store."

"What else do you need?" she asked. "I knew I was sending you to the wolves."

"It's not so bad. So far I've met a few people and with the exception of one . . ." I rambled as long as I dared. I didn't want Daddy to have a heart attack when he got the phone bill.

I must have apologized one too many times about the collect call because later that afternoon, as I stood in the bathroom, covered in droplets of paint, a knock came to the door. I stole a glance at myself in the mirror. One look told me I'd best pray no one from the church had come to surprise the reverend's wife with a little visit.

It turned out to be a representative from the telephone company from Hudsonville. He took one look at me, grinned, then held up a wall phone he carried in his right hand. "Afternoon," he said.

"Hello." I blinked at him. "I'm sorry; are you sure you have the right house?"

"I am if you are the daughter of a Mrs. Carroll Puttnam of Meadow Grove, Georgia."

I couldn't help but note he didn't need a notepad to look at in order to remember my mother's name. "I am."

He shook his head. "That's some demanding mother you have. I'm here to install a phone by six o'clock or else." He looked at his watch. "That gives me just a little under an hour."

I stepped aside to give him entrance. "Then by all means," I said. "I wouldn't want you to get in trouble with my mother."

He chuckled; the tools on his belt jingled. "Me neither. But if you're her daughter, you probably know that."

I closed the door. As I did, I spotted Alma peering out her kitchen window toward the cottage. Even with the distance, I could see she was frowning. I raised my chin and turned on my heel. "You think she's bad," I said to the telephone man. "You should meet my father."

"No, thank you."

A half hour later, I flipped through the phone book the man had left behind until I found the name of the one and only church in Logan's Creek. I dialed the number, then smiled as I waited, thinking, *Won't Thayne be surprised!*

When he answered I heard him say, "Goodness," as he

picked up the phone, followed by "Reverend Scott" spoken directly into the mouthpiece.

"Reverend," I said, lowering my voice so it sounded like the late Marilyn Monroe's.

"Um . . . yes, this is Reverend Scott."

"Oh, Reverend," I said, keeping up the ruse. "I'm desperately in need of spiritual counsel."

"Oh. Okay. Um . . . may I ask who is calling?"

I wanted to laugh out loud, but I managed to hold myself together. "I'd rather not say," I answered. "But . . . well . . . I saw you today when you were walking to the church, and I have to admit, I've done nothing but think sinful thoughts of you since."

There was a long pause. "Ma'am, I'm not sure what this is about," he finally said, "but I'm a happily married man. And a pastor. A pastor who is a happily married man."

"But, Reverend," I said, adding my best Marilyn pout. "I've never . . . um . . . *been* with a reverend before. I almost was . . . but then a knock came to the door . . . an old woman with a quiche . . ."

"Mariette!?"

I burst out laughing then. "Who'd you think it was? Marilyn Monroe phoning from the grave?"

"I thought it was my worst nightmare. The professors warned about women like you, you know."

"I'll just bet they did. Hey, we have a phone now. Compliments of my parents."

"Is that where you're calling from?"

"Mmmhmm. It's a wall phone in the kitchen."

"Let's hope we can afford the monthly bill."

"What does that mean?"

"I'll tell you later. I'm heading home in just a few minutes and I'm starving. What's for supper?"

"Supper?" I touched my hand to the bandana around my

head. "Oh, dear." I sighed. "Thayne? How do you feel about leftover quiche?"

While Thayne busied himself with getting acclimated, I kept busy with the interior of the cottage. My first few days were spent painting the place. The bathroom and bedroom: stark white. The living room and connected kitchen: creamy white trimmed in glossy white. There was a nook between the living area and the kitchen that I thought perfect for a home office for Thayne, and I painted it a muted shade of gold, a color Miss Carolyn had to read a manual to mix. I drove to Hudsonville one morning, found an old desk and chair at a junk store, then paid for it plus a little extra to have the owner transport it to Logan's Creek in the back of his truck. I bought some lemon oil at Boykin's, and when the desk arrived I polished it until it gleamed, then decorated it with a lamp and a photograph taken of Thayne and me with Ward and Missy at a community picnic.

Mama sent my sewing machine, which I set up in our bedroom. Then I went to the five-and-dime and purchased yards of material.

"I've always liked this red and white large check pattern," Carolyn Boykin said as she stretched it across the measuring table and prepared to cut it. "What are you going to do with it? Kitchen curtains?"

"No," I said. "I'm going to make a drapery for the bathtub."

"You mean, like a curtain to go around it?"

"Actually, no. Over it. I found three rods, which I painted white like the walls. Then Thayne mounted them to the wall for me, one high over the center of the tub and the other two, one on either side about two feet down and over . . . like this. . . ." I spread my arms wide. "Anyway, I'm going to sew a drapery that will drape over the tub. Like a canopy."

Carolyn shook her head. "Try hard as I may, I just can't

seem to picture that. I do declare, you young people have so much creativity these days." She patted the bolt of off-white gossamer tulle. "What are you doing with this?"

"I'll wrap it around the bedposts." When she looked at me strangely, I said, "Romantic, don't you think?"

She pressed her hand against her ample breasts. "Oh yes." Then she leaned closer to me. "You know, I guess one just doesn't think about the pastor and his wife . . . you know . . . being romantic."

"We can be," I answered with a smile.

Between Monday when we'd arrived in Logan's Creek, and Saturday morning, Thayne spent most of his days and evenings pondering over and studying for Sunday morning, when he would give his first sermon. He asked me what I thought the theme should be, and I told him honestly that I had no idea. "Aren't you supposed to ask God that kind of thing?"

"Depend on the Spirit to guide me," he affirmed with a nod. Then he walked out of the bedroom where I was busy sewing new slipcovers for the kitchen chair pads. I shook my head, partly in wonder, partly in confusion.

On Wednesday he expressed his displeasure that midweek services had been cancelled by the most recent pastor, then determined he would have them back up and going before the end of the following month. With all his stress over one sermon on Sunday, I couldn't imagine him wanting to preach twice in one week.

On Saturday night, with the decorating nearly complete and poor Mrs. Stoddard's neck nearly out of joint from craning it so much as she spied out her windows at my comings and goings, Thayne and I went to the Oglesbys' for a social, a welcoming from the town. I was informed via Carolyn Boykin that I "didn't need to bring anything, just show up."

"Wonder what I'd need to bring if we weren't new here,"

I said to Thayne as we readied ourselves for the evening. Thayne was dressed in his best dark blue suit and sitting on the sofa, listening to Elvis belt out the gospel while I dressed in the bedroom. I chose a slim sheath dress with three-quarter length sleeves in charcoal gray that gathered in little tucks at the front waist. The neckline, trimmed with black satin, dipped at my bra line in the back. I slipped my feet into matching pumps, my hands into black gloves, and was reaching for the red clutch lying on the bed when Thayne stepped in to tell me we'd be late if we didn't hurry. "Wow," he said. "You look too good to stay home and too sexy to go out."

I turned to face him. "Too sexy? Do you think this is too much? I've never been to anything like this, you know. Not as the reverend's wife, anyway."

Thayne pinked. "Nah, nah. You're fine." He looked at his watch. "Seriously, we'll be late."

I ran into the bathroom for a final look. I was wearing more makeup now, mostly black eyeliner to accent my eyes, a pat of powder, a kiss of rouge, and the pinkest pink lipstick. "Do I look okay?"

"You look great, honey. Seriously. Come on!"

I ran out of the bathroom and through the bedroom. Thayne was already at the front door, which was wide open. Bursts of cold air blew past him and into the room. "The temperature is dropping," I said. "Will I need a coat?"

"You'll be fine, you'll be fine," he said. He jerked his head a few times toward the car in a "come on" motion.

I stopped short. "What about my hair? Does my hair look okay?" It had grown out again. I wore it teased around the crown; it fell in a precise flip just below my jawline.

"You're as cute as Natalie Wood. Come on."

"Natalie Wood?"

Thayne started to shiver. "Okay. It's cold." He shut the door. "I'll get our coats."

He ran past me, toward the bedroom. I was right behind him. "I'll get mine."

I had found a coatrack on sale at Boykin's. It now stood in the corner of our bedroom, perfect for hanging our coats and jackets. I'd also found, behind the store, an old and rusty circular clothes rack that Carolyn said was from "back when we used to sell clothes here." I asked her if I could have it, and she said I could. I brought it home, sanded it—something I would have never dreamed I'd know how to do—then wrapped the poles with batting followed by wide ribbon. It thus became our closet, a place for us to hang our clothes. Even Mrs. Stoddard—who'd managed to stop by more than a dozen times—had to admit the idea was pretty ingenious.

Thayne grabbed our coats, helped me on with mine, jerked his arms into his, then escorted me to the door.

"Are you sure I look okay?" I asked again.

He stopped long enough to kiss my cheek. "You look great. Everything is great. And you look fine. Everything is fine." He smiled and I smiled back.

But before the night was over, I wondered if I should have sent Thayne to the social and just stayed home alone.

22

The social was held in the home of Edward and Viola Oglesby, the patriarch and matriarch of the church. I'd yet to meet them, but Thayne had. He spoke highly of them both. "Oscar White was right about one thing," he said to me on the way to their home. "You can tell Mrs. Oglesby is a prayer warrior."

"I'm not sure I know what that means," I said. I laced my gloved fingers and squeezed.

"It means she prays and prays hard. She advances the kingdom of God on her knees."

"Oh, I see."

He stole a glance at me from the driver's seat. "Do you, Mariette?"

"No, not really."

I heard him sigh. It wasn't exasperated; it was just a sigh. "Do you pray, Mariette?"

I jerked my head toward him. "What kind of question is that? Of course I pray. Every Sunday, just like everyone else."

His brow furrowed. "Now I'm confused. On Sunday?"

"Sure. The preacher says, 'Bow your heads,' and I do. Then he prays and I listen. Isn't that praying?"

"Well, not exactly. I mean, it *is* praying, but . . . what I'm asking is, don't you pray when you're alone with God?"

"Alone with God?" I unlaced my fingers and then pressed my index fingers against my temples. "Thayne, seriously. Do you believe that? Really? That you can pray and God can hear you?"

"Absolutely." He paused. "I'm kind of disappointed that you don't."

I shrugged. "Of course he hears *you*, Thayne. You're a preacher now. But what I mean to say is that I'm not so sure he hears me."

"Why wouldn't he, Mariette?" His voice was coaxing, but I wasn't sure what he wanted from me.

"Because," I said as though that one word held all the answers.

"Because?" He lifted a hand from the steering wheel, then placed it back.

I shook my head. "Oh, I don't know, Thayne. Who am I to try to talk to God about anything? When I am in church I certainly try to be respectful of who he is. When I was at school and we went to mass, I was quiet and reverent toward him. But who am I to bother him?"

"You're his child!" Thayne's voice squealed.

I laced my fingers again. "I don't want to argue about this."

"Neither do I. But if my own wife—the wife of the reverend—can't understand who God is and who she is to God . . ."

"What?" I challenged.

He shook his head. "I don't know what." He pointed to a small dirt road that jutted out to the black asphalt we were driving on. "This road leads to the Oglesbys' so we're almost there."

I felt myself stiffen. The conversation—the theological debate—was over. I pressed my lips together and wondered

213

if, right now, Thayne was sorry he'd married me. I felt tears spring to my eyes, and I blinked them back. I took a deep breath, blew it out slowly until my nerves calmed and the two-story, rambling farmhouse came into view. With darkness settling in like a thin blanket, I could still see how impressive it was in size, much more than the houses I'd seen within Logan's Creek's city limits.

"Nice, isn't it?" Thayne said as though he'd read my thoughts.

"It's so big," I said. "I mean, compared to most of the houses here. Compared to Daddy and Mama's, I'd have to say it's about the same, but . . . as Mitch would say, 'Gee, boy.'"

Thayne chuckled before saying, "Story goes, it was built by her father on the same site as the original homestead built by Jeremiah Logan, Miss Viola's ancestor."

"And founder of the town."

"That's right."

We rambled across the ruts in the driveway until Thayne brought the car to park.

"And," I continued, "Miss Viola and Miss Carolyn are sisters."

"Two out of four. There's Miss Leila—she's a widow, remember?—and Miss Edith too." He reached for my hand, squeezed it, blew out a pent-up breath, and said, "Okay. Here we go. You'll be fine."

I nodded.

"I'll be fine."

I nodded again.

"Kiss me for good luck," he said, and I happily complied. Then he got out of the car, came to my side, opened the door, took my extended hand, and led me toward the front door. He rang the bell and we waited. Then he said, "Don't be nervous."

"Okay."

He looked at me with a grin. "I wasn't talking to you."

Five seconds later we were being escorted into the spacious home by its owner, Mr. Edward Oglesby, a gentleman in his mid-sixties. His hair, neatly cut and combed over, was white; he sported a trimmed mustache and wore round specs. His complexion was pale, and his throat folded into the neck of his shirt. He reminded me of a turtle, all dressed up for church. He shook Thayne's hand, pumping it up and down, then took mine coolly in his and squeezed. No sooner was this done than his wife came up behind him. She was short, round but by no means overweight, with hair the color of the cotton on a Q-tip. She also wore glasses—black cat eyes—and the blueness of her eyes stood out behind them.

Before I had time to react, Viola Oglesby had instructed me to hand her my coat, which she then handed to her husband. She took me by the arm and led me through the house toward the kitchen, where the women—including Alma and Minerva—had gathered to finish dinner preparations. The room—warm and intoxicating with the aromas of fried chicken, pecan pie, and tea leaves brewing on the stovetop— was buzzing with activity. It seemed to me that every woman, whether young or old, knew the room well and her place within it. For a fleeting moment I wondered if I'd ever feel so comfortable within my own kitchen, much less another woman's.

"Ladies," Miss Viola called out. Her voice commanded attention, and she got it. All conversation ceased, and then every face turned to the two of us standing in the room's threshold. "Ladies, this is the new reverend's wife, Mrs. Thayne Scott."

"Mariette," I said, my voice barely above a whisper. "Please call me Mariette." I was momentarily transported to the September morning Sister Benedict stood before my ninth grade class and said, "Girls, this is Mariette Puttnam. Please make her feel welcome."

A woman, slender and pretty with coiffed light brown hair and dark peach lipstick, stepped forward. She wiped her hands on the pink apron that hung from her waist, then extended one in greeting. "Mrs. Scott, I'm Rose White. Oscar's wife."

Again I said, "Call me Mariette. Please." I released her hand. "Nice to meet you, Mrs. White."

"I will be happy to call you Mariette, but you must call me Rose."

I gave her a smile. "I can do that."

Another woman approached, and I felt Miss Viola's grip loosen. "I'm Leila Freeman," the woman said. "That's my sister you're standing next to." Leila Freeman appeared to be in her fifties. Her black hair bore a shock of gray running from the forehead to the temple and was styled like Mrs. John F. Kennedy's. Her brows were dark and arched as though she were in a perpetual state of suspicion or disbelief. "My son," she said, not giving me time to respond to her introduction, "is Charles Freeman. He and his wife are teachers."

"I believe Mr. Oscar told Thayne and me about them and their children," I said.

"I am both the pianist and the organist at the church," she continued.

"I see."

"Yes." Her voice was curt. I wasn't sure if she was verbally sizing me up or it was always like that. "I understand from your husband that you also play the piano."

I felt my cheeks warm. I pulled off the gloves I still wore and stuffed them into my clutch. "I'm sure not as well as you, Mrs. Freeman."

"I just wasn't sure if you were going to want my place at the piano."

"Me? N-no."

A young woman, pretty with a radiant smile, came up behind Mrs. Freeman, placed her hand on the older woman's shoulder, and said, "Mama, are you intimidating this young lady? Hi, I'm Jane Freeman, Charles's wife. Goodness, you *are* young. How old are you?"

"Twenty-two."

"Twenty-two?" She laughed easily. "My gracious alive, honey, I've got lettuce in my fridge older than you."

I looked away from her and toward the back door where a woman, stylish with porcelain skin and dreamy dark eyes, was slipping out. She cut a glance over the room as though she were trying to walk out unnoticed. Jane Freeman's gaze followed mine then turned back to me. "That's Charlotte Knight."

Mrs. Leila Freeman suddenly declared, "Viola, let me do that!" then spun away from Jane and me and toward the stove, where Viola was adding what appeared to be milk to a pan full of something that smelled delicious.

Jane looked at the two women, then back to me. "Gracious. Those two in a kitchen. Do you like to cook?"

"Not really," I said honestly.

"That'll change," she said matter-of-factly. "Oh, look! There's Carolyn."

I saw Carolyn Boykin, followed by two women—obviously twins and therefore, I assumed, her daughters—all carrying armloads of covered dishes. Before I could respond, Jane hurried over to them, saying, "Gracious! Look at all this food. Did you see Mrs. Scott is here?" She jutted a thumb toward where I stood, still in the doorway.

Behind Carolyn's daughters came another woman, older, tall and slender, with fading blonde hair and pencil-thin lips. She, too, carried dishes of food. Someone in the room said, "Edith, please tell me you brought some of your chicken salad." To which she replied, "Would I dare come here without it?"

I stepped over to the door where I'd seen Charlotte Knight go out, then similarly followed suit. The chilly air wrapped around where my coat should have been. I crossed my arms and gripped my forearms, then rubbed. The night had closed in since we'd been inside; it was dark now. I glanced up at the sky. The stars and half moon were shielded by night clouds and therefore provided little light. Only the glow from the kitchen window kept me from falling as I stepped down the three or four steps leading to a grassy lawn and cautiously moved to the left of the house. From inside I could hear the laughter of men; Thayne's laughter too. I looked down and smiled, wondering what had the men so merry. No doubt dreaming of the food the women in the kitchen were preparing.

I missed my mother then. It came on me suddenly. I'd been so busy the last few days I'd hardly had time to miss anyone. But now, in the night's coolness, following after a woman I didn't know, walking around a yard I couldn't see well, I found I missed Mama very much. I stopped, cocked my hip, and looked up to the sky in wonder. Was God really up there? Was praying to him as simple as speaking words? "I want to go home," I said aloud, to test and see, I suppose, if he heard me.

"How well I remember those feelings." The voice came from in front of me. I jumped, blinked, then watched as Charlotte Knight stepped from behind the trunk of a pine tree.

"I didn't see you," I said. "You scared me."

"I know," she said. The smell of a cigarette being smoked wafted toward me. "I just came out to grab a smoke." She held the cigarette up toward her face. "Or two." Then she laughed; it sounded throaty and almost glamorous. She inhaled on the cigarette, then ground its tip out on the trunk of the tree before dropping the butt onto the ground. "Do you smoke?" she asked.

"No."

She shook her head. "I didn't expect so. I shouldn't. Then again, there are a lot of things I shouldn't do."

I stepped closer for a better view. "Like what?"

She snorted a laugh, then without answering the question said, "Twenty-two, huh? I was twenty-two when I came to this town." She took in a breath then released it. "I met Milton in college, fell madly in love, and the rest is history."

"Your husband, he grew up here?"

"Yep. And, if you can imagine, he actually wanted to come back. He's the choir director at your husband's church; did you know that?"

"No."

She grinned at me. "You should hear him and that old biddy Leila Freeman going at it over what music is going to be played and in what tempo." She shrugged. "Oh, well. It gives him something to think about."

I didn't know what to say, so I said nothing.

She ran her hand over her styled hair and said, "I'd best be getting back in before they miss me and call the rumor committee."

"Pardon me?"

She put her arm around my shoulders and turned me toward the door from which we'd escaped. "You, too, little missy. They'll eat you for lunch if you're not careful." She squeezed me, tipped her head toward mine, and said, "Hey, I understand you've done some pretty marvelous things with that guesthouse of old lady Stoddard's."

"How'd you hear—"

"There are no secrets here in Logan's Creek." Then she chuckled. "Well, not many, anyway."

23

If there was one redeeming thing about that evening, it was meeting Rowena Griffith.

Nearing the end of the evening, when I was all but exhausted from the women's small talk and the men's rambunctious laughter and chatter, I had stepped away from the gathering in search of a bathroom. I stepped quietly around the first floor, peering in one door after the other.

The house was immaculate; I could say that for Viola Oglesby. Each room was simply decorated, leaning toward the era of the earlier years she'd been a bride. There were plenty of doilies on the furnishings, and I wondered if she'd crocheted them herself. The walls were barren of framed artwork, boasting only large gold-framed black-and-white photos of people I assumed were family members.

There was a single bedroom downstairs; its bedcovers were simple, made of pink chenille. From the looks of the room, it was where Viola and Edward slept, so I didn't linger long at the door. Finally, in desperation, I slipped up the stairs, where I heard women speaking—two or three, I could not tell—somewhere at the back of the second story. The thick rug running the length of the hallway muted my steps as I walked toward them, figuring if women were talking, there was surely a bathroom nearby.

". . . pretty, but my goodness, so young," I heard one say. I stopped, realizing immediately that I was the topic of conversation.

"I hear," the other voice replied, "she comes from money. My, my, I can only imagine what she must think of us here in Logan's Creek."

"Personally," replied the first speaker, "I find him completely charming; I can't wait to hear him preach. But her . . . not a lot in the personality department, I'd say."

"Doesn't even cook, I've heard her say." I tilted my head then, straining my ear to recall their voices. They were most definitely familiar, but try hard as I might, I couldn't place them. "Alma says she's been working on the house night and day. I guess what we had to offer just wasn't good enough."

My mouth dropped open to retaliate, even if it meant revealing my eavesdropping. But before I could speak a word I heard a shushing sound from behind me. I whirled around to see a young girl I'd noticed earlier—teenaged, I supposed— looking to be about the same age as Tommy, though with girls and boys it was harder to differentiate. Her dark blonde hair fell in crimped waves to her shoulders. Her eyes—Bette Davis eyes—were a sad shade of blue. Her skin was like a china doll's, her lips full and pouty. She held her finger up to them and gave the "be quiet" sign as she shook her head.

"What are you doing?" she whispered.

"The bathroom," I mouthed.

She crooked her finger—follow me—then led me down the stairs and toward the back door. There was a large flashlight on a stand to the left of it; she reached for it, flicked it on, then led me to the outside. Only then did she speak. "It's this way," she said.

"This way? We're outside, for heaven's sake."

221

"I know. Viola and Edward have yet to add a bathroom to their house. The outhouse is just right here."

I stopped. "An outhouse? You expect me to go to the bathroom in an outhouse?"

She stopped too. She turned, the beam of light following at her feet. "Well, if you don't like it, you can hold it until you get home."

I blinked. *Could I?* No, I couldn't. "This is positively primitive."

She licked her lips. "Maybe what those women up there were saying is true. Maybe what we have to offer here in Logan's Creek isn't good enough for you."

"It's not that," I said, rising to my own defense. "It's just . . . well, I've never . . . I mean, I've not ever . . ." I swallowed. "I've never ever *been* in an outhouse."

"Not to worry. You'll be okay. Leastways, as far as I know, no one has ever died in one." She started to walk again.

I moved quickly to keep from being left in the dark. "It's all just a little spooky for me."

"You'll get used to it." She jerked her head backward. "And don't let those old biddies up there rile you none, either."

We arrived at the outhouse—a spacious single unit, I was soon to learn—and the girl pointed the flashlight toward it, then extended it to me. "You might want this."

I took it, then walked cautiously to the building, opened the door, stepped inside. It wasn't bad . . . considering it was *outside* and was for the purpose of doing something I thought should only be done *inside*, in rooms built just for the function. In fact, it was not at all what I'd been picturing since stepping out the back door of the Oglesbys' home. Like the house, it was white clapboard. Even the inside was whitewashed, a nice touch—for an outhouse. I scanned the interior with the flashlight, first upward, then to my feet. The ceiling was slanted, the floor cemented. There was a metal box on a small ledge. I opened it cautiously, pointed the light toward it, and spied toilet paper.

"Are you all right in there?" I heard the girl ask.

"Fine. Just trying to get my bearings."

I did what had to be done, then returned to my waiting guide. "Thank you," I said.

She took the flashlight from me. "My turn."

A minute or so later we were on our way back to the house. "By the way," I said, "what's your name?"

"Rowena. I'm Rose White's daughter."

"Rose and Oscar's daughter?"

"No. Just Rose's. Oscar is my stepfather. My real father died when I was five."

"I'm sorry."

"Not your fault."

"No, but . . ." I sighed. "How old are you, Rowena?"

"Seventeen."

"Are you in school?"

"Mmmhmm. Senior year. Mrs. Freeman is one of my teachers."

"Oh? What does she teach?"

"Home ec."

I smiled inwardly. No wonder she'd asked me if I like to cook, and then told me I'd learn.

"But I don't really care much for cooking and sewing and things like that," Rowena continued.

"What do you like?"

"Woodworking. And I'm good at it too. Would you like to see?"

"Very much so."

"Then I'll come by on Monday after school. Okay by you?"

We reached the back door. I reached for the handle of the screen door and smiled at the young woman. "I look forward to it," I told her.

Thayne talked a hundred miles an hour on the way to the cottage while I stayed relatively quiet. There wasn't a whole lot to say. (Yes, the food was good. Yes, they all seem like fine people. Yes, I thought the outhouse a little outdated for 1963, and no, I didn't think it was funny at all.) When he'd finally said all a human being could say in one breath, he asked, "Did you meet anyone special? I want you to make friends here, Mariette."

I nodded. "I did, actually." I told him first about Charlotte Knight and then Rowena Griffith.

"So you had a good night?"

Electing not to tell him about the overheard conversation, I lied and said, "It was nice."

The next morning Thayne preached his first sermon at the church. After nearly a week of being in town, it was my first time inside the structure. It was everything Thayne said it was: tiny, tidy, and it exuded an aura of God's holy presence. Even I, with as little a relationship as I had with the Almighty, could feel it. It was peaceful. Ethereal. When we walked in, an hour before Sunday school was set to begin, I felt as if I were entering a picture postcard and whispered so to Thayne.

"It does have that kind of feeling to it, doesn't it?" he responded. Then he grabbed my hand. "Come on. Let me show you around."

There were only a handful of Sunday school classes: Tiny Tots for the younger children, Junior Apostles for those between ages six and ten, Disciples for eleven- to thirteen-year-olds, and then Young for Christ for the teens. Adults were divided into two groups: those under the age of forty and those over. Edith Willoughby taught those forty-one plus, and her husband taught those in the younger group. Thayne and I assumed we were to be in Mr. Willoughby's group.

Mr. Willoughby was a fine class leader as Sunday school teachers go. He used a lesson plan provided by the denomination's publishing company; we each got a student copy of the magazine-styled book while our teacher had the leader's edition. I noted that Thayne was a little antsy throughout the forty-five-minute session, no doubt ready to preach and see if his congregants thought he was impressive enough. I'd heard him on Friday as he practiced in front of the bathroom mirror. I stood on the other side of the closed door, shoulder against the doorframe, and listened. From what I could surmise, the title was "All Things New"; it focused on how God's love washes his children clean, but also on new beginnings, such as the one Thayne and I— and I suppose the church and town—were now experiencing. For forty-five minutes Thayne rehearsed the fifteen-minute sermon—over and over—until he felt confident enough (I suppose) to say the same words to the citizens of Logan's Creek who might come to hear him. If he did half as well from the pulpit as he did in the bathroom, I knew he'd be just fine.

But in spite of his best efforts, Thayne's nerves overtook his performance. He read from his notes and often lost his place. He dropped his Bible twice, tripped over his feet once, and nearly choked on his tongue more times than I could count.

That afternoon, after lunch with Alma Stoddard (she'd invited us on Wednesday) and her family, Thayne made a beeline past me and into our cottage where he stripped out of his clothes and crawled into our unmade bed. By the time I got to the house he'd already managed to pull the covers over his head and was moaning as though dying.

"Thayne," I said, standing near the foot of the bed. I reached down for the pants that lay in a heap at the toes of my pumps. "Thayne."

"Go away," he said.

"I know what you're thinking. I know you think you didn't do well this morning, but you did just fine." I shook the pants free of wrinkles and folds and then laid them across the hope chest. Next I reached for his shirt.

"I never should have come here."

I was halfway to the dirty clothes basket in the bathroom. I stopped, turned toward the lump in the bed, and said, "You don't mean that." I continued on to the bathroom.

"Yes I do."

I leaned my head out the opened doorway. "No, you don't."

Another moan escaped the mound of linen, blanket, and bedspread. "Yes. I do."

I stepped out of the bathroom and into the bedroom. "All right then," I sighed as though resigned. "I'll be right back." I started toward the door to the rest of the house.

"Where are you going?"

I turned toward my husband, whose face now appeared encircled by linen. His eyes were actually wet with tears. "I'm going to get boxes."

"What for?"

"We'll need to pack, won't we? You don't want to stay and I don't want to be here, so why not leave this evening. We can be back at Daddy and Mama's by early morning if we start packing within the next couple of hours. We didn't come here with much and we won't leave with much so . . ." I turned as though leaving.

"Mariette, wait," he said.

I turned again. He was now sitting upright in the bed, his near-naked body exposed to the chill of the late September afternoon.

I purposefully cocked a brow. "Yes?"

His shoulders drooped, and his head hung between them. "I didn't mean it."

To which I smiled as I came toward him. "Okay," I said, then sat on the edge of his side of the bed. "So you didn't impress them. This time. Next week you'll do better."

"If anyone comes back."

I touched his bare shoulder, ran my fingertips down his

arm, then back up. "Oh, they'll come all right. They'll want to see if you can act any more like Barney Fife next week."

He grabbed me from around the waist and threw me onto my back next to him. "Very funny," he said, then gave me a sweet kiss.

"Made you smile."

He nodded. "Yes, you did." He kissed me again. "Hey," he said. "Would you really have gone to get boxes?"

"Would you really have left?"

He didn't answer and he didn't have to. We both knew the answer and we sealed it the best way we knew how.

Blessedly, no one showed up on our doorstep all that afternoon. They probably didn't know what to say. Mama called to see how Thayne had done in his preaching debut, and I told her he'd done fine. I looked out the window, expecting a lightning bolt to come slamming through the pane at any moment. Perhaps God spared me because I was honoring my husband, but only God knows the answer to that.

Alma had sent us home with enough leftovers for dinner. We ate quietly, then Thayne went to his "study" and pored over some paperwork while I cleaned the kitchen.

The next morning Thayne and I walked together to Main Street. He gave me a lingering kiss on the cheek then went on ahead to where the church stood waiting for its young, inexperienced shepherd. I turned left, heading for Clarence's grocery store, where I'd pick up a few items for that night's supper. It was a pleasant two block walk and there was a spring in my step. I spied Will Willoughby—William Jr., to be precise—entering the local post office. I called out a greeting to him; he turned and waved back. "You should come set up a post box," he said.

At that, I crossed the street to where he stood. "Really? How come?"

Will Jr. was a handsome man. He reminded me of a young Cary Grant, including the deep cleft in his chin. His eyelashes were long and dark and he batted them slowly. "Well, most folks around here who live within the city limits don't have a home box. I've been happy to bring your mail to you this past week because you're new, but if you can walk here, it's a whole lot easier on me."

I cocked my head. "Who do you deliver to, then?"

"Those who live out a ways. You know, farmers and such."

"Oh. I'd be happy to set it up then."

Over the next few minutes I stood at the counter of the tiny post office and filled out a pre-printed card with our information. Name, address, number of people living in the household—that sort of thing—thinking the whole time how truly grown up I now was. I'd been a wife since the age of eighteen, but was no longer a bride who lived in her old home-town or in her parents' house. We were officially on our own as a couple, and the white card with blue ink proved it.

Will Willoughby handed me two small keys from the other side of the counter, then walked around it. "Come over here," he said, pointing to the wall of ornate brass-covered boxes. "You're number fifty-nine."

"Fifty-nine," I repeated.

He grinned down at me—he being well over six feet tall—and said, "Is that all right with you?"

I felt myself blush. "Oh yes. Fifty-nine is just fine." I blinked. "Should it not be?"

He chuckled. "I can't imagine why not."

He then showed me how to use the key, standing so close I caught an easy whiff of his aftershave. I took a step forward and he did the same, pinning me near the wall. I felt my heart race uncomfortably; I wasn't used to a man other than my husband being so near my body. I held my breath as my mind raced for an easy out, but before I could make up my mind,

Will moved back. "Sorry about that," he said. "You surely can't open the box if you're pressed against it."

I exhaled, grateful the closeness had not been on purpose. *Had it?*

I turned and sidestepped him just in case. "I think I can open it with no problem." I pointed toward the glass door with the large brass handles. "I'd best get to the grocery store. Thank you, Mr. Willoughby, for your help."

"Call me Will." He blinked. "My father is Mr. Willoughby."

I took a deep breath, blew it out, and said, "All right then. If you call me Mariette."

He gave me a half smile that brought dimples to his cheeks. "Mariette. I look forward to seeing you the next time you come in. Please let me know if you need anything." He paused. "Anything at all."

I walked out, now unsure more than ever as to whether Will Willoughby was a flirt or just kind. As I crossed the street I dropped the keys into my purse, then entered the grocery store, where Minerva Stoddard stood behind the cash register near the door, a smug look on her face. "My, my," she said. "He's quite something, isn't he?"

With those words, I knew the identity of one of the women in Viola's upstairs bedroom.

24

I ignored Minerva with a flash of a smile, then grabbed a shopping cart and pushed my way down the first aisle. I intended to have fried-up slabs of ham for dinner and serve them with warmed cinnamon applesauce, sweet peas, and slices of bread. It wasn't much compared to the feasts I was sure the other wives of Logan's Creek set out each evening on their dinner tables, but it would be warm and filling.

From a shelf on aisle 1 I grabbed a can of sweet peas and tossed it to the bottom of the cart. It clattered along the meshed wire. I looked behind me to see if anyone might be there to notice, but I was alone. I shrugged, then moved on to aisle 2. It was there I heard the second voice from the bedroom as it spoke from aisle 3.

"I know he's young. I told William last night that the only reason we should consider giving him another chance is because he *is* young. My gracious alive in the morning, he's hardly old enough to vote."

I looked from the small section of spices—where I found the cinnamon—to the front of the store. Minerva Stoddard was standing with her hip against the cash register counter. Her arms were folded and her face wore the same smirk as she'd had when I'd first entered. I narrowed my eyes at her then turned back to the voices on the other side of the aisle.

"I thought it was endearing," Carolyn Boykin's voice returned. "And if you look close enough, you can see that spark in his eyes. He's got the Lord's Spirit all over him."

"Sister, say what you will. I now wish Reverend Dorn had stayed."

"You mean that you hadn't run him off."

"Me?"

I decided to continue down the aisle, then back up the next. A surprise attack, of sorts. As I did, Edith Willoughby gathered her bearings. I heard her shoot back, "I cannot believe a member of my own flesh and blood family . . ."

I spotted a can of applesauce on a bottom shelf, hoisted it up and into the cart, then—with one final look at Minerva—came around the end of the aisle.

"Edith, only members of your flesh and blood family would dare . . ." Carolyn Boykin's voice trailed off as her eyes locked with me.

"Mrs. Boykin. Mrs. Willoughby," I said, pushing my cart toward them. "How are the two of you this morning?" From somewhere in the recesses of my mind I thought, *Gee, I sound just like Mama.*

Carolyn had the good graces to blush, but Edith Willoughby was having nothing to do with shame.

"Shopping for supper?" Carolyn asked.

"Yes, ma'am. I'm not much of a cook," I said as I gave my attention to Edith. "But you probably know that." I took a deep breath, blew it out. "Still, hot ham and warm applesauce, peas and some bread. It's not bad."

"What about dessert, dear?" Carolyn asked. "Did you think about dessert?"

I gave her my best smile. "Yes. There will be dessert." I started to push my cart past the two of them.

"And what will that be?" Edith asked, though I doubt she really cared.

I looked over my shoulder. "Me." To which Carolyn burst

out laughing. Edith raised her chin, and I disappeared into the next aisle, quivering like a coward the whole way.

It was I who was curled under the bedcovers when Thayne came home for lunch. By this time I'd cried until hiccups had taken over my body.

Thayne rushed to me, sat on the bed next to my body, draped an arm over my hip, and said, "What? What happened?"

My words were hardly comprehensible; they were caught between English and gibberish.

"What?" he asked. "Mariette? Did someone die?"

I shook my head.

"Did someone get hurt?"

I nodded.

"Who?" When I didn't answer right away, he asked again, "Honey, who?"

I turned my face to his. "Me!"

A strange look came over him then. Angry yet protective. A man's glare. A husband's face. "Oh, my." He grabbed my shoulders. "Mariette, don't move. I'll get a doctor. I'll find one. I knew I shouldn't have brought you here." He ran out of the room before I fully understood his misunderstanding, his assumption that I'd been assaulted. I rose on my elbows and hollered his name, which brought him back to the bedroom.

"Where are you going?" I asked.

"I have to find a doctor."

"Thayne, no. No one has hurt me . . . like that."

Relief fell over his entire body, and he returned to the bed. "Then, what?" he asked, sitting beside me again.

I told him what I'd heard in the grocery store, explained to him what I'd left out when I told him about Saturday evening's events, even shared my catty comments to the sisters.

"Are you sure you heard them correctly?"

I nodded.

"It's me, Thayne. Not you. I've known this feeling before, believe me. I lived with it for four years at Saint Margaret Mary."

He grabbed my shoulders again. "Oh, Mariette. Don't say that. Give them time. They'll come to love you like I love you."

I felt my eyes widen. "I should hope not."

He blushed.

I shook my head. "Thayne, I'm no good for you. That's why I've been crying. Feeling sorry for myself, I suppose. You want to be a preacher, but I'm no good at being a preacher's wife. I don't even know how to pray properly!" And, with that, I fell flat on my back and burst into another fit of tears.

This time Thayne's look was almost entertained, which didn't amuse me at all. He shook his head, got up from the bed, and walked toward the bedroom door.

"Where are you going?" I demanded between sniffles.

"To get the boxes," he said. Then winked and left me to suffer alone.

By the time mid-afternoon arrived, my outlook had changed. Thayne had gone back to work—my cue to get out of bed, wash my face, and comb my hair. I brushed the thick tresses into a Gidget ponytail tied off with a wide ribbon, then applied a light coat of pink lipstick. From there I walked back into the bedroom, made the bed, and put away clothes that hadn't been properly hung over the last twenty-four hours.

I opened the plantation shutters in the kitchen and ran hot water in the sink. I plugged the drain, squirted some dishwashing liquid into it, then swished my hand back and forth until a frothy foam had formed. A few minutes later, with the dishes draining dry, I wiped down the white tile countertops, then gave the white cabinets a once-over as well.

I opened the shutters on the dining area window, which

had a ledge so wide that it provided the perfect place for the potted plants I'd purchased at the Feed and Seed the week before. I got water in a glass, soaked the soil in each pot, then went to the small utility closet and brought out a broom, mop, and bucket.

For the next half hour I cleaned the floors, fluffed pillows in the living room, and straightened papers on Thayne's desk, though not too much. One thing I'd learned while we were living at Mama and Daddy's was about Thayne's displeasure when Daisy tried to right his desk.

It was nearly four o'clock when I heard a knock on the front door. By this time I was sitting comfortably on the floral sofa, working on a counted cross-stitch pattern Mama Lena had sent me just before we'd moved to Logan's Creek but that I'd hardly had time to give attention to.

I sighed, thinking surely this wasn't the ladies' welcoming committee from the church or, worse yet, Alma Stoddard. I shoved my needlework to one side, then ambled over and opened the door.

"Hi."

It was Rowena Griffith, looking fresh—like a schoolgirl (which she was)—and somehow pleased with herself. Cradled in one arm were her schoolbooks. In the other, an intricately cut birdhouse with tiny doors and a chimney jutting from its roof.

"Hello," I said, taking a step back. "Come in. Please come in."

Rowena entered, extended the birdhouse to me, and said, "This is for you. I made it."

I took the tiny white-painted structure in my hands and said, "You made this?"

"I hope you like it."

"It's . . . it's . . . lovely. I had no idea when you said . . . you made this?"

Rowena laughed then, a sort of sad giggle.

"Put your books on the table there," I said, pointing to the dinette area as I placed the birdhouse on Thayne's desk. "Can I get you anything to drink? I've got Coke. Iced tea?"

"Coke would be good."

"I'd offer you a snack, but I honestly don't have anything here. I'm not a big eater and Thayne isn't a big snacker." I giggled. "Unless it's pie. Thayne loves pie."

Rowena placed her books on the table then followed me into the kitchen area. "Do you like to bake pies?" Her voice, I noticed, was quiet and gentle, but oddly sure. Just as it had been two nights before.

"Goodness, no." I got two glasses from an overhead cabinet, then an aluminum ice tray from the freezer. "Haven't you heard?" I asked with a smile as I walked over to the sink. I ran warm water over the underside of the tray. The ice cracked and popped.

"Oh yeah," Rowena said, coming up beside me. "That's what you were listening to when I found you eavesdropping upstairs at Miss Viola's." She looked from my eyes to the tray in my hand and then back up again. "Can I help?"

"Coke's in the fridge." I watched her as she walked over to the small refrigerator. She yanked the door handle, then bent over at the waist and peered inside. My attention returned to getting the ice out of the tray and into the glasses. "And, is it really eavesdropping if they are talking about you?"

Rowena returned with two Coke bottles.

"Opener is in the drawer to your left," I said.

She opened it without a word, then drew out the bottle opener and used it on the sodas. I held the glasses of ice toward her and she poured slowly, tipping the glasses slightly so as to lessen the amount of foam. As the dark liquid neared the top of one glass, she stuck her index finger in.

"What are you doing?"

"It fizzles the foam," she said. She nodded toward the other glass. "Try it in yours."

235

I did. It did. I'd learned something new from a high school student. "Hey, what do you know?"

"My mama taught me that when I was a kid."

We took our drinks into the living room and sat near each other on the sofa. In silence we sipped our drinks—once, twice—then Rowena said, "No."

"No?"

"No, it's not eavesdropping if they are talking about you."

I laughed lightly. "Glad to hear it. I do know now, at least, who the women were. Minerva Stoddard and Edith Willoughby."

"I know," she said. "I recognized their voices right off." She brought her glass to her lips—they were naturally ruby and downturned—and took another sip of her drink. I noticed then the watch around her wrist. A man's watch.

"You wear a man's watch?" I asked.

"It belonged to my father," she said. She slipped it over her slender hand and laid it in her lap. "I don't wear it at home. Just to school."

"Why not?"

She shook her head. "I don't want to upset Oscar. You know, make him think he's not daddy enough." She looked around the room. "You've sure done a lot with this place."

I allowed my gaze to follow hers. "You like?"

"Yeah. Did you do it all by yourself?"

"Mmmhmm." I pointed to the birdhouse. "But I'm more impressed by your handiwork than mine."

She pointed to the cross-stitch still on the sofa between us. "You do this?" She picked it up.

"Yeah. Thayne's aunt got me started on it. I've always been kinda good with a needle and thread but she . . . well, she's quite something."

She looked up at me again, tilted her head to the right, and said, "Do you like being married?"

I felt my face grow hot. "Well, yeah. I . . . well. Yeah." I coughed out a laugh. "My goodness, you surely asked a personal question for someone so young."

"Sometimes life makes you older than your age."

I blinked. She had a point. "That's true." I took a sip of Coke. "And yes. I like being married."

"Been married long?"

"Ahhh . . . since we were eighteen and nineteen. It seems so young now, but so old then." I laughed.

"How old are you now?"

"Almost twenty-three."

"So . . . twenty-two."

"Yes." I waited a beat. "And you're seventeen, if I remember correctly."

"Yes."

"A senior in high school."

"That's right."

"Do you know what you want to do when you graduate?"

She looked toward the window, beyond it. "Get out of Logan's Creek and never come back."

25

Settling into life in Logan's Creek came with a price, some-times happily paid, sometimes not. I'm not sure who it was more difficult for, Thayne or me, though Thayne certainly seemed to draw more approval with each Sunday that passed and, eventually, Wednesday evenings.

By the middle of October, he'd reorganized the midweek suppers, followed by a prayer service. There was no preaching. No teaching. Just the faithful of the church bringing their covered dishes and prayer requests; some of which sounded more like gossip, others shrouded in secrecy. "Unspoken re-quest," they would say from their seat in one of the pews. Thayne would solemnly pen something in a desk journal he kept while I wondered why—if the prayer request was to be secret—bother to bring it up at all.

But, prayer services gave both of us—Thayne and me—the opportunity to learn more about the people of Logan's Creek and their history. Prayers for family members neither spoken to nor seen since who-knows-when seemed to be a common offering. There were illnesses—some curable with a prescription from one of the two doctors in Hudsonville, others terminal.

Such was the case of Bessie Thurman, an eighty-seven-year-old widow who died after a prolonged illness not too long after we'd moved to town. Bessie Thurman was, of course, not to be confused with Bessie Truman, who, at ninety-four, was the oldest person alive in Logan's Creek. She was also vitally active. "Spry," Alma called her. Personally, I thought she was simply adorable.

Apparently, Thayne thought she was dead. As he preached Bessie Thurman's funeral, he repeatedly lifted the soul of "our dear sister Bessie Truman" to the bosom of God. From my pew—four back from the front where the family sat, teary-eyed and gasping—I tried to catch Thayne's attention, but he seemed to look right over the top of my head the entire service.

As we made our way outside to the cemetery, I leaned over and whispered, "You're burying the wrong Bessie!"

"What do you mean?" He looked over at me as he buttoned his all-weather coat at the neck. It was the beginning of November and the cold was already slicing bitterly in and through us.

I reached over and plucked lint from the shoulder of his coat, then adjusted the wool scarf around my head. "You keep saying Bessie Truman. It's Bessie Thurman who died." I glanced over at a few of the horror-stricken parishioners who were exiting the front door from the back aisle and granted them a smile, hoping to ease my husband's embarrassment.

"Please tell me you're kidding," Thayne whispered in my ear.

"Take a look at the faces around you, hon. What do you think?"

Thayne recovered nicely. At the gravesite, yards from the northern side of the clapboard church, where generations of Logan's Creek residents had been laid to rest, Thayne cleared his throat and righted his wrong. Looking to the mortified face of Miss Bessie Truman, he said, "Miss Bessie, my wife tells me I've just spent the last half hour burying you." He smiled, and his dimples cut into his cheeks. "I do apologize." Miss Bessie blushed like a schoolgirl.

He then looked to the grieving family and said, "And I do apologize to Miss Bessie Thurman's family." They all nodded; he took a deep breath, looked heavenward, and said, "And Miss Bessie, if you are watching from the good Lord's presence, I apologize to you, most of all."

Everyone chuckled then, and I thought that, once again, Thayne had righted his stumble. Once again, he'd gained adoration from those who called him "Reverend."

It was also in early November that Thayne told me that the balance in our checkbook was nearing zero. "Honey, I know you've enjoyed fixing up this little place, but quite frankly, if you buy one more knickknack or yard of fabric, we'll be in the poorhouse." He winced. "Actually, we already are."

He was sitting at the desk where he'd pored over the most recent bank statement and unpaid bills. I had been drying the last of the supper dishes, putting them away in the cabinets. I walked to him, peered over his shoulder at the checkbook register. The deposit column seemed to be fairly vacant. "When were you paid last?" I asked.

He looked up at me. His face flushed, then he looked back down. "It's been a month."

"What? You're supposed to get paid every other week." I stepped over and leaned against the wall, which allowed me to gain a better view of his face.

"Tell that to Oscar White."

I crossed my arms. "Oscar White? What's he got to do with your paycheck?"

"He writes them, Mariette. He's got everything to do with them."

"I don't understand."

"We've sort of had a falling out, Oscar and I. Not that either of us have let on to anyone outside the board."

240

I almost commented that Rowena hadn't mentioned any-thing of the sort but caught my loose tongue in time. "What kind of falling out?"

"Oscar isn't altogether pleased with the way I'm doing things around here."

"Why not? Attendance is up on Sundays. Wednesday nights are a success."

"It is and they are."

"You work so hard, Thayne. You study to prepare yourself, you visit the people in their homes, you've brought people back to church who swore they'd never step foot back in."

"That's true. But I'm also wanting to do some things that have Mr. and Mrs. Willoughby up in arms. Apparently, the first rule around here is *not* to upset Mr. and Mrs. Wil-loughby."

"Like what?" I pointed to the sofa, encouraging him to join me there, which he did. "Do you want some coffee?"

"No. No, thank you."

We both got comfortable, him drawing one knee up onto the sofa, me kicking off my house slippers and tucking my feet under my backside. "So, like what have you done?"

"At one of the board meetings I mentioned that I'd like to see each one of the Sunday school classes on the same page. You know, so that we're all learning about the same thing and the study topic ties into the sermon. I'm more than happy to alter my teaching to go along with the studies. More than happy. And even though a few of the members thought it was an excellent idea, Mr. Willoughby was quick to tell me they'd been using a particular Sunday school guide since God put the tree in Eden and they weren't about to change."

"He actually said that? About the tree in Eden?"

Thayne shook his head. "No. I added that part in."

"Oh." Thayne remained quiet, so I added, "I don't under-stand what's so wrong with your idea."

He shrugged. "All I can tell you is that Mr. Willoughby

looked at me and said, 'Preachers come and preachers go, but we're staying. So you'd best get used to our ways rather than trying to conform us to yours.'" Thayne raised his right hand as though taking an oath. "Verbatim."

"Goodness, Thayne."

"Then there's the issue of the song service."

"Oh, this I might know something about."

He gave me a hard look. "Like what?"

"Like Charlotte Knight telling me that her husband and Leila Freeman go at it when it comes to the songs being sung and all that."

"Be careful not to be caught up in gossip, Mariette."

I felt myself grow hot. "I'm not gossiping. She told me; I didn't ask her."

Thayne sighed. "Just be careful. The last thing you need is anyone thinking you're taking sides."

I wondered what he meant by that exactly. The last thing *I* needed. Not *we* needed or even *he* needed, but *I* needed? Did he know something I didn't? Was the fact that I'd hardly been accepted as the pastor's wife, much less a citizen of the town, starting to wear on him? "What do you mean by that?" I finally asked.

He touched my hand, but I drew it away. "Look, Mariette. You might want to try doing something *at* the church from time to time."

"Meaning?"

"Meaning . . . I don't know, take something other than deviled eggs on Wednesday night. Fry a chicken. Bake a pie."

I shoved my arms across my middle. "I don't know how to fry a chicken or bake a pie. Every time I try, the chicken comes out raw in the middle and the pie doesn't firm up properly. I'm not bad with the basics, but I'm no good at the rest."

"Mrs. Stoddard has offered to teach you, how many times?"

"I wouldn't let that old biddy teach me how to blow my

nose!" I stood, pounced over to the front window, and pointed toward her house. "I don't know what she has against me, but whatever it is, it's a doozy."

Thayne stood, placed his hands on his hips, and jutted his head forward. "You're being ridiculous."

"Oh, am I? Ridiculous, am I? Tell me the truth, Thayne. How many friends do I really have in this town? Huh? I'll answer that. Three, and two of them I would hardly call my friends. Carolyn Boykin is kind, Charlotte Knight is dangerous, and Rowena Griffith is a child. These are the three people who have made me feel welcome here, not that you—Mr. Reverend Popularity—have noticed!"

There was another party who'd made me feel at home but, in reality, more uncomfortable than welcome. Will Willoughby, the postmaster, was always kind whenever I went to town to get the mail. But, perhaps, too much so. His eyes always seemed to sweep over my body as though he were inspecting it. His words were spoken too slowly, as though he were whispering sweet nothings rather than simple greetings and such. He simply made me nervous, not that I would ever mention it to Thayne, or to anyone else for that matter, though Charlotte Knight had certainly noticed. One Sunday morning, after spending an entire church service feeling as though I were being undressed by the junior Mr. Willoughby, who sat two rows back and one aisle over, she approached me. "Be careful." She spoke her words quietly, then nonchalantly glanced over to the postmaster, who was helping his mother on with her coat.

I pressed my lips together, then said, "I'm not doing anything to promote it."

"You don't have to." She raised an eyebrow. "Believe me." We were then joined by her husband, thereby stopping any and all conversation about Logan's Creek's Casanova.

The argument I'd had with Thayne that evening wasn't the last we'd have after moving into the home of Alma Stoddard.

I tried to be the helpmeet I kept hearing the other women insist I was supposed to be. I called Mama and asked her to send some recipes. She did, and even included some from Daisy, but try as hard as I might, my talents in the kitchen were limited.

To make things easier financially (Oscar White finally handed over Thayne's check, but a meeting of the Scott Financial Board—as Thayne called it—revealed it just wasn't enough to cover our day-to-day expenses), I began teaching some of the young girls what I'd learned from Mama Lena and Aunt Harriett about needlework. Most of the women in town were more gifted than I, but having seen what I'd done with the cottage, they were more than happy to hire me for a pittance. I held "classes" on Saturday mornings and Tuesday afternoons. Four girls, including Rowena, came faithfully, and with Thanksgiving and Christmas nearing I decided we'd tackle cross-stitching holiday linens. It was simple, and it made for practical gift-giving.

In the meantime, a man named Mr. Johnson—the old cemetery caretaker—died, leaving his position open. Oscar White, knowing we were in dire straits financially, suggested Thayne take the job. The pay was nearly as meager as what I made teaching needlework, but the salaries combined helped tremendously, though not enough to get us back to Meadow Grove for Thanksgiving. Mama cried inconsolably when I called her to break the news. "Thayne says to tell you we will absolutely be there at some point during Christmas, though."

"What do you mean 'at some point'?"

I sighed as I looked down at the glass of ginger ale clasped in my left hand. "Well, Mama . . . I guess surely you understand that, as the pastor, Thayne has to be here on Christmas Day. And, this year it falls on a Wednesday, so all the more reason." I choked out the best laugh I could muster. "I'd say the four of you could come here, but honestly I don't know where I'd put you!"

"So, 'no' to Thanksgiving and 'no' to Christmas?"

"I'm sorry, Mama." I took a sip of my soft drink as my mind scrambled for a change of subject. My eyes came to rest on the projects my sewing class had been working on just days before. "Oh, Mama, you should see the Thanksgiving gift baskets my girls and I have made for the shut-ins here. They've been stitching little turkeys on large linen napkins, which we then laid in the baskets donated by Miss Carolyn. And Mr. Clarence is providing the meat and fixings in exchange for the girls doing some work around his and Minerva's house. You know, to get it ready for the holidays."

Mama didn't say anything.

Finally, I said, "Well, it's a Friday afternoon and not quite five o'clock. Thayne has asked that I keep our weekday calls to a minimum. To help with the expenses."

Mama sighed. "Why didn't you say something? I'll always be happy to call you back."

"I know, but . . . Mama, again, I'm sorry."

I heard the front door open. I jumped; it was mid-afternoon and Thayne was not expected home for another few hours. "Goodness! Thayne just walked in and scared . . ."

The look on my husband's face was nearly unreadable. Shock. Horror. Disbelief. "What?" I asked. "Thayne, what is it?"

"Who are you talking to?" he asked.

"Mama."

Mama, misunderstanding, said, "What?"

"No, not you. Thayne just walked in and . . . Thayne, what's wrong?"

By now Thayne had reached me, had placed his hand on my shoulder and begun to cry. "Thayne?"

"Tell your mother"—he said between breaths—"tell her . . . tell her someone has shot the president."

26

In the days following President Kennedy's assassination and the murder of his accused killer, the country reeled as I'd never witnessed. Logan's Creek was no exception. Although fully Republican and Protestant, the citizens there were first and foremost Americans. As I passed by their clusters, either along Main Street or at the church where Thayne called for a special prayer meeting, I often heard, "I didn't vote for him, but I didn't want him dead." Or, "I didn't care for him much, but he was still the president."

Early on the Monday following the president's death, I answered a knock at our front door to find a deliveryman with a package—rather large—from Daddy and Mama. Thayne helped get it inside; I signed for it and then waved good-bye while Thayne went in search of a box cutter. When the binding had been slashed, Thayne pulled back the cardboard flaps to reveal a portable television set still in its container.

"It's a color set," Thayne said, his tone almost reverent. He was now on his knees before it, most definitely like an awed child on Christmas Day.

I spotted a small envelope with our names scrawled across it in Daddy's handwriting. "We have a card," I said, pointing.

Thayne retrieved it and handed it up to me, then continued to cut away at the box housing the actual set. I opened the card and read out loud, "To Mariette and Thayne. To help you keep up with the news."

"The news?" Thayne shook his head.

"Never mind the news. I'm thinking we can watch *The Wonderful World of Disney* in color now. No more Sunday nights at Alma's after church watching it on her old black-and-white set."

"We'll have to have Alma and her family here," Thayne said. "After all, we have a color set."

My shoulders sank. "Oh, Thayne. Let's not ruin this moment."

He gave me a look of warning, then chuckled. "Do you think we can keep it a secret?"

"I doubt it." I pointed to the ceiling. "The antenna we'll be forced to install will be a fine clue."

This wasn't the only secret we would soon be unable to keep. In fact, I'd not even told Thayne, but every morning and throughout each day, as the nausea only seemed to increase, I knew I was expecting again. I also knew the timing couldn't have been worse. Our finances would hardly allow for doctor bills or getting a place large enough for a nursery. On a more public note, Thayne was so busy with trying to increase the church's membership, as well as focusing on his own spiritual journey, he'd hardly have time for tending to me should there be complications as we'd had with Rachel.

Still, I knew I could hardly keep quiet about it forever. My lower belly had begun to swell, not that anyone—including Thayne—had noticed. I wondered if I could keep it to myself, at least until Christmas, which would keep the doctor's visits at bay until after New Year's Day.

On the Tuesday afternoon, the day after JFK's funeral, Rowena arrived at the cottage—early, as always—to help prepare for the other three young ladies who were attending the sewing class. As had become her habit, she walked into our bedroom, dropped her books on the hope chest, then moved on to the bathroom. When she returned to the kitchen I placed a prepared glass of Coke over ice in her hand, then set about putting cookies on a plate, which I then handed to her. As she walked them over to the table, she said, "I can smell Alma Stoddard's laundry all the way from her backyard in your bedroom."

"How's that?"

She shrugged. "Your window is open. It actually smells nice in there. Fresh. Like clean laundry."

I giggled. "Glad to hear it doesn't smell like dirty laundry." She laughed with me and I asked, "How was school?"

"It was school."

I could have bet on that answer. It was the same one I got every Tuesday afternoon.

"Nothing special? I mean, with it being so soon after the assassination?"

"Not really. Morose, of course, but what's to be expected?"

Over the weeks, I'd tried to pry her for stories about friends—including possible boyfriends—but she seemed to never have any to share. "I guess I'm not much of a people person," she said when I'd asked her to tell me about her girlfriends.

"But I'll bet Oscar is having to keep the boys at bay . . . polishing his gun . . ."

She looked at me queerly then. Her eyes narrowed, then widened, and she said, "No. I don't date, really."

"Don't date? But Rowena, you're so pretty. I don't understand."

She shrugged. Only shrugged. No answer, not then, not ever.

"Of course," I now said, returning to the earlier subject. "I'm sure everyone is going around, speculating about what happened . . ."

"Yeah. Completely morbid. Everyone is going around act-
ing like they knew him personally or something. Mama hasn't
stopped crying yet."

I nodded. "I know. I saw her at the post office today. She
looked just dreadful, though don't tell her I said so."

Rowena smiled at me then—a half smile—and I thought
how I'd really never seen much more out of her. "What are you
and Reverend Scott doing for Thanksgiving? Mama said she'd
asked you to join us, but you already had other plans."

I nodded. "Yes. Thayne accepted an invitation to the
Boykins'." I didn't add how relieved I'd been when Carolyn
had asked before Alma had the chance. I felt as though I
had already spent enough hours entrapped by the Stoddards.
Clarence was all right, of course, but Alma and Minerva
were cut from the same cloth, and that cloth—for whatever
mysterious reason—just didn't match mine.

Rowena looked around. When her eyes came to rest on the
television in one corner of the living room, she stopped and
said, "Hey, man, what's that?"

I had poured myself another glass of ginger ale, which I took
a sip of before answering. "A television set. Ever seen one?"

The teasing lilt in my voice brought the half smile back.
She rolled her eyes and said, "Ah . . . yeah." She walked over
to the set, leaned from the waist, and undoubtedly noticed
the color wheel above the channel dial. "Color?" She shook
her head. "This is a first; nobody here in Logan's Creek has
a color set."

"Don't be overly impressed. We don't have an antenna yet,
so at this point, it's just another odd piece of furniture."

She stood upright. "Well, I wouldn't mind having a house-
ful of odd furniture as long as the house was mine and I lived
in it alone."

I leaned my backside against the kitchen counter. "You
make comments like that from time to time, Rowena. Do you
not like your brothers?"

Her brow furrowed then leveled out again. "They're all right as brothers go."

"I have two, myself," I told her. "Tommy and Mitch. I bet you and Tommy would get along great."

Her shoulders slumped forward. "Well, I dunno." She looked around again. "Hey, where are the baskets? I thought we were delivering them today."

"We are. They're in the bedroom against the wall. I'm surprised you didn't see them when you were in there."

Again she shrugged. "I guess I just didn't notice." She set her glass of Coke on the table and said, "I'll go get them."

"I'll help," I said, following her. "Next meeting we'll begin working on the Christmas tablecloths and napkins for your mothers and grandmothers."

"Sounds good," she said, looking over her shoulder at me, then returned her attention to getting the baskets.

The girls and I delivered baskets to seven homes. It was past dark when we arrived back at the cottage; their mothers were all there in parked cars on the street in front of Alma's, waiting for their daughters. I waved to each woman, then followed Rowena up the path to my front door, avoiding any conversation.

Rowena turned to me and said, "If you don't mind, would you get my books from your bedroom? I'm sure Reverend Scott is home by now, and it wouldn't be right for me to go in there."

"Of course. But if he's at his desk or in the kitchen, feel free to just go on in."

She shook her head. "No. Really. That wouldn't be right."

I nodded. She slowed her pace, which allowed me to walk past her and enter the house first. Sure enough, Thayne was sprawled on the sofa, already in his pajamas and reading a book. He jumped up when we entered, immediately criss-crossing his legs on the cushions, dropping the book. "Oh!"

I exclaimed at the same time, then turned to face Rowena, whose lips were pressed together and whose eyes were focused on the floor. She wrapped herself in her arms and whispered, "Could you get my books, please." Then she turned and stepped back out into the cold of the evening.

"Thayne," I hissed as I sped past him and into the bedroom, where his suit had been haphazardly thrown across the bed. I collected Rowena's things and then brought them outside to her. "Here you go," I said. "Sorry about that."

She kept her eyes averted from mine. "Tell Reverend Scott I'm sorry," she said.

I watched her as she walked briskly to her mother's car, then turned and went back inside to find Thayne stretched out again, his nose buried in the book. "Thayne!"

He looked up. "Sorry about that."

I threw my arms up. "That's all you have to say?"

"Well, gee, Mariette. What do you want me to say?"

I put on my best Goofy voice and said, "Well, gee, I dunno, Thayne. Maybe stay out of your pajamas until bedtime."

He narrowed his eyes at me. "What's that about?"

I waved him away as I walked into the bedroom, where I laid face down on the bed.

He was right behind me. "Seriously. What's that about?" His voice declared his frustration, I supposed with me.

I moaned into the bedcovers. "I need a nap. Don't start with me right now."

"Start with you? And what does that mean? Honestly, Mariette. I'm exhausted. Do you have any idea what it's been like to be me—'the Reverend'—since last Friday? All I wanted to do all day was come home, get out of that suit, get into my pajamas, and read. Because goodness knows we're not watching television yet."

I pushed my upper body up with my elbows and looked over my shoulder. "What does that mean?" So far, I thought, we sounded like two parrots.

"Your parents send us a television knowing good and well we can't afford to buy an antenna. When are we supposed to do that, huh?"

By now I was on my feet with my arms crossed. "How in the world would they know that, Thayne?"

His ears turned red as he jutted his chin toward me. The deep blue of his eyes went darker than usual as he said, "Oh, don't even think to tell me you haven't told your mother that I'm not able to provide enough for you."

I coughed in mock disgust. "Why in the world would I do that? It's not my fault you decided to leave the Fox & Hound. I certainly wasn't the one calling you to ministry. And it wasn't my fault you got handed this joke of a town as your first assignment."

"Joke? You think Logan's Creek is a joke?"

I widened my eyes. "It doesn't have a library, for heaven's sake. If it weren't for Mama sending books and having my needlework, I'd probably die here. Oh! Oh! And it doesn't even have sidewalks, Thayne. It's a town of two blocks and not a single sidewalk."

Thayne glared at me. "Oh, that's rich. No wonder you think no one here likes you. They can probably guess how you feel." Thayne turned and started back for the door.

"Not no one," I said, tears threatening to spill from my eyes. "Miss Carolyn is kind to me, and Charlotte is nice. And . . . and . . . Rowena is my friend."

Thayne turned in the doorway and crossed his arms as he leaned against the doorframe. "She's a high school senior, Mariette, and you're a grown woman. Don't you think it's a little strange that you feel so comfortable palling around with a girl in bobby sox when you're in nylons?"

"She's got more maturity than most of the grown women in this town."

Thayne sighed. "That's another thing, Mariette." His voice

lowered. "I can't put my finger on it, but there's something not right about her."

I shoved my fists into my waist with such force I figured there would be bruises the following day. "Thayne Scott. You take that back."

"I don't mean that in a cruel way."

"Well, it certainly came out that way." I pointed a finger at him. "I will not have you talking about my friend like that." I stomped my foot. "I won't!"

Thayne rubbed his forehead with the fingers of his right hand as he said, "I'm not going to get into this with you. My head hurts and I'm hungry. What's for dinner?"

"Tuna hash. It's cooked and in the fridge. You'll just need to heat it." I turned toward the bathroom door. "And make a couple pieces of toast to serve it over."

"You're not eating?" From the sound of his voice, it was obvious the fighting wind was out of his sails.

I shook my head. "I'm not feeling well. I'm going to take a hot bath and go to bed."

"I hate tuna hash," I heard him mutter.

I rolled my eyes as I turned to look back at him. But he had left the doorway. It was then I noticed the window across the way, still open, drapes pushed back. I sighed and slumped my shoulders as I trudged back across the room. When I reached the window, my breath caught in my throat.

There stood Alma Stoddard, illuminated by the moonlight at the gate to our front walkway, arms crossed, hip cocked out. She'd heard every word of our argument, no doubt. Including my feelings about Logan's Creek.

27

Thanksgiving Day brought two surprises.

The first came just as the sun made its brilliant arrival over the horizon. Thayne and I were still asleep, our bodies wrapped around each other to ward off the cold of early morning. With finances so tight, we'd agreed to turn off even the small gas wall unit in our bedroom at night and to instead lie under a pile of blankets and quilts. Between them and body heat, we were keeping warm enough.

Even when we were angry. Especially when we were not.

On Tuesday evening, after our snippy argument, Thayne came into the bedroom, looking sheepish and—even though I was still in no mood to deal with him—boyishly adorable. "Look, Mariette," he said after sitting on his side of the bed. Although he spoke to me, he kept his face to the door and pretended to be busy taking off his bedroom slippers, replacing them with thick socks. "The Bible says that we should not go to bed with anger in our hearts."

I didn't say what I was thinking.

"So, I'm sorry for what I said."

I was lying on my left side, my back to the bathroom, from where a stream of light shot across the bed and faintly illuminated the bedroom. I watched Thayne's face through the veil of my lashes. My head ached, and without food in my stomach, acid was building at the core of my abdomen.

"Which part?" I asked.

"Any of it. All of it."

"Including the part about Rowena?" I asked, not moving.

Thayne nodded. "Yeah. But . . . seriously, Mariette. We need to talk about her sometime. I don't want people getting the wrong idea about you."

I sighed, then opened my eyes fully to look at the draperies shrouding the telltale window across the room, the window that had provided Alma Stoddard with a front-row seat for one of our rare arguments. "What kind of wrong idea?"

His shoulders fell forward. "I don't know, Mariette." His hand rose and then came to rest on my hip. "I know you like her, and goodness knows there's nothing wrong with the pastor's wife mentoring the young ladies of the community. Especially with where you come from and where they are."

"Thayne, I have no idea what you're saying."

His hand stroked from my hip to my knee and then back up. "You know. Your background. You've been raised with some of the finer things life has to offer. Even your time at Saint Margaret Mary taught you something you can offer to the girls that they'd never get from anyone else here. Do they even know you spent four years in a boarding school?"

"Goodness, no."

He scooted closer to me. His hand now came up my spine, which would ordinarily have felt wonderful but tonight only brought pinpricks. "Today was awful," he said. "Just awful. Nothing in seminary prepared me for this. Nothing I can think of, anyway. And I was so tired when I came home. I just wanted to relax. I knew you were out with your girls and I thought . . . well, it would be nice to have some quiet time. Just me and a good book. Reading. I didn't stop to think that Rowena Griffith would be walking in at any minute."

I tried to shift—a subtle hint that I didn't want my back rubbed—but Thayne didn't catch on. He came closer, leaned over and kissed my exposed shoulder. "You smell great," he whispered near my ear, then pressed his lips against my temple. "I love you, Mariette. I don't ever want us to fight like that again."

I knew where this was going. "I love you too, Thayne." Then I pushed him away. "But I really don't feel well. Please. Just let me get some sleep, okay?"

His face showed noticeable disappointment. Understandable, but if I'd welcomed him into my arms, I would have puked all over him. Unfortunately, that feeling only intensified over the next twenty-four hours with Thayne concerned I was coming down with the flu and saying he wasn't sure we'd be going to the Boykins' for the holiday.

Then, Thanksgiving morning—when we could actually sleep late—we heard activity outside our bedroom back window.

"What now?" Thayne groaned as he rolled away from me.

I opened my eyes and turned onto my back as he threw the covers away from himself. "Thayne?" My voice was filled with sleep. "What is that?"

Thayne reached for his robe at the foot of the bed, shoved his arms into the sleeves, and then jerked the sash into a knot. "I don't know," he said. "Surely we don't need new screens."

I watched as Thayne pulled back one side of the drapes, then said, "Good morning, Mr. Boykin."

"Mr. Boykin?" I groaned from the cubbyhole where I stayed snuggled up.

"Hello, Reverend," I heard Wilbur Boykin call back. "Listen, I might need your help here. I was going to knock in a few minutes."

"Help with what, Mr. Boykin?"

"I'm putting up your TV antenna," came the jovial too-early-in-the-morning voice.

"My TV . . . how'd you know about our TV?" He looked to me. I shrugged. "I didn't say anything." Then he turned back to the window. "Mr. Boykin?"

"Mrs. Stoddard told the missus and the missus and I decided to surprise you. So, surprise!" I pictured Wilbur Boykin, handsome by every definition of the word—tall, slender, tanned, with black hair that had silvered on the sides of his head, which only added to his good looks—on the other side of the window, most likely holding a ladder against the side of the house. I'd seen him often enough in a suit—at church, at the store—but figured that for this job he'd be casually dressed and bundled into a thick hunter's jacket to ward off the cold.

"I'll make coffee," I mumbled as I stretched. The movement brought a wave of nausea; I clasped my hand over my mouth, then scooted out of the bed and into the bathroom, where I vomited into the toilet.

"Mariette?" I heard Thayne call from behind the door I'd managed to shut.

"Everything all right in there?" Mr. Boykin called from beyond the outside wall.

"Oh, God help me," I whispered as I flushed the toilet, meaning every word of my haphazard prayer.

"Mariette?" The door opened slightly. I peered up as Thayne's face appeared between the door and the doorframe. "Here, let me get you a washcloth."

"Thank you," I said, standing. The wonderful thing about morning sickness is that—at least for me—once I threw up, it was over. It was just getting to the throwing-up stage that was agonizing at times.

Thayne handed me the cold wet cloth, and I immediately wiped my mouth. "Should I tell Wilbur we won't make it today? I mean, you obviously have a bad bug."

"Everything all right in there?" Wilbur called again.

I glanced toward the bathroom window. "You'd best get dressed and go help. And, no. I think I'm fine now."

Thayne started for the door then stopped and looked back at me. "Say, how do you think Alma knew about the television?"

Probably by eavesdropping into our argument, I thought, but said, "She was probably watching when it was delivered."

He bought the white lie, then left me to wash up.

After the men were done putting up the antenna and had played with the TV and the antenna box that now sat on top, the three of us sat and watched about five minutes of *Captain Kangaroo* in glorious black and white before I said, "I have coffee made."

Thayne and I arrived at the Boykin home at about 11:00 that morning. Thayne brought the Detectives board game for anyone who might want to challenge him. When we'd lived with my parents, Thayne often played board games with Mitch, who had gifted Thayne with this particular one when we left Meadow Grove, and—as I suspected—Thayne missed the occasional challenge of his game-winning skills put to the test.

I brought my usual deviled egg plate, the smell of which brought a new wave of nausea. As soon as my feet hit Carolyn's kitchen floor, I turned what I'm sure was a lovely shade of sea green. Miss Carolyn turned me and pushed my body toward the hallway and said, "That way," and I ran for the bathroom. Ten minutes later I was back, good as new, but still of little help in the kitchen. Miss Carolyn politely handed me a stack of plates and napkins and instructed me to set the table. "That's your job," she said. "I'm sure you'll do well at it."

The festive table was soon occupied by Wilbur and Carolyn,

who sat at either end, their daughters Sylvia and Helen, both adorably and annoyingly dressed alike even at nearly thirty years of age, Sylvia's husband Pearson (who I guessed to be closer to Wilbur's age than Sylvia's), their daughter Penni, a pixie child who was ten-going-on-fifteen, and Helen's husband Jimmy (a truck driver who looked more like a college-aged linebacker with his broad shoulders, wide face, and naturally red cheeks that only looked more ruddy next to his white-blond crew cut).

After Wilbur had said grace and the food was being passed and oohed and ahhed over, Carolyn spoke from her place near the swinging kitchen door. "So, Mariette, honey, when are you due?"

"Due?" I asked.

"Due?" Thayne repeated. He laughed lightly as the table, which not two seconds before had been filled with chatter and clatter, went silent.

I bit my bottom lip as I looked from Miss Carolyn to Thayne and then to everyone else at the table, including little Penni.

"Due for what?" Thayne asked. His eyes followed the path mine had just made.

I watched as he turned red, then white, then red again. I noticed that the large bowl filled with fresh white acre peas seemed to grow heavy in his hand so I reached for it, lest he spill what the locals called pot liquor all over his nice pants. "Thayne," I whispered.

"Oh, dear," Carolyn said.

"A baby!" Sylvia squealed. "Oh, how lovely!"

Jimmy, who was sitting next to Thayne, slapped him a couple of times on the back and said, "Way to go, Reverend," as though Thayne had just made a touchdown or hit a home run or shot a basket from the opposite end of the court.

"Pipe down, everyone," Wilbur said. "I don't think the Reverend has had a chance to digest this news."

Thayne continued to stare at me, mouth half open, eyes wide and filled with both question and fear. "Mariette?" he finally breathed out.

"Yes, Thayne. I'm . . ." I looked over to Penni. "Expecting."

"Take a breath, my man," Pearson said from the other side of the table. "You look like the first man to ever hear these words." To which everyone but Thayne and me chuckled.

I knew—deep in my heart—I knew we were thinking the same thing, repeating the same name. *Rachel.*

Thayne took my face in his hands, kissed me lightly on each cheek, and then whispered in my ear, "Have you seen a doctor?"

I shook my head no.

"Seriously, Reverend," Jimmy bellowed. "You all right here?"

Thayne nodded so faintly, I may have been the only one who noticed. I kept my eyes locked on his, then blinked and smiled, my way of telling him I wasn't sure about much, but I was sure things would go better this time. They'd certainly been different so far. I'd not been this sick with Rachel.

Thayne's lashes fluttered several times as though he were waking from a deep sleep. He turned to face the others at the table, then laughed lightly and said, "I'm sorry. I just had no idea." He pinked as he said, "I guess ol' Dad's the last to know, huh?"

"I'm sorry, Reverend," Wilbur said as he reached for the bowl of dressing next to him. "I figured it out this morning, came home and told Carolyn." He winked. "My can't-keep-a-secret wife."

"I most assuredly can," Miss Carolyn said with a feigned pout. "Not a word of this will go any further than this table—oh . . . well, I might have mentioned it to Sister on the phone earlier . . ."

"Which sister?" Wilbur asked.

Carolyn's brow rose as she answered, "All of them."

Everybody laughed then, Thayne and myself included.

But later that night, as he held me close in bed and stroked my face, he whispered, "I want you to have the best doctor, Mariette. We can't take any chances."

"We also can't afford the best doctor," I said. "There are two to choose from in Hudsonville, and I'm sure they're both fine. I'll find out which one is the cheaper and see if we can set up a payment plan." I turned my face toward his. "And I'll take real good care of myself, Thayne. I promise."

He sighed. "Mariette . . . I just don't want anything . . . not like last time."

I snuggled closer to him, kissed his chin, and said, "Thayne, the best obstetrician in the world couldn't have stopped what happened last time. And you know as well as I do that chances are slim that it will happen again." I kissed his chin again.

He leaned back and said, "Careful there. You know how I feel about you, little girl. I might not be able to control myself."

I wrapped my arms around his shoulders and drew him close. "What's to control?" I asked. And then I giggled as he sighed, giving in to my feminine wiles.

Part 4

Baby Love

28

In the weeks preceding Valentine's Day 1964, I taught the girls to crochet heart-shaped doilies that could easily be sewn into table covers or even bedcoverlets, were they to stitch enough of them. As the girls grew more adept at their needlework, it seemed to me that with each meeting, Rowena and I grew closer. She also seemed more than a little curious about the child growing inside me.

"Were you this inquisitive when your mother was expecting?" I asked her.

"I was too young and too busy to notice really," she answered. "There's seven years between Sidney and me and nine between Jason and me."

"Oh, I see," was all I could think of to say.

I did a lot of sewing in those days. During our holiday time with family, when we'd told my parents about our expecting again, Mama whisked me off to downtown Meadow Grove. "We can shop for clothes or patterns," she'd said as soon as we got into the car.

"Patterns," I said. "I like to sew, and to be honest, it'll give me something to do."

She patted my hand and said, "Come June you'll have plenty to do, but I agree with you for now."

Since then, I'd sewn several adjustable, cut-out pouch-front pencil slim skirts and a variety of scoop-necked over-blouses to match. For relaxing at home, I'd made an oversized but fashionable pants dress that seemed to grow tighter with each wearing. I'd also sewn a pair of Gidget sleepover pajamas, complete with smock top, pants, and matching duster peignoir robe, which Thayne said I looked adorable in.

My new condition had brought changes to the way most of the women (and even some of the men) in Logan's Creek looked at and treated me. Even Alma had become more tolerable, though Minerva continued to keep her distance. I tried to tell myself I didn't care—one way or the other—but the truth was, I cared very much. No one likes to feel rejected.

By early March, when I was in my sixth month, my morning-to-all-day sickness was but a vague memory. And, according to Dr. Kathleen Meredith—the less costly of the two doctors in Hudsonville—I was the picture of health. My weight gain was good and my blood pressure was deemed appropriate. Dr. Meredith sent for my records from Dr. Franklin's office in Meadow Grove, studied them carefully, and then met with Thayne and me, telling us she saw no reason why I would miscarry again.

"But I'm going to say this," the young doctor said. "I'm not God. He makes these decisions, not me. So while I can tell you I see no reason, it is ultimately up to him."

Thayne assured her he both understood and agreed.

I said no such thing. I had yet to understand Rachel's death, nor did I think I ever would. I might not have been the most perfect or influential Christian, but I wasn't a bad person, and it just made no sense that God would have wanted to punish me so. And, if not me, then surely Rachel had been innocent. Surely she had deserved a chance to live.

But I kept these feelings to myself, speaking to no one about them. Not even to Thayne or to Missy in our once-a-week gab session.

By now, Missy and Ward had three children in addition to Ward's son by his first marriage. "I told Ward this was it," Missy said one recent Saturday afternoon. Then she laughed. "But he says 'Oh, come on, Missy. One more.'"

"What did you say to that?" I asked.

"I told him I was too tired and he was getting too old, though honestly you'd never know it the way that man runs his life."

I smiled. Missy was happy; this was good.

On the first morning that dawned with an edge of warmth to it, Thayne declared he'd walk to work, something he had not done since just after the first of the year.

"I'll join you," I said, pulling my apron strings from the place where my waist had once dipped in so gracefully. "I need to get some things at Stoddard's."

Thayne placed his hand against my swollen belly. "Are you sure you're up to it?"

Adorable, thy name is Thayne, I thought. But I said, "I promise you, I'm fine."

I wrapped a scarf around my head, tying it under my chin. We both donned light coats and then headed out of the cottage. We passed Alma in her backyard, hanging out her clothes. She called to us, we waved back, then she reminded me to be careful that I didn't slip and fall if I was walking "all the way up to town and back."

"Thank you, Mrs. Stoddard," I returned. "I will."

"Amazing, isn't it," Thayne said from beside me, "what the impending birth of a child will do?"

Again, I said nothing. I was grateful for the change but was still puzzled as to why she'd been so cold initially.

At Main Street we parted with a kiss; Thayne continued on, and I turned to the left. My first stop was the post office to retrieve our mail from the little box with number fifty-nine on it, and to say my customary good morning to Will Willoughby, who'd managed to keep his eyes from roving too far along my body since the announcement of my pregnancy.

"Good morning," Will said. And then, as always, "How's the little mother?"

"She's good," I said. Our words rarely varied.

I collected our mail—mostly bills, a letter from Missy, and another letter that looked official in a legal-sized envelope with a gold-embossed return address. I studied it for a moment. It was from the church's head office in Atlanta. My eyes dropped to the addressee. It was to Thayne and addressed to the church's address rather than our personal one.

"Something wrong over there?" Will asked.

I looked over my shoulder at him. "Not really, no." I waved the envelope. "This was placed in our box by accident. It goes to Thayne at the church."

Will came from behind the counter and reached for the outstretched correspondence. "Sorry about that," he said. "I was probably just looking at the name."

I shrugged. "No big deal. I'd be happy to take it home."

Will shook his head. "No, no. I'll just put it in the right box. The reverend usually comes by on his lunch break. Gives him one more thing to do, I think."

I nodded an okay, then left the post office and ambled over to the grocery store. I felt a moment of elation when I spotted the new signs in the window announcing that bananas, which I love, were on sale for ten cents a pound, beef chuck roast was forty-nine cents a pound, and—better yet—Banquet frozen dinners were thirty-nine cents each.

So far I'd managed not to make TV dinners more than a couple times, but I figured it never hurt to have them on standby in the freezer. In spite of Thayne's obvious aversion for them. "Everything tastes like the container," he said. "And the peas and carrots taste like wax."

I just rolled my eyes. "Tuna hash tomorrow night then," I said, to which *he* rolled *his* eyes.

Inside the store, Minerva was standing in her usual spot; without a customer to ring up she was grooming her long nails with an emery board.

In spite of her attitude, I said hello. She raised her chin; I grabbed the handle of a shopping cart and then made my way to the back, where the Bishop Sisters—all four of them—were clucking over the price of chicken, which was twenty-nine cents a pound. They stopped their chatter as I approached, all four suddenly beaming toward the pregnant woman as though they were, each of them, the baby's grandmother.

"Good morning, ladies," I said. "I suspect your tables will be graced by chicken tonight." I laughed inwardly at my choice of words and the way I spoke them.

"Mariette," Carolyn said. "You are just glowing, my dear. Just glowing." She looked toward her sisters and said, "Isn't she, sisters?"

Edith Willoughby, who looked as though she'd just stepped from the beautician's chair, commented, "Oh, how I remember the way it was when I was expecting my Will. I do believe I was healthier than I've been at any other time in my life. Not a moment's trouble, my son. Not then, not now."

I silently groaned. From what I'd come to learn—mostly from Rowena—Will Willoughby the adult had another well-deserved name, and it was spelled t-r-o-u-b-l-e. He used his Cary Grant good looks on nearly every woman he came into contact with, and it didn't much matter if they were married or not.

"How is the reverend this morning?" Viola asked. But before I could answer she added, "Oh, I do declare, that was one fine sermon yesterday morning."

"It surely was," Leila chimed in. "When Reverend Scott gave me his sermon notes so as I could pick out the music . . . well, I just have to tell you, I got goose bumps."

I drew my shoulders back with pride. "I'm sure Thayne will be happy to hear this," I said. To which Mrs. Freeman touched my arm and said, "Oh, honey, you really must remember to refer to him as Reverend Scott when you are speaking to members of his congregation."

I felt like a scolded child and an angry woman all at the same time, torn as to whether to drop my eyes and say "I'm sorry" or stare the staunch older woman in the eyes and say, "It's hard for me to refer to a man I've seen naked as 'The Reverend.'" But I simply nodded and said, "I'll try to remember, Mrs. Freeman. Thank you."

My good upbringing rose to the occasion, and I thought at least Mama would be proud.

Carolyn, who didn't seem the least little bit affected by my choice of names for my husband, jumped a little as she said, "Oh, my dear, tell Sisters what you've done with the bedroom at Alma's guesthouse."

I smiled at her, then at the others, who inched forward as though I were about to tell a ghost story. "Well," I said. "Obviously, Th—Reverend Scott and I cannot afford to move right now. You know, to get a place big enough for a nursery. So, I have turned part of the master bedroom—well, the only bedroom—into the nursery. It's no more than a tiny corner in a small bedroom, but . . . well, it will have to do. I decorated with Winnie the Pooh, of course."

Viola looked at me strangely. "Why, 'of course'?"

"It's Pooh's Corner, Sister," Carolyn said before I had a chance to clarify.

The ladies all laughed lightly before Viola added, "Well, I for one would love to see it. I declare I would."

The matriarch of the community had just invited herself to our home, and she didn't mean later in the day. I tried to remember if I'd washed the breakfast dishes yet or made the bed. No to the first, yes to the second. "Why don't you finish your shopping," I said, "and meet me back at the cottage?" I pointed to my shopping cart. "I only have a few items to purchase. I'll be done here in a jiffy."

The sisters nodded, agreed to come back to the house with me, and then Carolyn insisted she drive us all in her new dark blue Plymouth Belvedere. We placed our grocery bags in the trunk, everyone found a place to sit (me sitting in the front passenger's seat), Carolyn turned the key and said, "Road trip, girls! It's like we're taking a road trip!"

"Honestly, Carolyn," Edith said. "What would you know about a road trip?"

"I'd know plenty," Carolyn said. "Wilbur and I take a vacation every year and you know it."

"I think I'll take a vacation," Leila said. "Osborne left me plenty of money to do with whatever I want to do."

The car moved smoothly along Main Street toward Railroad Street.

"The good Lord knows Osborne never took you anywhere. Might as well let his money do it now," Viola said. The way she spoke Mr. Freeman's name told me in no uncertain terms she'd held him in low regard.

"You can say that again," Miss Leila said. I turned my head slightly toward her, shocked by her own disdain toward her late husband.

She frowned at me, then said, "I don't expect you to understand, Mrs. Scott." At the sound of my name I turned and looked out the windshield. Carolyn turned on Railroad as her sister continued. "I was never loved by my husband the way the reverend loves you." I took a deep breath, feeling a level of discomfort I wasn't familiar with. I wasn't accustomed to older women sharing such intimate details about their marriages. I prayed silently that she'd stop, but she kept going. "Osborne was a mean man," she continued. "He ran my daughter off in '53, and I've not seen her since."

I looked over my shoulder again. "Why'd you let him do that?" I asked before I could stop myself.

"Our parents always said, 'You make your bed and you lie in it.'" She turned to look at Viola and Edith, who sat next to her. "Mama and Papa never liked Osborne, but I wouldn't listen."

"No, they did not," Viola said. "Oh, that was one sad day when you married that scoundrel."

"But you do have Charles and Treena," Carolyn said. "Treena may not be living here, but she has called you since Osborne died and she did say she'd think about coming home sometime soon."

"She didn't come for Christmas," Leila said. I heard the deep sadness in her voice, and for the first time, my heart went out to her. I wished there was something I could do to make it better for her, to change the course of her life. But I couldn't.

"She will for Easter," Viola said, then reached beside her and patted her sister's knee. "You just wait and see."

Carolyn pulled the car into Alma's driveway, directly behind the De Soto Thayne had washed and hand waxed on Saturday. It gleamed as the mid-morning sunlight reflected on its shiny paint, looking nearly as new as it had the day Daddy and Mama had given me the keys to it. Alma's car, which was always parked under a little shelter on the side of the house, was missing, for which I was grateful. It was enough that I had these four sisters traipsing into my home with dirty dishes in the sink. I didn't think I could bear Alma too.

"Come on in," I said as we all moved toward the door. "I'll warn you, though; I haven't had a chance to do the dishes this morning."

Carolyn said, "Don't think a thing of it" as Edith said, "I never leave my kitchen dirty."

I was sure she didn't.

When we walked into the cottage, I set my single bag of groceries on the table where Thayne and I ate our meals, then pulled the scarf from my head. The sisters pointed to the various changes I'd made to the front room of the cottage and made quiet compliments.

I stepped over to them as they admired the needlework seat cover I'd recently completed for Thayne's "office" chair. "Such a nice place for the reverend to study," Viola said, keeping her voice low, as though to be so close to where Thayne studied was tantamount to being in the church.

I looked at them and said, "Let me take you into the bedroom."

They followed as I led them past the dining table, through the kitchen, and into the bedroom. I'd no sooner started to say, "Here it is," than I noticed Thayne's clothes—the ones he'd been wearing earlier—thrown in a heap near the foot of the bed. I said "Oh goodness" just as the bathroom door burst open and Thayne stepped out, wearing nothing more than a towel wrapped around his waist.

I'm not sure who screamed the loudest, Thayne, the Bishop Sisters, or me. There was a flurry of activity as the four older women squealed, turned, and bumped into each other before making it through the door to the kitchen. Thayne doubled over and backed into the bathroom while I threw my hands over my face as if to do so would just make the whole scene go away.

I scurried after the sisters, two of whom were sitting on the sofa laughing while the other two, hands clasped over their mouths, stood at the front door, looking outward. "I am so sorry," I said, attempting to sound as horrified as I was sure I looked.

Carolyn and Viola—the sitting sisters—spoke simultaneously.

"Well, that was unexpected!"

"It's a first, that's for sure."

The other two stood motionless.

Suddenly, as though taken by some unknown force, I began to laugh. I wrapped my arm around my round belly, then stumbled over to the table and collapsed in a chair. A few minutes later Thayne came out, looking red and sheepish, to explain that he'd spilled coffee all over his clothes at the office and had come home to clean up. Mrs. Freeman and Mrs. Willoughby kept their backs to him, but within a moment or two of hearing his excuse for nearly exposing himself to them, I noticed their shoulders quivering with laughter.

"Oh, come on, sisters," Carolyn finally said. "We can now say with certainty that this good shepherd has nothing to hide from his flock."

A line which only left us all laughing until tears fell like rain on parched earth.

29

Thayne was unusually quiet when he returned home that night. At first I thought it was due to his . . . *exposure* . . . to the Bishop Sisters, but he assured me otherwise.

"I'm just tired," he said. He'd already taken his bath, and while I continued supper preparations, he slumped on the sofa to watch *The Huntley-Brinkley Report*.

"You're unusually quiet," I said to him as we ate our meal at the table. "What's wrong, Thayne?"

He shook his head. "It's work related. Nothing for you to worry about."

"But I'm your wife," I said, setting a bean-filled fork on my plate. "If you can't share with me, who can you share with?"

Thayne pulled the linen napkin from his lap and laid it beside his nearly untouched plate. "I'm not hungry," he said. Then he stood. "I'm going to go for a walk."

"Thayne?"

He walked over to the chair the Bishop Sisters had admired earlier and pulled his jacket from its back then slipped his arms into the sleeves. "It's okay, Mariette. I just need time to think." He stepped toward the door. "And to pray."

After he'd left—after I'd watched him walk down the path

that snaked between the garden, which was beginning to look more a place for weeds than flowers—I went to the phone and called Mama.

I didn't begin my conversation with any fanfare. I got right to the point. "Mama, does Daddy share with you the things that bother him? You know, the ins and outs of his day at the office? Things like that?"

Mama didn't answer right away, as though she was thinking before speaking. Finally she said, "Mariette, men think and do things differently than we do."

"I know that, Mama. It's just that . . . well, when Thayne worked for Daddy, he came home at night and talked to me about the people from the factory and what he did all day, and when he was in school he talked to me about his classes and his professors and even the subjects that went way over my head. But since we've moved here, I get 'I'll tell you later' more than I get explanations."

I heard a sigh from the other end of the line. "Mariette, darling. I'm sorry, but you've called just as we're about to sit down to dinner and—"

"Oh, I'm sorry," I said. "I didn't think about the time."

"I'm sure whatever it is that's going on with Thayne at work is nothing for you to worry about. After all, you've got a baby to stay healthy and worry-free for." Another pause. "Where is Thayne now?"

"He went out for a walk." This time it was I who broke for breath. "And to pray."

"I'm sure that's appropriate . . . *I'm coming, Carroll* . . . Mariette, honey, I'm sorry but . . ."

"I know. Dinner. Tell everyone I love them."

"Will do. And we love you too."

I hung up the phone and set about cleaning the kitchen and dining area. I'd washed the last of the pots and pans when I heard a knock at the front door. I reached for the drying cloth hanging from a hook to the left of the sink, called out, "Just a moment," and then walked toward the door. I peered out the front window and saw that Rowena was my unexpected guest.

"Rowena, hi," I said as I swung the door wide. "What brings you here?"

She poked her thumb over her shoulder and said, "Oscar's truck."

"Ha ha." I stepped back. "Come on in. I was about to make some coffee. Would you care for any?"

Rowena ambled over the threshold as she said, "Yeah, sure. Is the reverend here?"

I was halfway to the kitchen when I looked over my shoulder at her. "Thayne? Oh no. He's out walking."

"It's getting a little cold out," she said, coming out of her coat. "I hope he wore a sweater or something."

I pulled the coffee tin from the red and white checked canister set and began the coffee preparations. "He wore his jacket, yes. So seriously, why are you in town at this hour?"

"Oscar had something that needed to be delivered to Mr. Knight and asked me to bring it." I caught her as she shrugged. "Gave me a chance to get out of the house, so I didn't mind."

I plugged in the coffeepot and then pointed to the sofa. "Let's sit," I said.

When we'd gotten comfortable, I asked her, "Rowena, you aren't very happy at home, are you?"

Her Bette Davis eyes clouded with ambiguity. "It beats living on the streets, I guess."

Rowena was a mystery to me. She was pretty in the classic sense; earthy and ethereal at the same time. I knew she felt a void where her biological father was concerned, but in spite of some of Thayne's disagreements with Oscar White over church finances and his own paycheck, Oscar appeared to be a good stepfather. He provided well. Thayne and I had been to their home on more than one Sunday afternoon for dinner.

The white framed house stretched near the back border of well-kept acreage and boasted both an inviting front porch lined with rockers and ferns and a large bay window in the living room that overlooked a gracious flower garden, tended by Rose's own hands. The house was more contemporary than any other house I'd been in since moving to Logan's Creek, and I'd often thought Rose and my mother would get along famously when it came to furniture shopping. And, of course, each being the mother of a daughter followed by two sons would give them plenty to chat about.

The difference between Rowena and me—when it came to our brothers—was that I found mine to be adorable while she seemed to only tolerate hers. There was a distance between them I couldn't quite put my finger on, and it appeared to be brought about by more than just their being half-siblings.

"Rowena." I spoke her name slowly. I was the reverend's wife, for heaven's sake. I should be able to help my husband in his work reaching the citizens of Logan's Creek, and it seemed pretty logical I could begin with a young girl who was standing on the brink of womanhood. "I want you to know how glad I am you're my friend and that I feel privileged you want me to be yours."

She actually laughed at my efforts.

I laughed too. "I'm sorry," I said. "I'm trying to be mature here." The aroma of the coffee slipped into the living room area as the pot coughed and gurgled.

"You're doing an okay job. I just can't help but remember you the night I met you, seeing an outhouse for the first time."

I stood to go into the kitchen. "Don't remind me. Thayne said the Oglesbys are actually considering having indoor plumbing brought in."

"I'll believe it when I see it."

"Me too," I said. "Come prepare your coffee."

Rowena joined me.

"So, did you already go over to Charlotte and Milton's?"

"Mmmhmm. I was hoping to get out of the house before Charlotte pegged me to babysit on Friday, but no such luck." Rowena went to the refrigerator and pulled out the cream.

"Oh? You don't like to babysit?" I poured our coffee in the delicate china cups; part of the set Mama and Daddy had given us last Christmas.

"Those kids are wild things." She touched the rim of her cup with the tip of her finger. "These are pretty."

"The pattern is called 'Francine.' Made by Sango China out of Japan." I smiled. "I like the pretty pink rose with the gold and silver stems." I looked over my shoulder. "And look. It goes nicely with the sofa, don't you think?"

Rowena's eyes followed mine. "I guess. If you're into that kind of thing."

We took our coffee back to the sofa. "How's the wood-working going?" I asked her.

She nodded her head. I watched the blonde waves that tumbled to her shoulders bob up and down. "Good. There's a store in Hudsonville that started carrying my birdhouses."

"Really?"

"Yeah. The owner said he wants to introduce me one day to some man who owns a company up in Atlanta. He said the man would probably want to talk to me about designing a line or something like that."

"Rowena, that's wonderful news."

"Yeah," she said, then took a sip of her coffee.

"Just think, you could be a businesswoman one day."

"Beats being a wife," she said.

I was stunned. "What?" I lowered my coffee cup, gently holding it in place with both hands. "What did you say?"

"I'm sorry. I just . . . I mean, I don't intend to get married."

"But why? Being married is wonderful, Rowena. I can't imagine being anything *but* married. In fact, when I was your age—or just a little bit older—my parents were practically at war over what I was going to do after high school. Personally, I had no clue what I wanted to do, so you're one step ahead of me, but when I met Thayne—Reverend Scott—I knew immediately what I wanted out of life. He was everything and more than enough for me."

She sipped her coffee nonchalantly. "I'm going to graduate high school in a few months and then I'm going to check out my options with my woodworking. Who knows where it will take me, but as long as it takes me out of Logan's Creek, I don't care where my feet land."

I felt sad then. My friend—my only true friend in Logan's Creek—was looking forward to leaving. I'd not felt any kind of connection with any of the women here (though I had to admit Charlotte Knight made me laugh with her dramatic way of looking at life). I'd only felt a kinship with Rowena, and now she was telling me how anxious she was to leave.

The doorknob rattled then, causing both Rowena and me to look up as Thayne walked into the living room. He looked startled at first to see Rowena there, then nodded and said, "Rowena, how are you this evening?"

"Probably in need of leaving now," she said, handing me her half-emptied coffee cup and standing.

I stood too. "Oh, Rowena. Don't leave. Just because—"

But she was already shoving her arms in her coat sleeves. She pulled the ends of her hair out from beneath the collar; I watched it spill over her shoulders like a cascade of water over smooth stone. "Nah. Oscar will have a fit as it is." She worked the zipper up to her throat, then turned to me and said, "Thanks for the coffee."

"Thank you for stopping by."

I stood at the front door and watched as she disappeared up the path, to the gate, and then on around the side of Alma's house before I closed the door behind her. When I reentered the house, I found Thayne in the bathroom, brushing his teeth.

"Thayne," I said from the doorway.

"Mmm?" He spit into the basin then rinsed his mouth with a cupped handful of water.

"Have you ever noticed that Rowena doesn't look at you?"

He wiped his mouth with the towel hanging on the rod. "Yeah."

"You have?"

He locked his eyes with mine. "Yes, I have."

"Why do you think that is?"

Thayne sighed. "I don't know, Mariette." He pushed past me. I turned to find him closing the Venetian blinds and pulling the drapes together. "Maybe she's shy."

I couldn't think of a shy thing about Rowena Griffith. "I don't think that's it."

I watched as he pulled his shirttails from the waist of his pants then pushed his feet out of his shoes. "Do I smell coffee?"

"Mmmhmm."

Thayne turned toward the kitchen and out the door, leaving me standing in the doorway of the bathroom still, leaving me wondering what it was my husband was avoiding sharing with me.

And speculating what it had to do with Rowena.

30

The following morning, as we ate our breakfast of hot grits and butter, Thayne informed me that he was taking the car into Hudsonville.

"What's going on in Hudsonville?" I asked.

"I have a meeting with the school's superintendent."

I took a sip of my coffee from the Francine china cup. The morning sun, which was pouring between the ivy growing in the window, winked against the gold in the leaves and stem. "The superintendent?"

Thayne wiped at his mouth with the napkin clutched in his left hand and, just a moment before, held against his thigh. "He's talking to me about a job for next school term."

I felt an internal quiver, though whether it was optimistic or foreboding, I couldn't tell. "What kind of job?"

Thayne slipped another spoonful of grits into his mouth, his eyes focused on the Francine bowl before him. "You're getting pretty good at making grits," he said, then looked up at me. "One time, when you and I were at the Freemans' for Sunday dinner, and Charles and I were watching a game of baseball, I happened to mention that I played right field in high school . . . you know, and I mentioned some of my stats

. . . and . . . well . . . anyway, he said Hudsonville has a pretty good team, but they were losing a coach and . . ."

"You're applying for the job?" I leaned back in my chair. The baby inside my belly was awake and moving as if to get in on the conversation.

"I am." This time, Thayne shoved the spoon of grits into his mouth.

"You're leaving the ministry?" I placed a hand against the top of the swell in my abdomen and pressed. *Not now, baby. Be still.*

"Heavens, no."

"Then, I'm confused." I took a deep breath, then let it slip out between parted lips.

Thayne pointed to my stomach. "We can't live here, Mariette. Not once Junior comes."

"Junior? Thayne . . ."

He laughed lightly. "You know what I mean. You want a house, don't you? You don't want the baby sleeping in that tiny Pooh's Corner the rest of his life, do you?"

"No, but . . . how are you going to fit another job in? Between your work at the church and the cemetery . . . when will you have time for me? For us?" The baby kicked against my hand then. I wasn't sure if he was asking me to move my hand or affirming my thoughts.

"My visitation work at the church . . . I'm going to form a committee. It's time some of the others took on the work of guiding the flock." He wiped his mouth a final time, then stood and carried his dishes over to the counter by the sink. I turned in my chair to follow him. "If we have a committee of, say, four of the parishioners, the majority of my visitation work will be eliminated."

"Good," I said. "I hate it when you visit."

"Mariette." Thayne gave me his best look of rebuke.

I turned back in my chair. "Well, I do." There was good reason too. Once he'd visited an elderly member of the church in the hospital in Hudsonville. Just before time to leave, he asked if he could pray with her and her visiting family, had been granted permission, then stepped over to the head of the bed, laid his hand on the elderly woman's shoulder, and prayed. Unbeknownst to him, he was standing too close to a vital tube hooked to a nearby tank, and his knee, pressed against it, cut off the flow of oxygen. Although the patient survived both the lack of oxygen and the prayer, I worried for days that we'd be sued. Another time, after he'd visited another of Logan's Creek's elderly, we received a phone call that the man's favorite "huntin' gun" was missing. The call had come from Mr. Willoughby Sr., who'd been called by the man Thayne had visited. "Don't worry about it, Reverend," the church's patriarch said. "Fred Drummer is not known for being altogether there. I'm sure the gun will turn up."

But it never did—or at least we never heard that it did—leaving me wondering if Thayne was being fully trusted by his board and by the church's home office or not. Which reminded me . . . "Thayne, did you get a letter from the home office yesterday?"

Thayne returned to the table and sat in one fluid movement. "What do you know about that?" he asked, as though I were the one who'd taken Fred Drummer's gun.

The baby kicked again, this time so hard I winced. "This baby . . . Nothing. The envelope was placed in our personal box, and I gave it to Will Jr. to put in the church's, and I just wondered . . . why, what's the big deal?"

Thayne blew out a pent-up breath. "Nothing. It's just business."

"Does it have something to do with why you hardly ate last night?"

He stood again. "I need to wash up and get to Hudsonville." He placed a hand on my shoulder as he finished the conversation. "Don't worry, Mariette. I've got it under control."

He had *what* under control, I wondered the rest of the day, most of which I spent sitting on the sofa, watching one TV show after the other like some old indolent housewife. Early morning game shows gave way to afternoon soap operas, and in between were commercials that either made me feel like a lazy pig for not getting up and cleaning like all the good homemakers in the commercials or like a fat pig because my figure could no longer measure up to those of the models used to advertise products.

Does she or doesn't she? one commercial jovially asked. *Only her hairdresser knows for sure.*

I sneered; that model had a professional hair job, and anyone with an inkling of personal care knowledge knew it.

Nearing 3:30, just as an infectious voice announced, "This is Ed Chandler inviting you to tune in tomorrow and every weekday for *General Hospital*," the phone rang. I jumped as though caught doing something naughty, sprang as gracefully as a woman nearing seven months of pregnancy possibly could to turn the television off, then waddled to the kitchen and answered the phone. "Hello?" My bones were stiff from having hardly moved all morning. I pressed my fingertips between my lower back and hip and arched to knock out the kinks.

"Mariette?"

"Hi, Mama."

"What took you so long to answer?"

"I was sitting on the sofa watching—uh, I was sitting on the sofa and it just takes a while longer to get up these days." I faked a giggle.

"Oh."

"What's up?"

"You were on my mind . . . after your call yesterday . . . I've been worried."

"I'm okay." I turned to press my back against the countertop and leaned in to it.

"But what about Thayne?"

"Thayne's okay too. He's actually in Hudsonville right now . . ." I filled Mama in on what I knew, leaving out the part about the letter from the church's home office. "Won't that be something?" I asked, keeping my voice upbeat as I ended my explanation of Thayne's behavior. "Thayne a high school coach?"

"He'll work too hard," she said. "And you'll never see him."

"Don't worry, Mama. We're fine."

But even as I hung up the phone, I wondered if we were or not.

Another call came about an hour later. It was Thayne, calling from a pay phone at the county's school offices to tell me he'd be home in a half hour. "I didn't want you to worry," he said. "I know I've been gone all day."

To be honest, between the television watching and intermittent napping I'd done, I'd hardly noticed. "How'd it go?" I asked.

"Good. I'll tell you all about it when I get home. I'm starved. I didn't have lunch today."

I frowned. I not only hadn't thought about supper, I had nothing to prepare. "Thayne," I said. "I've kinda been laying down most of the day."

"Are you all right?"

"Just tired. The baby and all. It's nothing. Can you live with sandwiches and soup?"

"I could eat the can, I'm so hungry," he said.

I hung up, walked to the food cabinet, and opened the doors. There was nothing even resembling cans of soup. I would have to go to Stoddard's, and with Thayne using the car, I'd have to walk. A thought occurred to me then. I'd seen it on one of the commercials earlier in the day.

I called Stoddard's number. Minerva answered, and I boldly said, "Minerva, this is Mariette Scott. Do you deliver?"

"No," she said. "I'm sure your mother was used to having her groceries delivered, but we don't do things like that here in Logan's Creek."

My mother doesn't have her groceries delivered, I thought. At least, not that I knew of.

"I'm afraid I need some things and Thayne—Reverend Scott—has the car. My back is bothering me a bit today and—"

Minerva sighed into the phone. "You did just fine walking up here yesterday," she said.

"Minerva." I attempted to keep my voice calm. "I'm not sure what your problem is with me, but I need two cans of tomato soup, some sliced ham for sandwiches, some white bread, a tomato, and a head of lettuce. Do you think you could possibly, possibly bag those items up and send them my way?"

Another sigh was followed by, "Let me see what I can do."

I hung up the phone with a "gracious" then went to the bathroom to freshen up, after which I planned to make the bed.

I had just tucked the bedspread under the pillows when a knock came to the door. Answering it, I was surprised to see Oscar White standing on the front stoop, a brown bag stuffed with groceries cradled in his left arm.

"Oscar," I said, reaching for the bag and smiling at the sight of him. "Are you working for Stoddard's now?"

Oscar stepped over the threshold while still holding on to the groceries and without returning the smile. "I've got it," he said. "You may not need to be lifting anything quite so heavy."

I turned and watched him as he walked the bag to the kitchen counter, where the day's dirty dishes were still stacked, ready for washing. "I apologize for the mess," I said, feeling heat rush to my cheeks. "I've not felt well today and . . . well, I guess you know that already."

He looked at me then and pointed a finger, like a father scolding a child. "You need to be careful," he said. "We can't have the little mother risking the life of her unborn child, now can we?"

I felt my heart flutter, and I wondered if he knew about Rachel. Maybe, I thought, he was just being overly cautious. He was, after all, on the board of directors at the church. He probably thought of Thayne like a son, or if nothing else a kid brother. That would make me something akin to a daughter-in-law or a kid-sister-in-law.

My face must have registered my thoughts and concerns. The next thing I knew Oscar was standing beside me, steadying me, leading me to the sofa. "There ya go, now," he said.

I pressed the palm of my shaking hand against my forehead. "I don't know what's wrong with me today," I said. "I don't remember this from before."

"Before?" he asked. He seated himself in the white wicker rocker sitting catty-corner from the sofa.

I shook my head. "It's nothing."

"You've been in the family way before?"

I nodded. "I thought you knew. I thought that was why you said something about . . . Thayne and I had a child a few years ago. She died right after birth."

It seemed to me that Oscar's face didn't change one way or the other. He simply said, "I'm sorry to hear that, Mariette. We'll be praying for a happier ending this time."

I kept my focus on his eyes. They'd always held a twinkle, but tonight they seemed steely and cold. I shivered, though I wasn't fully aware of the movement or the reason for it. "Thank you," I said.

He clapped his hands together and stood. "I'd best be heading out," he said. He made his way to the door, opened it, then turned back to me. "Be sure to tell your husband I was here," he said, then left.

Thayne arrived home within minutes of Oscar's leaving and found me still sitting on the sofa where I'd been deposited. He shirked out of his overcoat as he looked from me to the bag of groceries and dirty dishes on the counter and back to me again. "What's going on here?" he asked. "You said you haven't felt well?"

I shook my head. The air in our home had changed, but I couldn't put my finger on when or why. Was it Thayne's actions— or lack thereof—over the last few days or was it Oscar's unplanned appearance?

I licked my lips and said, "No. I'm sure it's nothing. I'm mostly just tired."

Thayne joined me on the sofa, cupped his hand over my belly, and said, "Did you walk to town?"

"What? Oh no. I called Stoddard's and . . . Oscar White must have been there when I called because he brought the groceries I ordered."

Thayne's face turned pale and he leaned back. "Oscar was here?"

"Yeah. You just missed him." I blinked. "Thayne, is there a problem with Oscar? He was . . . I don't know . . . different than usual."

Thayne shifted his weight onto the cushion next to mine, rested his elbows on his knees, and cracked his knuckles before asking, "In what way?"

"It was weird. He was cold. I mean, he said all the right things. You know, about the baby and all. Even about Rachel—"

Fire came to Thayne's eyes. "Rachel? What does he know about Rachel?"

I jumped at Thayne's sudden outburst. "Nothing . . . I thought he knew and . . ." I felt tears stinging the backs of my eyes. "Thayne, what is it? What's going on?"

Thayne stood, walked over to the sack of groceries, and began to empty them onto the counter. "It's nothing, Mariette. Leave it alone."

I scooted to the end of the sofa then heaved myself off. "Is he holding your checks again?" I asked as I walked toward him. "Here, let me do that. I'll have dinner ready shortly."

Thayne stepped away, loosened his tie, and then came out of his suit coat.

"Is that it?" I asked again. "Is he holding your check?"

"He's held a few," Thayne answered. His voice sounded strained.

"Have you talked to anyone at the home office?" I pulled open a drawer, retrieved a can opener, and began to open the soup cans.

"Uh . . . yeah. But I have to be careful here." He jerked his head toward the bedroom door. "I'm going to wash up. At dinner I'll tell you about my trip to town." He took a step forward, then stopped, came back to me, and kissed my cheek. "By the way, I'm the new baseball coach."

31

Thayne was to begin work at the county's high school the following Monday.

On Sunday he preached to the congregation as he usually did, but this time his sermon was brooding, full of damnation. As he spoke his jaw was set, his eyes were cold. This was a Thayne I'd never seen before, and I was sure the community of Logan's Creek would rise up against him and demand his resignation as soon as the service was over.

Instead, for the most part, he received accolades for his message.

I stood next to him, outside the front doors of the church, as always after services, shaking hands with the members, the numbers of which had doubled since Thayne had come to preach. I listened, amazed, at their comments.

"Good service, Reverend."

"About time you brought a little hellfire into your talks."

Miss Carolyn seemed taken aback, though she smiled as she took my hand and said, "Goodness me. That was something, wasn't it?" And Miss Viola commented that "Reverend Scott reminded me this morning of a preacher we had back years ago. Many years ago."

We were invited to Charlotte and Milton's for Sunday dinner after church, which I dreaded. Mainly because I wasn't feeling well, and in part because I didn't want anyone else picking up on the dark cloud that seemed to hover over Thayne's head. Charlotte, of all people, would be sensitive to it; she seemed to pick up on everything.

But once we got to the Knight home, Thayne's mood lightened. He was his old self again. For the next few hours the tension that had built in my shoulders and chest over the past week seemed to dissipate. That evening, at home, his good humor continued.

On Monday morning Thayne got dressed for his work at the church. Before he left he kissed me hard, told me he loved me more than he could ever express, then ambled out the door to walk up Church Street.

At noon he returned home for lunch and to change into proper clothing for the high school and brought with him the dark cloud once more. I fed him in silence and then watched him change into sweats and sneakers, the laces of which he tied while sitting on the sofa. He looked up at me—I stood nearby, hands resting on the rise of my belly, and just stared and said, "I'll be back around suppertime."

"What will you be doing?" I ventured to ask.

"Not sure, to tell you the truth. I guess today will be more about getting to know the team and the team getting to know me."

I nodded.

He left. This time without the kiss.

The first Sunday in April Thayne preached a sermon on the love Jesus had for children, a lesson taken from Matthew 18:10.

"Take heed," he bellowed from behind the podium. "'Take heed,' Jesus said, 'that ye despise not one of these little ones; for I say unto you that in heaven their angels do always behold the face of my Father which is in heaven.'" Then he looked across the congregation, his eyes finally resting somewhere in the middle. "So let me ask you this today, are you following the command of the Lord Jesus? Are you treating your children as Jesus himself would do were he their parents?"

That night in bed, I snuggled as close to my husband as my swollen body would allow. "Thayne," I whispered.

"What, baby?"

Baby, I thought. It was the first endearment he'd used in days.

"Thayne, love me?"

He kissed the top of my head. "You know I do."

"No," I whispered. "I mean, will you *love* me. Make love to me. Now."

I heard him sigh. "Not tonight, sweetheart."

I arched my neck and looked up at him. "Why, Thayne? Why not? You haven't touched me in weeks. Is it because I'm fat and disgusting?" It had been this way when I was pregnant with Rachel, but back then Thayne had been so busy with school and work. This time, I couldn't comprehend the change in our relationship. Or in Thayne.

Thayne cupped the palm of his hand against my cheek. I watched his face; it was soft. Kind. "Mariette," he said. "I love you so much. I just . . . I have some things on my mind and . . . everything's okay, honey. I promise."

"I don't understand."

"Just sit tight. You will soon enough."

"When, Thayne." It wasn't a question.

His eyes squeezed shut. "Soon. Now, shhh. Get some sleep."

But sleep didn't come easy. Nor would it for some time.

On Tuesday, when the girls gathered at the cottage for their handwork lesson, we were one shy.

"Where's Rowena?" I asked.

Carla, a sweet girl with long brown hair and a sprinkling

of freckles across her nose, spoke from her seat at the dining table. "She was in school this morning, but then she got called into the office and I didn't see her after that."

"Where were you at the time?" I asked.

"English Lit. She didn't come back for her books or anything." Carla shrugged but didn't seem overly concerned.

"Maybe she was sick," Janice, another one of my girls, said.

Carla shook her head; the sunlight from outside the window shimmered copper in her hair. "Nah, I don't think so. Like I said, one minute she was there, the next she was gone."

"Well," I said, "let's get started, and maybe she'll show up later."

But she didn't. When the last of the girls left, I started slow-cooking rice on the stovetop, then went to the phone and dialed the Whites' number. Rose answered on the first ring.

"Rose? This is Mariette Scott."

"Oh. Hello, Mariette. How are you? I suppose Rowena is on her way home."

I felt a wave of fear and concern rush through me. "Actually, no. I . . . Rose, Rowena didn't come to the group today and . . . I thought maybe she was sick or something."

"What do you mean, she didn't come today?"

I wrapped one arm around my middle as though to do so would steady the quivering that had begun deep inside me. Something was wrong. Something was horribly wrong. "Rose, she didn't come to the group. Carla Evans said she was called to the office during English Lit and that she'd not returned, not even to get her books."

I heard the panic rising in Rose, even without her saying anything. "Oscar!" she bellowed. I heard Oscar's voice from somewhere nearby his wife. "Rowena didn't show up for the needlework group at the Scotts."

There was a rustling on the line, then Oscar White's voice came on, asking, "Who is this?"

"Oscar," I began, willing my voice to stay calm, all the while thinking, *Is this what it's like to be the pastor's wife? Involved in the lives of all those who call your husband "Reverend"?* "This is Mariette. Rowena didn't show and . . ." I retold the story, reiterating Carla's information, all the while hearing Rose weeping in the background.

There was a pause before Oscar said, "I'm sure she's fine. I'm sure it's nothing at all to worry about. *Rose, do you hear me?*" Rose mumbled something between sniffles, something that sounded a lot like *She's been so moody lately.* Oscar came back to our conversation by saying, "Thank you, Mariette. I'll call the Evanses' residence and see what Carla can elaborate on."

I hung up the phone but didn't move from my place in the kitchen, of resting my back against the countertop. I went over every word, every syllable, of conversation between Rowena and me as of late. Disappearing like this was something young lovers did when they'd planned an elopement. True, Rowena had asked questions about being married, but she seemed more set against it than for it. Besides, Rowena had sworn she was not involved with any of the boys, either here in Logan's Creek or in Hudsonville. She also seemed to have a plan, an exit plan, to graduate from high school, to discover her options with her woodworking.

Our front door opened, startling me. I gasped. "Thayne," I sighed.

He looked worn out. Barely into his second week of working three jobs and already he was frazzled. But his facial expression—of which I knew better than anyone—bore something more. Something heavier than mere fatigue. "Hi," he said. He didn't bother to come out of his coat. Instead, he walked over to the sofa and collapsed onto it. His elbows came to rest on his knees, his head in his cupped hands.

"Thayne?" I pushed away from the counter and walked toward where he sat. "Thayne?" I asked again.

He looked up at me; his eyes were watered down. "Sit down, Mariette," he said. "We need to talk."

I sat next to him. He took my hands in his. But before he could say anything, I said, "It's Rowena, isn't it." It wasn't a question. I knew. I didn't know what it was, but I knew it was something awful and it had to do with my young friend. She was hurt. She was sick. Or worse, she was dead.

"How'd you know?" His voice was raspy and strained.

"She didn't show up today. Carla said she was called out of English Lit and didn't return. Tell me, Thayne. Tell me. What is it? Why are you making me wait? Just say it. Say it!"

"But you don't know . . . you couldn't know . . . no."

I began to cry. "Know what, Thayne? For heaven's sake, please just tell me."

He sighed. His tongue took a swipe at parched lips. He hung his head then turned it enough to cut his eyes up to mine. "Rowena is gone."

My weeping became screams, gut-wrenching, feeling as though they were tearing through the core of me. My words were unrecognizable; they were not of this world. I felt Thayne's arms around me, his knee against my hip, the other leg around my lap as he tried to hold me in place, to stop my thrashing, to keep me calm.

I threw my head back as I cried out, "Oh, God! Why? Why did you take her?"

"Stop, Mariette." Thayne's voice was firm. "Stop. She's not dead."

I gulped as I pushed my husband away from me. "But you said . . ." I was angry and I was sure my face showed it. How could he have let me think . . . ?

Thayne grabbed my hands, clasped them together as though we were in prayer. "Listen to me." He kissed my hands. He breathed in deeply. Exhaled. "Listen to me," he said again.

"I'm listening, Thayne."

His eyes caught mine and I saw the seriousness they held. "Mariette, I've done something . . . something that could change everything for us. Rowena . . . I helped her, honey."

"Helped her what?"

"Get out of here. Out of Logan's Creek. She's gone, yes, but she's not dead, Mariette."

I jerked my hands out of his. "Why would you do that?"

"She had to go, to get out. I made all the arrangements, put her on a bus."

"A bus? My gosh! I know she wanted to get out, Thayne. She had a plan. Graduation. Woodworking." I stared at him. He said nothing. "She's a minor, Thayne! A *minor*! Oscar White will have you in jail! He'll have your job!" I pushed myself off the sofa, paced in front of my husband as I continued. "What were you thinking? Were you thinking at all?"

Thayne leaned back, his body stiff against the floral pattern of the sofa. He looked odd to me. A stranger and yet vaguely familiar as an older version of the boy I'd married. Older in years. More mature, perhaps, even than he should be at only twenty-four. "You have to listen to me, Mariette!" he bellowed. "He was *hurting* her."

"Hurting her?" I sat in the wicker chair. My breath came in shallow waves now. "Who hurt her?"

"Oscar." The name was hissed from Thayne's mouth. Elongated by several syllables. Spoken as though he'd said the name of Lucifer himself.

I could only stare at him. My thoughts ran amuck. How could Oscar hurt Rowena? Had he spanked her when she was a child? Did he beat her, maybe? No, no. Oscar White hardly appeared the type to lay a hand on his children. But Rowena wasn't his child. Not really. Then again, he'd raised her as his own. Didn't that count for something? Anything at all?

"Mariette." Thayne pulled my thoughts back to the room. He'd leaned forward again, elbows resting on knees, hands clasped between them. "Mariette, you know what I'm saying, don't you?"

"No."

"He's been hurting her, Mariette. Touching her. Treating her like his second wife."

"No," I said again, this time meaning something altogether different. "You're lying."

Fire rose to his eyes. "I wouldn't lie to you, Mariette."

I swallowed the bile rising to my throat. The tears began again, this time without any sound from my soul. "How long have you known?"

He cracked his knuckles. "A month, maybe more."

I gave him a hard stare. "And you didn't tell me?"

"I couldn't."

I said nothing. Then: "How is it that you knew and I did not? I was her friend."

"You still are."

"No." The smell of nearly cooked rice filled the room.

"The girl in college."

"What?" I felt the baby kick; he was awake now.

"Leslie was her name. The girl I dated in college."

"What does she have to do with this?"

The room had grown darker, it seemed to me. It must have felt that way to Thayne too. He reached over and turned on the table lamp to the left of the sofa. It cast light across half his face. The other half remained clothed in shadows. "You asked how I knew." He slipped out of his jacket and tossed it to the cushion beside him. He was in his gray sweats and maroon Hudsonville High School tee. The blond hair on his arms was wet with sweat. "I told you about her. When we first met."

"That she wanted to get married."

"It wasn't love she was after, Mariette. It was a way out. I realized it . . . almost too late. Look, I was a kid back then. She was pretty. She was . . . *willing*. There aren't many boys who could turn that kind of girl down, and I didn't feel God's call on my life. Not like now."

I didn't want to hear this. "Why are you telling me this now?"

"Listen. Okay?"

"I don't care for the details, Thayne." I'd always wondered if . . . and now I knew. Knowing, I wished for ignorance again. "I'd like to pretend I was your first, if you don't mind. You certainly know you were mine." The baby fluttered about, then settled.

He raised his palms toward me and pressed the cold air between us. "Don't make this about us, Mariette. You have to listen. Trouble is going to pour down on us within the next few days, and you need to know this story. Start to finish." He took a breath then blew it out. "Now, do you want to hear it or not?"

I told him I did, though deep down I wasn't altogether sure that was true.

"Good," he said. "I'm going to tell you everything. Then I want you to go into the bedroom and pack."

"Pack? For what?"

He looked at his watch then back up at me. "Your father will be here soon. He's coming to take you home. Back to Meadow Grove." He swallowed hard. "Where you belong."

32

For the next half hour Thayne poured out his story, leaving no stone unturned, explaining to me the relationship he'd had with Leslie, the relationship she'd had with her father, and how he'd come to recognize—finally—the dysfunctional relationship between Rowena and Oscar White.

"He's a man who thrives on control," Thayne said. "Holding my paychecks over my head unless I saw things his way, preached the sermons he wanted to hear, had the song service he felt best reflected those messages . . . these were clues. But there was something in Rowena's eyes. The lack of contact between hers and Oscar's, the way she kept hers downcast when I walked into the room."

"But you said Leslie was promiscuous. Rowena isn't."

"I've done some reading, though I have to tell you, there's not much out there. Some girls are like Leslie. They see a way out. Have sex, get pregnant, get married, get out. Never mind the list of problems marriage and unplanned babies might cause. Whatever they are, they're better than being used sexually by someone you live with."

"Thayne . . ."

"I'm sorry, honey. I'm truly sorry." We were sitting next to each other on the sofa now, clasping our hands together,

300

pleading with our eyes. "I'm just trying to be honest. To explain fully."

"Keep going, then."

"Okay. Others focus on being overachievers, appearing to be nothing shy of normal. Others develop some other plan to get out. They have the first step but not a single step more. These are the ones who end up on the streets, which I'm afraid is where Rowena would have landed."

"Her woodworking. She had hopes that her work would get her out of town. It makes sense now."

"Plan A is out for her because Rowena doesn't date."

"How do you know that?"

"I talked to her. One afternoon . . . I was getting ready to come home. I had turned out all the lights in the back of the church and was coming through the sanctuary when I saw her sitting there, back row left side, at the aisle. I walked up to her—it had been raining and she was plastered wet through and through—and when I asked her if she was all right, she just stared at me with those eyes of hers."

"Bette Davis eyes."

"Yeah." Thayne sighed. "Anyway, when I asked if she was all right, she said no she wasn't, and then I asked if she'd like to come back to my office. To talk. It was cold so I took off my coat and helped her into it. She kept her head down the whole time, all the way to the office, in the office. Just sat there with her head down, looking like a whipped dog."

"Poor Rowena . . ."

"I asked her if she had some sort of spiritual question I could answer or a prayer need. She shook her head no. She said she knew all the answers and that prayer was only for the weak. I said, 'And you are strong?' 'Yes,' she said. 'Stronger than you know.' I asked, 'What makes you so strong? So strong you don't need prayer with God?' She raised her head then and said, 'God doesn't hear my prayers, Reverend. But that's not why I'm here. I'm here because I like your wife and you seem like a nice guy. I'm here to tell you not to trust Oscar. He's not at all who you think he is.'"

"Just like that? No lead-up, just bam! Here it is?"

"Not on that part of it. I decided that for her to tell me something like that, I needed to know where she was coming from. I started asking her questions. About her life. Friends. Boyfriends."

I nodded. "And she has none."

"That's right. Oscar would have a fit if she did. But there was more; Rowena had distaste for men, even boys her own age. She wants nothing to do with parties or dances, and I noticed she often dresses *down* rather than up. She's beautiful, no two ways about it, but she does nothing to accentuate that beauty. She told me she was going to graduate from high school and get out of town, but then she looked down at her hands folded there in her lap and back up again and said, 'I'm never getting out of here, Reverend.'"

"How did you get her to admit it? About Oscar?"

"I told her I had a friend once, a girlfriend, who reminded me of her. I told her this girl's father did unspeakable things to her, mostly when he was drunk, which seemed to be more and more often as the days went by. Rowena told me then that drunk men do things like that, but sometimes good men—the kind who go to church and sit on boards and have office jobs—do things like that too. That's when I knew. I came right out and asked her." Thayne hung his head. "I have to tell you, Mariette. It took every ounce of courage I had."

I didn't say anything for a moment, then asked, "Where is she?"

"I can't tell you."

"Why not?"

"Because I don't know."

I pulled my hands from his and jerked back. The baby moved again; I wrapped my arm around my belly. "How can you not know? You're the one who pulled her out of class, aren't you?"

"Yes."

"So?"

"So, I pulled her out. I drove her to the bus depot and put her on a bus. She's heading to Atlanta, to the church's home office. From there they'll send her somewhere, but they won't tell me where. Somewhere where she will hopefully be able to finish high school, then get a job and have a fairly decent life." He breathed out heavily. "The odds are still against her, Mariette. But they're a heck of a lot better than if she stayed here."

I swallowed back reality. "I'll never see her again."

"Maybe. Maybe not."

I stood then, and Thayne stood with me. He reached for my hand, but I pulled away. "Don't, Thayne. You've known this for how long and you didn't tell me. I can't forgive you right now for that. You've obviously told the people in Atlanta and you've told my father. But you didn't tell me. Me. Your wife. Rowena's friend." I raised a hand and took a ragged breath. "I have to go pack now." I walked halfway to the bedroom, then turned. "How are you going to tell Oscar White this?"

"Simple. I'll make a phone call. Tell him I put Rowena on a bus to nowhere and that if he has any sense, he'll let it go. I'll tell him I know the truth about him, that I want his resignation from the board—that the home office expects it—and that the only reason he's not being prosecuted is that Rowena swore she'd kill herself if I went to the law. I'll tell him he can tell his wife and family whatever he pleases and that maybe, one day, Rowena will contact her mother. Then I'll tell him that if he has an ounce of decency, he'll beg God to forgive him and get help, wherever that might come from."

"God," I said, then snorted. "Can God forgive him for this, Thayne?"

"Yes, Mariette. As hard as it is to understand, he can. And he will. If Oscar will just ask."

I blinked. "I would have never guessed, I don't think. He seemed like such a nice man, most times."

Thayne said nothing in reply.

I took another step toward the bedroom door, turned again and asked, "Do you think Rose knows? Even a little?"

Thayne stared at me for a moment. His face was expressionless while his eyes showed exhaustion. "I don't know."

I nodded. "Okay, then," I said, then went into the bedroom to pack my clothes.

I understood everything and nothing. My head was moving forward while my heart screamed to go back. Back to Meadow Grove and the days before we'd come to Logan's Creek. Back to Thayne and me the way we were when we were newly married, living in the apartment, or even living with Aunt Harriett. But then my heart rushed forward. Forward to this town and these people who, though I hardly understood them, I had come to have affection for. Forward to believing in my husband's mission to come here, the passion he had, and then standing beside him in that, no matter what. Come what may.

There was a chance, he said, he could be arrested, should Oscar challenge him.

"Will he?" I'd asked.

"God alone knows what that man is capable of," he replied.

When Daddy arrived, my suitcase was packed and standing next to the front door. Daddy shook Thayne's hand, told him he was doing the right thing, and that even though he knew it had to have been a difficult decision, it was one Daddy was proud of on his behalf. "You're more man now than you've ever been," Daddy said. Then he turned to me and said Mama was looking forward to having me at home, for however long I needed to be there, and that he knew this wasn't going to be easy on my part and that he was proud of me too. "I know you love your husband," he said. "You aren't leaving him, Mariette. You're protecting yourself and your child."

Thayne walked us to the car, shook Daddy's hand one last time, then walked me to the back passenger door, which he opened to place my luggage inside. Daddy slipped into the car as Thayne closed the door and then wrapped me in his arms as best he could. But our child was not the only thing coming between us at the moment. For me, it was everything that had occurred in the last few years. His decision to put God before me. Before our marriage. His choice to move me to this town, where my acceptance had come only after I'd conceived once again. And finally, his keeping from me the awful truth about Rowena. About Oscar. About the filthy things he had done to her.

Still, when he kissed me—long and hard, like a man drowning and gasping for air—I kissed him back with the same passion as I'd always shown. It was the one thing we had in common, this passion. Everything else was a mystery. Thayne's outgoing ways shadowed my somewhat reclusive ones. His love for God outweighed my indifference. But passion, the good Lord knew, we had.

When Thayne broke the kiss, his hands cupped my face and he brought my forehead to his. His breathing was ragged and so was mine; the condensation of warm air meeting cold formed clouds between us. He spoke finally, saying, "I love you so much."

"I love you too." I did. I loved him. I just didn't understand him anymore.

"I'll call in the morning," he said. Then he pushed my head back so as to make eye contact. "I know you don't pray much, Mariette, but pray for me now. I need it more than ever."

I nodded, still aware of his fingertips spread wide against my skull, his thumbs at my cheekbones, catching my tears. "I will. I promise."

He gave me a swift kiss, then added, "I've got something for you." He dipped his hand into his coat pocket then pulled it out again. With the other hand, he took my left, then slipped his grandmother's wedding ring—the one he'd given me before telling me he was going to seminary, the one that had been too big and that I'd never worn—onto my third finger.

"It fits," I whispered.

He snorted, his eyes twinkled, and he said, "That little bit of extra weight you're carrying, I'd wager. But after you have the baby, we'll have it resized." He kissed the ring then. "Wear it, Mariette. And don't ever let me, or what it stands for, go."

I shook my head. "I won't."

Then he opened the front passenger door and eased me into the car. Leaning down, he looked past me and toward my father. "Take good care of her, sir."

"Thayne," Daddy said with all seriousness, "you know I will, son."

Then Thayne closed the door and Daddy backed out of the driveway. All the while I watched the figure of my husband, standing there alone in the cold, hands shoved into the pockets of his coat. When the car's back wheels hit the road, Daddy turned the steering wheel hard right, easing the car onto the street. I rolled down my window, raised my hand to give a silent wave good-bye. Thayne pulled one hand out of his pocket and did the same.

Just as Daddy put the gear shift to drive, I caught movement at the side window of Alma Stoddard's dining room. Thayne saw it too. He looked back to me and I to him. Even with the distance, I knew our eyes read the same.

Mrs. Stoddard had witnessed the whole thing.

33

Oscar White was arrested two days later, but not for abusing Rowena.

He was arrested for beating up Thayne. Word came to me through my parents, who'd been called by the church's main office in Atlanta. They'd been called by Edward Oglesby, who'd been called by the sheriff from Hudsonville.

I'd been napping when Daddy came into my room, with Mama close at his heels. Sensing their presence, I opened my eyes. Startled, I sat up and asked, "What happened? What is it?"

Daddy cleared his throat and gave me the news. "He held his own," he said finally. "From what I understand, this White isn't in any better shape than Thayne."

I swung my legs over the side of the bed. "I have to go to him," I said. "Daddy, get the car ready."

But Daddy grabbed my arm and, drawing me to him, said, "No, sweetheart. Thayne said you are to stay here."

I looked up at my father, saw the steeliness in his eyes, and knew he had no intention of allowing me to leave Meadow Grove. "Where is he?" I asked.

"He's in the hospital in Hudsonville and promised to call you later today. I spoke to his doctor there—a Dr. Kathleen

Meredith, who says to tell you hello, by the way—and she assures me he will mend just fine and that you don't need to be there right now."

"Why not?"

Mama stepped around Daddy and answered, "Apparently your little Logan's Creek is in quite the upheaval right now, Mariette. Thayne spoke to Dr. Meredith and explained everything to her, and she explained to us . . . about the ripple effect on the town." She touched my arm. "It's best you are here. I know it won't be easy, but it is best."

I looked at my father. "Then, Daddy, you go. Go help him."

But Daddy shook his head. "I offered, sugar. But Thayne's his own man now."

I went downstairs and into Daddy's office, sat in his chair and waited for the promised phone call from my husband, which did not come for another two hours. He sounded weak but confident still that he'd done the right thing. He was assured that Rowena was safe, he said, so it didn't matter that he'd had the "hound beat out of" him.

"Thayne," I whispered into the phone. "I can't bear being away from you now. You need me there."

"I don't, Mariette. I don't need you here. I need you to stay out of this and to take care of yourself and the baby. This isn't over yet, not by a long shot."

"Thayne." I said his name again as though repeating it brought us closer in distance. "Does Rose know the truth?"

"I don't think so. I honestly hope not. I hope no one knows . . . for Rowena's sake. She might want to come back one day." He paused. "I'm not real sure of the effects something like this has on a mother-daughter relationship, either. I'd hate for Rowena to lose that too."

I leaned my elbows onto the shiny surface of my father's desk. "I've been thinking about that, Thayne. Do you think . . . maybe she knew? She knew and didn't do anything about it for . . . I don't know . . . whatever reason a mother wouldn't do anything in this case?"

I heard Thayne sigh, then answer, "I hope not, Mariette. For the sake of her soul, I hope not."

I blinked. "But God can forgive that?"

In my mind I saw him smiling—face battered and bruised, lips curled higher on one side than the other—into the phone. "Yes, Mariette. God can forgive that."

I leaned back then in Daddy's chair, swiveled it around toward the rear wall of the room, and said, "That's just as difficult for me to understand, Thayne. How could a father do such a thing? How could a mother let him? And how could God be so willing to forgive the heinousness of the crime of abuse and neglect?"

"Because he is a God of love, Mariette." I heard him swallow. "Honey, what's the worst thing you ever did in your whole life?"

I had to think about that. I'd never been what I would call a saint, but I'd not been a high-ranking sinner either. "I used to fight with Tommy a lot when we were little," I said. "I guess that counts as a sin?"

"I hardly think God is holding that against you." I thought I heard him wince, but he continued anyway. "I mean as an adult. Conscious sin."

My answer came to me quickly. "I lied to my parents about seeing you."

I heard a faint chuckle. "Somehow I knew that was coming."

"It's true."

"I know it is. Have you asked God to forgive you for that lie or *those* lies?"

I said I had not; I hadn't thought to do so.

"You should," Thayne said. "Sin is sin, Mariette. Your white lies and Oscar's child abuse are both black and ugly in God's eyes."

"I hardly think you can compare my fibbing to Mama and Daddy to what Oscar White did."

There was a long pause before he answered. "In all honesty, Mariette, I can't. Not me personally, anyway. I'm not hammered out that way. But I'm not God either."

"No," I said.

The ensuing silence did more than separate us in time. It reminded me again that this one thing—this one very important thing—which was of such importance to Thayne, was an absolute mystery to me.

I called Missy the following morning to tell her I was in town and why; she insisted I drive myself over pronto to see her. "I'd come to you, but with this brood . . ." Then she laughed. "Your mother would skin me alive if I brought them all over."

She probably would. I told Missy I'd be over after lunch. Then I went to tell Mama, who said she wasn't altogether sure I should be driving.

"I'll be fine. Besides, I need to spend some time with Missy. She has a way of putting things into proper perspective for me."

Mama frowned. "I suppose," she said, dismissing any further comments.

I took Mama's car—the family car—to Missy's. I drove slowly, taking in the old sights and sounds of home. As I looked from one landmark or Main Street shop to the next, I found myself thinking about Logan's Creek's small collection of businesses. As I passed the Piggly Wiggly, stretched out and boasting a façade with the two words of the store's name separated by a smiling pig in a white butcher's cap, I thought suddenly that I missed Stoddard's with its handmade signs, and oddly I even missed Minerva, who was probably even at this moment resting her hip against the counter, sharpening her nails. I wondered again what it was about me that Minerva didn't like, wishing I'd worked a little harder to get to know her. Clarence was certainly likable enough. Why not his wife?

As the car eased down the roads and streets, passing people standing in clusters or walking along their way, I started searching for familiar faces among them, but there were none. In Logan's Creek, I thought, you rarely saw anyone you didn't know.

A traffic light up ahead turned red, and I slowed the car, stopping directly in front of our church. I turned my neck to study it. Large. Rambling. Old stone walls and a bell tower that pealed out a tune every weekday at noon and on Sundays at 10:45, calling the members to worship. Inside, long pews boasted velvet-cushioned seats and floors made of shiny terrazzo. Not like Logan's Creek's small church. The seats were hard and worn, the floors scarred.

I sighed. The light turned green, and suddenly I found myself outside the town and heading toward Missy and Ward's country home. *Now this*, I thought, *reminds me of Logan's Creek*. Thick foliage and narrow roads.

I turned off the newly installed air conditioner and rolled down my window, breathed in the warm fresh air, then threw back my head and gasped back tears. By the time I pulled into Missy's driveway, I was nothing short of a mess.

She must have been waiting by the window because I'd no sooner shoved the car into park than she ran out, arms stretched wide, looking tanned and more beautiful than I'd ever remembered. I stumbled from the car, taking no more than three steps before she'd wrapped me in as tight a hug as my body would allow. "Oh, Mariette. Mariette. You're okay, honey. You're here now. Here with me." I shook against her as great sobs wracked through me, and I half-wondered how it was she—such a tiny thing—could even hold me up.

"Oh, Missy!" I cried. "You have no idea . . . no idea . . ."

"Come on inside," she said, slipping her arm around my

shoulder and drawing me toward the house. "Now, you and I are going to sit out by the pool and drink Coca-Colas and talk and laugh and scream, and it'll all be okay before you head back to your mama's."

"Promise?" I sniffled.

"I promise," she said. "You just wait and see."

Missy's children—all four of them—were scattered about the house. I couldn't believe how grownup Ward's oldest—now thirteen—had become in the months since I'd seen him. Her three youngest ranged in age from eighteen months to four years. The two younger ones were napping while the older pair were sprawled out on the den floor, watching television.

"I'm going to be outside with Mrs. Scott," she informed them. "Cookies and milk only, you hear?"

"Yes, ma'am," they both chimed as Missy led me to the patio, where two Coca-Cola bottles were perched atop the umbrella table, next to a large bucket of ice and two gold-colored tumblers. The pool's water shimmered in the sunlight, its blue-green color interrupted only by a child's pink inner tube that bobbed at the edge of the shallow end.

I sighed as I closed my eyes and tilted my face toward the sun. "My goodness, it feels good to be back here."

"Sit," Missy said. "I've got Coke, but if you want anything else . . . I know with all three of mine, all I wanted toward the end was Coke and peanuts."

I smiled at her. "Coke is fine."

As we sat she asked, "Do you want some peanuts?"

"No," I said. "I just want to sit here and soak all this up." I squinted an eye at her. "You know, all the way over here, I found myself comparing Meadow Grove to Logan's Creek, thinking that I have somehow, insanely, fallen in love with that little place and all her quirky people."

Missy laughed as she poured our drinks. "How are the Stoddard ladies?" She extended my Coke to me.

I took a sip, then said, "Oh, Alma's not so bad . . . I guess something about me being pregnant broke the animosity. But Minerva is just as put out with me as she's ever been."

"One of these days I'm going to have to come to Logan's Creek," Missy said. She looked out past the pool and toward the lake. "I think it's time for me to meet these people."

I didn't say anything. Missy in Logan's Creek was just about as odd as me in Logan's Creek.

"A penny for your thoughts," she said from the opposite side of the shaded table.

"I'm just thinking what a slap in the face I must have been for them, is all."

"In what way, Mariette?" She crossed one slender brown leg over the other.

"Look at you," I said. "You look more like a high school cheerleader, what with your hair all pulled up in a ponytail and tied off with a ribbon. And *how* have you managed to stay so slim, even after three children?"

Missy threw back her head. "Have three children of your own, plus one teenager in the house, and you won't have to ask that. And as for this ponytail, it's called 'quick and easy,' my friend." She furrowed her brow. "But that can't be what you were thinking about."

I shrugged. "Sort of. I was thinking that you and I come from a different place than most of the people in Logan's Creek. Other than Charlotte Knight, I mean. I think maybe I stood out from the get-go. Not Thayne, though. Thayne is just a good old farm boy, and they knew it the minute they met him. But people like us, Missy, like you and me, we were born with that proverbial silver spoon in our mouths and there's really no way to get it out."

"Why would you want to?"

I took another sip of my cold drink, let it ease down my throat in that stinging yet refreshing way it has, then answered, "To fit in."

Missy wisely stayed quiet. She swung her crossed leg a little as she nursed the drink held loosely in her hand. Finally she said, "How is Thayne?"

"Okay. He's home. He says all the ladies are trying to mother him, but Alma has gained and maintained full control over the situation." I snickered. "I can just imagine she has."

"And his injuries?"

"He's going to be all right. No broken bones, only bruises and some swelling."

"That must make you feel a little relieved."

I drained the last of my drink and returned the sweating tumbler to the table. "I tried to be insistent that I was going back, but he won't hear of it. He said until we know, really know, how the people are going to react to all this . . . a board member arrested for beating up the pastor. I can't say that I blame him, not wanting to take any chances with this baby."

"Has he heard from Rowena? Do you know?"

I blinked then shook my head. "No, I don't know. If he's heard anything from her—anything at all—he's keeping that from me too."

Missy stared at me for a moment before saying, "You have to forgive him for this, you know, Mariette."

Again I shook my head. "No. I love him so much, Missy. But I'll never forgive him for keeping this from me." I looked down at my belly just as the baby performed a somersault. "It was tantamount to a lie."

"It's his job, Mariette. As a pastor—"

"He is my husband *first*," I said, cutting her off.

Missy stretched her arm across the table, hand up. "Oh, honey," she said.

I slipped my hand into hers, and she squeezed. "I guess I've still got a lot to learn, don't I, Missy?"

"We all do."

"I mean if I'm going to be a pastor's wife for any true length of time."

Missy shifted in her seat, drawing her hand away from mine. She pressed her elbow against the tabletop then rested her chin on the pad of her palm. "You still don't get it, do you?" she asked. "What it is about God that drives Thayne with such passion."

"No," I said. "I've listened to his sermons, been to all the Sunday school classes, and heard all the stories, but I've yet to *feel* anything, Missy." I sighed. "Oh, Missy, what is wrong with me?"

Her back straightened as her head came up and her arm dropped to the table. "Not a thing." Then she winked. "Do you know what I think? I think it's the old 'fitting in' thing again."

"What do you mean?"

"You never felt as though you fit in at Saint Margaret Mary and you felt that you stopped fitting in here, and then you met Thayne. With Thayne you totally belonged. He didn't care who you were or where you were from; he just loved you to pieces. Then he goes and gives his life totally to God and is called into a life you don't understand. Once again, Mariette is on the outside looking in."

"That's so true," I said, my voice whisper soft. Tears stung at the back of my eyes as Missy continued and I listened.

"Logan's Creek. Once again, you're the outsider. The pastor's wife who can't fry a chicken." She smiled at me then, and I in turn giggled.

"See, Mariette, God has a family. Yahweh is our Father. Jesus is our Brother. And we're all brothers and sisters *in him*. But you don't think you belong. You somehow believe that you *should* be on the outside looking in, rather than inside the family home, enjoying the party." She took a breath. "Do you want to know what else I think?"

I wasn't sure, but I nodded anyway. "I think you know

all that; you just don't know how much God loves you and wants you inside the house." Her face was as serious as I'd ever seen it. "But one day you're going to see a door swing open and God standing there, and you're going to run to him, Mariette. You're going to run inside the house."

34

I remained in Meadow Grove for the next two months, not because I wanted to and not because being in Logan's Creek held any danger.

Mama had made an appointment for me to see Dr. Franklin, who was now in semi-retirement but whose son Dr. Rodney Franklin was working full time and alongside his father. I told Mama I wasn't altogether comfortable seeing anyone but Dr. Franklin Sr., though truth be told, most of my resistance came from remembering Rodney from my earlier days in school. He was older than I, but not by enough to count.

Still, Mama insisted, and so off we went for a late Friday afternoon appointment, just after my return from Missy's.

Dr. Rodney—as I soon learned he liked to be called, so as to separate his name from his father's—went over the records from my pregnancy with Rachel, then left the room and returned some time later to tell me he'd just had a long conversation with Dr. Meredith. "She and I agree," he said.

"About what?" I asked. I was still sitting on the examination table, draped in a light blue cotton gown and covered by a pink blanket. Dr. Rodney stood before me, back against the closed door, the metal chart holder stuffed with papers in his hand.

"About your not traveling back to . . . where was it again?" He looked down at the chart as he flipped it open, searching his notes. I noticed then a small circle forming at the crown on his head. Like his father, he would be half bald one day. But, like his father, it wouldn't detract from his good looks, sharp features, and muscular physique. The thought of being undressed and exposed to him was nearly more than I could comprehend. Pregnant or not.

"Logan's Creek," I supplied.

He flipped the chart shut. "That's right," he said.

I sighed. "And why is that?"

"Mariette . . . do you mind if I call you that?" He laughed lightly, exposing two dimples in his tanned cheeks. "I can hardly think of you, little Mariette Puttnam, as Mrs. Mariette Scott, to be honest."

I felt my brow raise. "To be honest with *you*," I said, "I can hardly think of you as Dr. Rodney Franklin."

"Touché." He winked at me, I suppose in hopes of helping me to relax.

It had the completely opposite effect. "So, back to Logan's Creek . . ."

"That's just it. We don't think you should go back to Logan's Creek."

"But, why?"

"The risks involved. Dr. Meredith and I both think the chances of your having the same complications as before are slim, but they are there just the same, and better safe than sorry, right? Meadow Grove has more to offer than . . . where did she say she was located . . ."

"Hudsonville."

"Yes, that's right," he confirmed.

I squared my shoulders. "Not to be argumentative," I said, "but being here in Meadow Grove didn't save Rachel's life, now, did it?"

He crossed his arms and sighed. "You're right, Mariette.

But still, we think it's best. You'll just have to trust us on this, okay?"

Mama—whom I'd left in the waiting area—was for it, of course. She practically danced in the driver's seat all the way home. At dinner, Daddy said it was practical, and on the phone later that evening, Thayne said he didn't want to think of not being together for two months, but he had to agree.

I was left, as usual, the odd "man" out.

"You'll come here," I said to Thayne. "Right?"

"As much as I can, sweetheart," he answered. It wasn't what I wanted to hear, but it was honest.

Thayne called on Sunday afternoon to tell me he'd started a new series of sermons from the book of Joshua, then encouraged me to read them for myself. "I'm heading for chapters 7 and 8," he said. "Sin in the camp costs Joshua and his army the lives of innocent men and the first battle at Ai."

"Thayne, you might as well be speaking Greek to me," I said with a sigh.

"Or, Hebrew, huh?" he joked back.

"So what are you getting at?" I asked, leaning back in Daddy's office chair.

"When God sent Joshua and his army into the Promised Land, he told them not to take anything for themselves, and that they would always have victory in war. But this guy named Achan didn't listen. He took some sacred objects, thereby bringing sin into the camp, if you will. The next battle—the fight against the city of Ai—was lost to them. Sin in the camp will always bring defeat. That's what I'm preaching."

"I see," I said. "Well, you seem pretty excited about it. I take it this has something to do with Oscar?"

"It sure does. As far as I'm concerned, Rowena was a sacred thing, and Oscar White took her for himself. God won't stand for that kind of behavior from his people. Eventually, this church would have collapsed had it not been for cleansing it of him."

I tried to take in his words, but it was difficult for me. I wished so badly that it wouldn't be that way, but it was. "Have you heard anything more about Oscar?" I asked, changing the subject.

"Rose wasn't at church today," he said. "I'm going to go out there and talk to her tomorrow. Kinda feel the whole thing out. Let her know I don't hold her responsible for her husband's actions. Her own are another matter."

"And Oscar?" I asked again.

Thayne was quiet before answering. "I'm going to Hudsonville later today to see him, Mariette."

I sat up straight. "Have you lost your mind, Thayne Scott?"

"No," he answered. "It's what God would have me do."

God again. That one thing that always kept us separated, one way or another. "I'll never understand this, Thayne. Never." I felt myself grow tense and stubborn.

Thayne must have felt it too. "I know you don't, Mariette. Maybe one day." Then he sighed. "I love you. I'll talk to you later tonight."

And with that, he hung up.

There would be no jailhouse confessions from Oscar White. He wouldn't even see Thayne or talk with him.

Rose, on the other hand, was full of words. Venomous words. She told Thayne in no uncertain terms that Oscar had told her of the insane and sick accusations he had made against her husband, that she believed not a single word of them, and that Rowena was an often difficult, headstrong, and imaginative child. "She'd make up anything to leave Logan's Creek," she said. "She never wanted to be here, never loved Oscar the way he deserved to be loved, and never truly got over not being an only child."

After Thayne relayed the conversation to me, I hung up the phone, went upstairs to my bed, and cried. In part because now, with her words of doubt, I was left to wonder if Rowena might have made it all up, just to get out of Logan's Creek, the little town *I* couldn't wait to get back in to.

Over the next few weeks, as I grew in size physically, Thayne was happy to report that, just as he'd suspected, the attendance at the church had increased. At first, he said, people came to see the pastor who'd been beaten up by his parishioner. Then, he said, they returned because he was getting better and better at preaching.

"I can just feel it," he said.

To which I laughed. "Don't get so full of yourself," I warned. "That just might bring sin back into the camp."

"Hey," he said, nice and slow. "You should be a preacher." To which we both laughed.

But we didn't laugh when he told me that Oscar had been released from jail after being sentenced to a fine and some community service. "Don't worry about me, though," Thayne said. "He and Rose have packed up the boys and moved away. I have no clue as to where."

It was for the best, I figured.

Of course the community wondered what had really transpired between Thayne and Oscar, but Thayne never shared the truth with anyone other than me. "Charlotte Knight is suspicious," he said. "What with Rowena being gone. But all she has is her female intuition, and eventually she'll put her suspicions to rest."

No, she won't, I thought. But that much I kept to myself.

Thayne did hear that Rowena had made it to Atlanta and that, from there, she'd been sent to live with some of the church family in Tennessee. The reports were that she was doing well and that, in time, we'd hear from her again.

Thayne felt relatively sure this was true; but I wondered. Rowena wasn't one to just "get over" anything, I knew. She was lovely and funny, but she was also tough as nails.

Thayne came only once to Meadow Grove. Between the church, the cemetery, and the high school, his ability to cut loose was just shy of nil. But he wrote every day and called several times a week, and always on Sunday afternoon.

It was, he said, our time.

35

2:35.

I waited, resting against the ladder-back chair for a moment, then reached for the knob on the transistor radio—white, of course—that sat perfectly straight on the right back corner of the desk. I flipped it on. Brief static was replaced by the clear voice of Connie Francis cooing "Who's Sorry Now?"

The irony wasn't lost on me.

I switched the radio off. "Oh, Lord, help me." I whispered a prayer. "If I've ever meant anything to you at all, help me."

I stood without waiting for a divine answer, walked over to the window, and peered down to the thick carpet of grass stretching from the white frame of the house to the sidewalk out front and driveway to the right, where my brother Tommy was washing an old jalopy he'd purchased with the money he'd earned as an usher down at the Liberty movie theater. I looked past my own reflection—the dark blonde hair pulled taut, the ghost of a face in spite of the extra pounds I carried, the full lips that, without lipstick, disappeared into peachy skin—and smiled at him. Sensing my stare, I suppose, he looked up and waved, soapy suds running down the length of his tanned and muscled arms.

When did he get to be so handsome? So grown up?

He motioned for me to come down and join him, but I shook my head then shuffled away from the window and toward the closet where my purse, draped with a pair of gloves I'd worn to town that morning, hung on the glass knob. I pulled them off the purse and slipped them onto my hands, adjusting one finger at a time while humming a familiar tune. Without thinking about it, the humming gave way to its lyrics.

The tears began. I choked as I continued, this time speaking rather than singing. "Come with me . . . for thee . . . I *love*."

Oh, Thayne! How do I get to where you are?

I closed my eyes against the pain returning yet again from deep within, took a deep breath, and exhaled as I'd done earlier. I opened my eyes, looked down at my watch, then slipped the strap of my purse over my wrist. I stepped over to the desk and reached for the pen still lying across the open diary.

I leaned over the desk and penned "2:57." Twenty-two minutes.

"Time to go," I whispered. I closed the diary and slipped it into the purse. I wet my dry lips with the tip of my tongue, took one more deep breath, and then ambled toward the door as a lingering question pounded from deep within.

I slipped down the stairs unnoticed, into Daddy's office and over to his desk, where a cluster of keys hung from a single ring. I cupped them in my hand so they wouldn't jangle, then studied them, hoping to spot the one that went with the family car. None of them looked the part. I set the keys down on the desktop and sighed.

Mama and Daddy, I knew, were napping. Sunday afternoons were made for that, and for long family drives, Daddy always said. I wouldn't wake them. I sat in Daddy's chair for a few minutes to think. What I needed now, what I needed most, I would ask my younger brother for. I walked out the back door and over to the driveway, where Tommy was putting away the rags and bucket.

"She's a beaut, isn't she?" he asked. His eyes twinkled with pride toward the hunk that needed way more than a washing to be called "a beaut." But, I supposed to Tommy, she was an absolute Cadillac.

"Tommy, do you mind if I borrow her?" I asked. "I just need to run an errand." I took in a deep breath, exhaled.

"Well . . . I mean, I was gonna meet some of the guys down at the Bean."

I laid a hand on his wet arm. "Tommy, please. I promise I'll make it up to you. I'm not sure how exactly, but I will. I just . . ."

He gave me a hard look, then. I'd never seen such maturity and compassion rise up in his face before, but there it was. My little brother, a man. "You're going to Thayne, aren't you?"

My hand slipped from his arm as I nodded. "Please don't tell."

He looked back at the house. "You're not telling Mama or Daddy?" he asked, shifting his eyes back to me.

I shook my head.

"Should you drive that far?" His eyes fell to my belly. "In your condition?"

"Probably not, but . . . I just have to get to my husband, Tommy."

His eyes locked with mine. "Then I'll drive you," he said.

"No! I can—"

Tommy pulled the car keys from the pockets of his jeans and said, "Either I drive you, or you go inside and tell Daddy you want to borrow the family car."

"Your T-shirt is wet." It was a statement of acquiescence.

"Give me five minutes to change."

"Okay," I said. He started to walk away, but I placed my hand on his arm again. "Leave a note on the kitchen counter for them, okay?"

"Sure, sis." He winked and was off.

I slipped into the warmth of the front passenger seat and closed the door quietly behind me. Waiting, I ran my hands around my distended middle as it drew to a peak, and forced breath from my lungs to keep from crying out. A look at my watch told me it was now 3:15. Maybe 3:16; my vision was blurring.

"You can do this," I said. "Missy's deliveries always took at least twenty-four hours, so you can do this." I pulled the diary out of my purse.

Within a few minutes Tommy rejoined me, pushed the key into the ignition, turned it, and listened as the engine purred. "She's such a lady," he said, patting the dashboard, which made me laugh.

"Do you know where you're going?" I asked when the car came to a stop at an intersection a block from the house.

"No," he answered. "But I have an idea you're going to tell me."

"Do you have a map in the glove compartment?" I asked, reaching for it.

"Nope," he said.

I leaned back again. "Well, for heaven's sake, why not? This is a car; it should have a map of the state of Georgia in it."

He gave me a sidewise glance. "But I wasn't planning on driving all over the state of Georgia. Everywhere I was planning on going, I knew how to get to."

Well, if that didn't just make sense . . .

I gave him the directions as best as I could recall them, feeling fairly confident we were heading in the right direction, keeping my eye on the path of the sun in the afternoon sky. Wherever it was headed was west.

The opposite of where we were heading.

We pulled over two hours into the drive, at the same restaurant where Thayne and I had stopped our first trip to Logan's Creek, because Tommy declared he was starving to death. He ordered a fried chicken plate, heaping with mashed potatoes and green peas. When I told the waitress I wasn't hungry, Tommy looked at me funny.

"Since when aren't you hungry? Man, lately you've practically eaten us out of house and home."

"That's rude, Thomas," I said. Then, to keep him from being too nosey, added, "I'm just not wanting to eat and have another two hours in the car. You know . . . this baby does crazy things to my digestive system."

Tommy paled. "Just don't go throwing up in my car, you hear?"

With a smile I promised him I wouldn't. Throwing up was the last thing I was worried about, though. The contractions were coming faster now, no more than ten minutes apart and consistent. So far I'd managed to keep myself from crying out with the pain, but I knew from having done this once before that if we didn't get to Logan's Creek soon, I'd be in a world of trouble. "You just hurry up and eat, *you* hear?" I teased back.

Three contractions later, we were back in the car, windows down, warm summer air passing between us at fifty-five mph.

An hour later, with another hour to go, my water broke.

"Ohhhh!" I screamed.

"Sweet Aunt Martha!" Tommy cried out, staring at the water soaking the front of my dress and spilling down my legs. The car swerved and bounded onto the shoulder.

"Tommy!"

Tommy jerked the car back onto the road. "What *is* that?" he asked.

"It's my water—"

327

"Your what?" Tommy looked at me with terror-filled eyes.

"It's . . . it's water, Tommy. From around the baby. Ohhhh!" I arched, blew air from my lungs, then cried out, "It means the baby is coming!"

Tommy's head swung from the road to me, back to the road, and back to me again. "What do I do? What do I do?"

"Just keep driving." I wondered if the intensity of my voice was carried away by the breeze gusting between us. I lay my head in the space between the car seat and the window; the warm air blew across my face. Another contraction hit. It felt as if a hot poker had been driven through my middle then just as suddenly ceased. I gasped. My fingers curled in, my hands formed fists, and my teeth ground together.

"Mariette?"

"It's okay, Tommy. I'm fine. Just get us to Logan's Creek." *Drive as fast as this old car will go.*

And then, as if on cue, the sky opened up and showered the car and the countryside around us in a heavy summer's rain. I laughed out loud, though I was hardly tickled. "Just like before," I called across the front seat. "When Thayne and I were coming here the first time." The rain blew in, splattered across my face, washing the sweat and heat away. Another contraction. I arched my back. "Ohhhh, Tommy!"

"I can stop at the next town," he said.

I looked over at the speedometer; Tommy was barreling down the road at sixty-five now. "Tommy," I said once the contraction ended, "don't go too fast."

"But you want me to hurry, don't you?" Tommy's face had turned an angry shade of red. "You want me to get there."

"I do," I said. "But I don't want your car to break down."

Tommy's smile was broad. "Thanks, sis," he said.

I opened my mouth to answer, to flippantly say I wasn't holding any concern for his car in general. I only wanted it to keep going until we made it to Logan's Creek or to the next town if necessary. But then I thought how selfish labor had made me and how good my little brother had been to have even offered to drive me in the first place.

I looked out the windshield. The gray in the sky grew darker as the rain pelted against the car. I rolled the window up halfway. By now I was soaked from the waist down with water from below, and on my face and chest from heaven above.

My body arched again; my belly peaked in the middle as though my baby was raising his hind end into the air, preparing for a quick exit. I blew out another breath, then another and another, until the pain subsided. I looked at my watch. The contractions were coming every two minutes now.

"Well?" Tommy asked from the seat beside me. "How close are they?"

"Two minutes."

"Is that good?"

"It's according to how you look at it." I mopped water from my face with my fingertips then raked my bottom lip with my teeth. "I'm so thirsty."

"I told you that you should have eaten dinner back there."

"Not hungry, Tommy. Thirsty!" I all but barked at him.

Tommy's hands were clenched at ten and two on the steering wheel. I kept my focus on his face—his chiseled and handsome face—willing myself to concentrate on him rather than the pain due back at any moment. He looked at me, eyes ablaze. "Hey," he said. "You knew, didn't you? You knew back there at the restaurant and—hey! You knew before we left the house!"

"I'm sorry, Tommy. I thought I had time. Plenty of time. Missy's always took more than twenty-four hours and . . . and, for pity's sake, Tommy, I just wanted to get to Thayne! You can understand that, can't you?" Another contraction, another arch, another peak. "Great golly," I groaned.

"Man, just wait until I tell Mama," he said, ignoring my pain. "You're gonna be in some kind of trouble."

"Oh, Tommy, for pity's sake! I'm not ten." A sign on the road indicated that Hudsonville was twenty-seven miles ahead. Twenty-seven. If I could just make it another half hour, if Tommy could get this old jalopy to make it all the way to the county hospital, everything would be all right. I'd have the baby in a nice, sterile delivery room with Dr. Meredith in attendance and nurses dressed in white. Tommy could use the pay phone to call Thayne—he'd meet us there—and Mama and Daddy too, who would yell that they were grounding him as soon as he got home.

If we could just make it . . .

But then the pain was replaced by pressure and the immense need to push and push hard. I sat upright, grabbed Tommy's arm, and cried out, "Pull over, Tommy! Pull over!"

"Why?" The wild panic in his eyes had returned. "What?"

"Just do it!"

He followed my command; the car bumped and jostled until it came to a stop. I opened the car door, stepped onto the rain-soaked grass of the shoulder, and then closed the door. "What are you doing?" Tommy's voice strained against the words.

I opened the back passenger door and crawled in. "Okay," I said. "I just need to stretch out. You can put her back on the road now." Another desire to push pulsed through my body. Tommy was still staring at me. "Drive, Tommy!"

Tommy jerked around to face the front, shoved the car into drive. As he eased onto the gas pedal and released the clutch, the car stalled and died. I laid my head back against the rock-hard armrest. "Oh, dear God . . . dear God . . ." I prayed. "Please. Not now."

Tommy tried to restart the car. Again and again he tried until he looked over his shoulder at me and said, "She's dead, Mariette. I think she might be flooded."

Another need to push . . . "Oh, Tommy! Get out of the car! Get out!" Tommy bounded from the car and onto the road, where the rain fell steadily against the asphalt, the smell of it assaulting my senses. I wrestled myself out of my underwear as the front door slammed and then the back door opened. I watched my little brother's face elongate, his mouth form an oval, as he looked down to the car seat where I'd sprawled myself out and prepared myself for the worst.

"Mariette!" He pointed toward where I knew the baby's head was crowning. "I can't do this! I can't do this!"

I strained my neck to look at him. "You have to, Tommy. You have to help me! I'm going to have this baby and I'm going to have it now, do you hear me?"

Tommy took a step back, wiped the rain from his face by rubbing the palm of his hand from his forehead to his chin. "Mariette!" He shook his head then looked from the right to the left. "Where is the traffic around here? We need help."

"Tommy, do you have any rags or anything in the trunk?"

His eyes widened. "I got an old blanket."

"Get it!"

I laid my head back again. I remembered reading a book Mama had sent me the year before. It was called *Joy in the Morning* and had been written by Betty Smith, who wrote *A Tree Grows in Brooklyn*, one of my all-time favorites. In *Joy in the Morning* the main character, Annie, thinks she is going to die during childbirth, then remembers a verse in the Bible about God's eye being on the sparrow. I'd heard Thayne talk about that same verse in his sermon about not hurting a child. Now, it ran through my mind like a chant: *Fear not therefore: ye are of more value than many sparrows.* "Oh, God . . . God," I prayed out loud. "Thayne says you watch over even the little sparrows, so I know you are watching over me. I believe it, God. I do. I do! Please, I beg you, Lord, watch over me. Or, if I'm not precious enough to you, then at least love my baby. My baby has done nothing wrong, and I already love him so much. I can't . . . can't bear . . . not again . . ." I burst into tears as another desire to push seemed to tear me in half. "Not like Rachel, Father," I groaned. "Not like Rachel. Show me you love me! Show me I'm your child too!" I gritted my teeth, then screamed, "Tommy!"

"Mariette?" A woman's voice called my name.

I blinked.

"Mariette?"

I dipped my chin toward my chest.

"Child, child . . ."

"Miss Carolyn?" I stretched my arms and fingertips toward her. "What are you doing here?"

She caught my hands in a firm grasp and pulled me up slightly. She reminded me all at once of a drowned rat and haloed angel. I'd never seen anyone more precious in my life. "Lucky for you, I've been visiting a friend at the hospital in Savannah," she said.

I groaned through a pain, then said, "I prayed, Miss Carolyn. I prayed for God to help me."

"Well, looks like he heard you, sweetheart," she said with a laugh. She let go of my hands. "Come on now; brace yourself on your elbows."

I followed her instruction. As I did, from over her right shoulder, I saw Wilbur with his hands on Tommy's shoulders, pressing down as though trying to keep my brother steady.

"I think . . . I've got . . . to push!"

I felt her hand pressing against my bottom. "I'm doing this to keep you from tearing, honey. So you just push!"

Something guttural—almost animalistic—escaped from the soul of me. It cried out against everything from the moment of my birth to the one I was currently in. It cursed life for the hurt and the doubt, and blessed God for the love and the fortune. It reached out of my heart to a place I couldn't see or hear and yet where I was keenly aware of every color

332

and every chord of sound. And, for a moment, I touched the face of God and then watched him smile as he blew life into the nostrils of a writhing baby . . .

"Boy!" I heard Tommy shout.

"It's a boy!" Miss Carolyn declared. And then, between the patters of rain on pavement and another shout from a teenaged young man, came the sweet sound of a child's first cry.

Part 5

Return to Me

36

In 1971 Thayne had been the pastor of Logan's Creek's one church for eight years and I had been the pastor's wife—*truly* been the pastor's wife—for seven. The church's membership had grown from the handful of parishioners who scattered themselves among the pews to standing room only, thanks in part to Thayne having cleared "sin out of the camp" combined with his increasingly charismatic preaching style.

Added to that was the fact that my father had decided to expand his enterprise. He built the second Fox & Hound Manufacturing Company on the outskirts of Logan's Creek, thereby giving jobs to the people who lived there and in neighboring Hudsonville, while it brought in a whole new population of citizens. With the explosion of townspeople, additional new businesses were established: clinics, department stores, a car dealership, a barber shop and beauty parlor, a library full of books (Praise God from whom all blessings flow!), and even a movie theater. When the S & H Green Stamp store opened next to the Sears and Roebuck catalogue center, Thayne declared we were bustling like New York City.

As though he'd ever been there.

Two other significant events occurred in 1971. The first was that Thayne and I became the proud parents of twins, Mark and Melanie. They rounded out our family nicely, bringing the number of children to four.

Or five, according to how you look at it. Rachel's name would always rest near the top of our family tree, preserved in my Bible.

First was Gabriel Johnson, whom Thayne called Gabe but I called Sparrow. Then, two years after his roadside birth, we had welcomed Lena Sue (named for her grandmothers), a sweet girl who grew to look like me but who was graced with the disposition of her father. She never met a soul she didn't love and who, in return, didn't adore her. (She also had both her father and her older brother wrapped around her little finger—a fact in which I took no small amount of delight.)

The other thing that happened in 1971 was that, with the increase in parishioners, Thayne was forced to write a formal letter to the church's district offices, asking for funds to expand the current building. The church had managed to raise five thousand dollars, and he was hoping for matching funds from the denomination.

For days after he sent the letter he hovered near the telephone. On the days and nights he had to go out, he rushed right home, bounded into the house, and said, "Well? Any calls?"

Two weeks passed. One morning, while I was feeding my family a hearty breakfast of cereal and strawberry Pop Tarts, the phone rang. I'd just risen from the table to get more juice for Sparrow and Lena Sue. "I'll get it," I said, then answered the kitchen extension that hung on the wall near the back door.

By this time we were living in Alma's old house. Miss Alma had died in 1965, and in her will had left the house to the church for the pastor's residence. Our cottage home was now a guesthouse for visiting preachers or the denomination's higher-ups from Atlanta when they came to town. Mostly, though, it was Daddy's "home away from home" whenever he needed to visit the Fox & Hound's second factory, which Tommy managed for him.

A voice asked for Reverend Scott.

I sighed. So early in the morning and someone was already calling for him at home. "Thayne," I said while placing my hand over the mouthpiece. "For you."

Thayne rose from the table. He was already dressed in a pair of slacks and a short-sleeved white shirt. His tie—wide and thick—hung loose, not yet knotted. He wore his hair longer now, with curls licking the tops of his ears and playing havoc with his forehead and the nape of his neck. I wasn't sure how I felt about this new look, but Thayne thought it gave him an edge with the young people at the church and at the high school, where he continued to coach. "Who is it?" he asked with a quick glance at his watch. "It's not even eight o'clock."

I shrugged. "My thoughts exactly."

I returned to the table with more juice for the children, whose cherub faces were a mess of strawberry jam. Sparrow—evermore his father's son—said, "Why can't I just stay home today, Mommy? I don't like second grade all that much."

To which Lena Sue chimed, "Second grade! I'm in second grade!"

I pointed to her playfully. "You, my adorable little muffin, are in kindergarten. Sparrow is in second grade."

"It's just no fun," my son said, sinking his chin into the palm of his hand.

I started to say something motherly, that school "was not meant to be fun," when Thayne returned to his chair. "State office of the church," he said. His voice sounded tight, like a rubber band twisted and pulled as far as it could go. "They're coming to the church today. Eleven o'clock."

"This is good, no?" I rose to clear the breakfast dishes. "Children, go wash your hands. I'll be in there in a minute." Sparrow and Lena Sue scrambled from the table and tore off down the hall. "Thayne?"

339

"I don't know," he answered. "That was Dr. Andrews. He sounded so serious." He breathed a long sigh. "What if I've made a mistake, Mariette, asking for that money?"

I patted his arm. "You've done no such thing."

My assurance earned me a kiss and a smile. But, deep inside, I wondered the same.

A little after noon, Thayne had returned home with the news. He found me in the kitchen, ironing clothes. It was, after all, a Tuesday. "Dr. Andrews wants me to consider another church."

I felt my brow knit together. "What other church?" I asked, as if there were only one church in the entire world.

"It's a church just outside of Columbus. They already have a membership of about five hundred."

"Five hundred?"

Thayne slumped at the table, then pulled the knot of his tie loose.

"Take off your coat," I told him. "I'll get you some iced tea." I set about doing my wifely duty and listened as Thayne continued.

"Their numbers are actually slipping. The pastor there—a Dr. Lee—has been battling depression." Thayne waved his hand in the air. I brought the tea to him, placed it on the table, then sat across from my husband. "The home office is thinking I might be the ticket to bring the membership up while Dr. Lee takes an early retirement."

"Can they do that? Make us leave Logan's Creek?"

Thayne took a long swallow of his drink then shook his head. "Oh, I don't think so, no." He seemed to ponder it for a moment before adding, "I think they want to give me the option, though. It's a nice offer."

A nice offer. "So then what did you tell Dr. Andrews?"

Thayne smiled. "I told him I'd pray about it. And I will." He straightened then, looked me in the eyes. "What do you think? How do you feel about it? It'll mean a bigger salary, more money to help take care of the kids' futures. And Dr. Andrews says the pastor's home is quite nice. Two story. Brick. Five bedrooms, three baths. Has a balcony running all across the front of the house. Big white columns."

I looked around me. After Alma had died, the church members had gotten together and done everything they could to bring the old house up to a more modern standard. Once completed, Thayne and I had spent every spare minute renovating it to our personalities. Still, the kitchen was in need of a new floor, new appliances, and even a new ceiling. The countertops and cabinets weren't anything to write home about either. There were only three bedrooms, which meant that, for now, Sparrow and Lena Sue were sharing one, the babies shared the nursery, and Thayne and I had the master.

But leave Logan's Creek? I couldn't imagine.

"I vote no," I said, then patted Thayne's hand. "But you pray and I'll pray too. If God says move, then we move."

"Sounds like a plan," Thayne said. Then he reached into his pocket and pulled out an envelope. "This was in our mailbox today."

I recognized the handwriting immediately; the loops, the lines, the slanting to the left. "A letter from Rowena," I said. I took it from him, then walked it to the counter and laid it there. "I'll read it later. With a cup of coffee."

Letters from Rowena were not to be rushed. They were to be savored while curled on the end of the sofa sipping hot tea or coffee. She now lived in North Carolina and was working for a woodworking company where her furniture designs brought a nice paycheck and had won her several awards. I'd seen photos of some of her work; it was both stunning and impressive.

She'd yet to marry—yet to date anyone seriously, really. She'd also never seen or spoken to her mother or brothers again. *If she ever cares to write or call*, she once wrote, *she does know where to find me. Until then, I have a job I love, friends who make me smile, and I'm walking close with God every day. For a girl with my past, that's not a bad combination.*

In the years since her sudden departure from Logan's Creek, we'd not seen each other. But she wrote once a month and called twice a year, on my birthday and at Christmas. One year, she surprised us by sending a personally hand-carved cherry bookstand for Thayne's office and a free-standing needlepoint hoop for me, both intricate and lovely to behold. And, one time for my birthday, she sent a birdhouse that looked like the outhouse behind the Oglesbys' home. I laughed till I cried.

In the years since we'd moved to Logan's Creek, I'd made many new friends, and some initial acquaintances, like Charlotte (who Thayne called a "rascal"), had become dear friends. But never would there ever be another Rowena Griffith in my life. A girl in so many ways like me—living on the outside looking in, wanting to be left there alone, and yet desperately wanting to belong.

We'd prayed, Thayne and I. Together. Separately. We gave the decision to God and trusted he would let us know in his own way what we were to do. And then, a week after the offer was made, Thayne gave a solid "no" to moving to Columbus. Dr. Andrews was, he said, initially disappointed when he went to the Atlanta office to personally give his answer. But then he'd chuckled, shook Thayne's hand, and said, "You know, in my heart I hoped you'd say this. Logan's Creek's in your heart, son. Our thoughts for sending you to Columbus were selfish, but God knew better." He then informed Thayne that the powers that be had considered the need for expanding Logan's Creek's little church building and were granting him $15,000. Thayne nearly soared on eagle's wings for the month after. In those that followed, he oversaw every detail of the renovation and, when all was finished, announced to the congregation that we'd have an official ribbon-cutting ceremony the following Sunday, followed by dinner on the grounds.

"My wife," he said from the pulpit and with a wide smile, "will *not* be providing the fried chicken."

To which the congregation, in unison, offered back, "But she will bring the deviled eggs!"

From the place where I belonged on the first row pew, directly in front of my husband and to the left side of the sanctuary, I threw back my head and laughed.

And they all laughed with me.

Eva Marie Everson is an award-winning author and a successful speaker. She is the coauthor of the Potluck Club series and the Potluck Catering Club series as well as *Things Left Unspoken*, the first in her solo line of Southern novels. Reared in Georgia, she makes her home in Central Florida with her husband, daughter, two dogs, and a cat who allows them to live there.

"A lovely and deeply moving story.
I didn't just read this story, I lived it!"

—ANN TATLOCK, award-winning author
of *The Returning*

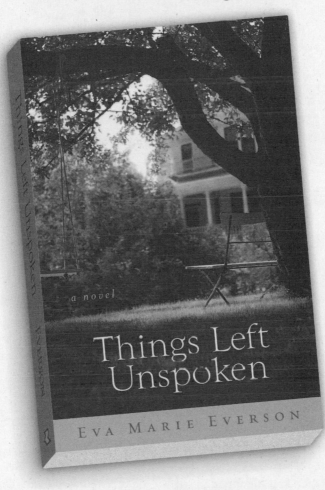

Jo-Lynn isn't sure she wants to know the truth—but sometimes
the truth has a way of making itself known.

 Revell
a division of Baker Publishing Group
www.RevellBooks.com

Available Wherever Books Are Sold

"Make sure you have a tissue nearby, because you are going to need it!"

—Terri Blackstock, bestselling author

A young boy's prayers, a shoebox full of love letters, and an old wooden soldier make a memory that will not be forgotten. Can a gift from the past mend a broken heart?

Revell
a division of Baker Publishing Group
www.RevellBooks.com

A Reluctant War Hero Returns Home . . . and Encounters a New Chance at Love

A HEARTWARMING STORY of tender love
and fresh starts will capture your heart.

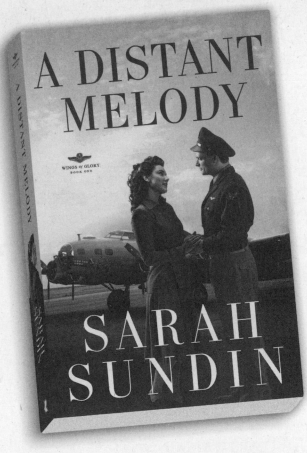